ALL THIS TALK OF LOVE

ALSO BY Christopher Castellani

A Kiss from Maddalena
The Saint of Lost Things

All This Talk of Love

A NOVEL

Christopher Castellani

ALGONQUIN BOOKS OF CHAPEL HILL   2013

Published by
ALGONQUIN BOOKS OF CHAPEL HILL
Post Office Box 2225
Chapel Hill, North Carolina 27515-2225

A division of
Workman Publishing
225 Varick Street
New York, New York 10014

Edna St. Vincent Millay, excerpts from "Well, I have lost you; and I lost you fairly;" from *Collected Poems*. Copyright 1931, © 1958 by Edna St. Vincent Millay and Norma Millay Ellis. Reprinted with the permission of The Permissions Company, Inc., on behalf of Holly Peppe, Literary Executor, The Millay Society, www.millay.org.

"How Some of It Happened," © 1998 by Marie Howe from her collection *What the Living Do,* published by W. W. Norton & Company, Inc.

This is a work of fiction. While, as in all fiction, the literary perceptions and insights are based on experience, all names, characters, places, and incidents either are products of the author's imagination or are used fictitiously.

Library of Congress Cataloging-in-Publication Data
Castellani, Christopher, [date]
  All this talk of love : a novel / by Christopher Castellani. — 1st ed.
      p. cm.
  ISBN 978-1-61620-170-8
    1. Italian American families — Fiction.   2. Immigrants — Fiction.
3. Children of immigrants — Fiction.   4. Nostalgia — Fiction.   5. Loss
(Psychology) — Fiction.   I. Title.
PS3603.A875A55 2013
813'.6 — dc23   2012030841

10 9 8 7 6 5 4 3 2 1
First Edition

For my parents, my family, and Michael,
who make everything beautiful

—One day it happens: what you have feared all your life,
the unendurably specific, the exact thing.

—MARIE HOWE, "How Some of It Happened"

ALL THIS TALK OF LOVE

Part 1 ∽ *Fall 1999*

1   *La Famiglia Grasso*

FRANKIE GRASSO AND HIS mother watch the same soap, but they root for different women. He likes the deranged ones: the pregnancy fakers, the poisoners, the tramps. They are necessary research for his chapter on the legacy of the gothic in the construction of female identity. His mother favors the patient, dutiful wives—they of the shellacked hair and pantsuits and unshakable faith—and looks to them as examples of proper behavior in 1990s America. Frankie shouldn't be surprised. His mother's life has been a jeremiad in two languages and two countries, and her seventy-two years have taught her to distrust romantic passion. Precious minutes on the phone with Frankie she spends wishing doom on the amoral women of daytime, shocked that some network executive has allowed them to stray so far from decency in the middle of the afternoon. "In life," she says tonight, after Frankie praises the pregnancy faker for her resourcefulness in finding her long-lost identical twin sister and persuading her to carry the baby she can't admit she lost, "you have the truth or you have nothing," and what he wants to tell her is, by that formulation, not a single member of the Grasso family, not to mention anyone he knows, has a blessed thing.

Instead he says, "I'm exhausted. I've been working all night on this chapter. My phone bill's ten pages long. Wait until she has that baby, then we'll see."

"I call you back right now," she says. "I have the money. Daddy put me on a plan: ten cents a minute. If you can call your cousin in Avezzano twice a week, I tell him, I can call Boston for a few dimes."

"I need sleep," Frankie says. Then: "All right, call me back." He hangs up and takes a sip of whiskey. The light comes on in the window of his neighbor's house, an identical triple-decker but better maintained. Recently, in his German immersion course, Frankie invented the adjective *zusammengedrängt,* or "thrown together crowdedly," to describe his neighborhood. He loves his word, which looks and sounds like the claustrophobia it conveys, and connotes the grime and desperation of those thickly settled towns that surround a city. His street is populated mostly by low(er)-class Italian and Irish families jealous of their countrymen in the North End or Charlestown, who step from their front doors onto charming streets lit with gas lamps and lined with exposed-brick restaurants.

"This is your home now," his mother said the one time she visited. She stood on his crumbling front stoop with her arms outstretched, facing the vista of chain-link fences and vinyl siding. "It's ugly, but it's yours. You'll never want to leave."

"It's only a six-hour drive," he said. "I'll be back all the time." Instead they settle for Frankie's nightly phone call at 11:01 no matter where he is in the world, one of their many promises to each other.

Frankie's friends call their parents once a month and fly home twice a year, less often if they can swing it. Like him, they toil in obscurity in the service of literary scholarship. They have advanced degrees and drug habits and a love affair with irony. Unlike him, the toil (or is it the obscurity?) has soured them on distractions like family and authentic human connection. "You really talk to your mother every single night?" they ask him. "How? *Why?*"

"Because she's alive," he says.

"But what do you talk about? I haven't spoken an honest word to my mother since kindergarten."

"Who said anything about honesty?"

He lets the phone ring five or six times, imagining his mother on the other end staring into the receiver. When he finally picks up, she says, "What's wrong with you?" and though he thinks of three things off the bat, he treats the question as rhetorical and lets her talk.

Maddalena Grasso switches the phone to her left ear and again takes up her husband's pants, which she has been hemming off and on for hours. She's been on the phone since eight o'clock: first with her daughter, then her friend Arlene from the dance studio, then Sister Mary asking another favor for the church, then a wrong number with a friendly voice, and now, finally, always finally, her Frankie.

"Your sister was here this afternoon," she says. "You should have seen: she had my old sweat suit on, the pink one with the rhinestones on the cuffs your *zia* Ida gave me thirty years ago. She's like a hurricane, your sister, never any time to sit and have a conversation.

She ate a bowl of soup and some pasta leftover standing in front of the sink the whole time like a peasant. I said, 'Sit down one second! It's not good always to rush,' but she has no time. She's going to call you this week, she said. She's going to tell you she and Tom got that plot, the one with the water. They had the meeting with the builder, and they got it."

"The *lot*, you mean," says Frankie. "Not the plot."

"Lot, plot, whatever. And you know the land next to it, you saw it last time, it doesn't have any water, but it has those tall trees like you like. It's an acre, almost, for sale. And I was thinking, Daddy, too, how beautiful it would be for you to live next door to your sister. And you won't have to throw away your money on rent anymore."

"Who's got that kind of cash?" Frankie says, though if he doesn't shut her down now, she will offer at least a down payment, a cut of the money she and his father have been saving in his name since the night of his conception—a night she's told him about in more detail than was necessary. For a moment, Frankie allows himself to imagine the unimaginable: he and his girlfriend, Professor Birch, clearing the brush from their little strip of yard, she in her tank top and hairy armpits and army-issue boots, waving to his sister and brother-in-law from across a koi pond. Professor Birch is not the type for big Sunday dinners cooked and served and cleared by women, for shared acreage, for lawn care. She is the type who phones her husband while Frankie's inside her to remind him to mail the insurance bill, who makes Frankie call her Professor even when she's naked and sullied and rummaging under his bed for her socks. She is exactly the type of woman his mother was afraid he'd meet in the big city.

With or without Professor Birch, Frankie has no plans to move back to the suburbs of Wilmington, Delaware, a fact he can never admit to his mother. He has been called to a bigger and deeper life, far from the narrow bed in which he was planted. And yet it is a stipulation of his unspoken contract with his parents that he treat this stint as a graduate student in Boston as temporary—a regrettable but necessary period of time away from home that will allow him to return in triumph as a doctor of philosophy in English literature, secure a highly paid professorship at the university, marry a sweet Italian girl, and start a family like his sister did and his older brother would have done, had he lived.

When Frankie is quiet for too long, Maddalena worries: he is jealous of his sister and brother-in-law and all their money, he is falling in love with Boston and will never come home, he is too young and confused to think about plots. Let him be, she thinks, but how impossible that is! So she tells him her stories over and over again, in different words but with the same lesson at the end of them, stories about how it was for her to be brought to America from her village across the ocean like a piece of furniture, in love with one man but married to another, a stranger, and just a teenager she was, without a word of the language, and none of it by choice, not at all like for Frankie, who left his mother in Wilmington four years ago not for love or money or a better life but for school, as easy as you'd leave a movie if it wasn't making you laugh.

"You know Prima saved you a place at the table for the confirmation," she says. "She has to tell the catering how many people. Every person who doesn't show up, she still has to pay forty-five dollars."

"I told her I wasn't coming."

"You should come," she says. "To respect your sister. Not because you want to or don't want to."

"To be honest, I'm disappointed Patrick's getting confirmed at all. I had high hopes for him when he became a Buddhist and gave away his stereo."

"Don't even mention that," his mother says. "He's normal again now, and I've never seen your sister more happy." She takes a pin from between her lips. "You know, you can bring somebody if you want. I pay for the train for both of you. Prima put you down for two just in case."

"I don't need train money."

"Forty-five dollars a person," she repeats. "And that's without the open bar. Can you imagine? And if you don't belong to the country club, you can pay a *hun*dred dollars a person and still they don't let you have the party there." She lets that sink in for Frankie, though elegant things have never impressed him.

Maddalena held all three of her children's First Communions at the Al Di Là, the Grasso family restaurant, where there was home cooking and plastic red tablecloths and white crepe paper hanging from the walls. First the party for Prima, the first child, her daughter, the angel; then for Tony, the first son born in the new country; then, seventeen years after him, for Frankie, who saved her. Every night when the phone rings and he's there to say, "Hey, Ma, what's up?" he saves her again.

Frankie rubs his eyes. Even if Professor Birch could ditch her husband, he knows exactly what they'd do at this silly fete: chug free cocktails, gorge on the buffet, and spend the rest of the time on the lobby couch sneering at Prima and Tom's unexamined embrace of Catholicism.

Worse, Prima's already called to inform him that the confirmation isn't all the Grassos will be celebrating. She has a big announcement, one of her famous surprises, one she wants Frankie to hear in person because it will affect the entire family. She offered no more details, convinced he'd blab to their mother.

"Turns out I have to present a paper that weekend," he says to Maddalena. "Not that anyone ever asks me about my schedule. It's kind of a big deal, actually."

"They just tell you now?"

"The university's not very organized. Harvard. What do you expect?"

"Harvard?"

"Yes, Harvard. Does that make it all right? I can miss the formal induction of my innocent nephew into the racist, sexist, xenophobic institution known as the Roman Catholic Church if I'm speaking at Harvard?"

"Do they pay you?"

"Something like this you don't do for money," he says. "You do it for the prestige."

The truth, of course, is that there is no paper and no invitation from Harvard, which won't even let Frankie into its fortress of a library, let alone the "Millennium Reproaches: Anxiety and Authorship in the

Fin de Siècle" conference. There is certainly no prestige. Despite employing some well-connected and widely published professors (Dr. Birch among them), Frankie's graduate school is solidly second tier, and Frankie himself is passionately meeting but not far exceeding its modest expectations. Upon earning their PhDs, he and his classmates can expect not tenure-track positions at coastal universities or the Seven Sisters but—if they're very lucky—Comp and Rhet jobs at mega state schools in Des Moines or Tallahassee or some other regional-airport city, where their bitterness will thrive like kudzu. As far as Frankie knows, he is the only one sleeping with a professor, an advantage he counts as distinct in the job market.

"Your sister will be devastating," his mother says. "But school is more important."

"I'm sorry," Frankie says. "I really am. This semester's strung me out. I'm not myself. Tell everybody I feel terrible."

"Do what you have to do," Maddalena says. "That's why you up there. Work hard. Stay straight. Drink some whiskey—it helps you sleep."

"Excellent idea," he says.

"Good night," she says. "I love you."

"Love you too, Ma. Good night."

"Good night, Frankie," she says. "I love you, I love you." It's important to her to say the words until she's sure he's hung up.

"Bye, Ma," Frankie says. "I love you. Bye." It's important to him to say the words until he's sure she's hung up.

And once again she has spared him, this time as so many before. How easy life can be, Frankie thinks, when your mother knows so little of the world, and you are not her favorite son.

PRIMA GRASSO BUCKLEY and her mother look like sisters. They have the same hairstyle, the same slightly crooked noses rounded at the tip. They once had the same figure, but Prima's hips and backside have widened, and her thighs—well, her thighs bulge in the areas where Maddalena's are slim. She is twenty-seven years younger than her mother, but she's not embarrassed when someone calls out, "Maddalena!" and rushes toward her at the mall. It's a compliment to be mistaken for a woman so beautiful. From a distance, at least.

Maddalena, in her ivory slip, holds a crushed-velvet sleeveless dress to her chest. She lifts one of her long dancer's legs to see how it falls. Prima bought her this dress last year, for her seventy-first birthday. She's considering it for Patrick's confirmation party, along with a hat and gloves, but in the end she decides the hat and gloves, and the crushed velvet itself, are old fashioned. She doesn't want to dress classic, like Sophia Loren, like people expect her to. She wants to dress "in." That's her word. So she ends up choosing a knee-length black-and-white number Prima found her at King of Prussia, one that's sure to knock everybody out.

All Maddalena's clothes she gets as gifts from Prima. Birthday, Mother's Day, Christmas, even Easter. Her favorite thing in life, she says, is for Prima to take her to Christiana Mall and for them to window-shop for a while, stop for a bite to eat at the sit-down restaurant, get their nails done if they have a coupon. Maddalena does have a few friends her own age, Italian ladies who came over after the war, but their idea of a good time is to sit at kitchen tables and gossip and show off vegetables from their gardens and tell each other how old they're getting. They're round and fat, these Italian ladies; Maddalena calls them *le patate,* the potatoes. They prefer terry cloth housecoats to sleeveless velvet; they don't color their hair or pluck their moles or learn to drive. Maddalena has never enjoyed cooking, never planted a garden, and never left the house without makeup. She's worked in factories and drapery shops. It is one of Prima's many promises to help her mother stay young, to keep her from what they call *la vita patata.*

The surprise Prima's planned for the confirmation party fulfills that promise. Prima is such a junkie for surprises that even this one, which will make her mother furious, gives her a buzz. The juggling of information, the giddy expectation of her sons' hands thrown in the air, of her father's happy tears and fierce embrace, thrill her. It's the stuff of life! It will take willpower to keep the surprise to herself for three more days. When she reveals it, her mother will put up a big fuss before Prima can even get all the details out, but eventually she will come around. Prima has studied her mother's patterns all her life, talks to her many times a day, knows her better than she knows herself. They are bound both by that sacred covenant between every mother and daughter and by a cord of grief. The grief is like a living thing, silent but always present; they stand guard over it the way they would a child of their own, which, in a way, it is. It comforts Prima that the surprise is something Tony would have loved.

"Frankie should be at the party," Maddalena says. "You need to call him. He listens to you."

"Since when?"

"He tells me he had some speech to do at the Harvard, but he made it up. I can tell. Not once he mentioned it this week. He forgets to cover up when he lies."

Prima has never understood her youngest brother, and not only because he was born so late, when she was already a teenager. He's had dark curtains over his heart from the beginning and rarely gives anyone a peek behind them, least of all his sister. Unlike her and Tony, who were born two years apart and had dozens of other friends their age around them, Frankie was a loner as a kid, never played sports, never even broke curfew on the weekends. The night of his senior prom, Prima found him sitting at home in bed, still in his school uniform, reading a book of Polish poetry. Prima sat next to him and acted Big Sister as best she could, asked if he wanted to go out for pizza. But Frankie just kept reading. When Prima finally asked if he was OK, he said, "Of course I'm OK. Why wouldn't I be OK?" and read her a poem out loud from the book.

"Aren't your exams over by now?" Prima asked, which really meant, What's a healthy red-blooded Italian American boy doing at home reading Polish poems on prom night? His solitary existence worried her. She was, and still is, looking for any sign of trouble. But again Frankie ignored her, so she stood, kissed him on the forehead, and let him be.

"Keep an eye on Frankie" is what her parents have begged her to do since Tony died, so she does. Patrick's confirmation is a big deal, not only because the kid finally came to his senses, but because she and Tom are spending a fortune on the party, not to mention the surprise Frankie should be there to hear. If he doesn't show up, it will be another crack in a family that could fall apart at any moment. You have to tend to family like you tend to a garden. That's what's wrong with America, if you ask her, why no one's as happy as they used to be, like in the fifties.

Prima raised her own boys the old-fashioned way. All four of them kiss their *nonna* and *nonno* and say "I love you" every time they leave them, whether their buddies are around or not. It's a requirement. She's dragged them with her and Tom to Mass every Sunday, and to all the sacrament parties and birthdays, and they've given up meat on Christmas Eve and on Wednesdays and Fridays during Lent no matter how much they've bellyached. Ask her boys about their mother, and they'll say she's their best friend, one of their buddies, like they're on the same team. Zach calls her his "wingman." She's gone to all their games—Ryan and Matt's football, Zach's soccer and tennis, Patrick's baseball—and watched how they act with the guys, and the truth is they act no differently than they do with her. It's almost a shame to say, but they're closer to her than they are to Tom, and maybe even than they are to each other. She's picked them up from parties after they've passed out drunk. She's paid more speeding tickets and police fines than she can add up. Where were their buddies then? Where was their father? She's the one person they can trust without hesitation, she's told them, so they share everything, sometimes more than she wants to know. Ryan, the oldest—it's like it's his life's mission to shock her with his stories. He doesn't realize how much it would take to shock her.

The past few years, with Ryan and the twins away at college, Prima has had to work extra hard, spend more money, make more phone calls, to keep everyone together. Just because your kids grow up and don't live at home anymore doesn't mean they stop being members of the family. And sometimes, to fall asleep at night, she pretends that this isn't Patrick's last year of high school, that he won't be leaving them next fall. She likes to imagine Patrick at the other end of the kitchen table, his hands folded in front of him, nervous and guilty maybe, telling her and Tom that he's decided not to go to college right away, that he wants to take a job in Wilmington for a year, live at home, save money. If Prima doesn't pretend this is at least a possibility, then all she can see is Tom and her alone in their big house—the TV on but no other voices, no boys in the yard hitting chip shots, nobody in the basement sneaking swigs from the bar—and she feels like she's tied to train tracks and a big one's coming at her full force.

Patrick's at her bedroom door, knocking and turning the knob. "What's this locked for?" he calls out.

Prima and Maddalena slip on their dresses and let him in. He's still in his school clothes—blue blazer and tie and backpack—with his shirt untucked and his Phillies cap backward.

"Check you two out," he says. "Very fancy." He kisses his *nonna* on the cheek and asks her, "You wanna be my date tonight?"

"If we go dancing, yes," she says. She takes his hands in hers, pulls him close, then pushes him out to arm's length, then pulls him back to her again. He picks up the rhythm right away.

"You've got a one-track mind," he says, giving her a twirl. "The dancing track."

Maddalena smiles. Her life is dancing, yes, she thinks, but more than that, it's Frankie and Prima and her husband and keeping up her house and some sewing work on the side for extra money. For many years she wanted more, or different, or to go backward—once, long ago, she wanted romance and adventure, like a woman in a movie—but then she lost Tony, her beautiful son, and after that, she stopped wanting anything and needs one pill to sleep and another to wake up, and what may be true, what the years have taught her, is that a son and a daughter and a husband and dancing and a little house and some paying work and to sleep through the night are as much as anyone has a right to ask for in this life. More.

"Handsome boy like you," she says to Patrick now, and she pats his cheek. She stares at him a moment, her hand still on his cheek, struck by his smooth skin, his big blue eyes, broad shoulders, blond hair. She wants to say more, to tell him he is one of the lucky ones to be good looking and strong and young, but his sudden beauty, and the explosion in her heart, have stopped her mouth. She can't form words. His name disappears from her lips. She just stares.

"I am a swordsman," Patrick says. "It cannot be denied."

"What on earth is *that* expression?" Prima asks.

"Think about it," he says.

Prima shakes her head. It sounds dirty. She looks over at Maddalena. "You still with us, Ma?"

"Of course," says Maddalena. The spell breaks. She takes her hand away. "I was just thinking, Prima, you need to bring your handsome son here to the dance studio. We get lots of young men from the University of Delaware. They take lessons and practice for the competitions. More the young men these days than the old men are coming. When I dance with the college ones, I feel like I'm a teenager again, back in my village before your father took me—"

"Yeah, too bad all those dudes are gay," Patrick says, laughing. He walks over to Prima, gives her a peck on the cheek, and rests his elbow on her shoulder. He's more than a head taller.

"Some, yes, it's true," Maddalena says. "Not every one of them, though. I can tell. I see everything. The ones that look like you, they not. Just the funny-looking ones. I don't dance with the funny-looking ones. Or the geezers. You should see how the college boys ask for me. All those pretty young girls around, and they ask *me* to dance—an old lady!"

"See what I'm saying?" Patrick says. "Gay."

"Go take a shower," Prima tells him. "You've got BO." It's beer on his breath, actually, and she needs him out of the room before her mother notices. "You weren't running around outside in those pants, were you?"

"I was just over at the Gooch's," he says.

"The Gooch," says Prima. "Don't you love these kids' names, Ma?"

After the door's closed and the music starts up from Patrick's room, Maddalena says, "He's so full of life, that one. Two big things you did right in your life: marry Tom and raise those boys."

They take off their dresses and Prima covers them with plastic. She sits with Maddalena on the deck for a while, watching Tom trim the hedges. She has come through life OK after all. A quiet childhood with a thousand friends and weekends at the shore and the lead in *Saint Joan* even though she was just a sophomore. Then, the morning of opening night, Tony went missing, and for years after, there was just a kind of blankness she never imagined could be filled. Until Tom. Until her boys. And now she considers herself one of the lucky ones to have seen through the blankness—blessed, in fact, smiled upon by the God she visits each and every Sunday. Her tragedy came early in life, and since then other tragedies have sideswiped her but never crashed full on. A lump in her mother's breast, suspicious at first, diagnosed as benign. Tom almost getting transferred to Omaha, then finding a new job here that paid twice as much. And just last month, a boy on Patrick's team—the shortstop, All-American kid, stands next to Patrick in the all-star photo—drops dead swinging at strike three. Prima should thank God a hundred times a day, but she forgets, and then on Sundays she has to ask his forgiveness for forgetting. She wonders whether anyone can be grateful enough to satisfy him and, if they are, whether God rewards or keeps testing you.

These are the questions Prima asks herself that night, and the night after, and the night after that, the one before the confirmation, when she's awake at 1 a.m. next to her husband, so tired from the day that her eyes burn and the pins and needles pinch her legs, and she gets that train-track feeling again and hears the whistle screaming closer and feels the vibration on the rails beneath her, and sleep—that fickle hero—won't cut her loose.

FRANKIE LIGHTS THE front burner on his kitchen stove. He fills a medium pot with water and watches it come to a boil. He takes a small box from the cupboard, slices it open with a steak knife, and pours pasta shells into the water. Eight minutes later he drains the shells, returns them to the pot, and pours in a half cup of milk, a tablespoon of butter, and a packet of powdered orange cheese. He brings the pot to the couch and turns on the television. The bottom of the pot warms his lap. He's not tired. It's past 1 a.m. and he can't get tired as hard as he tries. He flips through the six channels that come with basic cable and settles on PBS. An old astronomer stands in front of a poster-size photograph and points to a blur surrounded by smaller, brighter blurs. It's a low-budget documentary on the Hale-Bopp comet, and though it's yesterday's news, it captivates him. The comet, the greatest natural spectacle of the nineties, is long gone and won't be back for two thousand years. The thirty-nine brainwashed believers who followed it into oblivion won't be back at all. Meanwhile, the earth remains in a perpetual state of loneliness, welcoming but never visited, a host whose friends drive by once in a while but don't stop in.

What's at play all those miles beyond him shouldn't matter. What should count, his friends might say—and doesn't he agree, officially?—is the here and now. And yet, in the here and now, with the screen flickering and the old astronomer circling the blurs with a red marker, Frankie longs to know, with the certainty of a scientist, a few more whats and whys of the cosmic plot. Like, what did he hope to find in this city, and when will he find it? Like, why did one son embrace oblivion and the other merely run away? Like, why does Frankie feel that the Grassos—his mother and father, Prima, his nephews, himself, and even, strangely, Tony—are at the end of something?

IN THE BALLROOM of the Wilmington Country Club, Prima buzzes from table to table. Each round holds eight of her gussied-up friends and family, whom she hugs and waves at in a blur of kisses and smiles. Before each course goes out, she rushes to the kitchen to scrutinize its preparation: first the arugula salad with its crispy Parmesan ring, then her father's lasagna trucked in from the

Al Di Là, then lollipop lamb chops with a mint sauce and sides of asparagus and rosemary potatoes. The chef and servers shoot her dirty looks, but too bad. She is Antonio Grasso's daughter.

She goes over again and again how she and Tom will bring the confirmation to its dramatic close. She'll wait until the desserts and coffee are cleared, and then just as her family considers heading for the coatroom, she and Tom will join hands and tell them to hold their horses. We have a second gift to give you today, she will say. By that point, the other guests will have gone; the three-piece orchestra will be packing up; the sunset will be spilling its pink light through the French doors of the terrace; the only missing element will be a film crew, a sound track, a bubbly host/model/reporter shoving a microphone in each of their faces, asking, How do you feel? What does this act of love and generosity mean to the Grasso family?

All that, and Frankie.

Prima can't help looking for her brother in the crowd, but she sees no shock of dyed jet-black hair, no John Lennon glasses, no silver bracelets. She should know better than to expect Frankie to rise to the occasion. She regrets having bribed him with the promise of the surprise, but at least she didn't reveal it. Besides, it's not Prima's role to begin with—or at least it shouldn't be—to enforce Frankie's obligations, to make him a better man. It's her father's. It would have been Tony's. Whatever the case, once you prompt a person like Frankie to do the right thing, it's impossible to gauge his sincerity; and then you have to put up with his sullen "I'm here, happy now?" whiny self-righteousness. Who needs it? And what would Prima even say to him? Even though you've ignored your nephews all your life, I appreciate your presence at Patrick's official transition into Christian adulthood?

But that would be stooping to his level. Sarcasm. It seeps into you like a stain; it blinds you; it makes you think you're superior, but Frankie is not superior to anyone, not even to Prima, who might never have gone to graduate school but has just as much of a college degree as he does, and in something practical. She shouldn't have to defend herself or her choices to anyone, let alone Frankie, and another thing—

Zach, her quietest, appears. "Ma," he says, "dance with me?" He holds his arms out. He wears the suit she bought him on his sixteenth birthday, made of imported English wool hand-cut by their Italian tailor, Ernesto, who looks proudly over from his seat near the grand piano. Like every Ernesto suit before it, this one infuses Zach with strength and pride in the way it hugs his arms and slims his waist and falls sculpturally at his ankles, announcing its quality to even the most casual observer. If you didn't know Zach, you'd think he was the teen heartthrob from your soap opera or the class president; you'd be surprised to hear he's just a kid, not a man, barely a young man. He has his *nonno*'s ambition and long legs and his father's freckles; from his mother he has practicality and deep brown eyes and a head of un-ruly curls; with his twin, Matt, he shares not an identical face but a delirious faith that life is a carnival designed to amuse and delight them. Prima shared that same faith once.

Mother and son hold their hands on each other's waists, sway back and forth to "As Time Goes By." Four or five couples join them on the large square of hardwood: her mother with Tom; Mark Krouse from the firm with his new wife; and, on the periphery, ancient Aunt Helen with her son, Michael.

"So, Ma," Zach says, "don't get mad, but Dad told me the secret."

She stops moving for a moment, looks at his overeager eyes, then gets back to the sway. "No, he didn't."

"He did!"

"OK, then you tell me."

"You first."

"Son," she says, "you really think I'd fall for that old trick?"

"What old trick?"

Soon the song ends, Zach, defeated, kisses her on the cheek and strides off, and dessert arrives: generous sampler plates of pear-and-ginger tarts, apple cobbler, and chocolate-pecan truffles. The expression alone on her guests' faces when they notice the supplemental buffet with fresh fruit and cake and ice cream swells Prima's already bursting heart. Across the room, her mother catches her eye, mouths "Beautiful!" and folds her hands as if in prayer, as if the sweet little delights before her are too perfect to touch. Still Prima can't relax enough to sit with her. She paces in the back of the ballroom near the kitchen, watching and waving and occasionally crossing the dance floor to wish the early departures good night.

"A lovely affair," they say. And to Tom: "First class, Buckley. First class all the way."

"Thank you," they say as she squeezes their hands and kisses the cheeks of the overcologned accountants and their jittery wives. "Thank you so much."

All her life, Prima has put her faith in the grand gesture. In middle school she organized elaborate study parties with themed food and music and mnemonic games. As a child she reenacted Lucille Ball skits in the basement for her mother and Tony, memorizing the jokes and the pratfalls. On Tom's twenty-first birthday, after they'd been dating only a month, she filled his dorm room with twenty-one presents of various shapes and sizes.

"Excuse me," someone says, behind her. "You must be the mother of the bride?"

She turns and—no mistake this time—there's Frankie. Frankie in a wrinkled shirt, no tie, and khakis with frayed cuffs. Frankie after all. Her first instinct is to throw her arms around him, but she stops herself. He's two hours late. The look in his eyes is smug. She checks her watch. "How'd you get here?" she says. "You couldn't have called?"

"I drove," he says. "I got up at the crack of dawn and sat in traffic all day. That's why I'm late. But maybe I shouldn't have bothered."

Prima has steeled herself to fight her mother today, not Frankie. So she says, "You know what? You're right," and apologizes, thanks him for making the effort to drive all the way down, and offers him gas money, which he refuses. Finally she throws her arms around him like she wanted to when she saw him. He is her only brother. She's happy he's here, even two hours late, even smug.

"Did I miss the big announcement?"

"You're in luck," she says.

She takes him by the hand and leads him toward the head table. When they reach the dance floor, their mother spots him. It occurs to Prima at this moment—as Maddalena jumps out of her chair and runs to greet her son—that all Frankie needs to do to fill his mother's heart is walk into a room. There are tears in Maddalena's eyes like he's a soldier stepping off a warship. She's seen him as recently as the Fourth of July, when he came down to Prima's beach house for a few days, but it might as well have been a decade. When you have lost one of your own children, every day apart from the ones who survived seems endless. Prima lets go of her brother's hand, steps to the side as their mother embraces him, and searches the room for other early departures to bid good night.

Before long, the guests have all gone, taking with them the heavy glass vases of orange dahlias, the cake in wax-paper bags. Prima and Tom stand at the head table, her arm around his waist, her head on his shoulder. Their family sits before them: her mother and father, three of their boys, Frankie eating a warmed-up plate of lasagna. Behind them, the violinist snaps his case shut and shakes hands with the cellist. It is six o'clock, nearly dark, and through the windows they can see the last of the golfers carrying their gear to the parking lot.

"Oh well," says her mother, rubbing her arms and standing. "They're going to kick us out, I guess."

"Hold on one second, Mamma," says Tom.

Antonio puts his hand on his wife's leg. "What's your rush?" he says.

Ryan, shirt untucked, returns from the men's room, glances around at his parents and brothers and grandparents and uncle all sitting quietly. "What'd I miss?" he asks.

"Your mother has something to say," Tom tells him.

"Oh, right!" says Ryan. "The big finale."

The folded papers in Prima's hands suddenly take on a weight. For weeks she's been eager to hand them to the seven people gathered around the table, but now, inexplicably, she wants to keep them to herself a bit longer.

"Can I guess?" asks Matt.

"Sure."

"Really? OK, hold on. Let me think."

"You're buying a boat," says Maddalena. She's sitting up straight in her chair, ready to be proud of what her daughter can afford.

"Nope," Tom says. "But that's not a bad idea."

"You bought both those plots in Greenville," Maddalena guesses again. "So me and your father can live with you."

"Colder," says Tom. "We're selling that lot for a nice little profit, by the way. We'll need it."

"This news involves us all," Prima says. "Not just me and Tom."

Maddalena narrows her eyes. "Why does that make me nervous?" she says. "Don't tell me you're moving somewhere far. You can't go chasing your kids—"

"No, of course not," says Prima. "But actually, yes, temporarily we're *all* moving. Far, *far* away." She takes a deep breath, locks eyes with her mother. "We're going back to the Old Country, all of us. To the Grassos' ancestral village, Santa Cecilia, where it all began. For two weeks."

"Awesome!" says Matt.

"Talk serious," Maddalena says, crossing her arms.

"I'm very serious," Prima says. "It's not difficult. I buy the tickets. I call a few relatives. We get on a plane."

"I'm there," says Ryan.

"Oh yes, it's very easy," Maddalena says. Everyone's looking at her. She shakes her head, folds her arms more tightly across her chest, the way Patrick used to do when he wouldn't eat his peas. "You knew about this, Frankie?"

Frankie shakes his head.

"I didn't think so."

"It's like a resort now," says Tom, gently. "There are five or six hotels, right smack in the village of Santa Cecilia. And even if there weren't, there's so much to see in Italy. Prima's mapped out a bunch of day trips. We want the family to learn its history."

"I know my history," Maddalena says. "So does he." She ticks her head toward Antonio. "I don't tell you enough times I'll never go back there? You call it a gift to force me?"

"You weren't kidding," Tom says to Prima under his breath.

"I knew you wouldn't be thrilled," Prima says to her mother. "But this isn't only about you. There are other people at the table here today. Do you ever think about what Dad wants? How about your grandsons? Us? Do you know how embarrassed I get every time I tell somebody I've never been to my homeland?"

"Embarrassed?" says Frankie, again with the smug face.

"She's got such a sad life, doesn't she, Frankie?" Maddalena says. "She wants to go to Italy so bad, why doesn't she go herself?"

"I'm still here, Ma," Prima says.

"Nobody's stopping you, Prima. You've got money. I tell your father all the time, 'Let your daughter take you back. Don't drag me into it.'"

"You haven't heard her say that, Prima?" mutters Frankie. "Did you two just meet?"

Prima shakes her head at her brother. "I've heard it," she says. "I live here. I know her better than anybody. Without her in Italy, though, it won't be the same. And what, she's supposed to stay here by herself when we all go?"

"I don't have to go," Frankie says.

"I'll say one thing," Antonio says. He leans back in his chair, presses his fingertips to the edge of the table. "This is the best idea I've ever heard."

"Finally!" Tom says. "Somebody likes it."

"*We* like it!" Ryan adds.

"There's only one mistake you made," Antonio continues. "No way in the world you're spending all that money on us. I'm paying the tickets for everybody."

"Save your breath, Dad," says Prima. "Because—and hear me on this—it's *already done.*" She waves the folded envelopes at them. "Right here, eight prepaid travel vouchers. Nonrefundable. Departure date: August tenth, 2000. Return date: August twenty-fifth."

"No shit!" says Patrick.

"I told you I was serious."

"But Frankie has school," Antonio says.

"In August?" Prima answers. "Even Frankie doesn't go to school in August. The details we can work out as we go forward, but for now we're all going to clear our schedules for August tenth. That's ten months away, plenty of time to plan, cover the restaurant, knock some sense into you, Mom, whatever we need to do."

"All that money wasted," says Maddalena. She takes her fork and pushes a bite of cake around her plate. "It's a shame. I'm staying here. Call the airplane company and tell them I died."

"Jesus Christ," Prima says.

"This is supposed to be exciting," says Tom. "Prima and I have been wanting to make this happen for years, not just for us, for everybody. Since the day we met we've been talking about a Grasso-Buckley family trip to Italy. Doesn't it sound like a movie?"

"Good news is long overdue in this family," says Prima. "That's all we're trying to do: give the Grassos a happy memory."

Maddalena stops listening to this nonsense. Why bother? They speak for her. Always people speak for her, tell her what she really means, how to pronounce the words so they sound not only like correct English but less angry, less sad. First her mother and father spoke for her; then, when she was just a teenager—barely nineteen!— Antonio Grasso came along in his suit and his *zio's* car and did the talking. She has never been back to Santa Cecilia, not even for a visit, not once in the fifty years since Antonio married her and brought her to America, and she's not about to start now. Unlike him, she still has her people in that village. She remembers them how they were when she left them in 1946. Now most of them are bones in the ground behind the church. Mamma and Babbo, her sisters and brothers, Teresa, Celestina, Maurizio, Giacomo. Too much family to lose in one lifetime. It's not enough to bury your own son; now they want her to go back for the bones of the others, too? She has only one brother left, Claudio, and one sister, Carolina, but she hasn't spoken to them in twenty years. She won't see them old and sick, not after working so hard, every day, to keep them young and beautiful and full of life in her mind. No. She won't let that happen.

She could be loud about it now, but she won't, not here, not on her grandson's special day. Not with Frankie beside her. If she makes a fuss, she'll scare him off. So she pushes the slice of cake around her plate until it hardens to a paste. Her eyes wander the room. She notices the spill stains on the carpets by the bathroom, the chips in the saucers, the dust on the drapes. In the corners of Prima's eyes—look how she's talking now, on and on, her and her surprises—are a web of wrinkles, and not just when she smiles. Liver spots cover her once-perfect wrists. No, that's Maddalena's own face in the mirrored wall; that's her spotted, wrinkled old-lady skin. Santa Cecilia was the one place on earth where she was young. She was a beauty and a talker there, an expert at voices, an actress in the making. What belongs to her and her alone is that village during those nineteen years, her memories of it, of who she might have been, the view from the terrace above her father's store, the stairs to her bedroom made of marble, the tops of the trees scraping the sky. Go back now, see it all changed, and that, too, will be taken away.

"DON'T WORRY ABOUT my mother," Prima says to Tom on the way home. Patrick's in the back seat with his headphones on, staring out the window. The other boys are safely on trains back to Syracuse and to Penn State. "She'll come around. Who can't come around to a trip to Italy?"

"Her," Tom says. "Maybe it's wrong to push her. You saw her face—she went white. And she was *mad*. Like, *rage*. I've never seen her that way. You told me this trip would be a tough sell, but I wasn't expecting such an extreme reaction. You think she's hiding something about that village?"

"She's got nothing to hide, trust me. She's an open book. She needs that push. She doesn't know what's good for her. And she's so dramatic. Ryan got that gene, didn't he? Somehow it skipped me." She smiles and pinches him.

More than that, though, she explains to Tom, it's unhealthy for her mother to pretend Santa Cecilia stopped existing the day she left it, to treat her childhood in the village the way she and Prima have both treated losing Tony. It's time for that to change. She read in a magazine that decades of denial build up in a person, that closing yourself off, never giving yourself a release, pretending things are one way when they're another, is unhealthy, can even lead to cancer or Alzheimer's or high blood pressure. It makes sense. You hold something in long enough and it turns to poison.

"It was Tony's forty-third birthday last week," she says to Tom now. She's testing how it feels to say his name out loud, to make him a part of the day. It's never too late, the magazine said, to chip away at the buildup of denial, but mentioning his birthday to Tom so casually, the way she'd mention the birthday of someone in his firm, feels like a betrayal of the unspoken pact she's had with her mother.

Even so, she continues. "I went to my mother's house on the actual day," she says. "I didn't tell her why. I just stopped in. We sat at the kitchen table drinking coffee and talking about the party, and I said,

'Let's walk down to St. Mary's and light a candle,' but she pretended not to hear me. She got up and emptied the espresso maker."

"Like I said, maybe it's wrong to push her."

"If you don't push people, Tom, they don't change. What if I didn't push this one?" She ticks her head back toward Patrick, then leans in to whisper. "He'd be bald right now, begging for change at the train station."

Tom laughs. "That's a Hare Krishna, not a Buddhist."

"Still," says Prima. "If it weren't for me and Father Larson sitting him down, explaining his roots, you think he'd be confirmed today?" And here's another reason for the Grasso trip to Italy: to show her sons the beauty they came from, walk them through St. Peter's Square, fill them with a history that will ground them for life. Though Prima's never been to the Old Country, she's seen enough movies and read enough articles to know that it can transform and unite them, keep them from wandering too far from each other.

It's a school night, but Patrick's had a big day, so they let him stay up and watch TV in his room and go through his gifts. He's zonked, though, and Prima's not surprised when, on the way to the laundry room, she finds him asleep on his bed fully clothed, cards and un-wrapped boxes around him. She stands in the doorway a moment, watching his easy breathing, his hand still clutching the remote. He is her most precious, fragile, extraordinary gift, made only more pre-cious, more fragile, by the simultaneous existence of his extraordinary brothers. It seems that every time she looks at one of her boys, it's to fix him there before her, to stop time and fate and circumstance from stealing him away. Her mother must have looked at Tony this way, too, while he practiced the piano he'd begged for, while he cruised through his homework at the kitchen table in half the time it took Prima to finish hers, but it didn't work. Prima doesn't need a magazine to explain the guilt Maddalena will always feel for that, because it's a guilt that Prima shares.

2 *Two Lives*

ANTONIO GRASSO AND his mother loved the Ristorante Al Di Là like it was one of their own children. The last time he saw her alive, she was in her wheelchair by the window, at the restaurant's fortieth anniversary party. They had built this place together—he and his mother and his brother, Mario—and together they'd watched it grow and settle and slide into middle age. "Forty years!" his mother had said, amazed, clutching his hand, and he'd said, "*Che brutta cosa come passano gli anni.*" What an ugly thing, how the years pass. Twenty-two of them already, since Mario died. Two, since Mamma. Twenty-eight, since Tony. If he blinks, another year will go. He doesn't blink.

After a certain age, you're no use to the world. Everybody knows this, of course, but you're not supposed to put the words together out loud. What you're supposed to do is make enough money to leave to your kids. Set your wife up with a pension and annuities. Pay off your house and the funeral parlor. Get out of the way.

Antonio is seventy-nine years old. He can't work like he used to, can't keep as strong an eye on the cooks and the managers. He showed up this morning and directed Olindo, the newest manager, to open the drapes in the main dining room to let in the light, but if Antonio hadn't shown up and the drapes stayed closed, the Al Di Là would have made just as much profit. Each day when Antonio walks down Union Street, through the neighborhood once filled with Italians, he doesn't recognize the faces. They're all strangers, the men on the sidewalks and the young women leaning out the windows, and he is the last man standing from an era that matters to no one.

He wants to go home. One last time to the village, that's all. One last time to walk with his arm around Maddalena's waist through the streets where they met as children, to the church where he married her, to the terrace of her father's house. One last time in a place where people want him and where his memories are happy. In the three days since he saw the tickets in Prima's hands, Antonio has been in Santa Cecilia in his mind. He's left behind the country club, the arguments, the Al Di Là, all of it. When thirsty, he goes to kneel at the spring in the piazza. His *zio* Domenico waits in line behind him for the clear, crisp water, and behind Domenico his mother and father wait in their summer clothes, and behind them stands Antonio himself at the age of seventeen. A horse and carriage go by, driven by Aristide Piccinelli; beside Aristide is his youngest daughter, Maddalena, eighteen years old, hiding her golden hair under a wide-brimmed hat. They are on their way to Avezzano to buy supplies for their grocery store. And then it begins to snow, and he is seven years old, tackling his brother in a drift. Mario escapes and runs deeper into the woods, where it's summer again and the leaves are thick and he and ten other boys are playing war . . .

He sits in a booth by the window, with a view of sunny Union Street and the *Corriere della Sera* before him on the table. He has a lunch meeting with his lawyer, DiSilvio, but DiSilvio is always late, so Antonio keeps reading. There's another story—a different one every week, it seems—about the drop in the Italian population, the growing fears that the country will have no one to carry on its traditions, now that Italian girls feel no shame living childless with their boyfriends, choosing careers in politics and banking and the law over motherhood. The article confirms for Antonio that he will die at the right time: before Italy loses its Italian altogether. He circles the headline—ARRIVEDERCI, ROMA—to show DiSilvio.

Antonio's first years as an immigrant in America, he lived alone and single and with his back turned to the Old Country. It had served its purpose by giving him life, but after that, he'd asked himself, what good did Italia do? The Grassos' farm, stuck at the rocky bottom of the hill, struggled to produce enough to feed them, let alone trade. For every child born to Antonio's mother and grandmother, another died before the age of five. The wars came through like tornadoes, spinning good people and bad people together up in the air and spitting them out in pieces. The few left on the ground stayed dumb and believed whatever they were told, afraid of tomorrow, afraid of today, happy only when they remembered yesterday and tried to repeat it, even if yesterday punched them in the gut.

America, on the other hand, was never without a smile on its face and a big idea in its head. It did stupid things—the government was a bunch of crooks, of course, show him a government that wasn't—but the stupid things it did still put the country a step ahead. It knocked people over on the way, and didn't apologize, and kept that smile on its face the whole time, and that was how it earned respect. This is, at least, how his father explained America to Antonio in those first years he and Mario and their mother lived with him in the row house on Eighth Street. He convinced his sons that Italy was a dying world, that eventually everyone they'd known in the village would have to find their way across the Atlantic, and that they were lucky to have beaten them to it. Their mother was not convinced. Sunday afternoons at four, she would turn on Radio Italia, and the men would leave the room. Nostalgia was not allowed. Nostalgia was not honest, their father said; it got you drunk and tired worse than whiskey. It was better to pretend that Italy, and all their memories of it, had sunk into the sea.

When Antonio named the Grasso restaurant after the Al Di Là Café in Santa Cecilia, he meant it as a tribute not to his country or his village but to Maddalena. He had brought her to the café late one Saturday night, soon after he and Mario had returned to Santa Cecilia to find wives. He was twenty-six then, Mario twenty-four. The Al Di Là Café was the only place to take a girl dancing. By day, customers ate their meals outside on the terrace, surrounded by a wrought iron fence, but a few times a month, a band showed up from another town, colored lights were strung across the walls, and the terrace became a nightclub. That night, with her chaperone father watching, Antonio and Maddalena slow-danced across the stone floor to the music of a young guitar player from Terni. Maddalena was nervous.

The boy who loved her, Vito Leone, might be watching, too, she said, along with her father, so her body was stiff, and when the song ended she had tears in her eyes. She'd known Antonio less than a month at that point, but he'd made a good impression on her parents—the farm boy turned rich American businessman!—and they insisted she marry him, and then the boy who loved her married her sister Carolina, and in that village way, life started for them all. The only guilt he felt at the time was for separating her from her family, but he trusted that one day she'd thank him for giving her a bigger life. He's been waiting for that gratitude ever since, but she is stubborn and still angry, and maybe he deserves it, but maybe, too, this trip will show her he's been right all along.

He wishes he could see Maddalena as she was then, climbing the stairs to the terrace in her sister's blue sundress, holding her mother's hand. It was a cool night and she wore a shawl, but after she'd seen Antonio waiting for her at the bar, she removed the shawl. As they danced, cheek to cheek, left side, then right side, he couldn't take his eyes from her shoulders. That she had left them there, bare, for him to admire, was a sign. A week later, they were husband and wife.

Antonio and Mario opened the American version of the Al Di Là in 1955. Their father was gone by then, and with him went the daily reminders of the inferiority of Italy. Slowly, as the restaurant grew into a success, memories of the Old Country, the innocence between the wars, found Antonio. He and Mario talked about buying back their old house in Santa Cecilia, making it a second home for their families. More and more Italians, Antonio included, left the city for the suburbs and surrounded themselves with the Irish and Polish and, worse, people who couldn't even tell you what their blood was made of. In the years after moving out of Little Italy, Antonio came to feel fear, not pride, when Prima spoke perfect English to her friends without the hint of an accent. He searched through the basement for the trunk of clothes he wore as a child and asked Maddalena to dress Tony in his old short pants and jackets and noticed, as if for the first time, the high quality of the material. The American brands they paid a fortune for in the stores seemed cheap by comparison. He became one of those fathers who told the same stories from his youth long after his kids stopped listening, and as he got older, it occurred to him that he did not tell these stories to teach Prima and Tony and Frankie about their heritage but to keep the stories alive for himself. The Italy of the 1920s and 1930s—the mountains in his bedroom window, the young women in furs taking their *passeggiate,* the horse-drawn carriages bringing food and mail to Santa Cecilia from the cities—came to him in dreams, and when he woke he'd feel guilty, like he'd been cheating on America, until he learned that he could love them both, but differently, the way he loved his children.

He took nostalgia's hand, and it pulled him under. Then Tony died, and grief held him there. He's been drowning ever since. If Antonio can get back to Santa Cecilia, where his son never walked or slept or played the piano or looked up at his father with love and need, maybe he will breathe again. And if he takes his last breath there, so be it.

In the meantime, he has business to finish. The first call he made after Prima's announcement was to DiSilvio to set up this meeting. The way it stands today, Maddalena gets the Al Di Là and every penny of the savings. Then after she goes, the kids and grandkids split the savings that are left: 40 percent to Prima, 40 percent to Frankie, 5 percent each to the boys. Fair and square. The problem is the afterlife of the Al Di Là. He can't count on Prima or Frankie. They don't love the place the way Tony did. Worse: they have their own lives. They don't come to the Al Di Là much as it is. After he's gone, they'll let things go, make too many friends, trust the wrong people, lose trust in each other. So he will go over the will and the restaurant papers again. He doesn't know what the papers will tell him and DiSilvio today that they didn't tell them last year or five years ago, but he needs DiSilvio at least to help him think.

Antonio always thought both Mario and Tony would be around for this part. Since the day the Al Di Là opened, it was the two Grasso brothers running the show together, and their two sons who would take it over. He never imagined putting all three men in the ground, one at a time, his brother at fifty-five, his nephew at twenty, his son at fifteen. Without Mario, there'd be no Al Di Là in the first place. Antonio would still be working for peanuts on the assembly line at Ford.

Every Sunday, after he drops Maddalena off at church, Antonio drives to the cemetery. The cemetery is *his* church: the headstones and the dirt and the fresh air and flowers. Half a day it takes to visit the people he knows. So many Italians came to this country over the years. Some paid a lot of money to get buried back in their village, but most ended up here. Giulio Fabbri and Gianni Martino are on the far side near the highway, both waiting for their wives to join them. Mario's in the quieter part, under a thick stone with an angel and deep engravings that Antonio wipes clean of grime. For his son, Antonio chose a crypt in the St. Jude section, high up off the ground but not so high he can't place his lips and palms against it. Next to Tony is a spot with his own name. Beside him, Maddalena.

He doesn't believe in anything after, like she does. He won't see Tony or Mario or Mamma or Papà or his friends again in heaven. Maddalena and his kids won't see him or each other. There's no big garden party with butterflies and fountains and trays of pastries. He'd bet money on it, if he could ever collect the winnings.

How is Antonio spending his last days? First of all, he doesn't sleep. He puts his head on the pillow and closes his eyes, but sleep never finds him. At seven o'clock he gets out of bed to make the coffee. He eats two Stella D'oro cookies and sits in his chair in the den. He watches the local news and *The Flintstones*. Eight thirty he brings coffee to Maddalena. Eight fifty-five on the stove clock he makes sure she's out the door for church. If it rains or is too cold, he drives her. If the weather's good, she walks. He reads the American paper on the toilet for a good long hour, and by then she is home and has made the bed and started the day's cleaning. He showers and shaves and checks the VCR to make sure it's taping her soap opera. Then he takes the car to Union Street and eats lunch at the Al Di Là with the *Corriere della Sera*. Lunchtime is busy. They get a lot of businessmen, and most of the time he has to give up his seat, which he is happy to do. After the rush, he makes sure the tables are set for dinner and the silverware is clean. Sometimes he walks over to Eighth Street to visit Mario's widow, Ida, all alone in her big house. She has a broken right leg and a knee replacement in the left, and since her husband died and her son got killed in Vietnam she's never had a happy thing to say. "We had some good years," he reminds her. "When we lived here all together, us and Mario and Mamma and Papà. You don't remember the Sunday dinners and the bingo games and Nina's little dog?" But she makes a face and turns up her game shows.

For dinner, Antonio brings something home from the restaurant, or he just fixes it himself for the two of them. Little by little over the years, Maddalena stopped cooking. She's in the kitchen one day out of 365: Christmas Eve, to fry the fish. No other husband in America has cooked as many meals or washed as many dishes as he has, but he doesn't mind. He just wants a little credit once in a while.

After dinner he drives back to the Al Di Là, stays an hour to shoot the shit and look over the receipts, then hits the Amerigo Vespucci Club to play bocce. Yesterday he beat the new guy, Tomasso, who's ten years younger and some kind of champion from Trenton. If you win, the club buys you a drink, but Antonio doesn't drink much anymore. He lost the taste for it. Soda and iced tea and coffee are enough, and maybe that's why he doesn't sleep? The doctors don't believe him when he says he hasn't slept since Ronald Reagan was the president. Not that Reagan was ever *his* president.

Antonio should be grateful for these days, but he can't help it, he hates to be old. It's ugly and sad punishment for sins he never committed. He would prefer to live to see the next election, and the one after that, and on and on, mostly so he can keep reminding the younger generations that the working man built this country. He hates the sunset because it brings on the night, and the night scares him with its ghosts and silence. The night is thick with memories in a way that the day never is. Nobody wants to hear any of this. So he pretends

that he's happy and at peace, that when he closes his eyes he's not falling from the bridge with his arms out, reaching for his son just out
of reach, calling his name over and over. Only if he is "upbeat" (that's
Prima's word) will his kids and the customers talk to him for a few
minutes in a row, and for just that little bit of time he's supposed to
thank the Lord.

There's only one person Antonio should stick around for, one reason why he and Maddalena shouldn't move back to Santa Cecilia for
good, and that's Frankie. Prima is more than settled, but Frankie's up
in the clouds somewhere. Where he came from, where he's going, nobody knows. Thirty years old almost, and still fooling around with
school and master's degrees and jobs that don't pay. ("How can you
live on prestige?" Antonio has asked him. "Does prestige put food
on the table?") Sometimes he thinks it's a good thing Frankie lives
in Boston, so Antonio doesn't have to see his mixed-up life up close.

He would be very lucky to live long enough to see Frankie settled
and happy, with his own kids, out of danger from a lonely life, or
worse. If he could get DiSilvio to put that on paper, make it official
and guaranteed, he would, no matter what the price. But DiSilvio
is later than ever, and there are some things even a lawyer and all
the education in the world can't do. Maddalena prays every day, but
Antonio doesn't think that does any good, either.

MADDALENA PICCINELLI GRASSO and her mother talk every day. For ten minutes after Mass each morning, Maddalena stays
and talks to her, and then at night, while Antonio sleeps, she writes
her letters. One a month. From the day she arrived in America,

Maddalena's been writing to her. She keeps the pages—hundreds now—hidden in the back of the middle drawer in her dresser of fabrics. After she's gone, her kids will find the pages and think she was crazy most of her life. But she is not crazy. Her mind goes blank sometimes, and she'll forget a name or a face or the point she was about to make, but otherwise she's got it all upstairs. She knows her mother's been dead twenty years. The letters and the talking keep her close.

Domenica scorsa c'è stata la Cresima . . . , she writes. Last Sunday was the confirmation of your great-grandson Patrizio. She describes in detail the boy's pin-striped suit, the kind priest, the desserts. She doesn't mention Prima's surprise. The letter takes an hour, but afterward Maddalena's still not tired. Though she'll sleep through the night until Antonio wakes her for Mass, it is the act of falling asleep that gives her trouble. The little pink pill's not strong enough to stop her mind from going over all there is to do, to plan, to change, to check, to remember. She longs to redecorate this bedroom with new wallpaper—an ivory moiré, maybe, or something more modern—to replace the big blue flowers a generation out of style.

She pictures what each of her children is doing: Frankie at the library in Boston, Prima on one last walk through her big house to sweep and straighten up, Tony in heaven in his pajamas eating a TV dinner in front of *The Beverly Hillbillies.* Maddalena blesses them, one by one, at the start of her prayers. Then another hour it takes for her to pray for all the other people in her life, living and dead, in this country and in Italy. Seems like every week she makes a new friend—a lady from church or the dance studio, or one of her sewing customers who wants to take her to lunch—and each new friend is one more person who keeps her awake.

All the complaining about sleep her husband does, and listen to him now, snoring so loud he's waking up dead people. One night she'll put a tape recorder in front of his nose and the next day play him the snoring, but just watch, he still won't believe her. He'll keep singing his favorite song, the one about how he's too old to sleep, that he's no good to anybody anymore, why won't God just take him. Maddalena hates that song. She tries to lift him up. "We have to keep moving at our age," she's always telling him. "Once you slow down, you make it easy for God to catch you. You think it's no trouble for me to drive to the studio twice a week, with all those lanes to merge, and take lessons like a teenager?" And no matter what griping Antonio does, she knows he wants to keep living. Why else does he run to the doctor every time he's got a cough?

Maddalena is seventy-two years old, and in America that's a spring chicken. When she's dancing at the studio, when she tries on with Prima the new dresses of the season, when her children and grandchildren are sitting around her at the dining room table Christmas Eve, and she's able to forget what's come before, she's twenty-five again. She thinks, I'm too alive to ever leave this world. All the time people waste! Why don't they realize? It takes hard work not to look back. So she turns her bedside radio to the fast-music station, and if she gets three clean hours of sleep, that's plenty to give her the energy she needs to accomplish the day.

She wants to look especially fresh for tomorrow at the studio—the "fall fling," they call it—where she'll wear her new gold Dance

Naturals shoes. So she closes the light and lies down next to Antonio, who's wrapped like a sausage in the sheets even though the heater's on. She puts her arm around him and thinks of Frankie, whose voice tonight on the phone sounded sad, lost. She worries he's not eating enough, that he's drinking too much to sleep, and that somehow it's her fault. Each time she talks to Frankie, he's a different man. At the confirmation party and for days afterward, he agreed with her about the Italy trip, told her not to let Prima push her around; then tonight he snapped at her, told her she was acting selfish. Both times he was right. She knows she's making too much of the trip, but once she admits that to Frankie, to anyone, they'll have her. It's a shame Antonio was off the phone already; he would have liked hearing Frankie take his side for once. Nothing the boy does is good enough for him. It's right to discipline, but if you ask Maddalena, Antonio tries too hard to be tough.

People at the dance studio ask Maddalena to tell them about her kids, but she says there's no word for the feeling that her heart is full and breaking and refilling again, all at the same time, every moment of every day. If they know the word for that, would they tell her, please?

"No," they say. "Not how you feel to be a mother. We want to hear: Do your kids like to dance? Do they have good jobs? Why don't they ever come to the studio to watch you do the tango in the competitions? Why don't you ever mention them, never pull out pictures from your purse? . . ."

How can Maddalena explain? The studio is one life, her kids another. Santa Cecilia another. The years she had Tony, that was another, too, a separate life. In this way only can she understand how the pregnancy faker can do the evil things she does. When she explained this to Frankie the other night on the phone, he told her, "That's compartmentalization, Ma. It's not exactly considered healthy."

"Call it whatever big word you want," Maddalena had told him. "It's the only way a person can survive."

There are parts of her soul that are dark, like the room where Tony slept. When you walk into it, you can only throw yourself crying onto the bed. No one will ever convince her she's wrong to avoid that room, to pretend it doesn't exist. It's hard enough passing the door every day, remembering the life on the other side of it. She can forgive herself for pressing her body against the door, even for turning the knob once in a while, but afterward she always wishes she'd been more strong.

No one at the studio knows she once had a life that included a son named Tony, or if they do know, they don't ask about it. A long time has passed since anyone—usually a woman, another mother—looked at Maddalena and put her arms around her in comfort. It's a relief for Maddalena to be free of those stabs in the throat. The woman's comfort always came first, but then, before long, she'd add up Frankie's age and ask how Maddalena could have had another child so soon—two years, could that be right?—after losing her son, which would force Maddalena to say, "How could I not?"

These women weren't in the Grasso house in 1971, when Prima was taking the Chevy out without asking and sometimes not coming home at all; when Maddalena cooked for the three of them every day, then ate alone from the pots on the stove and put away the rest because Antonio would stay late at the Al Di Là and Prima disappeared for days without calling. Those nights, when Antonio finally got home, almost always after midnight and more than a few whiskeys, Maddalena would be in her rag clothes scouring the refrigerator or wiping down the shelves of the china cabinet. She'd begun to iron their underwear and towels and paint the skinny lines of grout in between the kitchen and bathroom tiles with a Q-tip. At the time, she was still working nine to five at the drapery shop, and Antonio would try to get her to rest during these late-night hours—watch TV, read one of her Italian romances—but she was afraid of having nothing to do but think, because when she had nothing to do but think, she dug her nails into her scalp. Besides, she said, a house could never be too clean. People were always stopping by to tell her how sorry they were and what a tragedy it was that Tony couldn't go to heaven. She'd scream at them until they left, and the next day they'd come back with more food.

One of those nights, Antonio was sitting at the kitchen table with her at his feet. She was on her knees scrubbing the ceramic tiles. It was almost one o'clock, and they were alone in the house. They didn't know where Prima was or if she'd be coming home. Maddalena wore a flowered housedress with holes in the underarms, looking, he said, like his peasant *nonna* in her old age.

"Have you ever thought—" He stopped.

She sat back on her ankles. They looked at each other.

"Yes," she said. She wiped her cheek with the back of her hand. "I've thought. I want to."

"You don't know what I'm asking."

"I think I do." She looked up beyond the doorway to the stairs. Their house was a split-level with the master bedroom on the first floor and three small bedrooms on the second. "After all these years, you still don't believe I can read your mind."

"I'm talking about another child."

"I know, Antonio. I've been asking you for three months now."

"When? Where was I?"

"Not out loud," she said. "Inside, to myself. I figured sooner or later you'd hear."

"Why not just . . . out loud?"

She bowed her head. She was an Italian wife of the old fashion. They had married when she was a girl. She might have learned to read his mind, but she still could not ask him to do what it took to make a child. He had not reached for her in the year since Tony died.

It didn't happen that night. Or the night after. She felt ashamed for wanting it to and worried what Antonio thought of her for agreeing to his suggestion, for not resisting, for dishonoring the memory of their son.

On a Wednesday afternoon weeks later, he came down to the basement, where she was measuring drapes, and handed her six white roses wrapped in blue and pink ribbons. In the past, the few times he'd brought Maddalena flowers, they were violets, her favorite. This occasion, though, did not call for violets. Roses had music. They gave permission. She stood at her worktable, the roses in one hand and a stick of chalk in the other.

They started there on the worktable, the drapes pushed to the side in a wrinkled heap. The next morning in their bed. He showed up early from the restaurant the night after that. The roses went brown in the vase on the nightstand. There was a new electricity between them, a live current trapped just under their skin. It was the force that connects husband to wife, keeps their hearts pumping, keeps one from spinning away from the other even when spinning away seems like the only way to escape grief.

They lay side by side, sheets pulled up to their chests, and spoke Italian, as they often did when alone, but they would not look each other in the eyes. Maddalena fixed hers on the burnt-out bulb in the floor lamp in the corner. To meet Antonio's eyes was to betray Tony. And to admit they were taking a big risk. Giving birth to Prima had left her in a coma for a week, and though Tony had been easy, who knew how her body had changed in sixteen years? The baby could be born deformed. Back in the village, women her age were already grandmothers.

If he'd been born a girl, they'd have named him Antonia. But he was Francesco, after Antonio's father, and from the beginning he was like an old man himself, quiet and serious and smart even though he moved slow. He was as different from his brother as two boys could be, wanting always to be left alone—first with his little toy cars, later his homework and his books and the noise he called music. He didn't seem to need or want to be around anyone but Maddalena. Like Tony, he got top grades in school, won all the awards for English and history, but unlike Tony, at the ceremonies only his teachers came up to congratulate him. He never brought any friends home. No sleepovers, no birthday parties. As a teenager he sat most summer days in the re-cliner holding a book in front of his face, blocking the sunlight like a vampire. His father came to think of Frankie as the sick child they'd feared he'd be, deformed from the inside.

"He's OK, you think?" Antonio would ask her. He meant in the head. He meant, You're keeping an eye on him, yes?

"Better than OK," Maddalena would reply. "He doesn't need any friends but us." And because Frankie belonged to her more than to him, and always would, since that night she looked up from her scrubbing, Antonio never argued. He gave him over to her. Tony had loved his mother, of course, in the way that all boys do, but what he'd felt for his father was stronger, deeper. There should be a word for that: for the different quality of love a child feels for one parent over the other.

What Tony was to Antonio, Frankie became to Maddalena: the first person he'd want to hear one of his stories, the last person he wanted to talk to before he went to bed. When the sixth-grade teacher asked his class to write about their heroes, Frankie chose his mother. For an art project, he traced an old Polaroid of Maddalena as a teenager and colored it in to make her look like a movie star. He couldn't stand to be apart from her the weekends she spent in the Poconos for dance competitions, not because he didn't get along with Prima, but because he worried he'd forget the things he wanted to tell her. "If I don't tell you about them," Frankie once said to her, "it's like they didn't happen."

To Maddalena, he might as well have said: I love you too much ever to leave this world. There was nothing better she could have heard from him than that.

Then something, somewhere, went wrong. It took Frankie over, like a brainwash. She can't reach him the way she used to, but she keeps trying, on their eleven o'clock calls, by telling him her fears and her opinions and all her secrets. She repeats the stories about Santa Cecilia and the boy who loved her, and the bike he made for her with his own two hands, and how the war came between them. She tells Frankie about his father, who started out a stranger and became a good man. She tells him whatever comes to her mind in the moment, to be like a friend to him because he's had so few, and it used to work: he used to tell her his secrets back. Then he became a man, and she lost her magic. His life would happen even when she wasn't in it.

So if she wanted to be honest, this is what she'd tell the people at the dance studio about Frankie: My son's the smartest boy; he's going to be a professor someday, a PhD; this nowhere city couldn't hold him; but I miss him the way he was when he was a boy and I was in the center of his life, and sometimes, God forgive me, I wish he'd been born deformed after all, living at home under my hand, where I could watch over him and talk to him face-to-face.

This thought rouses her from her anxious half sleep. She sits up against the headboard, in the dark, the fast-music station still playing on low. Her heart is pounding. She has to call Frankie now, even though she talked to him just three hours ago, even though it's late, because her heart won't beat slow enough to let her sleep unless she hears his voice again. This has happened before, and he's always forgiven her for disturbing him.

The phone in her lap, she dials the long-distance number, but it rings and rings with no answer. Where can he be? At eleven, he'd called from the library and said he was almost done for the night. He knows that all she needs is for him to say, It's OK, Ma, I'm fine, and she'll reach back over Antonio, put the phone down, close the light, breathe easy, and let sleep take her.

She keeps calling. One thirty. One forty-five. Two o'clock. Finally the roommate answers. "He likes to walk," she says. "Sometimes he leaves the library and just walks."

"Walks where?" Maddalena asks, but the girl has hung up.

When she calls again, at 3:30 a.m., he picks up. Finally. "Jesus, Ma," he says.

She's on the cordless, pacing the basement, where Antonio can't hear her banging on the walls. "Frankie!" she says, in tears. "Where do you go when you walk?"

3   *Resistance/Pleasure*

THEY HAVE A code, Frankie and Professor Birch. When she can make their standing date (Tuesdays and Thursdays from one to three, which, alas, preempts his soap), she leaves a note on department letterhead in his campus mailbox. "Dear Francesco—Finished chapter two—Coffee necessary—To discuss," or some such Dickinsonian construction. If she has to cancel, she'll leave a single yellow Post-it, blank or with a frowning, big-nosed cartoon face. The nose is metonymic of her husband, Dr. Amos Ziegler, chair of the Department of Engineering. Dr. Z. has not tapped her phone and does not monitor her e-mail; she just gets off on conducting a clandestine epistolary relationship. Birch's specialization may be in the field of postcolonial studies, but her heart, as best Frankie knows it, lies in a distant century.

He has never missed one of their dates. The Freshman Comp courses he teaches three mornings a week are his only blocked-out hours; the rest he spends grading papers or writing lesson plans or building additions onto the sprawling mansion of his dissertation zealously. Most nights, he's the last person out of the library at 2 a.m., and if it weren't for his walks and the shot of whiskey before bed, his mind would never settle. There are too many ideas, too many influences, too many phone calls from his mother and sister reporting and worrying and complaining and negotiating, too much distance between them all (the writers, the critics, the family) and him, and also not enough. If anything, he needs the structure—the distraction, the release—of his Tuesday-Thursday sessions with Dr. Birch. Between here and his PhD lies a chasm he must fill with just the right pages in order to cross, like a magic bridge, and once he skips across that bridge, his new life will unfold before him. In the meantime, Professor Birch and the whiskey are his only vices.

"Francesco—" begins Birch's note today. "Have the new Zizek— Useful for your diss?—See me to retrieve—Cheers—R. Birch."

Her first name, Rhonda, is forbidden in every circumstance but one. Only in bed is Frankie allowed to call it out, and only when he's close. Then she'll swivel her hips or wrap her legs around his back the better to receive him. It has taken some trial and error, but over the past semester he has learned advanced methods to achieve her pleasure, and also to resign himself to the fact that, though enthusiastic, she is an impatient lover who favors frequency over quality. Most days, he's not on his back five minutes catching his breath after the first time before she's fiddling with him and climbing on top again. If he calls her Rhonda in some other context—over cereal at the kitchen table after they've gone a few rounds—she'll reach across and tug his ear until he begs for mercy.

He tears up her note and watches the pieces flutter into the recycling bin. He has come to campus this morning for the sole purpose of checking his mail, the rest of which consists of flyers on brightly colored paper advertising various politically charged talks. He must resist such talks, and the spiraling conversations afterward, to avoid the possibility of new ideas and textures for the arguments in his dissertation. So he sends the stack of flyers, too, fluttering.

Frankie's first year, he attended every lecture he could fit into his schedule. He marked up the precirculated papers with a purple pen. He sent follow-up notes to the guest speakers and even maintained brief correspondences with a few. It was a happy year, his mind abuzz with theories and ideas. He lamented that he couldn't live long enough to finish all the papers jousting for attention in his head. Now, though, his charge is to focus, to shape. Not create. Not investigate.

According to the flyers, next week there will be another onslaught of programs: a roaring seventies feminist will speak to a half-filled auditorium; a prominent professor of history will posit a radical shift in US foreign policy to five ardent graduate students scattered across a lecture hall; wine and cheese will be consumed in a carpeted room here on the basement floor of West Hall, where, instead of discussing the paper just presented by the esteemed visiting Whitman scholar, the professors will gossip about the department chair's new Lexus. But for Frankie, the ideas might inspire new chapters, new takes, and so he must avoid them.

Inspiration, Frankie has learned, is the cheapest of the scholar's tools. Anyone can get charged up by the work of others, but what distinguishes true genius is the ability to sustain a thesis of one's own conception. His dream and intention is to contribute an enduring, crystalline text to the field of postcolonial studies, something to be read and studied by students as eager as he, ages and ages hence. Why else bother with the stale, endless hours in the library, the liminality, the suspension of normal life?

And if not now, when?

Stuck to the bottom of Frankie's mailbox, as if afraid to assert itself into the cacophony, is an official memo from Dr. Lexus. It's rare to get such a memo, as they're issued almost exclusively to announce that some university no one has heard of has offered a tenure-track position to a long-graduated PhD no one remembers.

This memo is different. Apparently the department has found, or been granted, $15,000 to give away in the form of a fellowship. Rather than divvy up the money into small awards for a handful of worthy graduate students, Dr. Lexus (in his typical all-or-nothing only-the-strong-survive absolutism, which, to everyone's surprise, has yet to distinguish him in the field of twentieth-century American poetry) will hold a competition to determine the most deserving scholar. Preference will be given to those graduate students who are more than halfway through their dissertation and who would benefit most immediately from the time away from teaching or other "financial pressures." The fellowship will be based strictly on merit, the first cut made by a panel of the university's own professors, the final round decided by a visiting judge named Felix Carr, from Princeton. The submission deadline for the first round has been set for next week—"deliberately short notice," Dr. Lexus explains, "to reward those who have done consistent work and who have something to show for their time"—and the finalists will be notified by Thanks-giving break. The application requires only a cover letter and as much of one's dissertation as is presentable.

Frankie has never wanted anything more. Also: he deserves it. Nobody works harder. He has turned down high-paying gigs (SAT and TOEFL prep, tutoring the spoiled daughter of a Saudi prince, bartending) to devote time to this work. A man of immigrant stock, he fully appreciates the decisive stamp of validation, and so will his parents, who, he might remind the committee, came to this country illiterate! Who toiled in factories! Once Frankie wins this, he'll have his own big announcement to make to his family, his own show-off moment. If he does make it to Italy next August, it will be as a doctor, another American success story coded into the Grasso genes.

He glances around, as if his fellow grad students—now the Competition—have already begun to mobilize. But there is only the empty hallway, the thin layer of beige carpet frilling at the seams, the muffled voices of office hours behind closed doors, the drone of the fluorescent overheads. He rereads the memo, looking for a clause that might disqualify him, but there is none. He has no excuse. In fact, the fellowship seems designed with him in mind, and he wonders if Birch had a hand in its design, if it was she who convinced Dr. Lexus, with whom she's always maintained a flirty antagonism, to swing the entire wad of cash toward a student who fits his exact profile. Oh, he could just kiss her!

Mentally he reviews his credentials. Two of six chapters complete and approved. Eight or nine more chapters in various stages of progress. A clever and potentially groundbreaking but still conclusionless take on Rushdie's *Midnight's Children*. The half-formed paper on the gothic and female identity, which he still must find a more elegant way to link to race. The Fanon chunk on which Birch has yet to give feedback, though he's nudged her twice over cereal. Can any of his colleagues beat that? Ann Highgate's not even finished her prospectus; Hector Billings has alienated and ditched his third adviser; Steve Doerr has two well-researched but histrionic chapters on the romantics; Chris Curran's on and off the wagon; and the pregnancies of Mary Kessler keep impeding her progress and prompting her to reimagine her entire project. Who's left?

Annalise Theroux, of course. Only Annalise, darling of the theoryheads, with her mod bob and inborn facility with French poststructuralism, poses anything close to a threat. Halfway through her examination of American film noir through a Lacanian lens (or something—Frankie doesn't quite get it), Annalise may just snatch this prize from his deserving jaws.

But he can't concern himself with Mademoiselle Theroux. Not at the moment, at least. He must get home and start crafting the most compelling cover letter in the history of the genre.

He dashes out the back door of West Hall before anyone sees him. The weather is perfect, as if nature itself won't let him corrupt the beauty of the day with further thoughts of his theoretical French nemesis. As he climbs the hill to the Great Lawn, he tries to think of a setting more exquisite than this New England college on this particular October morning, but he comes up empty. He's been to Niagara Falls, Key West, and the California coast, but the stately nostalgia of the university quad remains matchless. Hunched-over trees, backs heavy with history, line the grid of walkways. Perfectly molded bricks, drenched with two hundred years of knowledge and speculation and failure and triumph, quietly stabilize the buildings. He stops to look, now, as it rings, at the bell tower of the multidenominational house of worship, once an Episcopal church: the black, heavy stone against the brilliant sky. He loves the smoky, stale smell of the falling leaves and the whispers they make as he walks through them. All of it is enough to call forth a thousand innocent childhood hours in his old neighborhood, and the sense that autumn, that season of decay, marks the beginning of all good things.

Today the quad is thick with flannel blankets on which the undergrads lie, two by two, with books and notes between them, or doze with their backs against the trunks of the elms. He waves to a couple of jocks from his eight thirty, one of whom immediately holds up his textbook to show Frankie he's doing his homework; the other, in shorts and a tank top despite the weather, his book bag unopened before him, just shrugs and smiles. (Charm and good looks, Frankie wants to tell him, get you only so far.) He watches a girl—a redhead in a formfitting blue fleece—stop a moment in her rush between classes to squint and admire the show of colors. She is as lovely as the landscape, standing there rosy cheeked and awestruck, thinking, maybe, as Frankie is, of the bravery of nature—its choice to sing so magnificently in its final days. What human, Frankie nearly asks this girl, has died with such grace and left, in his going, a gift so grand? Not even his most beloved writers. He can't name one who comes close.

His ten-minute walk home takes him down College Avenue, over a bridge, past a coffee shop, a pizza place, two baseball fields, and the new gym, which has been under construction since the spring and may never be finished unless some serious cash is raised. If it mattered more to him, Frankie, who's never played a sport or cared to, would suggest that the university dispense with athletics altogether and use the money for need-based scholarships and make it a requirement for kids to watch the nightly news or read international newspapers. Teach them who the true heroes are, he would say. Nat Turner, Gandhi, Grandy Nanny. Tell them, If you want the thrill of victory and the agony of defeat, study the Algerian War. The *Iliad*!

"You're such a snob," Prima said to him last Christmas, after he ranted on this same topic to her and his brother-in-law and nephews— otherwise intelligent people who slavishly follow baseball and car racing and feel most alive during the inexplicable phenomenon known as March Madness.

"There are worse things to be accused of," Frankie told her.

"Like what?" Tom said.

Mediocrity, Frankie could have said, if the indictment weren't so direct. Instead: "Hypocrisy?"

"Cruelty to other people on purpose," offered Prima.

"All the best people are snobs," their mother said. "Snob means you understand what God made good and what he made ugly. It makes him angry when you don't pay attention to the difference."

If the Grassos were to have that discussion again today, after the announcement of Prima's Forced March/Sentimental Journey back to Santa Cecilia, he might add "ostentatiousness" and "showmanship"— not to mention "gross insensitivity to the feelings of one's mother"—to the list of sins more egregious than snobbery.

At Frankie's apartment, 25 Stowe Street (which he likes to pretend is named after Harriet Beecher), the outdoor steps are painted a faded blue and shot through with so many cracks that one day soon, as Frankie races up to catch the last few minutes of his soap, they will give way like an ice floe. The place is generic by design, a blank canvas on which tenants have been ordered not to make their mark. For its one distinct original feature, you must walk onto the porch and check out the elaborate railing: an expertly rendered piece of waist-high ironwork that features an intricate pattern of birds and branches between the slats. Somebody loved this place once. He'd planned to stay here forever, maybe leave it to his kids, and so he'd wrought these birds. Now the tenants, Frankie included, treat it like a motel room in a stopover city. They rarely venture onto the porch, let alone lean over the railing to admire the view.

For any other girl, Frankie would shower and spritz on a little cologne. But the Professor likes him raw. *I want to smell the sleep on you.* So he wastes no time and starts on the cover letter, writing and rewriting the first sentence, until he hears Anita's heavy footsteps on the stairs.

"Your company coming today?" she asks as she blows by his open door on the way to the kitchen.

"Yup."

"Don't worry. Just grabbing an apple."

"Do what you gotta do."

And that is his typical encounter with Anita. She is the flash in the hallway, the disembodied voice from the other side of the wall. A full-time nursing student, part-time roofer, part-time waitress, and nascent lesbian (unconfirmed), she spends little time at 25 Stowe. She knows about his walks from his predawn arrivals just as she's leaving for the hospital. She knows about him and the Professor from coming home sick one Thursday afternoon and catching their naked bodies scampering from the kitchen. If not for the fact that the Nursing and English Departments never overlap, and closeted Anita values discretion, the Professor would have ended their relationship the day Anita saw her. Or so she says.

He doesn't know how long Birch has been standing in the doorway—arms folded, shoulder against the dusty frame, sunglasses flipped up onto her head—before she deadpans, "Well, aren't you a sight."

This is her view: Frankie barefoot and cross-legged in his desk chair, wearing boxer briefs and a Jockey A-shirt, chewing his fingernails, his nose an inch from the computer screen. The tattoo on his left biceps—a Chinese character that, according to the artist, means both "resistance" and "pleasure"—winking at her.

Quickly he closes the document and shuts down his weary Mac Classic. The Professor lets drop her black leather bag, places the sunglasses on the bureau alongside her rings and hair clip, unzips her boots, and stands behind him rubbing his shoulders. "You're such a *worker*," she says as she pulls his shirt straps down over his arms. "It's very sexy to me."

That's all it takes. Before the screen goes dark, she's got him stretched out on the futon and burrows her head in his armpit. He is always naked before she is, as she makes it a struggle for him to unclasp her bra and peel off her formfitting jeans. Her skin smells of pencils. Frankie used to pretend he didn't see or feel the hair on her legs; now he's come to like the extra warmth of it, its whiff of perversion. For a long time he thought she didn't shave for feminist reasons, but it turns out she's just lazy.

The third time's the charm today, and by two thirty they're sitting at the kitchen table, two bowls of Rice Krispies loaded with raisins and sliced bananas between them. He keeps plenty of her favorite cereals and add-ins on hand, in all varieties, as well as the full-fat milk she prefers. Under the table, her right foot pokes around for a while and eventually finds a home on his crotch. This part, the candid free-form talk of literature and department gossip, is his favorite, less predictable and enervating than the sex. Today she reveals that Professor Audrey Wang, hired to bring some diversity to West Hall, will apparently not get tenure, and that a second-year transfer, Max Bradford, "creeps everybody out" with his glass eye. She does not mention the Fanon chapter, on which he's desperate for guidance, or Dr. Lexus's memo.

"And next week, I'm on that fucking panel in Chicago," she says. She lifts the bowl to her lips and drinks the rest of the milk. "Are you going to that, too? I keep forgetting."

"No," he says. "They rejected my paper."

"The gothic thing?"

"Yeah. It's not done, so—"

"They're idiots," she says. "I'll take a half-baked Frankie Grasso paper over their overwrought bullshit any day." She smiles. "You're lucky, though. Now you won't have to go. I'll end up writing my talk on the plane like I did last year."

"It would have been good for my CV," he ventures. "And it looks like a fairly decent lineup."

She shrugs. "I guess. To me it reads like yesterday's news."

"Still," he says, "I've never been, so I guess I have a glamorous notion."

"Oh yes, it's terribly glamorous," she says, laughing. "Pasty-faced English types in vintage suits sucking down cocktails, holding court on uninspired and irrelevant ideas. If they weren't so blatantly insecure, you'd hate them for their arrogance. Instead you just feel sorry for them, and for yourself—because all the shit you talk about them goes double for you." She reaches back, puts her hair in a ponytail, and suddenly looks a decade younger. Frankie's age, give or take a few years. "That's what you have to look forward to, my darling."

"Still," he says again, "it's the life of the mind."

"That it is," she says, with the feigned earnestness of a shrink. She digs her foot in deeper between his legs. "But the body is more honest."

"Honesty's overrated," he says. He thinks a moment. "No—not just that. That's too glib. I think honesty might in fact be the ultimate red herring. It's nothing beyond the literal—"

She's making an anxious face. "Can I be honest with you now?" she interrupts.

He looks at her. She has a wide, flat nose and a jaw almost manly in its severity but the smoothest skin his lips have ever kissed. There is a tiny hole in her right eyebrow where she sometimes wears a silver ring, and the faintest shadow of hair on one side above her upper lip.

She is beautiful in an unexpected way, like the angry little sister of the homecoming queen, and sometimes Frankie wonders if her rebelliousness is as put on as her jewelry.

"Why not," he says. Sunlight streams in from the blinds in the window above the sink, striping her skin.

"I'm really sorry," she says, squinting. "But don't count on that fellowship."

THE TWINS' PARTY—ANOTHER party! Because isn't life just a string of parties with dead air in between?—was Prima's idea. She planned it before the confirmation, when she noticed that Matt and Zach's twentieth birthdays fell on a Saturday. They'd go out and drink illegally that night, anyway, so what was the harm in having them and their friends drive out from Penn State to her house, where she could supervise and the cops couldn't bust them? Also, Zach didn't need another arrest on his record.

That first violation was just underage drinking, not DUI. The Buckley boys love their lives too much to drive drunk. In case their friends don't love their lives, though, Prima greets each of the drivers at the front door and puts their keys into a locked drawer in the master bedroom. She's already talked to the parents of the underage kids she knew from high school, and if they hadn't thought the party was a good idea, they wouldn't have let their sons come. A few of the moms do show up to check on things and deliver care packages to be taken back to the dorm in the morning.

Prima's at the kitchen table with her parents, half out of her chair, lecturing her mother for the hundredth time on why the trip to Italy must happen, there's no point protesting, when the front door flies open and Ryan appears out of nowhere.

"Where are those two candyasses?" he shouts. He drops his duffel bag in the foyer, runs down the hall, and hugs Prima so hard he lifts her off the ground.

"What on earth are you doing here?" she asks. His next break is not until Thanksgiving, and he was home for the confirmation just two weeks earlier.

"I don't miss a party."

Ryan loves his brothers. And maybe he's lonely, up in New York, the middle of nowhere, all by himself. He has a thousand friends and a scholarship and girls throwing themselves at him night and day, but he has a sad streak, too. Prima can't take her eyes off him. The blond crew cut, the sandals, the sunglasses—he looks just like Tom twenty years ago. She falls in love with her men every time she sees them.

"My favorite Italians!" he says to his *nonna* and *nonno*. He hugs them, too. Any other kid would rush to his buddies. Prima notices Mary Walsh, mother of Charlie (a boy with no manners at all), watching Ryan's respectful behavior from the living room with her jealous little mouth.

"You're half-Italian, you know," says his *nonno*, his arm around Ryan's shoulder.

"That's right," Ryan says. "The good half." The punch line in a routine they've done a thousand times.

"*Bravo.*"

"How'd you get so tan?" asks Maddalena.

"Booth," he says. His puts hands on his hips, posing. "Buy ten sessions, get one free."

She shakes her head. "Those things are poison."

"I live in *Syr*acuse, Nonna. The sun's out, like, four days a year."

"You risk your health, you get cancer, then how good will you look? Tell him, Prima."

"Mom, relax." Prima's no fan of tanning booths, either, but this isn't the time to get into it.

The cancer talk chases Ryan out of the kitchen. He presses himself up against the sliding glass door Prima just windexed until Zach and Matt notice him from outside. Then they all four hug, the twins and their younger and older brothers in a huddle. Prima rushes for her camera, but by the time she gets to them, they've broken up and Ryan has his arm around some girl.

The torches on the deck aren't throwing much light, so Prima turns on the floods. Still, as the night comes on and the kids spread out onto the lawn and into various rooms of the house, she has a hard time keeping track of where everybody is. Her mother and father disappear from the kitchen. She goes upstairs to look for Tom, finds him asleep on their bed in his underwear in front of ESPN, and pulls the covers over him in case one of the kids walks in by mistake.

She sits for a moment beside her husband on the bed, her hand on his shoulder, wishing, briefly, that he were the partying type. She checks herself. He works sixty hours a week. On Saturdays he takes care of the lawn and the cars. On Sundays they go to ten thirty Mass, then to brunch in the same corner booth at Klondike Kate's, then for a beer at Grotto's to watch the Phillies or to his brother's out in

Lancaster to play cards. On some Sunday evenings on the way back, Tom puts his hand on her thigh, which means they'll head straight to the bedroom when they get home. It makes her happy—thrilled, really, and, every time, relieved—to see his hand rise slowly from the steering wheel, to feel its warmth and to hold it there in her lap. No, Tom Buckley is not the partying type, but he and Prima have their own rhythms, and it's nothing to complain about, so she shuts off the light and lets him sleep.

Ryan's dragged the old Ping-Pong table up from the basement to the deck. He's gathering a group around him to pick teams, and drafts Prima onto Matt's the moment he sees her. This is the woman Prima Buckley has become: a forty-five-year-old housewife and mother of four, varsity shopper and JV gardener, playing beer pong with a bunch of teenagers. She does it for Matt and Zach, of course, not to get drunk. She doesn't drink much anymore. She'll have a strawberry daiquiri once in a while at the shore, but she hasn't had more than two beers in a row since college. Even so, she's glad Tom's upstairs and her parents are out of sight.

"You've got such a nice house, Mrs. Buckley," says the girl on the opposite team, a skinny flat-chested thing in painted-on jeans and a fuzzy pink tank top. Her squeaky voice, and her arm rubbing along Zach's, staking a claim, disrupt Prima's concentration.

"Thank you," Prima says. She holds the Ping-Pong ball between her thumb and index finger, aiming for the cup at the other end of the table. She prefers the bounce method rather than the direct-in-cup strategy. Everyone is watching. The handsome young men in their dark jeans and Eagles jerseys. The glossy lips of the girls. Matt. If the ball in Prima's hand goes in, mother and son will win.

"How many square feet is this place?" the girl asks.

"Dude, she's trying to throw," Zach says.

Prima releases. The ball bounces once, then plops into the cup. She pumps both fists, her bracelets jangling, and Matt gives her a high five. Everyone claps.

"She's a ringer!" says the guy on the other team.

"That's it for me," she says. "Quit while I'm ahead."

"No way!" Matt says. "We're defending champs. You gotta keep playing till somebody beats us, or you lose your honor. That's how it works."

Prima glances at the girl. She's holding Zach's hand now. "You're really good, Mrs. Buckley," she says. "Seriously. You really never played this before? It's, like, all they do at U of D."

Turns out it's just beginner's luck, though, because the next round Prima can't get the ball anywhere near the cup. Matt's expertise carries them; the other team can barely stand up straight, so they win again, but in the meantime the rules make her drink many, many cups of beer. She keeps one eye on the living room and kitchen through the sliding doors. She has no idea what's become of her parents but suspects they're in the garage inspecting Tom's new tractor. She checks the upstairs windows for spies. "All righty, then!" she calls out. "Next victims!"

Zach and the girl step up.

Her name, it turns out, is Allison. Allison Grey. She's a senior at Padua, the sister high school to Salesianum, where Zach used to go and where Patrick goes now. What would the nuns at Padua think of Allison, Prima wonders, a good Catholic with glitter on her cheeks, smoke breath, and a Coors Light in her hand? She's pretty enough for Zach—he likes blonds, all his girlfriends have been blonds—but she thought he was going steady with a girl in his biology class at Penn, or at least that he was done with high school girls altogether. Their teams take turns at the Ping-Pong table, and in between, Allison keeps grilling Prima about the house like she's a real estate agent. Does she have a decorator? Who picked the border on the wall-paper in the study? Prima wonders how grand a tour Allison Grey got, and when. All the back-and-forth with her makes Prima dizzy. Her yammering voice and sparkly face are like an overloud commercial for zit cream.

"I just love the lowboy in the hallway. Is it Ethan Allen? My mom and I saw one just like it in the showroom last week. That's what we do, me and my mom, go to sample houses and furniture stores and an-tique fairs." She says this as she flicks the ball effortlessly into the cup. She and Zach are beating them pretty bad, and now Prima's forced to take another drink.

"All right, Chatty Cathy," Prima says when it's her throw. "I'm hip to your mind games. You, too, Zachary Joseph."

Maybe if she doesn't concentrate so hard, Prima thinks, she'll make this next one go in. She guzzles the rest of her beer, steps up to the table, and tosses the ball with barely a look. It hits the Gooch square in the face.

"OK, she's cut off," says the Gooch.

"Oh yeah?" Prima says. "You gonna stop me?"

She senses her mother's presence. And when she turns, there are her fierce, accusing eyes behind the glass door. Daddy beside her. Both stand stone-still, arms crossed. Prima gives them a jaunty wave. No reaction.

Zach's next shot wins the round, and Prima and Matt's short but glorious reign comes to an end. Matt puts his arm around her. "Maybe you should take a break."

"You're saying I'm drunk?"

"You're the coolest mom ever," says Allison Grey. Prima looks over at her. It's possible that she's quite sweet. Is she going to marry my son? Prima can't stop staring at her cheeks. Then Allison turns away. "Break his heart and I'll kill you," Prima says under her breath, but it's louder than she realizes, and Zach hears her and shoos her toward the house.

You were necking in my guest room, weren't you? Prima thinks. No wonder the fringe on the Oriental rug was out of whack. She looks around her in all directions, up at the second-floor windows; the floodlights dazzle her eyes. Where'd Ryan go, anyway? And Patrick? Why's that group of kids walking into the field? They're being too loud. The neighbors will call. What if Tom wakes up? He'll be mad at her, like he gets when she's relaxed enough to enjoy a few drinks. Why doesn't he like her when she's relaxed? Why does he need two beers at Grotto's before he puts his hand on her thigh?

The door slides open. "Come inside right now," her mother says, the words a hiss. She takes Prima's arm and guides her over the threshold into the muffled quiet of the house and to the steady barstool of the kitchen island. The stool is high. Her legs dangle like a girl's. Her view is of the big, open living room, the back staircase, the fireplace. She has picked out every single piece of furniture, every plate and vase and candle and coaster, and the music they make together brings her calm.

"I don't like this one bit," her father says. He watches the games on the porch through the window above the sink. "You let those kids drink too much."

"They're *teen*agers," Prima says. "That's what they do. It'll wear off. Better they do it here than under some bridge like I used to."

"And you're proud of that?" he says.

"I thought you had more common sense now," says her mother, shaking her head. "How much did you drink, anyway?"

"Is Mary Walsh still here?"

"I been talking to her in the driveway," her mother says. "Good thing. Then I come inside and see what I see?"

"If you don't like it, you can leave," Prima says. "It's not your party. Not everything's designed for your comfort and joy."

"Watch it, girl," says her father. He gives Prima the stern look that still makes her stomach fall. "Show some respect."

She turns the other way and rolls her eyes.

"You're lucky your husband's in bed."

"Welcome to my world," Prima says, throwing her hands up in the air. "Ten o'clock on a Saturday night, Tom dead asleep, me in the kitchen by myself. It's a wonder I'm *not* a drunk."

She doesn't know why she says this. Compared to every other husband in her circle of moms, Tom's a good egg. He doesn't make many gestures, but when he does, he makes them big, like she does: surprise weekends in New York City, a BMW with a red bow on the hood, the diamond-studded watch on her wrist. So what if he doesn't smother her with kisses every time she walks through the door? Who has time for that stuff anymore? The last thing Prima wants is to be one of those 'merican wives who complains that her husband doesn't talk enough, doesn't romance her, doesn't appreciate her. But she falls into that trap without even trying. Maybe she watches too much TV. That's all you see: husbands snoring away in the hammock while their wives drool over the gardener. One thing Prima can't bear is a bored housewife who wants to be her husband's best friend. A man, more than a woman, needs his own life. Don't nag him too much, and he'll always come back to you.

"Poor you," her mother is saying. Her arms are opened dramatically wide. "In this big house like a princess."

"I'm not asking you to feel sorry for me."

"I don't."

"My life is perfect," says Prima.

"Don't be sarcastic."

"You don't understand."

Maddalena shakes her head. "I understand you have too much. Your problem is you have no problems. You make them up so you have something to do." She walks to the sink and starts washing the dishes.

"Use the dishwasher, for Christ's sake," Prima says. "That's what it's for."

Ryan and Patrick and a pack of boys stumble into the living room from the porch. Doubled over laughing, holding their beers steady, they fall onto the couches. They switch on the TV and turn on the baseball game full volume. Ryan's a Yankees fan now that he's at Syracuse, but he's the only one pulling for them over the Indians.

"The Indians'll skin you if you let them," Prima shouts from her perch. "Their pitching's been lights out."

Just then, like magic, Paul O'Neill hits a grand slam. Ryan jumps on the arm of the couch and raises his arms above his head like it's a touchdown. "Real lights out, Ma," he says. "You should be a commentator."

It hurts her, O'Neill's grand slam. It feels, in this particular moment, personal. "Cut me some slack, will you?" she says. Again her voice comes out louder, more anguished, than she intends. A screech. The boys look over at her, narrow their eyes. Ryan drops his arms.

"Are you *crying*?"

"*Am* I crying?" She covers her face. "Yes, Ryan. Maybe I am! Maybe I'm crying!" The darkness spins. The tears are hot on her palms. "I can't be right all the time, you know."

"Jeez, Ma," he says. "It's just a baseball game."

"Get your feet off the couch!" she shouts, though her eyes are still covered.

He hops down and says something to one of his buddies. The two erupt in laughter.

"Don't make fun of your mother," says Maddalena.

It's the first good point she's made all night. And then it's her unmistakable arm around Prima's shoulders, her warm, perfumed chest upon which Prima lays her head.

"If you ask me, she needs to grow up and not be such a wacko," Ryan says, and with that he and his buddies are gone.

"Come with me," says Maddalena. She guides Prima off the stool. Her father takes her other arm. Her body feels both unexpectedly light and familiarly sludge-heavy at the same time. The stairs are wobbly.

"Open your eyes," Maddalena says. "Move your feet!"

"Not my room!" says Prima. She goes limp. "Tom'll wake up!"

"So?"

"He'll think something's wrong. Nothing's wrong. I can't fall asleep. I have work to do." She tries to break free. "The party—"

"The party's over," says her father.

"Take her to the living room," says her mother.

And then she sits between her parents on the sofa for what feels like hours. Her drunkenness fades to a buzz, then to a dull throb behind her left ear. The cloud of negativity over her mother, which first descended early in the night when the subject of Italy was mentioned, lifts for a while as they discuss Mary Walsh's obvious eye job, new colors to paint the living room walls, and the upcoming season of Christmas shopping. Slowly the throb fades, too, and the night clicks back into place. At exactly eleven o'clock, Frankie calls, and mother and son gab like sorority sisters while Prima and her father flip through magazines.

When Maddalena finally hangs up, she's got a smile on her face like she's forgotten there's been any fighting or drunkenness at all. "How'd he know to call here?" Prima asks her.

"I told him last night. He pays attention."

And I don't? Prima almost says, but she lets it go. Still, she can't resist taking a shot: "So how is the little vampire, anyway?" And just like that, as Prima suspected, the cloud descends again, and mother and daughter look at each other through the fog.

"You don't take anything serious," Maddalena says. "No, that's not true. You take the wrong things serious and the other things—the right things—you don't pay attention to."

"Give me an example."

Maddalena shakes her head. "We fight enough for one night."

Prima can't admit to her mother that she, too, is worried about Frankie. His walks remind her of Tony, the weeks before, when he'd come home hours late from school with no explanation and clean his room top to bottom without doing his homework and get quiet and far away in the eyes. So she changes the subject to something safe, and soon it's time for her parents to go.

She stands in the headlights of her father's Cadillac, waving as he backs out onto the street. He doesn't see so well anymore, and the road from here to Graylyn Ridge is dark and windy and narrow. At least once a week somebody hits a deer or drives into a ditch. He'll call her in thirty-five minutes to let her know they made it home safe. In the meantime, the last remaining clouds in Prima's head evaporate. She paces around the yard, sandals in hand, cooling her bare feet on the grass. (Lately the soles have been burning in flashes, day and night. She knows what this means, that it's the end of one era and the beginning of another.) She stares at the oakleaf hydrangea, pulls some weeds, breaks off a sprig of the red chokeberry. Even in the shadowy light they are beautiful against the brick. One day she wants a moonlight garden, all white flowers. Daisies and honeysuckle and birch. She wants to step down from the back deck at night into a field of ghosts. On recommendation from her landscaper, she is also considering an English garden—"controlled wildness," he calls it. Violets, peonies, primroses, asters. Something to shake up the yards of box hedges and boulders of Fox Chase Estates. It's a pretty neighborhood and costs a fortune in civic-association dues and property taxes, but the front lawns and flower beds are a yawn.

Three thousand three hundred and eighty-five square feet. There's your answer, Allison Grey. Market value: four hundred thousand dollars. She didn't want to brag. Maybe the girl isn't from money. She could be at Padua on scholarship. She and her mother might walk through Ethan Allen just to daydream.

After twenty-five minutes, Prima heads back inside, takes two aspirin, and sits with a big glass of water on the main stairs next to the hall phone. Yanks-Indians is long over, but the games on the porch continue. The basement door opens and closes. There are separate sets of footsteps on the back stairs and moving slowly across the second-floor hallway. She has lost supervisory control. She needs to set up the sleeping bags in the family room and put out towels for morning showers and prep some of the breakfast so she's not overwhelmed by all the hungry mouths in the morning. She wonders if the keg is done. In her mind the whole time is the image of a deer and a ditch and her father's car flipped over. She imagines her life without them, the emptiness of it, how you are never too old to be an orphan. Her friends who've gone through it have started on medication and gained weight; their grief hangs on them like an odor. When the first parent goes, Prima wonders, will the other move in with her, or will Frankie move back, or will they insist on living alone in Graylyn Ridge? Neither will want to give up the house, and she won't be able to win that argument, either. A house is an impossible thing to give up. It is a display of your insides, whether you mean it to be or not. And when you surrender your house, half your self goes with it. Meanwhile ten minutes go by and the phone doesn't ring and doesn't ring, and then it does, and her mother and father are home safe, and Prima says she's sorry for how she behaved tonight, because she is, because she's a good daughter and has a good life, and they say to make sure to wish the twins a happy birthday and tell them to save the money they put in their cards, and she says, "I will."

When Prima looks out onto the porch, she sees that not only does the beer pong tournament rage on, but a group of kids are now on the lawn running some sort of race? With a tree branch? Whatever it is, Ryan's directing it, shirtless, and she resists the urge to pull open the door and shout, You'll catch cold! like some sitcom mom. There's no sign of the twins, though that might be Matt who's just been tackled by a guy in an Eagles jersey. It's hard to see. She climbs the stairs again to check on Patrick, who's invited some of his own friends over, younger boys. They've spent the entire night locked in his upstairs bedroom watching horror movies in the dark with family-size bags of chips and a cooler of soda (and probably, if she knows Patrick, some beers stashed under the Cokes). It's a full house, for sure, a peaceful one, with all her beloveds, awake or asleep, safe and happy, and for Prima, nothing could be sweeter.

She heads down to the basement for the sleeping bags. A few years ago, they converted one side of it to a guest suite and put in a treadmill and a small office and a bathroom so it would feel like a hotel. Nobody's ever slept there, though, because it's warmer and plenty spacious upstairs, especially with the twins and Ryan gone. Prima looks forward to the guests. She has a leather-bound guest book with "Hotel Buckley" embossed on the front, ready to be filled.

She finds the camping equipment right away, Tom having organized the other side by season. As she's reaching to pull down one of the plastic bins, she hears a noise. She looks across the room but sees nothing. The hotel side of the basement is dark, and the Chinese divider stands where it stood when she came down. She reaches up again for the bin, and for sure this time, there's someone or something moving just a few feet away from her, on the other side of the divider.

"Hello?"

She walks slowly across the basement and peers around the corner of the divider into the blackness of the hotel. She hears laughter, muffled laughter, a boy's laughter, but sees nothing. She takes a few steps toward it. She rests her hand on the seat of the stationary bike. She should turn around. It's not her business if two kids want to sneak off and neck. Did she not do as much at their age? She might have expected this to happen but is surprised that she feels charmed by it—yes, *charmed* is the word—thinking that her house will be the site of such memories, that years later a woman like her, a wife and mother pushing fifty, might drive by this house and suddenly remember, That's where I had my first kiss, in that basement there. I think his name was Buckley . . .

She steps closer. Her eyes adjust. She can make out the desk, the printer, the treadmill, the door to the bedroom suite half-open. Still barefoot, she makes no noise as she maneuvers toward the door. The sounds on the other side are clearer now. Furniture moving, the creak of the bed, breath. More laughter. Voices. The slap of skin.

"Your turn . . ."

"No, you—get it—"

There are three of them. She can see that now, for sure. Maybe? A boy standing. Two on the bed. Are there four? They're laughing. No clothes at all. Moonlight. Their skin glows. A girl's on the bed. Her long hair covers her face. The standing boy jumps onto the mattress, lands on his knees. The other boy, in profile, lifts his arm. The girl is giggling.

Prima can see them, but they can't see her. The moonlight stops at her feet. There are three.

"Shh," one of the boys says, "you're not so wasted." *Matt* says. One of the boys is Matt.

More giggling from the girl. "No, not me!" She keeps giggling. Allison Grey keeps giggling. Then she stops.

"That's the way to shut her up," the other boy says. The other boy is Zach.

Prima closes her eyes, opens them, closes them again. The girl says something she can't quite make out—"Sure" or "Here"—and sits up. Maybe it's not Allison? The girls all look alike. The boys stay on either side of her. Maybe those aren't her boys? But they are. She'd know them in complete darkness. Then the girl starts to sing. *I'll be gone till November, I'll be gone till November . . .*

"I gotta piss," Zach says. He goes into the bathroom. She hears his stream, the running water of the sink. While he's doing this, his brother climbs on top of the girl.

"Off—" Zach says when he returns. He takes Matt's place.

I'll be gone till November, gone till November . . .

Prima backs away and, as silently as she came, crosses the basement and rushes up the stairs, leaving the light on, the sleeping bags in their bins.

Ryan's a blur in the kitchen, guzzling Gatorade. "Good night to you, too, Ma," he says as she charges up to the second floor.

In her bedroom, the TV's on low and Tom's still asleep and the walls are loud with blue light flashing. She locks herself in the bathroom and sits on the edge of the tub in the dark, her palms pressed to her eyes. This is the woman she's become: a mother who spies on her sons from behind a door. She's not proud of the spying or what she saw or thinks she saw, but she's not ashamed, either, not of herself and not of her sons. The girl is beautiful. They are, the three of them, young. They should have everything and keep taking and taking until they get it. If not now, when? They just need to be careful. Controlled wildness. And she is the boys' mother, their best friend. She won't be surprised if they tell her the story in the morning.

If Prima were braver, she'd change the rhythm, unlock the bathroom door, pull the covers off Tom, and wake him with a kiss on his mouth and her hand between his legs. But she's not brave in this way. She used to be, back when she was the twins' age, in the years after Tony, when nothing mattered, which is maybe why she feels no shame for her boys now. The reason is of no importance. They just need to be careful. How can she make sure they're careful?

"YOU HAVE TO understand," says Professor Rhonda Birch, from the other side of the kitchen table. "This puts me in a very awkward position."

Frankie's Rice Krispies have gone soggy. And now, while she explains why he should not count on the dissertation fellowship that could change the trajectory of his career, possibly not even apply for the award at all, the bananas rot in their little pools of milk, the cabinet doors fly open, the wallpaper peels off in sheets, and the ceiling begins to buckle. His own little House of Usher. And for not having said, Let's just be clear: no one deserves this award more than you, my darling Frankie, but— as a preamble, before her litany of practical reasons, he'd like to strangle her and hide her under the floorboards.

"We can't risk even the illusion of impropriety," she continues. "This is my livelihood we're talking about."

"What about my livelihood?"

"You have a thousand more chances ahead of you. This is the *beginning* of your career. Mine's in its twilight, at best. If I lose this position, where do I go? How do I compete with the rising stars? Plus, Amos has a lot of influential friends."

"Twilight is pushing it."

"These days, the lifespan of an academic—a woman's at least, a vital woman's—is short as a supermodel's," she says. "And these ankles are weak, baby. My wrinkles are showing."

"You're *not* serious," Frankie says, because it occurs to him she might be teasing, or if not, that she can easily be swayed. The Professor's pattern—in the classroom, in her scholarship, in bed—is to rant and bluster and overreact and get all soap-operatic at the beginning, then step back, consider broader contexts, give the other side its due, and finally stake out the middle ground in a kind of shared understanding, the end result of which is mutual pleasure. It distinguishes her among the ideologues in her field, but it also makes her extremely defensive if someone questions the strength of her convictions, which they frequently do. Empathy is not a virtue in their social and academic circles. Exhibit it too often or at too intense a degree, and sooner or later someone will hurl at you the most damaging accusation of all: "You're not serious." That label immediately casts you in the subintellectual league of humanists, Comp and Rhet instructors, and contemporary novelists. But Frankie has always believed—and will continue to believe, no matter what—in Professor Birch's intellectual integrity and academic prowess. Her chapter on Ngugi, from her second book, nearly brought him to weeping. He believes that empathy and literary theory are not only compatible but can enrich each other and possibly even change the world.

What a meathead he is.

"This is a university fellowship," he tells her. "Not an arms deal. It's barely on the English Department's radar! No one else on campus has even heard of it!" As his voice rises with each new sentence, he realizes how much he's using his hands and the full wingspan of his arms. His Italianness is bubbling over, its unseemly passion on display. It could work against him here, he thinks, make him appear hysterical. She has claimed to admire his passion, but he knows that, in the academy at least, passion is sentimentality's ugly cousin, and neither is welcome at the party. So he lays his palms flat on the table, calibrates his voice. "And besides, Professor Birch, people *expect* advisers to play favorites. Why else do we kiss your asses?" He checks himself again. "No one would blame you for *advocating* for your advisees, is what I'm arguing."

"People are whispering," she says. "I think Amos might already suspect another man—not you, specifically, but this would raise those suspicions." She pulls her hair into a ponytail again, holds it there for a second, lets it fall. This time it makes her look like a middle-aged actress. "I'm so sorry, Frankie. What you're saying is probably true, and I'm just paranoid. I don't have the stomach for a scandal. I hate the idea of gossip centered on me. I just want to keep doing what we're doing, undisturbed. Don't you? Don't you think it would be easier for both of us if you just didn't submit at all?"

"How is that easier for me? I've earned that fellowship!" he yells. "I'm just as qualified as anybody! More! Not to mention how hard I've worked. Not to mention how alone I am here, no family, no friends, day and night in the library. You want me just to throw that away because you *think* we might get caught? How is that even remotely fair?"

She goes quiet, bites her bottom lip, releases it, bites it again. "You do work very hard," she says, with the tranquillity of a guidance counselor. "Harder than anyone, for sure. In that race, you've got pretentious twerps like Annalise Theroux and Hector Billings beat by a landslide. But Frankie—and this is my fault, I take as much of the blame as you—what you've got so far of the diss, it's not . . . how do I say this? *Up there,* you know? It's *safe.* I think, for this particular fellowship, the department wants to make a splash, bring an edgier voice to the fore, someone they can parade around MLA. Your stuff is solid, but it's, in some ways, old fashioned." She clenches her fists. "It's good, though, Frankie. Really good and solid, and *good,* as I said. I wouldn't be working with you if it weren't. You know that. You know my reputation."

He stares at her. She looks down. Her hair is parted down the middle, hippie-style, but the part is clogged up with curly gray roots like little pubic hairs. He crosses the room and stands with his hands behind his back, gripping the cold cracked porcelain sink. He wants to shut her up, but he's too stunned to figure out how. It's the first time she's questioned the quality of his work. He's fully aware that he has a way to go in terms of the organization and focus of the chapters he's written so far, but his faith in their quality has been like a jewel in his pocket. When he's felt low, the nights he's walked through the neighborhoods surrounding his university, he's taken out that jewel and admired it in the moonlight, told himself, You may be lonely, you may not know where you're headed, you may question why you're even bothering, but at least you have this, Frankie Grasso—at least this, no one can take away from you.

"I think about you when I'm not here," Birch says. "You might not believe me, but I do. I think about your brother who died. I wonder, Is that why Frankie tries so hard, so he can make up for the brother?"

"Don't say 'the brother,'" Frankie says. "His name was Tony. And you're wrong. Every time you make some point about Tony and me, you're wrong."

From the day Frankie told Birch about Tony, the third or fourth time she came over, over cereal, like today, she's been on a mission to convince him that every one of his problems are somehow tied to him, that Frankie's life is a desperate attempt to compensate his parents for the loss of their oldest son. Now, apparently, even his very practical need for a fellowship—for time and space to write, for perfectly reasonable validation and justifiable reward—has its roots in Tony.

"I remember his name," Birch says defensively. "Even though you've only said it once yourself. I've come to think that's why—he's why—you haven't finished the diss yet, why you keep revising chapters I've approved and writing new chapters you don't need, why no fellowship in the world is going to get you to put this thing to sleep. You're afraid that if you finish, and it's still not good enough, you won't have anything left." She comes over to him, puts her hands around his waist, but doesn't look him in the eyes. "Do you understand what I'm saying?"

"Why not just kick me in the nuts?" says Frankie. He breaks free of her embrace, grabs their cereal bowls and spoons, and tosses them in the sink with a clatter. With the water running, he says, "Better yet, give me *another* reason why I won't win that fellowship. Some more armchair psychology, if you please. Or are these all the reasons you've got? How many are you up to now, ten?"

"I'm on your side, Frankie. I promise. I'm your friend. I *am* your advocate. You don't realize what an advantage you have, being an as yet unknown voice. But you don't get an infinite number of chances to impress people. I want you to go out in the world putting your strongest foot forward."

He shakes his head. "You must think I'm really pathetic."

"Not at all, baby. The opposite. I don't put this much energy into a pathetic person."

"Well, I'm applying, anyway. And I'll win."

"I want to root for you."

"That's generous, Rhonda. Really."

"Frankie—" She stops. Apparently she's said all she's going to say, but he wonders—will always wonder, maybe—what she reconsidered telling him. If only she'd begun with that preamble: No one deserves this award more than you, my darling Frankie. If only she'd surprise him and say it was all a joke, a twisted attempt to rile him up for a good, punishing fuck. But she doesn't, and it isn't, and on Thursday when he finds her note in his mailbox, he'll still run home to meet her.

From the hallway, arms crossed, he watches her pull on her jeans, lace her boots, get on her knees on his futon to retrieve her sweater from behind it. By the time she's gone, it's the middle of the afternoon. There is nothing to do, no refuge, but his work. So he finds his pants, wipes down his chest with a warm, wet towel, grabs his coat and his box of floppy disks and his backpack, and treks uphill to the library to finish his letter.

4   *Scarabocchi*

ANTONIO GRASSO LOVES the game of bocce. God bless the man who invented it. He had to be an Italian, or maybe a Chinese, who they say invented pasta, too, which is hard to believe. The point is, a seventy-nine-year-old man, good for not much else, can play bocce for hours, three or four rounds in a night if he wants, with as much skill as he had when he was young. Antonio loves the deadweight of the ball in his hand, the perfect smoothness on his callused skin, the sound it makes when it spocks the other team's ball and sends it flying down the court. When he was a boy, he and Mario used rocks. Now the Amerigo Vespucci Club stocks three brand-new imported regulation bocce sets, in fancy wood carrying cases. He loves that one team is red, the other green, and the *pallino* is white, so that when the balls sit on the court together, they make the Italian flag. What will they think of next?

Antonio is happy at the club. He knows a lot of the men. Most are

two-faced and gossip worse than women, but they tell jokes and stories from the Old Country and some even sing, so he puts up with the
rest of it. Mixed drinks cost seventy-five cents, and wine and beer in
short plastic cups are a quarter each. Thirty bucks a year for dues. A
dollar for a plate of pasta and some salad. It's a good deal. More than
that: for every bocce game you win, you get a free drink. And the dues
count for two tickets to three parties: a summer picnic, a wine tasting
in the winter, and, around Thanksgiving time, a steak dinner after
the Memory Mass for all the members who died that year.

Tonight, the Tuesday before Thanksgiving, is the steak dinner.
Antonio doesn't care about the steak, which tastes like sawdust, or
the Mass for the Dead, which he skipped. He's here to ambush DiSilvio, who stood him up at lunch a month ago and who hasn't returned
his calls since. DiSilvio never misses the Vespucci steak dinner.

Earlier, while the other men were at St. Anthony's, Antonio
walked up and down Union Street on the opposite side from the Al
Di Là, watching the customers in the window seats. He does this
sometimes, on nights when nostalgia's got him by the balls, which is
most nights lately. He likes to see the customers' excited faces when
the plates arrive, the grateful expression they make at the first bite. He
wants to make sure that the waiters stand up straight when they recite the specials—with their hands behind their backs, like he taught
them, nothing written down—and that the busboys don't let the tables sit dirty too long. When Antonio's inside and the workers know
he's there, it all goes the right way; from the outside, though, he sees
what really is, like a camera. He keeps his head down and wears a
Phillies cap and an old pair of eyeglasses so he won't be recognized.

Dov'è il mio villaggio? Antonio wonders on these incognito night walks alone on Union, a bum up ahead asleep on the stoop, cars rumbling past, drowning out the church bells. Where is my village? He has to get through the winter, then a few short months of spring and a taste of summer, and then in August, no matter what Maddalena says, he will get on a plane with her and their children and grandchildren, and the plane will carry them in its belly all the way to the real village, the only village, Santa Cecilia, the village immigrants like him tried to make again in these square blocks of Wilmington but failed, because there's never two of anything.

The plan for Santa Cecilia is first to find his old house. The last he heard, from his cousin Vincenza in Avezzano, the pink stone walls had deeper cracks but were still standing, still attached to the little farm on the south side of the olive grove. No, the Grasso home was not in the center of town, at the top of the mountain, like Maddalena's family's, the Piccinellis; it was farther down, on a slope, all by itself. The Grassos were not rich then. Papà Franco used to borrow from Aristide Piccinelli. But things have evened out, moneywise. Not that it matters for what Antonio wants, which is to breathe the mountain air again, to stand on the stone wall at the edge of the gorge and listen to the water below. To kneel in the graveyard before the stones of his friends and uncles and cousins and pay his respects. There are stories locked in his brain, memories he can't find the key for, but that key can be found in the old village.

August. Ten short months. Ten long months. Enough time, either way you look at it, to put his affairs in order, arrange his papers with DiSilvio, just in case. Old people die on trips. He has to prepare. His kids call him morbid. Every time Prima or Frankie says the word, Antonio hears the Italian *morbido,* soft. They are the same thing, in a way. Is Antonio not softer now—in the brain, in the legs and stomach—than he's ever been? Maddalena says he depresses her, going on and on as he does about his age, about "the end," but that kind of talk does not depress him. The opposite. The more he talks, the less afraid he is. When Maddalena says, "With that mouth of yours, you'll live to be a hundred," he replies, "Don't do me any favors."

"Signor DiSilvio," says Antonio when his old friend comes through the door of the Vespucci Club, "what a surprise. You're too busy to call me, but not too busy for a free steak?"

"Antonio," he says with a red face, "I'm so sorry—"

He could make a crack about DiSilvio's giant belly, which hangs over his belt like dough, but it's too easy. "Come on, *compa,*" he says. "I've known you forty years. If you want me to start paying you, just ask. Don't hide from me like a coward."

"You didn't hear?" DiSilvio says.

"Hear what?"

"I should have known," says DiSilvio. "Nobody wants to bring up such a thing with you."

He pulls Antonio into a corner of the club, away from the men gathered at the bar. "Two weeks ago," he says, "my son-in-law, Patrizia's husband, drove his car into a tree. Drunk. But on purpose, Antonio. Thirty-eight years old. Father of my grandchildren. On *purpose.*"

"*Gesù mio, no,*" says Antonio. "I read the paper every day. I didn't see it—"

"He didn't die. But he's messed up in the head. Says he can't remember anyone, but he's a faker. That's what I think. He wants to forget he has a wife and three girls. He was trying to get rid of his life, why would he want it back? He's crazy, a maniac—"

Men come toward them to pat DiSilvio on the shoulder and back, to calm him down, to ask, How is Patrizia? How did this world get so terrible? The news is two weeks old, but it's DiSilvio's first time at the club since it happened, and because of this he gets all the attention, as he should. They look out for each other, even the two-faceds and the gossips. Antonio steps away. He should have known his friend wouldn't abandon him without good reason. He feels sorry for DiSilvio, but it could have been worse. It could have been Patrizia or one of the girls. Also, Antonio needs him. He wonders if Christmas will be long enough to wait until he can call on him again, sit his lawyer down, and ask his advice on how to make sure the Al Di Là stays in the right hands, or no hands at all, if Antonio dies in Italy.

At the bar, the men who just had their arms around DiSilvio are already gossiping. Was the son-in-law having an affair? Did he owe a lot of money? Married to someone else? In the mob? (No to that one, says Tomasso, the bocce champion from Trenton. He was an Armenian with an Italian-sounding name; they'd never let him in the mob.) There has to be a reason, the men agree. You don't just decide one day to wrap your car around a tree. What do you think, Antonio? asks one of the men. You're close with DiSilvio. You ever meet this son-in-law? What kind of man . . . ?

But Antonio has nothing to say to these questions, or to the man who asks them, one of the new guys, a *calabrese,* who must not know that Antonio's son was cut from the same cloth as this Armenian who married Patrizia. A maniac, DiSilvio called him. A crazy.

Tomasso rescues him. "We here to play bocce or what?" he says. "You're on my team tonight, Grasso."

"Not fair," says the *calabrese*. "The two best players?"

For the first few minutes, Antonio throws well enough, can concentrate on getting his green ball close to the *pallino*. As the game goes on, though, he loses his touch. Tomasso doesn't tease him. He must know, somehow, the way men do but never discuss, that Antonio is now lost in a jumble of years and the memories of his son, and that he won't find his way back for a long time.

When Antonio can shut the rest out, this is how he remembers Tony best: a boy who loved his father and the place his father built. From the age he could walk and talk, the only thing Tony liked more than walking and talking at Antonio's side was walking and talking at Antonio's side at the Al Di Là. No one, including Antonio, has loved the restaurant so strong since.

After school, Tony would come straight to Al Di Là and sit for hours in a booth doing his homework. When his homework was done, he'd help fold napkins, arrange the forks and knives on the tablecloths, cut the slices of cheesecake and store them in the refrigerator. He drew new logos and signs for the restaurant on the backs of the place mats and showed them to his father, joking that when he grew up and the restaurant became his, he'd make it more modern. He had a talent for design, for making the perfect crease in the napkins, for spacing the knives and forks exactly the right distance apart, for drawing heart shapes on the cheesecake plates with strawberry sauce. Prima worked a few shifts as a waitress, but she didn't have the knack for it, was distracted and too chatty with the customers.

By the time Tony was fourteen, in 1970, he was doing the work of a busboy, making better tips than Prima, because who couldn't fall in love with him? He was already tall, already handsome, the shadow of his first beard growing, his legs strong, his face lit up always for the old ladies; he was the owner's sweet, intelligent, smiling son, the hope of the generations to come.

There was a waiter that summer, Dante, the son of Marconi the electrician. Antonio hired him as a favor to his father, even though he had no experience. Dante was nothing special; worse, he had a tattoo on his left leg and big horse teeth and a ponytail. He was on his way to becoming a derelict, another of those children who wasted their parents' sacrifices. But he had charm. The customers asked for him by name and left him big tips, and Tony followed him around like a puppy dog. It was after Dante came, in June of '70, that Tony changed.

Dante brought him albums and taught him to do mean but perfect imitations of the managers, Gilberto and Lucio. Lucio had a high, girly voice, Gilberto a stutter, and both imitations made everybody laugh. Dante pushed Tony to play pranks on the dishwashers and cooks and his sister, to hide their aprons or their salt until they got so mad they started fighting with each other. He made it Tony's job to cover his tables while he snuck off for a cigarette with his long-haired friends, who hung around outside the restaurant near the bus stop, waiting for the end of his shift. Dante's act bothered Antonio from the beginning, but he put up with it because of his friendship with Marconi and the free electric work, and because Tony liked having him at the Al Di Là. When the two had different schedules, Tony sulked and yawned and sat in the corner, writing in a book of guest checks he carried around in his apron so he would feel like a real waiter.

One day, Antonio overheard Lucio asking one of the other bus-boys, "What's the Prince always scribbling?" He was the worst gossip of all, Lucio. Still is.

"Who knows," said the busboy. "He's a smart kid. He's probably doing his homework."

"In the summer? In the check book?" said Lucio. "It's not normal, all that writing. It's too many words."

"Ask the Princess," said the busboy, pointing to Prima, and the two men laughed.

Antonio ignored this at first. He couldn't blame Lucio for not lik-ing Tony or Dante because of all the teasing they did about his high voice. Then he watched his son more closely. Tony took that book of checks everywhere. Whenever he got a free second, he'd write in it, with a kind of concentration Antonio didn't see again in anyone until Frankie. At the end of every day, just before he and Antonio would get in the car to go home for dinner with Maddalena and Prima, Tony tore out a handful of pages, stuffed them in his pocket, and threw the rest of the book in the trash. Antonio fished it out, but there was nothing: *Table 6. 1 Lasagna, 1 Veal Scallopine, 2 House Red. $9.50.*

One day, the widow Ida called to say she needed help in her kitchen. Could Antonio send over somebody tall and strong? He sent Tony, who left his apron behind, on a hook in the kitchen, and in its front pocket the book of checks.

Ida did not live far. Antonio had only a few minutes. From the window of the Al Di Là, he watched Tony cross Union, jog over to Eighth Street, and turn the corner toward his *zia's*. He had long legs and thick dark curls and a smart head on his shoulders. He was so young, just fourteen, innocent and decent, with a long life ahead full of every possible good thing. This is another way Antonio chooses to remember him, his son who turned the corner that day and came back somebody else.

Antonio flipped through the lined green pages. First, more specials, more lists. A running tally of tips. The middle was blank. Then he got to the back pages. Tony's handwriting, small and scratched, filled the lines. He'd crammed his words into every inch, like he was a prisoner and these were the last scraps of paper he'd get. They were letters, some to himself, some to Dante Marconi. Dante's name was on every page. But as letters they made no sense. No boy in his right mind sent letters like this. *Tony Grasso, where will you go?* he wrote. *You can't go anywhere without him. There's no place for you. Stop yourself before it's too late. Go to the bridge before it's too late. Do SOMETHING before it's too late. Find a priest before it's too late. Your mother will be better off. It's too late already. Too late too late.* What was he talking about? Too late for what? What was Dante doing to him? *You have flour all over your legs today. You are the beginning and the end. Take me for a ride with Bruce and Mikey and the guy with the broken arm. Take me anywhere. Why aren't you talking to me today?* Then some kind of poem about a field in the spring. Then a dream about the ocean. *In my dream, a wave knocked you down, and when you came up for air you had a hole in your back like a whale.* At the top of the dream page, that name again: Dante.

Antonio didn't understand. The black and blue ink marks blurred into a loud mess of nonsense. *Scarabocchi,* his teacher back in Santa Cecilia used to call sloppy handwriting. *Scarabocchi,* she taught him, was a sign of disrespect. When Tony and Prima did their homework, Antonio sometimes stood guard over them as they wrote, watching like a hawk for *scarabocchi.* He couldn't necessarily help them get the right answers, but he could insist that their handwriting showed respect: straight rows of neat letters, clear numbers. Not this disgraceful mess of Tony's. You don't write so sloppy and small unless you are ashamed.

He tore out the last three pages and hung the apron back on the hook. He went to the dessert fridge, where Dante was scooping out portions of tiramisu onto a plate.

"Go home," Antonio said, grabbing the plate. "You don't work here anymore." Fuck Marconi and his free repairs. Who cared that Dante chased after him, asking why, saying, *Please, please, Signor Grasso! What did I do?* Antonio didn't say another word. All that boy's sissy begging made him want to punch him in the face.

Antonio left out the back door and walked down Union in the direction of the Delaware Memorial Bridge. If he stood at the top and stared down at the water, an answer would come to him. If he could stop time and think, think hard, Tony's words would make sense.

He shoved the pages back into his pocket. He wandered the streets, passed the old men in their folding chairs without a wave, made a left and then another left, forgot where he'd turned. At the next intersection, he got so confused, here in the Little Italy neighborhood he knew better than his backyard, that he couldn't decide which direction to take to the bridge. He stood for a long time, paralyzed, dizzy. Cars rushed past. The traffic lights blinked. Then someone called his name.

Giulio Fabbri stood on the other side of the street—Seventh Street, so he'd gone in a big circle—and waved. "Antonio Grasso!" he called again. He was standing in front of his house. "You here for a visit?" He walked toward him, arms out. "Come in," he said.

Giulio led him into his little empty row house. Helen was at the store. He talked on and on. Politics, the weather, neighborhood gossip. Antonio was paralyzed. Every month, Giulio said, more Italians moved out of the city. It made him sad to see them go. His stepson, Michael, Helen's son, had just left for college in DC, and her daughter, Abigail, applied to study music in London; their leaving made Giulio wish that he'd had children of his own, young children like Tony and Prima, and that he hadn't met Helen so late in life. "You and Maddalena got lucky," he said. "Two children, two angels. A boy and a girl. Balance. Did you hear, by the way, about DiSilvio's jailbird son—"

Tears were forming in Antonio's eyes, and Giulio stopped. "What is it, *uaglio*?"

Antonio took out the pages, now crumpled and smudged, from his pocket. "I'm sorry," he said. "I don't know what to do." He laid them on the table between the glasses of wine Giulio had poured. "Tell me what they mean."

They called Giulio Fabbri the Professor of Little Italy. He understood poems and dreams. Antonio hadn't ended up on Seventh Street by accident. The Professor would find a normal reason for Tony's letters, tell Antonio not to worry, they were harmless. The boy was so young; we all get crazy ideas when we're young.

Giulio put on his glasses. He read all three pages twice. Then he took a sip of wine, folded the pages in half, and slid them back over to Antonio. He looked Antonio in the eyes. "I'm sorry, *compare*," he said. "This is bad. Very bad, maybe. But it doesn't have to be."

"Tell me."

His son had an unhealthy crush, Giulio explained. An infatuation. What made it bad news, of course, was that the infatuation, the romantic idea he should have for a girl, was for the Marconi boy. This idea got him twisted the wrong direction. You see men like this on the news, he said; you read about them in literature—the Greeks, even some Romans; but you never think they can be someone you know, someone of your own blood.

The good news, according to Giulio, was, first, that Tony was young, there was still time for him to grow out of it. And second, that the Marconi boy didn't share his feelings. Nothing had happened between them. Giulio pointed to the bottom of the first page: *You don't even know I'm alive. You don't see me. You will never drive me to New York. Dante Dante Dante Dante.* "That tells me there's nothing happening from the other side."

"He's only fourteen," Antonio said. "What kind of feelings can he have yet?"

Giulio smiled. "What kind of feelings did you have when you were fourteen? And he's almost fifteen, yes? In two months?"

Antonio stood and walked to the other end of the kitchen. "This Dante, he's got a ponytail. He *looks* like a girl."

"That's a good sign," Giulio said. Then: "You know, some of the greatest artists in history . . ." But he didn't finish the thought.

"It can't be," Antonio said. "You can't tell anything from that mess." He waved his arm toward the checks, still folded on the table. "You can be wrong. It could just be a joke he's playing." He took the pages and tore them into pieces. "That part you read, it doesn't even make sense. 'You'll never drive me to New York.' That could mean anything."

"Like what?"

"Like he wants to go to New York!" Antonio said. "See the Statue of Liberty! It can't be what you're saying. You can't tell me there's no chance you're wrong. Just because you read books."

"I never said there was no chance. I hope I *am* wrong," said Giulio Fabbri. "That boy is like my son, too. And Helen's. You think we want this for him?" He folded his hands. "It's more common than you think, especially these days. It's a scary time, all those crazies in California. Sometimes, I think, kids get ideas that don't turn out to be real. Just keep an eye on him. It can go away, I think. It's not impossible. It can be what they call a phase."

"I know what a phase means," Antonio said. "I don't have as much school as you, but I know the basic words. And I have common sense. And common sense tells me this can't be."

There are always signs, they tell you. The newspaper and TV shows, all they talk about is signs. You're supposed to look for them and then know what they mean when you find them, but Antonio's never trusted himself to read signs right. He is a man, a father, easily blinded by love, by the faith that if you want something badly enough, for you or your children, and work hard to get it, it will come to you. After that day in Giulio's kitchen, he was as blinded as ever by love for Tony, more blind, if you can be such a thing, and wanted more fiercely than he'd wanted anything in his life for Giulio to be wrong, for his son to turn out normal. Healthy. Untouched.

So he watched him. He stole more checks, read more pages of the same *scarabocchi* about Dante, always and only Dante, long after Antonio chased him from the Al Di Là. He went through every scrap of paper in Tony's room, looked in the back of his dresser drawers, under his bed, in the corners of his closets. He smelled his clothes, checked behind the mirrors. He listened in on his phone calls. He followed him home from school, kept two blocks behind him in his car. He waited in the parking lot while Tony sat with his friends—normal-looking girls and boys—in a booth at the Charcoal Pit, looking happy enough, right up to the day.

When he didn't come home from school that Friday, Antonio drove straight to the bridge. But he was too late.

They searched his room. Prima pulled out his desk drawer and turned it upside down. Index cards, notebooks, and a stack of rubber-banded guest checks fell to the floor. Quickly, Antonio slipped the guest checks into his pocket. He kept them with him, reading them over and over for a clue to where his son might have run off. Two days later, they dragged his body from the river.

Tony left his family with ugly words. Antonio burned them in a garbage can in the backyard. At the funeral, he avoided Giulio Fabbri's eyes and never spoke to the man again. When Giulio visited the house at holidays, Antonio walked past him without a nod, talked over him when he tried to tell a story. After a while, Giulio stopped coming to the Grassos altogether, and not long after that, he was dead, too, and there wasn't a person left who knew Tony's heart the way his father did.

Lately, that miserable time keeps coming back to Antonio, like a movie in his head that he can't turn off. It doesn't take the men's gossiping at the club to remind him. The words on the guest checks won't stay down. They shout at him from the dirt behind the garbage cans. The flour on Dante's legs, the body falling from the bridge, Tony asking him, with his heartbroken face, when he got back from helping his *zia* Ida, why he'd sent his best friend away.

And then there are times, like now, when Antonio's walking out of the Vespucci Club without saying good-bye to anyone, not even Tomasso, when he feels—can he even admit it?—relieved, almost grateful, that Tony died when he did. As Antonio's learned more of the ways of the world, seen it change and rot before his eyes, he's come to convince himself that his son would never have survived it. Forty-year-old men dying from "pneumonia." Teachers at the dance studio prancing around in their tight pants unashamed. Protests in

San Francisco and DC, parades in New York, celebrating. Would that have been Tony's life? A Grasso's life? He'd have been forty-three this year. What does forty-three look like for that kind of man? Would he be wasting away, too, a talking skeleton, like Rock Hudson, who'd once been handsome and rich and on top of the world?

As impossible as it's been for Antonio to imagine Tony's adult life, as much as it turns his stomach and fills him with fear, it's worse to feel this relief, this sickening gratitude. So he pushes it away. He stands in the parking lot, jangling his keys, scanning the rows for his car. So many cars. So much fuss for a free steak dinner and a Mass for the Dead. He paces up and down the Union Street side. Where is his goddamned car?

"*Compa*," says a voice behind him.

"DiSilvio."

"You lost?"

"I played like shit."

"No—lost here. In the parking lot," DiSilvio says. "Never mind. Your car's over there." He points.

"Thank you."

"I'll come see you next week. After the holiday. *Festa del tacchino*. Only the Americans would make a holiday for a turkey."

"See me when you can," says Antonio. They walk toward the car. He pushes the button to make it beep and flash. "In the meantime, take care of your daughter."

"Thank you. I will."

"One thing I don't understand, though," Antonio says, turning to him. He can't let it go. "Why didn't you show up for lunch three weeks ago? We had a date. I had my papers ready. You've never missed a date in your life. It bothers me. And don't tell me your son-in-law. That was before."

DiSilvio shrugs. "I have a girlfriend," he says with a smile. "What can I say? I lost track of the time."

It's dark, the streetlight is weak, but still Antonio can see his friend blushing. "You?" Antonio says. And just like that, the dark spell breaks. The men are both laughing. "You fat thing?"

"She likes it," says DiSilvio. "I got lucky, huh? She has a big bowl of pasta waiting for me when I get there and then we—"

"*Che abbondanza,*" Antonio says before DiSilvio can go on. He doesn't need him to paint a picture. Then he puts his arm around him and they laugh awhile longer.

This is how Antonio's life has been since 1971. A long darkness lit up by flashes of light that come all of a sudden, then fade just as fast. If only he could go back to the day Ida called the Al Di Là and asked him to send over somebody strong. Instead he settles for Santa Cecilia, where the darkness never touched.

He drives down Union Street, toward home, the music loud to flood his mind.

AN EMPTY TRAIN at night puts Frankie in the mind of Hitchcock, of Wharton, of James. He loves the grimy rumble over miles of desolation, the potential secret of the mustached conductor in the black coat removing his gloves, the lonely tolling of the bells as they chug past abandoned stations. Frankie is his best self on an empty train. He can read undistracted. Recollect his emotions in tranquillity.

Anywhere else, his dissertation shoots up around him thick and noisy and unchartable as a rain forest, but on an empty train he's a conquistador, armed with a harquebus, out for blood and order.

A rain forest seems downright pleasant compared to the Wednesday-before-Thanksgiving Amtrak Northeast Direct, and if the crowds and smells and constant shoving put him in the mind of anyone, it's not a literary figure. Try Manson, or John Wayne Gacy, or Mussolini. Mostly he feels as though he's being slowly lobotomized over the course of the wobbly seven-hour trek from Boston to Wilmington.

Or something like that. He rolls his eyes at his own pretentious simile. What does Frankie Grasso know from lobotomies? His primary association is a story his father once told him about an old woman back in the village, someone called L'Abbandonata because her husband and daughters abandoned her for the new country. She went off the deep end waiting for them to return, and some traveling country quack tried to cut the crazy parts out of her, which, of course, killed her altogether. It made Frankie think of Dora—Freud's Dora—and how much better L'Abbandonata might have fared had she lived in Vienna instead of Santa Cecilia and had access to the kind of help Sigmund and his minions could have given her. Wretchedly ignorant as Freud was when it came to the complex sensibilities of women, at least he didn't advocate making mincemeat of their thalami and frontal cortexes, as far as he knows. If Frankie is guilted into going to Italy next summer, he will leave some flowers on the grave of L'Abbandonata, but he doubts he'll get that chance.

He is settled firmly on his mother's side in the trip tug-of-war. Much to his relief, he won't have to fight that battle over Thanksgiving dinner, which Prima and Tom will spend with Tom's family in Lancaster. It will be a quiet Thursday night at the Al Di Là, just the three of them and a few families from the neighborhood. When he reunites with the Buckleys on Friday, it will be the first time he's seen Prima since she delivered her edict at the confirmation, and while he expects her to harangue him with reasons and ultimatums, at least she won't spoil the turkey and stuffing and lasagna and broccoli rabe and strawberry cheesecake of a Grasso Thanksgiving.

Frankie would prefer to keep his homeland free of family tensions and obligations and the ghosts of his mother's sadness. The idea of watching her suffer pains him; why does it not pain Prima? In a few years, on sabbatical from whatever university hires him, he'll go alone or with his father. The two Grasso men: one in search of art and wine, the other of memories. Until then, Italy will wait patiently for them.

The train is pulling away from New Haven—site of another famous university at which Frankie will never present a paper on modern psychology and postcolonialism or whatever his dissertation is ultimately about—when a duffel bag falls from the overhead compartment and lands on his head.

"Oh no, that's mine!" says a girl behind him.

"Jesus Christ," Frankie says, clutching his skull. He picks up the bag, which weighs roughly six tons, and hands it to her. "Are you transporting gold bullion or something?"

"I'm so sorry," she says.

His first thought is that this girl looks like a Bryn Mawr tennis player—silky brown hair in a ponytail, lots of makeup, white mohair sweater. A gold cross hangs from a chain over the fuzzy turtleneck. His second thought is that "bullion" is an extremely dorky word to utter in her presence. "It's OK," he says. "I'm still conscious."

"Inasmuch as any of us are conscious," she says as she stuffs the bag back in the overhead.

"Excuse me?"

"I noticed you were reading *Being and Nothingness.*"

Being and Nothingness, facedown on Frankie's lap before the duffel-bag bombing, now glares up at him from the floor. The pages are dog-eared, with yellow slips of paper sticking out from the sides. He's rereading it after some library sleuthing revealed it to be one of Dr. Felix Carr's sacred texts.

"We just did that in philosophy. I bet you actually understand it."

"I wrote a paper once called 'For-Itself, In-Itself, By Myself,'" he says. "I got a C plus."

She's a senior at Boston College, she tells him, en route to her family's place outside Philly. In four years of college she's never missed a holiday, birthday, baptism, confirmation, or wedding. The day she graduates, she's moving back to find a job as a middle school teacher.

"What a regrettable era of life," he says. "Please tell me you're teaching kids to erase it from their minds."

"That's the thing!" she says, her eyes suddenly silver-dollar wide. "It doesn't have to be so bad! They're doing amazing things with that age these days, especially in language arts. Have you read John Gaughan? Or Atwell's *In the Middle*?"

He shakes his head.

"It's this new way of teaching where kids write letters to each other and keep journals and publish their stories. Not just spit back spelling words. Kids don't even sit in rows anymore."

"How do they sit?"

"In pods," she says.

"Pods?"

She laughs. "Group learning and cooperation build self-esteem and make better citizens."

"Sister Carmelita used to throw chalk at my face when I got an answer wrong," Frankie says. "I don't think self-esteem was her top priority."

"And you're still a good citizen?" she asks.

"You have me there."

They trade Catholic-school stories for a while, him turned backward in his seat, his legs sticking out into the aisle, her leaning forward. Every time someone squeezes by, their knees touch. But she is five years his junior, not to mention a firm believer in the sanctity of the sacraments, and draws her knees back the moment the path clears. I need a girl like you, Frankie thinks. Decent, salt of the earth. Someone who cares about things like the self-esteem of sweaty, hormonal eleven-year-olds. He's done with sex, anyway. With Birch, he's had enough to sustain him through the long fallow period sure to be necessary with a girl like this.

Kelly Anne McDonald is her name. He's put in mind of Irish fields, of green beer, of luck.

What I don't need, he thinks: A selfish careerist, a woman who stands ready to betray me just to preserve her already assured place in the polluted ecosystem of academia. A woman unwilling to take even the slightest (and frankly theoretical) risk if it means a potential threat to her reputation as an evenhanded scholar, a faithful wife. A willing slave to the whims of the body. A corrupter. But that's what he's got.

The holiday week began well. "Dear Francesco Grasso," began Dr. Lexus's brief letter, typed on department stationery, left for him yesterday, the Tuesday before Thanksgiving, in his campus mailbox. In a spirit of fraternity and camaraderie, Lexus had crossed out "Francesco" with a blue pen and, above it, written "Frankie." "Thank you for submitting to the 2000 J—— University Dissertation Fellowship. I am pleased to inform you that the selection committee— Professors Arbuckle, Birch, McLean, and Yarrow—has selected your application as one of three to move forward to the final round of consideration. I congratulate you on this significant achievement. As stipulated in the design of the prize, the winner of the fellowship will be chosen by a visiting juror, who will read the finalists' applications and meet individually with candidates the week of December 13. As you know, this year the visiting juror will be Dr. Felix Carr. Enclosed please find a sign-up sheet for interviews. The winner will be notified no later than January 20. Sincerely," et cetera.

Within minutes of having received the letter, Frankie had marked the first interview slot as his first choice and the last slot for his second choice and returned the form to the department secretary. No matter that both slots conflicted with his teaching schedule; it was important to make a strong either initial or final impression. He hadn't heard of this Dr. Felix Carr, but he'd already made it his top priority to find out all he could about him, read his books, bone up on whatever field he was in. Lexus's letter didn't reveal the other two candidates, but he had no doubt Annalise Theroux was one of them. The third candidate was inconsequential because whoever it was had no chance.

Birch had come through for him after all. In the weeks since their first discussion of the fellowship, she'd promised Frankie that if he had plenty of support on the committee, she'd join in that support. Recognizing her moral failings, she also promised that if a vote came down to him and someone else, she'd choose him.

It came as no surprise, then, that under the letter from Dr. Lexus was a note from Birch.

She arrived, as usual, just after one o'clock. Frankie lay waiting for her on his futon, wearing nothing but Dr. Lexus's letter. "I squeaked through somehow," he said, taking the letter from its artful arrangement between his legs and waving it at her. "How did this happen, I wonder?"

"Classy," she said.

"Come on," said Frankie. "Let me have my fun. We're celebrating. You did the right thing. And if Dr. Felix Carr of Princeton picks me, it can't possibly reflect on you. You're free and clear."

"That's true enough, I guess."

She was still wearing a lot of clothes, which was rare for her. Frankie felt increasingly silly and confused as each second ticked by and she stood above him, hands on her hips, surveying, in her coat and scarf, how excited he was by Lexus's decision and their chance to christen it. Then it occurred to him that she might have buyer's remorse.

"What?"

He covered himself with a pillow.

"No, no," she said, tossing the pillow aside. She looked from his crotch to his eyes, then back again. "You just keep going, don't you? You don't give up."

"That's why you keep me around, I thought," he said. "Plus, why would I give up now? If I were going to give up, I'd have done it two months ago. Or last year, when you took a hatchet to my introduction..."

"That was the *Hindenburg* of introductions," she said. She laughed, and Frankie laughed, too, because she was right and because it was during the protracted and contentious dissection of his introduction that they'd decided to walk down to Elm Street for a glass of wine. It was that glass of wine that led to her first trip to his bedroom.

"You've helped me every step of the way," he said. He reached for her.

She remained stiff and unbearably clothed. "Frankie, I have to confess something," she said. "I'm sure it won't surprise you, but I have to say it. I won't feel right if I don't. I won't be able to enjoy"—she looked down at him again—"*today* if I don't."

"Jesus," he said. He got up, pulled on a pair of sweats, and muted the Cure CD, *Kiss Me Kiss Me Kiss Me,* that he'd put in especially for this session. His gut already guessed what she was going to tell him, but he stood across from her, arms crossed, until she fessed up.

"I didn't vote for you," she said. "I told you I would, even if the committee was deadlocked, but I didn't. In fact, there was a deadlock, and I argued for Mary Kessler. You made it to the final three in *spite* of me. And don't ask why because I've already gone over it."

"I'm in *third place*? You had to debate between me and *Mary Kessler*?"

She crossed her arms and looked at him with some defiance. "The uninformed are not permitted to be dismissive. Mary's doing some really excellent and difficult recovery work with Native American folktales. You don't cast someone aside because she's had a few kids in between chapters. That's what got me riled up, actually. The way the men on the committee—Arbuckle in particular, your new champion—would react whenever her name came up. The sexism of that place—"

"But it didn't rile you up that your advisee was floundering in fourth place."

"Frankie, we've been down this road. It worked out in the end. I made my spirited defense of Mary, they chose you instead, and now we can just let it go. I wanted to tell you, not to launch us into some debate over the relative merit of your work or the absurd biases in English Departments across the land, but because I don't want to keep any secrets from you. That's the beauty of what we have here, right? The honesty of it, our flaws on display? You know what lying does to me."

She'd expressed her discomfort with lying before, as a way of explaining her unique (and, to Frankie's mind, primitive) code of morality. She and Frankie had had many discussions about her marriage, which, by Birch's code, was an honest one simply because she'd never officially lied to her husband. For example, she'd never told Amos she was in the library or grading papers when she was really in Frankie's bed. When he'd asked, she'd said, "I was in a long session with an advisee," or "I went for a nice walk," or whatever could tech-nically be considered true. Speaking the truth and lying at the same time had both thrilled and shamed her, she said to Frankie, and she ex-pressed gratitude that Amos rarely asked questions, rarely concerned himself with the details of her weekdays on the campus they shared. He had no reason. They spent plenty of time together. They drove in and home together from Chestnut Hill on the days she taught, and on the weekends they had their Vineyard house, and fund-raisers for various causes, and lots and lots of hours to sit beside each other and read. After twelve years, she was as demanding of Amos in bed as she was of Frankie, a fact she liked to brag about whenever Frankie acted "all lazy and worn out" in the afternoon. It was Birch's code, which allowed her to keep her lives with Frankie and Amos separate but still "honest," if not equal.

Yesterday, too, he was so relieved to make it to the final fellow-ship round, and so eager to celebrate a rare victory, that he willed himself not to blow her confession, or her blind spot when it came to the defense of women, out of proportion. Instead he nodded, un-wrapped her scarf, unzipped her jacket, grabbed her big, chunky belt, and pulled her to him. Other than her revelation that the third final-ist was none other than Chris Curran, the pothead, nothing more was said.

It was after she'd gone, as he lay naked on his rough sheets, the late-afternoon skies already darkening, that his fourth-placeness settled on him like a fine layer of dust. He did some accounting: fourth place in his third-rate department, second place behind Amos in Birch's at-tentions, and second place behind Tony in his family's affections. In only one competition would Frankie be declared champion: the marathon of self-pity. And yet—what did Birch say? *You just keep going, don't you?* She admired him for that. He admired himself for that. He was not Tony. Whatever design flaw had existed in his brother's brain did not exist in his.

And now there is Kelly Anne McDonald, his new friend on this wobbly trek down the Eastern Seaboard, who has a great respect for what she calls Frankie's "interesting perspective on things." BC people look and talk the same, she says. No one disagrees or is disagreeable. The college is an "orgy of politeness," she says, without blushing. She's tried to branch out—to BU, to Harvard—but claims to have no talent for meeting left-of-center people and keeps settling for clones of herself and her current circle.

Sometime around Trenton, Kelly Anne gives Frankie her phone number and campus address. She still lives in a dorm, though her friends have moved into apartments or sorority houses, because she's afraid she'll never get her work done otherwise. Tomorrow she'll be attending Thanksgiving Mass, and Frankie, a twelve-year veteran of Catholic school, has to admit he didn't even know there was such a thing. He'd always thought of Thanksgiving as free from religious overtones.

Her hand is soft and creamy white. He holds it a moment too long as the train approaches Thirtieth Street and they say their good-bye and "we should get togethers." He enjoys his first sustained gaze at her ass as she drags the bag of gold bullion behind her. She looks back once before stepping off.

He's glad Kelly Anne McDonald is not around to see him take the ring out of his nose, replace his Holden Caulfield cap with the Timberland hat Prima gave him for Christmas, drop his bracelets into the front compartment of his backpack, and put on a J.Crew sweater over his Dead Kennedys T-shirt. He now looks as agreeable and cooperative as a kid from BC.

Though it's past midnight, the crowd on the train remains thick, having disembarked and replicated itself at each stop for the past six hours. Only a scant few of these people will disappear with Frankie into the vast metropolis of Wilmington, Delaware, or, as his friends used to call it, "the Town Fun Forgot." On the approach, the view from their smudged windows is the charming oil refineries of Marcus Hook, twinkling and pumping noxious clouds into the air, the stadium-size lots jammed with cars, and the squat downtown office buildings blank and empty as Sunday in Brasília. A good place to raise your kids, they say about this town. A short drive to Philly, New York, Atlantic City, Baltimore, and DC, but without as many "problems," by which they mean "crime," by which they mean "blacks." Everything is postcolonial, even here. He should write a chapter on the neighborhood around St. Anthony's Church, dominated by Italians for decades, then abandoned for the suburbs. The Grassos are complicit in this narrative, of course, though Frankie has gained some distance from it. He is the first member of his generation of the extended family to live more than thirty miles from Little Italy, to have the luxury of Boston culture at his fingertips—the lectures, the readings, the ghosts of Emerson and Thoreau taking his hand as they cross the common in perfect exhilaration. In this way, he reminds himself, he's lucky. If he's even luckier, he can catch the train back Saturday morning instead of Sunday night, ring up Kelly Anne McDonald, and take her to *The Battle of Algiers* at the Brattle.

But then, as he struggles to wrench his backpack from between two boxes of anvils in the overhead, he sees his mother and father standing on the platform. They are holding hands, searching every window for a glimpse of their son, relieved, when they find his profile, that Amtrak has delivered him safely home. Their faces say how grateful they are for this silly American holiday that reunites them, how they're planning every meal they'll eat this weekend, every visit to his *zia* and *compari* in the old neighborhood. The moment he sees them, Frankie knows he will not catch the early train home. He will stay with them until the last possible moment.

His mother has had her hair frosted and her nails painted pumpkin-orange. His father wears his leather jacket with the sheepskin collar. Frankie embraces him and rests his head for a moment on the fur. His father has grown shorter. The tremor in his arm, noticed in the summer but never discussed, is more pronounced. They bicker over where they parked, which neither one remembers, and how long it's been since they've seen Frankie. His mother smells of Nina Ricci and baby powder. She felt tired for no reason all day, she says, her mind foggy, but now that Frankie's here, the fog goes away.

All his life, Frankie's kept his mother and father from the fog. Antonio denies they planned it that way, but Maddalena has told him many times about the nightgown with the holes in the underarms, the roses. It is one in her extensive repertoire of stories, beginning always with the village boy, Vito Leone, her first love, who romanced her with a bicycle he made from scraps he found lying around three towns. It was Vito who'd rebuilt her parents' house after the Allied bombing and who would have been her husband if he'd had as much money as Antonio pretended to have. She has no end of Vito stories or memories from Prima's and Frankie's childhood, but only a few stories of Antonio. Of Tony she tells no stories at all. She rarely mentions him by name, and sometimes Frankie feels her trying too hard to remind him that he may not have been the first son born in the new country, but he inherited the promise of a great future for the Grassos. The best idea they ever had, his mother likes to say, was to bring Francesco Grasso into the world. Frankie has seen a hundred pictures of Tony, heard his voice on the one audiotape that survives, been reminded many times by his father and Prima of the little boy's energy and piano playing and love for the Al Di Là, but he can't summon much love for his brother beyond the theoretical: Without him, I would not exist, is the most he can do.

"But what about guilt?" Birch likes to ask, but that, too, is theoretical. Once, in response, he quoted Emerson: "In the death of my son . . . I seem to have lost a beautiful estate,—no more. I cannot get it nearer to me . . . It leaves no scar."

Birch had looked at him, puzzled. "There's no colder passage in all of American Literature," she said.

"And you've never known me to be cold."

"My point exactly. It's so unlike you, in such opposition to the Frankie Grasso I've come to know, that I have to think it's some sort of block. I suggest psychoanalysis."

"I suggest we pretend you didn't suggest that."

If anything, Frankie strives to be colder, to keep his distances. He's already deep in emotion; the last thing he wants is to go down the rabbit hole of Freudian exploration. Emotion continually threatens to disarm him. Like all the Grassos, he's a junkie for it. It is to avoid wallowing in emotion, and to train his mind to focus on reason and analytics, that he walks through sleeping neighborhoods and abandoned parking lots until he's too tired to feel anything, until all he can do is stumble up the stairs and pass out on his futon. It was to avoid emotion that he chose to live apart from his mother and father in the first place. He'd have gladly leapt into their mouths. And if he'd stayed, they'd have swallowed him whole.

Frankie's problem is that already, in the first minutes of a five-day visit, in his parents' company, he misses them. They wander through the parking lot, his mother's arm around his waist, his father's hand on his shoulder. He doesn't realize until he's with them how unsteadily he's been walking. As the emotion junkie can't help doing upon homecoming, as Frankie does too often lying in bed alone in Boston, he adds up the years he's been given with his parents and compares them to those he'll spend on people and ambitions beyond their reach, like PhDs and selfish lovers and pretty Irish middle school teachers. These are years Tony both granted his brother and denied him, and they are too short. To be the youngest child, his mother has told him, is a curse of sadness.

Frankie imagines the day when the train will pull into Wilmington and no one will be waiting for him on the platform. It's always with him, that day. And so already—as he takes the wheel of the enormous Sedan Deville and drives out of the shadow of the Delaware Memorial Bridge and onto the highway—he wants to tell his mother and father, Thank you for letting me go, and thank you for welcoming me home, and if you ask me right now to stay for good, I just might say yes and never look back.

BLACK FRIDAY, AND Christiana Mall's all jazzed up. Prima drags Frankie and her mother here to help them with their Christmas lists—they're hopeless shoppers—but she's got an ulterior motive.

She loves the festivity of the mall, however manufactured it might be. She loves the archways of green garland above each storefront, the roving carolers in petticoats and top hats, the wraparound lines of kids jumping up and down waiting for Santa Claus. Even Frankie's eye roll at the human toy soldier that welcomes them to the food court doesn't kill her mood. As obnoxious as her brother is, it's a blessing that he comes home, and she remembers, once she spends a little time with him, that he has his charms. Though they have few everyday things in common, his very presence, his Grasso heart beating close to hers, calms her.

Caffè Mediterraneo is offering free samples of Sicilian pizza. Prima takes three. "Between the holidays and a month in Italy," she says, "I'll be fat as a house."

"Don't let that happen," says Maddalena.

"I'm just so hungry these days," Prima says. "It's all the planning. I need an assistant."

"Dancing's very good exercise," says her mother. "Instead of being so busy for no reason, you could take a samba class. They're opening a new studio up near you. I promise, the more you dance, the less tired you look."

Frankie grabs a slice of pepperoni. "You two are masters of

passive-aggressive antagonism," he says, which causes both his mother and sister to laugh, Maddalena because she doesn't understand the words, Prima because he's right.

"We're not going to fight today," Prima says.

"Who's fighting?" says Maddalena. "I'm looking for presents."

Maddalena's wearing her new brown leather pencil skirt, which Prima bought for her birthday in September. "You still have the figure," she had reminded her. "You should enjoy it." Prima would never have chosen the outfit for herself, but it works on her mother. Frankie's jeans are too tight and torn at the knee, and his hair's a goopy mess, and this, too, works, though she'd never let any of her boys out of the house looking like that.

They stand before a display of $200 orange and lime cashmere sweaters. "You need to wear more color," Maddalena says to her.

"These make me want sherbet."

"I'm serious," she says. "Look at you." Prima's got on her khaki-and-maroon ensemble, bought over five years ago, the most comfortable outfit in her closet. "You buy 'in' clothes for me, but you walk around in a sack. Your friends don't tell you to dress more—what's the word?—hip?"

Prima shrugs. "I'm not as hip as you, Ma," she says. "We're wasting time here. They're not even on sale." She guides them away from the display, toward the less pricey shops on the other side of the fountain.

"Whatever happened to those nice girls from college you used to go around with?" Maddalena asks.

"Linda and Audrey? What made you think of them? They're around. I think Audrey lives not far from here, actually."

"You don't see her?"

"We have our own families, Ma. We lost touch."

You should have friends, Maddalena thinks. If you did, you wouldn't say, at your sons' birthday party, "It's a wonder I'm *not* a drunk." Maddalena wrote about drunks in her letters to Mamma. She asked God about them in church. She thought back to the ones she'd known—an uncle in Santa Cecilia, a Russian lady at the dress factory—and remembered them as angry people, but Prima wasn't angry. Now, though, as they walk through the crowded mall together, she thinks, No, those people weren't angry. They were lonely.

"I'm getting you one of those cashmere sweaters," she says to Prima suddenly, interrupting whatever she's saying to Frankie. "So you better tell me which color you like."

"You're still on that, Ma?" Prima says. "They're a rip-off."

"I want to do something nice for you this year."

"There's only one thing I want from you."

"Frankie, what do you think? Which color?"

"I'll take a medium," he says. "In cantaloupe."

Prima shakes her head. Then she can't help herself, she has to ask: "So, do you have anybody special in your life who'd look good in that sweater?"

Again the trademark Frankie eye roll. "Subtle segue there," he says. "Please change the subject." He picks at his fingernail as they walk, and won't look up at her or his mother. "I think I'd rather hear you fight about Italy."

"Come on, Frankie," Maddalena says. "I tell you *my* stories. You never tell me yours."

"I don't have any."

"I don't believe you," his mother says.

"I'm sorry," he says. "You have a boring kid. I'd think you'd want that."

That's anger, not playfulness, in Frankie's voice. Prima's finely tuned to how quickly, and without warning, a man can cross the line from one to the other, especially when he's being teased or probed. She's learned how to push Tom and her boys close to that line, get the information she needs or make the point she needs to make, then retreat at the last second before they blow up. This approach leaves them thinking they got away with something, and what man doesn't glory in that?

"Leave him alone, Mother," Prima says.

"You brought it up."

"Let me put it this way," Frankie says. "I'm not lonely."

Later they sit and rest awhile on the benches by the fountain. They're surrounded by shopping bags. At Prima's direction, Frankie's bought a monogrammed pullover for his father, a tie clip for Tom, and various gift cards for her sons, all gifts thoughtful enough to be appreciated but cheap enough for Frankie to afford. Frankie buys nothing for anyone in Boston, though Prima reminds him, gently, that Delaware is tax-free, and if he was going to get something for a certain nameless special person, now would be the time. She even offers to make the purchase herself if he wants to hide it from their mother, but he ignores her. She's helped Maddalena finish all her shopping, too, except the gift she'll get for Prima on her own steam, which better not be one of those sweaters or she'll return it immediately. Again,

Prima reminds her mother that for Christmas she wants only her blessing—which includes her cooperation with the Italy trip—but this, too, is ignored.

She finds a handful of pennies in her purse and gives them to an adorable little girl who sits beside her, looking even more bored than Frankie. Her grandfather looks over, smiles, and thanks her. The girl casts her arm back and pitches each penny as far as her matchstick body can make it fly, delighted by the splash and the ripples it makes on the water. In a year or two, Prima thinks, she'll be too old to enjoy this. She'll be too self-conscious. For a moment, Prima sees not the little girl at all but the twins at her age, at five, maybe six. They had the chubbiest little hands then, couldn't keep their balance, could barely outrun the neighbor's dachshund. Now Matt's an all-state pitcher, written up in the *News Journal* for his finesse and speed around the bases; now Zach's the team's most reliable goalie. What will become of this little girl in ten years, when she reaches Allison Grey's age? Does her grandfather have any idea how much the world has changed, how dangerous it's become? Yet another reason Prima should be happy with what God gave her. Sons. The world was made for sons.

Allison Grey is everywhere. All the girls Prima sees have her shiny, innocent-seeming face. Every boy stops to check her out, consider her, tick his head in recognition and invitation. In the mall today, Prima spotted her listening on a headset at Sam Goody, and again pulling apart a pretzel at Auntie Anne's, and again in the ladies' room coughing into a clenched fist. She's always singing that same song, always stretching her naked limbs. What Prima saw in the basement shocked her, turned her stomach, and yet she can't stop herself from playing the scene over and over in her mind—the moonlight on Matt's muscular back and behind, Zach strutting fully erect to the bed, their playful confidence and ease, all three of them. The next morning, Allison gone, Prima couldn't look Matt or Zach in the eye, but by the afternoon she watched with pride as they devoured the egg-and-sausage sandwiches she'd fixed them. After they conked out on the couch wearing only their boxers and a T-shirt, she brought down blankets, laid them over their gently breathing bodies, turned down the TV, and kissed them both on the forehead.

And then—it has to be said—as the evening came on and Ryan flew back to Syracuse and the boys woke and she vacuumed and prepared dinner for them to take in the car to Penn State, Prima felt closer than ever to her twins. Closer and, strangely, relieved. She had seen everything. And after everything, what more could they hide?

At Allison Grey, though, Prima's still mad as hell. Every time she sees her—driving her beat-up Toyota down Concord Pike, pumping gas, in the school newspaper running for student council, bagging her groceries—she wants to grab her by the neck. She should be warned. But the girl is never there quite long enough. She's always turning the corner. Prima's gone so far as to look her up in the phone book, but there are too many Greys in Pennsylvania and Delaware, and she has no friends in common with her parents, and to ask Matt or Zach is to risk their not having gotten away with something. Last Saturday, Prima went to Ethan Allen and wandered the showroom for an hour, just in case Allison and her mother wandered in. It's possible the girl lied about that, too, in some boneheaded attempt to impress her. Who does she think Prima is, anyway? Her future mother-in-law? The thought of this made Prima angrier than ever. She has a plan for this week, once school's back in session, to observe her—just observe her—and if the girl can stay still for one minute, maybe Prima will figure out what it is about her that she can't shake.

"Somebody's done for the day," Frankie says. He points his thumb at their mother, now dozing beside him on the bench.

"I'm just resting my eyes," says Maddalena, without opening them.

"One last stop," Prima says. "Come on." She pats her mother on the thigh, gives Frankie a wink. "We can do it." It's time to reveal her ulterior motive, even though she herself feels sluggish. For a moment she considers abandoning the surprise, worried that it will ruin an otherwise pleasant afternoon, but the junkie in her will not let her.

She leads them to Macy's. They weave among the fragrance counters, then up the escalator to the home section.

"What did we lose here?" Maddalena says.

Prima finds Arnaud, the flouncy fellow who helped her earlier in the week and promised to be working today from two to eight.

"Miss!" he says. "I'm ready for you!" Then he rushes off.

"What's this, now?" says Maddalena. She crosses her arms.

"An early Christmas present from the Buckleys to the Grassos," Prima says.

"Am I included in this present?" asks Frankie.

"Aren't you a Grasso?" says Prima.

In seconds, Arnaud is back, grandly wheeling two sets of luggage—one two-piece, one five-piece—on a big plastic cart. The first, Frankie's, is black, to match every article of clothing he owns; the other, her parents', is a rich burgundy. Both sets are fashioned from the finest leather.

"Jesus, Prima," Frankie says. "Your subtlety continues to amaze."

"Take it back," Maddalena says to Arnaud, waving him off. "We don't want it. Get it away."

Arnaud's big, toothy smile fades. An old lady behind him stares. He says to Prima, "Miss?"

"OK, Mom," says Frankie. He puts his hand on her shoulder. "Now you're being dramatic."

"I'm sorry," Prima says calmly to Arnaud. She takes her mother's arm and pulls her out of the aisle, away from the staring old lady, toward a dimly lit display of china. Frankie follows close behind her. "You're going to have to explain this to me again," she says.

"We haven't explained it enough?" says Frankie.

"Oh, I forgot. You're a united front."

"I just understand where she's coming from, and you can't seem to."

"Because where she's coming from is just plain stupid. We're doing this *for* her, Frankie, not *to* her. And definitely not *against* her. I tried to tell you that, but you're the one who can't seem to understand."

"It will only make her sad," Frankie says. "You don't think she's sad enough? You want her to be worse than she already is?" His expression is pained, like she's the enemy holding his loved one hostage. "There's an expression, 'You can't go home again.' It's from a novel—"

"Do *not* start quoting shit to me, Frankie. I'm not an idiot. I know that expression. I think he was wrong, whoever wrote it. I think you can go home anytime you want. You just have to be a grown-up about it."

"Her whole family over there is either sick or dead. I can't imagine what that's like."

"We're her family," Prima says. "We're not sick or dead. That should count for something. For *everything,* actually. Not to mention what Dad wants. You saw how excited he got when I told him."

"Dad, who basically had to kidnap her to get her to come here? I find it rather ironic that he's trying so hard to bring her back to the village now."

"Nobody kidnapped anybody," Prima says. "You only hear her side of the story. I talk to Dad."

"And Mom talks to me."

"That's enough," Maddalena says. "We both talk to you both. Can I say what I feel now?"

"Unless you changed your mind and aren't going to be so selfish, then I'd prefer not to hear what you feel."

Maddalena stares at her. "I'm saying, listen to this: Frankie and I had a good idea the other night. We were talking, and we said, Let's go somewhere else, all of us. California. Canada. Or Paris. If all you want is for us to be together, we can be together in Paris."

Prima shakes her head. It's the only response she can muster. She has a specific reason for Italy over Paris or Canada or California or anywhere, and an argument she could make, but not now, not here. She can't acknowledge the reason to herself, let alone to her mother or Frankie. Her hunch might not even be true. She's tried to put it out of her mind as a possibility, but nothing stays down for long, and when it comes up, it surprises her, and she starts to cry.

"Well, this has been great," says Frankie.

THEY WALK TO the car, Frankie and Maddalena a step or two behind Prima, without saying more. They pass a trio of animatronic elves, a dozen Allison Greys, a long mirror in which Prima spots herself and looks away. The harder she tries, the less her plans come together. The breakdown in logic infuriates her.

Between putting the keys in the ignition and turning them, Prima says, "Fine. We won't go. You win."

"It's not about winning," says Frankie from the backseat.

"We'll go to Paris," Maddalena says. She puts her hand on Prima's shoulder. "My friend Arlene says Paris is better, anyway. You can switch the tickets?"

Prima shrugs off her mother's hand. "I'm driving," she says.

She drops them off without coming in to say hello to her father—an act of rebellion she'll pay for later—and heads straight home. Tom is outside in the drizzle, stringing lights on the holly bushes. He's wearing a pair of old jeans, a Syracuse sweatshirt, and a baseball cap that offers little protection from the icy rain. "I'm almost done," he says before she can scold him. As he fiddles with the cords, knees in the mud and rain pelting them both, she tells him what's been decided.

"The luggage really freaked them out, huh?" he says. "I gotta say, I didn't think that was such a great idea. Not everybody likes being put on the spot."

"My intentions were good," Prima says. "If they'd only trust me—" She stops. She doesn't want to cry in front of Tom, not over the trip, not out here in the rain like a hysterical housewife, for the neighbors to see. And yet she can't seem to control the waves of emotion swelling and crashing inside her. She wonders if this acute, uncontainable emotion, like her burning feet, like the weight she's put on, can be blamed on the change of life. And suddenly she's furious again.

"Your intentions are always good, Prima. I'm sorry."

Prima looks up at the gray sky, watches the ice fall and settle onto the red berries, making them glisten deliciously, looks at Tom crouched under the bay window. He's stringing these lights for her, on the first possible day it's OK to do so, despite the rain, because he knows how much she loves them. Some nights, she'll bundle up and take a walk around the block just so she can turn the corner onto their street and come upon their house aglow. Watching Tom, his strong back, his full head of blond curls, his act of kindness, something in her stirs. It's a rare urge these days, and this, too, she blames on the new season of departures and decay in which she finds herself.

"Let's go out tonight," she says. "I don't feel like cooking."

"Really? In this weather?"

"Why not? We're not so old yet."

He looks over his shoulder and gives her a quick smile back. "Sure," he says. "Give me ten minutes."

"You don't have to finish this tonight," Prima says, and when he turns back to her again, his smile widens. He hops up onto his feet and brushes the dirt from his knees.

"Thank you, Sergeant," he says, and he kisses her.

They decide to try a new place called the Bourbon Street Café, out on Kirkwood Highway. There's live jazz on Fridays and half-price appetizers and a soft-shell crab entrée that won Best of Delaware. Prima would have preferred a longer drive, even in the rain, but Tom's a big fan of Cajun food and she never cooks it, so she's happy enough with the pick. Like her mother, Prima finds car rides soothing, especially when her husband's behind the wheel. She could ride all the way to New Orleans, him beside her with his eyes fixed seriously on the road, her with her head resting on the window, shoes off, heat blasting.

Tom doesn't fiddle with the radio, never drives faster than the speed limit, and doesn't talk much unless he's safe at a stoplight. He's driven this way ever since his twin sister, Amy, was killed in a car wreck when they were twenty-four, a year after he married Prima. It's a wound that opens each time he steps into a car. Prima understands this. It's one of the many reasons she's confident they will be together forever, why the cord that binds her to her husband is as strong as the one that binds her to her family.

Tom still dreams about Amy, he's said, still talks to her on his drive to work. He keeps her photo on the wall behind his desk and talks about her with his clients. He comes from the kind of family that believes in this type of public mourning, of making your lost loved ones part of your daily life. The Grassos—like most Italians Prima knows—are different. After you say your good-byes, after you've thrown yourself on your brother's or your son's body for one last touch as the casket closes, you keep your grief to yourself. The rest of your life is a long silence.

At the Bourbon Street Café, Prima and Tom sit side by side at the one available booth, closest to the stage, where an old black man with a white goatee blares a saxophone in their faces. They yell their orders to the waitress—conch fritters, two soft-shell crabs, and two hurricanes— then sit with their legs up and crossed on the opposite side of the booth, his arm around her shoulders, like they're in bed watching

TV. Prima's not a jazz fan (she likes the singer to tell a story, and here there's no singer, much less a story), but Tom loses himself in it. She watches him close his eyes and let the music wash over him. It's nice how at peace he is. When the set ends and the sax player drifts outside to smoke, she tells him that they'll come to this place more often, once a month if he wants, that he works too hard and could use a little music.

"You know," he says, midway through his second hurricane, "the more I think about it, the more disappointed I am about Italy."

"Me, too."

"The food, the historic stuff, the boys all together, your mom and dad in their native habitat. I don't think I'll ever understand why it's so complicated."

Prima can't bear to go over her mother's reasons again. Anyway, the layers of family dynamics are all lost on Tom, who grew up Irish Catholic. When the Buckleys had disagreements, they simply stopped talking; no wonder they don't know each other's hearts the way the Grassos do.

"I'll tell you this," Prima says. "I'm not dragging my parents and Frankie to Paris just to go somewhere. Not if they're going to be ungrateful. If it's not Italy, it's nothing."

"OK," Tom says as Prima sips her hurricane.

"We should take our own trip," Prima says. "Just us."

"You read my mind," Tom says. He sits up straight, his hand still around her shoulders. "I was just thinking as you were talking: my buddy from college has a cabin in northern Michigan. He tells me it's gorgeous up there. You have to take a little plane from Detroit, but once you get there it's . . . like Paradise. Unspoiled land and all that. Romantic. I'd love to see you in hiking boots."

"Oh," says Prima. "You mean, just the two of us?"

"That's not what you meant?"

She can't come up with a decent answer, and luckily the sax player's back. What would they talk about, she wonders, just the two of them in the Michigan woods for a week? It's one thing to take a Sunday drive or splurge on a hotel room overnight in Philly, but it's another to stretch out all that alone time over a week. When they were dating, they had a circle of friends to gossip about, career decisions to deliberate, wedding and honeymoon plans to make, and, until Amy died, only happy memories to bring forth in conversation. Now they have the boys and the house and baseball, but those only go so far, and besides, Tom, who was never a talker to begin with, has gotten even quieter in his forties.

"You take care of other people enough," Tom says at the next break. "Let me take care of you for a change. I'll teach you how to fish. I'll buy you the entire L.L. Bean catalog. It'll be an adventure." He leans over and whispers, "Plus, you'd look sexy in flannel. And the hiking boots. Or just the hiking boots—"

"Where's this coming from?" Prima interrupts, blushing. The people in the next booth can hear.

"What do you mean?"

"It's not like you."

"Is that bad?" He puts his hand on her thigh.

"No. It's just not like you."

"I saw the way you looked at me back at the house," he says. "It's been a while, but I still recognize that look."

"Tom!"

"'We're not so old,' you said."

"I was talking about driving in the rain."

"Listen," he says. He pulls her closer. "Next fall's gonna be strange as hell. Alone in the house. I know you're worried about it. The truth is, I am, too. So let's take some steps. Isn't that what we're supposed to do? Empty nest, second honeymoon, all that jazz?"

Prima can almost see Tom checking off the "second honeymoon" box in his head. He has always been conscious of life's schedules, and holds himself and his family to them. When he turned forty, he took up golf. At forty-five, he bought a sailboat. At forty-six, he sold it. His predictability has been a comfort to Prima over the years, but she didn't expect him to check off this latest box so soon. She's not quite ready.

"I don't know," she says. "It doesn't feel right to abandon everyone so soon. We should see how Patrick does in school. It'll be a big transition for him. You remember how Ryan lost all that weight his first term? What if Patrick needs to come home all of a sudden, and we're in some cabin in the middle of nowhere? Does this Michigan place even have a phone?"

Tom narrows his eyes at her. The waitress stands awkwardly behind him, trying to get their attention. "Never mind," he says, and suddenly there's a space between them. Their legs meet but don't touch. They watch the stage for a while, the crew adjusting the lights and arranging the chairs and various instruments for the headliners. When the waitress goes by, he signals for the check, even though Prima's hurricane is still half-full.

"It's still early," says Prima. "We don't have to go. You're enjoying this."

He shrugs.

"I screwed up again, didn't I?" she says.

Again he says nothing.

"How much was it?" she asks him as he hands the waitress his Amex.

"All I asked you to do," he says, "was spend one week with me and be excited about it—as excited as you were about spending two weeks with your family in Italy. I didn't even ask you to *do* it, just to *consider* it. But I guess that's asking too much."

"I'm excited about the idea. I'm just—the timing. Remember Ryan, when he left—"

"You're too close to those boys," Tom continues. "I love them just as much as you do. I pay attention. I remember how Ryan was at Syracuse that first term. I argued religion with Patrick for two years, even drove up to that monastery he was infatuated with! But there's such a thing as being too involved. You have to let go."

"I'm sorry, that's not possible," Prima says. "I don't even want it to be possible."

Frankie has accused her of the same crime, of being too close to her kids. Her mother, too, and her magazines. But Prima's not going to change, not one little bit. Because if she lets go of her boys, she'll have to replace them with something else, and nothing else compares. Not even you, Tom, she thinks. I'm sorry.

He keeps talking, painting the picture of their bright future as "empty nesters," but as soon as Prima hears that awful word, she tunes out. Cruises? Golf? A time-share in the Keys? She has little patience for relaxation. Volunteering? As a Catholic, she's as loyal as Tom, but she's unmotivated to nurture the poor if neither the Buckleys nor the Grassos will benefit directly. She'd rather sweep the sidewalks outside the Al Di Là than serve soup to homeless strangers. Unlike every other Grasso, Prima has never embraced paid work. She's been more than content as a mother and housewife, compensated with trust and gratitude. Retirement from such a career, with such benefits, might as well be death.

For a short time, at sixteen, Prima thought she might have a passion for the kind of career her father had—the management of a busy restaurant, which, it turns out, is much like running a family—but in retrospect that passion had everything to do with Dante Marconi. They used to kiss in the alley behind the Al Di Là. They fell in love there, the summer before Tony died, when Prima had no reason to think life wouldn't keep handing her one beautiful thing after another. In the blur of years that followed, it was Dante who helped numb Prima's mind. Memories of him keep coming back to her lately, in dreams and in her waking life, more often in the past year than in the twenty-seven before. Like tonight, after too many hurricanes and with Tom talking romantic getaways, she is thinking of the weekend they spent in Wildwood in a sleeping bag on the floor of Dante's cousin's beach house. There was no planning that weekend, just Dante surprising her one Friday at the door of her parents' house, his car packed with the sleeping bag, a cooler of beer, a swimsuit, and little else. Dante Marconi was my great love, she once thought. Now she wonders if love can earn its greatness only with history.

"We'll leave after the next song," Tom leans over to say, without opening his eyes. Since the band retook the stage, he's been one with the music, rocking back and forth like a man in a trance. She wills herself to put Dante out of her mind for now, here beside her husband. It's not right. A sin. Instead she tries to see in the jazz what Tom sees, but it's lost on her, a haze of seemingly random notes strung together with gibberish lyrics. In this way, too, she has disappointed him.

She should do something to smooth things over. Maybe later tonight—as soon as they get home, before her buzz wears off and Tom falls asleep—she'll go down to the basement, slip on an old pair of hiking boots, strip down, and stand before him in their bedroom. It's the least she could do.

She won't chicken out. She'll summon that sixteen-year-old girl who dared to let Dante Marconi hold her and kiss her against the alley wall while her father and brother worked on the other side of it. What a thrill it was—not the fear they'd be discovered, but the risk that Dante, who needed that job to make his car payments, took on her, a girl he barely knew, who wasn't even the prettiest waitress at the Al Di Là. Her father fired him, anyway, of course, without explanation, a few weeks after their first kiss, and Prima has always wondered whether he'd come upon her and Dante himself, watched them from behind a stack of empty boxes in the alley, or whether one of the managers snitched. She and her father have never spoken about it, but she knew Dante was not the kind of boy she'd ever be allowed to bring home. Still, for a year afterward, Prima and Dante met in secret, in his car, at Wildwood, under the Hagley Bridge after school.

She's lost focus again, takes another sip of her hurricane, tries again to love the music. No luck. After a while she takes a chance and puts her arm around Tom's shoulders. He opens his eyes immediately— had he fallen asleep already?—and turns to her. "Last song," he says. "I promise."

5   *Turn Up the Music*

I T'S THE MORNING of Christmas Eve, and no one is speaking to Maddalena because she has broken their hearts. This is a day of God, but how can she concentrate on him when Antonio's playing the silence game, Prima hasn't returned her calls since the Black Friday trip to the mall, and Frankie's train's not coming for six more hours? Frankie's the only one who will talk nice to her, but he won't be here long, and when he leaves it will be winter in every way.

There are worms in the flour she's set aside for the batter. They are signs: the worms, and Frankie's late train, and Prima's giving up on the trip so soon without more of a fight. Signs of what, Maddalena doesn't know, but they can't be good, and she is worried.

At Mass she asked God her questions, but because of all the work she has to do today, she left early, after Communion, like the teenagers do, before he had a chance to answer. As she walks home, she checks off what's done and not done: The dining room table was set the night before, the house is clean, and Antonio's shirt ironed. There are seven fishes to cook—two to fry, one to chop into the sauce, three to bread, one to fillet. *Contorni* to prepare. Wine to dust off and uncork. Traditions. As long as she's alive, her children will spend Christmas Eve in her house, no excuses. She made them promise this long ago, and even though she hasn't spoken to Prima for two weeks, she knows without a doubt that she and Tom and the boys will be here at five thirty tonight, just as they were here at five thirty last year and the years before.

In the kitchen she finds Antonio on the telephone, face guilty. "Is it Prima?" she asks, removing her gloves.

He shakes his head.

"Francesco?"

The counter is a mess of flour and salt and dripped egg yolk from Antonio's trying to finish the pasta before she got home. The call must have interrupted.

He holds the phone up to her ear, and there is the voice of her brother, Claudio, in Santa Cecilia, talking like he thinks Antonio is still listening. She pushes the phone away, runs down the hall, and locks herself in the bathroom.

"*Scema!*" he calls to her. Crazy woman! It's the first word he's spoken to her in a month.

She holds her hands over her ears and paces from one end of the room to the other, but still she can hear Antonio's voice in the kitchen shouting, "*Auguri, Auguri!*" to her family across the world, so she climbs into the empty tub and pulls the glass door shut.

Scema, Antonio has called her, since June 6, 1977, the day Claudio's voice on the phone said their mamma was dead. That was the last conversation she's had with him or any of her sisters or nephews or cousins in Italy. There were eighteen of them at last count, from the babies to the old ladies, enough for their own little village. To the grave with Mamma went them all.

Twenty-two years of their letters unopened and shoved to the back of the fabric drawer with Tony's pictures and Mother's Day cards, of looking away from the photos of their weddings and christenings that Antonio left on her dresser, of rushing down the hall every time he got on the phone with one of them. Can no one but Frankie understand her when she says it's easier to pretend they're all dead?

She doesn't deny Antonio the connection to her family, doesn't insist he abandon Santa Cecilia the way she has. His own brother gone, let Antonio have her brother and her sisters, too. He made his peace with them long ago, and they've forgiven him for taking her away from the village, so let him be the one worrying day and night about their cancers and their broken hips, their daughters pregnant without husbands, how their long lives of suffering and regret will finally end. Not her. She wants only the here and now.

Prima asks her what kind of person can talk like this, can give up her entire family and never look back, but if Prima knew how the death of a child changes a mother, she wouldn't have to ask. Prima knows only a sister's grief, and that bleeds you, it does, but not the same way.

I hope you never find out how different it bleeds, Maddalena has told her.

After Tony died, Maddalena came to fear the ringing telephone, even though Mamma was still alive and called her a few times a month from Santa Cecilia. Antonio went along, explained to everyone for seven years that the last time she picked up the phone, the policeman on the other end told her they had found her son. Then Mamma died, and with her went Maddalena's last reason to think that anyone could be calling for a happy reason. Since then, twenty-two years have gone by, and not once has she picked up except at 11:01 when she's sure who it is. Evenings, she sits sewing next to the ringing downstairs extension as Antonio jumps out of his recliner and, muttering "Crazy woman," marches into the kitchen to grab the phone.

She blesses the wonderful invention called the answering machine. It's given her a system that respects everyone. These days, when the phone rings and she's home alone, Maddalena climbs the stairs from her basement workroom, stands over the machine, and listens first to Frankie's voice telling the person that no one is home (Frankie's voice because they don't like to hear their own accents) and then to the person's message. If it's a voice from Santa Cecilia, she pushes Mute, calls for her husband, and disappears. If it's Frankie or Prima or the dance studio or someone from St. Mary's, she happily interrupts them.

All these years, Antonio has put up with her system without much argument, but not today, not Christmas Eve 1999. A bad sign. "Open up!" he says, losing the silence game. He pounds his fist on the bathroom door. "God's watching you. You hear me? Get out here and say 'Merry Christmas' to your brother. If you won't go see him, you can at least tell him 'Merry Christmas.'"

Twenty-two years she's spent blind and deaf to Italy. But lately, since the spring, it's been coming back to her in flashes when she doesn't expect it. She can't stop the flashing, she doesn't even know how to try to stop it, and when it comes, all of a sudden she's walking on the dirt road to the spring in the early morning with her empty water pail, and the sun coming up over the mountains is warm on her neck, and when she wakes up in real life sometimes she's in a different part of the house, or it's nighttime when it was daytime just seconds before. Antonio took her to the doctor, but all he could do was tell her to sleep more or see a psychiatrist, so she tells Antonio she's trying to sleep more, and because he's always asleep before she is, it's an easy lie.

She opens the bathroom door and takes the cordless, but not without shooting her husband an angry look. "*Pronto!*" she says, making her voice sunny. Antonio watches her, arms folded. "*Buon Natale, Claudio!*"

No one is there. She hears only a beep, then an echo of the beep, then the shaky four-thousand-mile-away voice of a different person, not Claudio, but a woman. Carolina. Carolina, her only sister alive. The sister who'd married Vito, the boy Maddalena loved, the boy of the bicycle and the secret meetings in the back of her father's store. He had married Carolina, the sister of spite, who in thirty-five years never gave Maddalena the chance to ignore her letters, because she never sent a single one.

"*Sorella mia?*" Carolina's voice asks. "*Sei proprio tu?*" My sister, is it really you?

She should throw the phone at Antonio for tricking her. But once you're pulled underwater like this, you lose strength in your arms.

"Carolina," says Maddalena, to which her sister replies, "Maddalena!" and at first all they can manage is to repeat their names over and over, like they're convincing each other they're real. What else can break a lifetime of silence? They were once the best of friends. First a man came between them, then an ocean, then the grudges and pride of sisters. Mamma and Babbo and the twins, Celestina and Teresa, all died before them, and now it is just the two of them and Claudio. They have grown children neither has met.

"*Ma dove sei?*" Carolina asks. "*Dove sei andata?*" Where are you? Where did you go?

"You know where I am," says Maddalena, in Italian. Carolina's voice sounds deeper and scratchier than she remembers. To hear it is a miracle. She wants to ask: Do you smoke now? Do you drink hard liquor, like Mamma used to do, to kill germs? She has so many questions that she can't get them out fast enough. The most important: "Tell me: Are you well? And your children?"

"*Che cosa stai dicendo?*" says Carolina. "*Quali figli?*" What are you talking about? What children?

"It's OK," says Maddalena. "I know about them. A boy and a girl. Sergio, Donatella. I follow your life even though I don't say."

"*Non ho figli,*" Carolina says. I don't have any children.

Maddalena looks at Antonio, confused. By now he's on the other cordless and has been listening along with her. His face, all smiles two seconds ago, goes guilty again.

There are other voices in the background of Carolina's house. It's midafternoon in Santa Cecilia, and the *Vigilia* guests must be starting to arrive. They must be carrying covered dishes packed with fish; they must be removing their fur coats; they must have sugar on their lips from the cookies they ate on the walk over.

"What happened to your son, Carolina?" Maddalena tries again, but there's no response, only the voices behind her getting louder and music switched on. "Your son, Sergio. What happened to him?"

Carolina says something Maddalena can't understand, but she thinks she hears the word "*tedesci.*" Germans. She seems to be talking half to herself, half to someone else in the room, but not at all to Maddalena. Still, Maddalena tries again.

"Is your daughter helping you cook? Donatella is such a pretty name. Does she have a *fidanzato* yet? Carolina?" Then the line goes dead. "Carolina!"

She shakes the phone at Antonio's face. In English she says, "What's going on? What are you trying to prove? What's wrong with her?"

"I'm sorry," he says, head down. He goes into the hallway to escape her, but she follows him. He moves around as if looking for something to do—change a lightbulb, dust the grandfather clock. But the house is in perfect order, as always. Finally she corners him, forces him to meet her eyes.

"I'm so sorry," he says again.

"I don't understand," she says. "You're punishing me?"

"No," he says. "I wouldn't do that."

"Something's wrong with her, isn't it?" says Maddalena. "Tell me."

"You don't want to know. You're better off."

"Tell me."

"Goddamn it," he says. "Claudio told me she was OK today. 'She knows where she is,' he said. I talked to him an hour ago. 'She knows *who* she is,' he said. I thought, I'll show Maddalena life is still beautiful there. I'll show her she can go back and everything will be the same. She'll make up with her sister. I'll be the hero for once."

"What are you talking about?" Maddalena says, though she can guess. She steps closer. They're pressed up against each other in the narrow hallway, the glass Nativity set on the lowboy beside them, the Christmas lights blinking around the mirror.

"Her mind's gone," says Antonio. "She's like a little baby. Worse."

"Old-timer's?"

He nods.

The first thing Maddalena thinks is that their nephew, Marcello, Celestina's son, is a doctor. Maddalena doesn't know what kind, only that her sister took great pride in him, called him a genius. "Marcello doesn't help her?" she asks.

"What can he do?" says Antonio. "His mother had the same thing. It's backward over there. If you get sick, all they do is take some of the pain away. They don't try to stop anything, to turn it around."

Already it's starting to come out, everything Maddalena's tried to keep on the other side of the ocean since Mamma died, a lifetime of miseries and diseases and deaths. This is what she tried to tell Prima, what her trip would have made happen.

"Not just Celestina," Antonio continues. "Teresa, too. And your mother. The same way."

"All of them, then. Why not just say 'all of them'?" She's been afraid to ask, to imagine. Every time she's been tempted to pick up the extension and listen to Antonio's conversations with her family in Santa Cecilia, she's reminded herself, You don't want to hear about cancer, strokes, old age, all the different ways they are being taken away. So she never listened. She's thought of old-timer's, but she figured one of them might get it, not all three.

Next it comes for me.

Antonio looks at her. She's the youngest in the family. He reads her mind: "Don't be scared, *tesoro,*" he says. "You live in the United States of America."

"What's that have to do with it?"

"You lived a different life."

"But I was born there. My head is the same as theirs. The same blood. Sometimes my head goes blank. I don't remember things. What's it matter where I lived?"

"The brain is a muscle," Antonio says. "Do you know that? I bet you don't. I asked that doctor we saw. I've been worried. You don't think I got worried, with your spells, knowing this all these years?" He moves closer, but she has her arms folded against her chest and is biting her lip, her body so stiff nothing can reach or relax her. "Every brain starts the same way—equal, like you said—but it can grow as big and strong as you make it. You have to exercise it to make it strong. Like a weight lifter. Your sisters, your mother—they did nothing with their brains. They let the muscles go to fat in the kitchens and fields of Santa Cecilia. Look how you're different: you learned to speak a new language, even to read and write a little; every day you use math when you're sewing; you learned the fox-trot and the tango and all those other complicated dances at the studio. That's exercising your brain, believe me."

"Teresa worked in the butcher shop."

"Wrapping up pig parts?" he says. "That's not enough. Not even close."

He takes her hands. His are a knot of veins, dry as paper, and cold, the hands of an old man.

She lets them go. "We have a lot of cooking to do," she says.

"Believe me," he says. "I know more than you. I won't let you suffer."

She goes downstairs to her fabric drawer, takes out the letters from her sisters and brother and from Mamma. She arranges them on the table and ties them in bundles with a colored ribbon. She presses her fingers to the handwritten names on the backs of the envelopes and places them behind the ones to her mother at the back of the drawer.

In the years before Prima was born, when Maddalena was in her early twenties, the possibility that Vito Leone might find his way to America gave Maddalena something to hope for. She dreamed of his finding her and returning her, like a princess in a maid's dress, to her real home, that magical village, with much celebration. She'd find Carolina there, in love with a German soldier maybe, or a widower from another town, and all would be well. But Vito turned out to be as ordinary as any other man. Maddalena, too, was ordinary, not a princess at all. She stopped dreaming of rescue. What she has wanted, above all, from her life, from this Christmas, is peace. Calm. To ask for happiness is to ask for too much.

It's 11:02 a.m. on the stove clock. In four hours and six minutes, Frankie's train will pull into the little station in Wilmington, where Antonio will greet him and drive him home. While she's been in the basement with her letters, he's washed the kitchen countertops clean. On the table the little nests of pasta dry in rows. Two coffee cups, washed, sit upside down on a dish towel. He's set out the ingredients for the fish batter and covered the bowls with the old linen napkins they use as rags. He filled the fryer with oil and turned it on high, knowing that she would be up soon from the basement.

GET FRANKIE ALONE in his old bedroom, and before long he'll raid the shopping bags at the back of the closet. On this day, Christmas Eve, he chooses the one magic-markered "9." He dumps its contents—letters and photos and notebooks from ninth grade—at the foot of the bed and sits cross-legged among the artifacts. The less preciously he treats them, the more likely he will be to uncover a gem, to spark a revelation. Instead he finds a mawkish poem he composed on the back of an algebra test, his first checkbook (blank), and a pink construction-paper Valentine from Charlotte Lemke, who drowned in the Atlantic the first night of senior week. He summons Charlotte's face from the newspaper photos—freckles, frizzy hair, spokesmodel smile—and wonders what might have happened if he'd reciprocated her freshman-year Valentine, asked her out, dated through the proms. She might never have taken up with the senior-week crowd. She might now be a grad student herself, on her way back to Wilmington this rainy afternoon, in traffic on the interstate, singing.

He tosses Charlotte's heart back on the pile. What's wrong with him, anyway? What compels him not only to seek the sad stories but to wallow in them?

"You're a child of tragedy," Birch told him soon after their first drink on Elm Street, her arm around his shoulder chummily. They were walking in the woods, one of their rare trips out in fresh air. "But you don't acknowledge it. You don't let it touch you. Once you do, you'll have enough tragedy, and you won't go courting more."

"I'll have so much time on my hands."

"It's not funny," she said. "And don't get excited. You won't use the extra time wisely. You'll waste away watching TV. Sports. James Bond movies."

"I loathe sports."

"I'm being serious."

She's right, he thought. The death by suicide of his older brother has not touched him. Isn't that a lucky break? Hasn't he been spared?

"I misspoke," Birch said. "It's not that it hasn't touched you. It's that it's touched you and you don't realize how."

"Why don't you tell me?"

"I don't know you well enough yet," she said.

With the door closed and the drapes drawn, Frankie's old bedroom—which was Prima's, not Tony's—is pleasantly hermetic. The aroma of garlic and fish, which will permeate every square inch of the house by the end of the night's holiday feast, can't find him here. His parents' raised voices, debating parsley distribution on the *baccalà* and the crispiness of the *frittelli,* come through the walls muted and garbled, as if from an adjoining movie theater. Here in his own theater, Frankie's been granted two luxurious hours to himself before Prima and Tom arrive with their brood and the Al Di Là managers stop by with their wives and their obligatory panettone and boxes of Italian chocolates.

He could call Kelly Anne McDonald, but they've already set and twice confirmed their plans to meet for a late movie tomorrow in

Philly. Movies are what Frankie and Kelly do together. Movies followed by a thoughtful exegesis over dessert and coffee, followed by twenty minutes of jerky over-the-sweater action in the front seat of her car, as if they are teenagers in 1953. "OK, that's a wrap," she'll say, flushed, when they've gone far enough. And yet, after they part, Frankie feels not frustrated but exhilarated. The delay, her coy deferral, thrills him; and if it's part of some elaborate plan, some kinky *American Graffiti* role-play, all the better. In the meantime he's still got Birch, with whom thoughtful exegesis (in bed or at the kitchen table) is strenuously avoided. Some days they barely utter a greeting or farewell, and even then, each empty phrase—each "see you" and "take care"—wields the destruction potential of a grenade. He would enjoy pointing out to her the irony of two literary scholars communicating primarily in Neanderthal-like grunts, but he can't seem to break from this new code they've established. For future reference/ammunition/amusement, he has been transcribing their entire conversations in a spiral notebook. He's kept the journal faithfully every Tuesday and Thursday over the past month but has yet to fill two pages.

Frankie hates to cop to this sentimental streak of his, but it keeps revealing itself. As it should, the academy frowns on sentimentality, that last refuge of the lazy and shallow minded. Among English lit types, sentimentality is a cancer that distorts the analyses of all texts, in particular those authored by marginalized or oppressed peoples. Frankie ruthlessly excises any and all traces of it in his work, but in life he saves every card and letter, every passed note, every flimsy token. The vestiges of the first twenty-three years of his life remain in this bedroom closet in the shopping bags arranged by academic year (he knows no other type of year); the most recent he keeps in neatly stacked plastic bins in the basement of 25 Stowe.

What would Birch say if she knew this about him? What about Kelly Anne?

One would laugh in his face and then, aroused, wrestle him to the floor. The other would squeeze his hand, look down, and ask, "So what have you saved of us?"

(Three ticket stubs. A cappuccino-stained napkin from Caffè Vittorio. Her phone number on a page of notebook paper from the night they met on Amtrak.)

Frankie Grasso, ninth-grade version, had no friends, certainly no girlfriends. In summer in Graylyn Ridge, the fifties-era suburb to which his parents had fled, he suffered in silence among mute trees, the white noise of lawn mowers, and the absence of kids other than the mongoloid, who never left his fenced-in yard. Frankie spent long hours in the woods behind his neighborhood, building little huts with sticks and mud, then exploding them with firecrackers. By August he'd destroyed every plastic toy in the house—the generic green army men, the Smurfs, Prima's bald and dented Barbies.

It was also in ninth grade that he saw Zio Giulio die.

Zio and Aunt Helen looked after Frankie in the afternoons while his father worked at the trattoria and his mother at the drapery shop. They lived in a little brick row house around the corner from St. Anthony's grade school, in Little Italy. There were real books on their bookshelves, not picture frames or figurines or extra plates. Aunt Helen, the only non-Italian in the Grasso family before Prima married Tom, taught piano at St. Ann's but could play any instrument:

guitar, clarinet, even harp. On holidays, Zio Giulio would break out the accordion and she'd sing traditional Italian songs for everybody like a *paesana*.

When Frankie arrived at their house each afternoon, he'd find them sitting on the porch or in their living room, reading. Zio Giulio would look up, startled, and say, "Oh, Francesco! Is it that time already?"

Giulio and Helen rarely watched television. They shrugged at exercise. They fed Frankie, made him finish his homework, double-check his arithmetic, revise his compositions, and, if time permitted, read aloud to them from his religion primer. From time to time they'd fight loudly in front of Frankie, who absorbed every word. This is how he learned that Helen had saved Giulio from a life of loneliness and disorder, that he did not deserve her, and that it was she who earned every penny of their meager savings; he also learned that Giulio had saved Helen from her own lonely and unbearably routine life, that she did not deserve *him,* and that if it weren't for Giulio's inheritance they would be sleeping in the gutter.

They were Tony's official godparents, they had stood beside him in the church a month after he was born and poured water over his head, but they, too, rarely mentioned him. Like his mother, they insisted to Frankie that he was worthy of great love. They saw something special in him. They made him promise he'd someday move to New York and open a bookstore/art gallery/jazz lounge, where nonames could perform alongside the celebrated. Helen believed that fame rotted the soul. Giulio believed in the underdog. They weren't hippies, they said; in fact, they'd voted twice for Reagan and disapproved of women who'd traded their God-given maternal destiny for careers. And yet it was Giulio who introduced Frankie to Amnesty International and Helen who admired Neruda's poetry and activism. They made Frankie read *Inherit the Wind* together with the Bible. If you asked them what they were—Libertarians? Reformed Catholics?—they'd say simply, "We're *educated.*"

It's what Frankie decided he wanted to be.

Though by ninth grade he no longer required a babysitter, he frequently walked the few miles to Little Italy at the end of the school day. He'd do his homework at the kitchen table while Helen taught piano in the dining room and Giulio napped in the leather recliner beside the bay window. It was in the unexpected harmony of these three rooms—the stuttering piano, Giulio's snores, Helen's exaggerated coos, the metronome ticking—that Frankie filled a journal with sappy sestinas, read C. S. Lewis, and traced the barbed-wired Amnesty candle logo on the front of all his notebooks. It was the least lonely place he has ever known.

One February afternoon, Zio Giulio came home carrying a large burlap sack stuffed with chestnuts. He dropped the sack on the coffee table, reached in, grabbed two handfuls of the chestnuts, and let them slip through his fingers like diamonds.

"Five bucks!" he said to Helen. "For all these!"

She stood over the sack, hands on her hips, picking over the contents with her eyes. "Full of worms, I'll bet."

"Say half are no good," he said. "It's still a steal. For five bucks? And Frankie loves them. Don't you, *uaglio?*"

Frankie didn't. They tasted like burnt rubber and made him thirsty. "I do," he said. Lately, Giulio had been getting little things mixed up, and Frankie didn't want him to realize he'd misremembered this, too. It was Tony who'd loved chestnuts.

"See?" he said to Helen.

"Well, I'm not roasting all those," she said as she walked back to the sour-faced girl at the piano. "Frankie will help when he's finished his homework."

So they cleared the kitchen table, Giulio handed Frankie a knife, and they sat cutting slits into the chestnuts for an hour by the heat of the oven. They arranged the chestnuts on trays and rotated them in and out every twenty minutes. While one tray cooked, they peeled the roasted ones and distributed them among brown paper lunch bags. Giulio marked the bags with the names of friends to whom he'd deliver them later that night.

Frankie had imagined a good, educated man like Giulio Fabbri fading away in his recliner, Emerson's essays clutched to his chest, Julius LaRosa on the turntable. Or in his sleep beside Helen, who'd rescued him from one life and could ease him with fortitude and tenderness into the next. He didn't expect him to drop a tray full of chestnuts and then—scrambling on his hands and knees to gather them before Helen caught him—collapse on the kitchen floor, splaying his arms and legs every which way. He didn't expect his cheek smashed against the greasy linoleum, his eyelids twitching, his fist around a burnt, tasteless chestnut. Frankie wanted a final blessing from the man, an assurance that the world he was leaving him was not vicious. He wanted his uncle's life to come to more than the sum of his days and nights in his little house.

But it didn't. As he watched Helen lay her body beside her husband's, her arm across his back, waiting for the ambulance, Frankie wondered what would become of all the words and stories and lyrics and notes Giulio had accumulated in his now-stopped brain. At the time, Frankie imagined it all melting out of his ears, invisible, irretrievable, wasted. Thirteen years later, in his bedroom on Christmas Eve, he has yet to develop a more sophisticated or philosophical or mystical grasp of the afterlife. All he knows is that he wants more from his years of study than to die an anonymous Soldier of Literature. He wants something to outlast him—a body of work. If not, then one book, one definitive text that shows ambitious ideas, something that says *Frankie Grasso's Life Meant Something.* Is that too much to ask? Is that not why his father opened a restaurant, and Kelly Anne McDonald seeks to transform inner-city youth? For what other reason do people have children?

His mother knocks on the door, then pushes through before he can respond. She holds a forkful of *baccalà,* white and flaky and parsley-perfect, her hand cupped under it to catch any crumbs. Without either of them saying a word, he takes the fish in his mouth and hands back the fork. She leaves, and minutes later, his father appears with three *frittelli* wrapped in a paper towel. Soon after, his mother again, with a single smelt impaled on a toothpick. One after the other, for the rest of the two hours Frankie was promised undisturbed solitude, the offerings keep coming, and how can he refuse them?

CHRISTMAS EVE, PRIMA drives alone to Graylyn Ridge, the middle car in the caravan. Tom and Patrick are in the BMW in front, and the older boys follow in Ryan's Jeep. Wrapped boxes fill her trunk and backseat, along with trays of home-baked cream puffs and sugar cookies. In her rearview mirror, the three boys are singing;

through the windshield, she can see Patrick's head turned toward his father, listening closely. She turns down the radio and, in the luxurious quiet, says aloud, "I am surrounded by gifts." She could keep driving to the ends of the earth in this formation, never stopping, never growing hungry, never needing any blessing other than the safe passage of her men.

Someone—a woman—once told her, offhand, that the secret of a happy life is to live for yourself. "Forget about other people," she added, finger wagging, bracelets jangling on her wrist. "Any businessman will tell you to pay yourself first," or some such nonsense. Prima was too shy to disagree to her face, but if she'd had a daiquiri or two she might have told this woman—Nadine was her name, some hippie receptionist at Tom's office—that her husband and children, those people it was her job to feed, had kept her full her entire life. As long as they're alive, she'll never go hungry.

Prima does not love her sons and Tom with her heart only. The heart—she might have told Nadine, after the daiquiri—is inadequate. It tears and skips without warning. It's open to attack. Everyone knows where to find it, how to break it. No. Prima loves with her soul, that chamber protected by God. There is no such thing as a broken soul, not for a person of faith, anyway, which she is.

Prima was not surprised when she learned not long ago that Nadine had gotten divorced and lived alone in a one-bedroom apartment behind the Tri-State Mall. She seemed like the type who would max out her credit cards, smoke pot before work, and spend the Christmas holiday on a Caribbean cruise. Prima should have felt pity, but instead she felt—still feels—a nagging prickle of alarm at the thought of the woman, as if she were the carrier of a deadly virus who should not be permitted on board her ocean liner.

Prima turns up the music, which helps to push ugly thoughts away. It's five fifteen. Five thirty on the dot when she pulls into the driveway of her parents' house. The Buckleys are right on time, as usual. Prima is still furious with her mother, but for her father's sake, she's decided to put that aside tonight and tomorrow.

Earlier, her father had called from the Al Di Là so Maddalena couldn't eavesdrop. "You have to make peace with her," he told her, his voice thin and agitated. "Please, Prima. She's wrong, you're right, no question, but not talking to her, not calling her back, is the wrong way to fight. You don't know how it upsets her."

"I want her to be upset," Prima said. "It's the only way she'll change her attitude. Besides, how many times have I watched you two play the silence game over the years? Where do you think I got the idea?"

"I talked to my mother every day of my life," he said angrily. "Even in the middle of a fight. Even when she didn't know my name. It's about respect."

If there was one thing her father could never tolerate, Prima knew, it was a lack of respect. And yet respect was what she hoped to show by bringing her family, especially her sons, to Santa Cecilia. Why could no one understand this? She waited a few moments, listening to the clang of pots and pans in the Al Di Là kitchen. "I'll see what I can do, Dad," she said. "I'll try and act normal. But I can't control what I feel. I'm not Irish, you know."

At this he laughed. Another thing Prima learned from her father is that she could always break the tension with a crack about the Irish.

He's stressed out tonight, standing before a ten-quart pot of tomato sauce, adding pinches of last-minute herbs. The dining room table is set with a new red tablecloth, gold reindeer candlesticks, cut-crystal wineglasses, and garland strung around the chandelier. It's the one night of the year that they don't let Prima help cook, that they've insisted she relax "like a queen," and so Maddalena and Antonio run in circles, testing each other's food, straightening knives and forks and lighting candles, as if expecting a food critic. It's like this every year. If it weren't, something would be wrong.

Prima gives her mother a kiss on the cheek. "Merry Christmas," she says.

"*Buon Natale,*" Maddalena says. "*Figlia mia.*" She steps back. "You see I'm wearing the dress you gave me." It's the red one with the three-quarter sleeves and the sequined flower at the left shoulder. On her feet are flats, but as soon as the first course is on the dining room table, she'll switch to heels.

"You don't want to wear an apron?"

"I don't spill," she says. "Not like that one." She ticks her head toward Antonio. "You should see his pants when he comes back from the restaurant. More food on his lap than in his mouth. But I make them brand-new again."

Frankie walks in, a glass of whiskey in one hand and a smelt in the other. "You just missed Aunt Helen," he says to Prima, embracing her. "And Zio Gilberto. And Lucio. It's like a relay race. When one shows up, it's the other's cue to leave."

Prima inspects the fruit baskets and wine bottles and poinsettias on the kitchen table. "Looks like they brought some good stuff."

"Frankie tell you the new guy came by?" says Antonio. "Olindo. He's a good kid. Pretty young wife, too, don't you think, Frankie?"

"She was all right. And he's kind of a suck-up, if you ask me, but whatever."

"All the managers are brownnosers," Antonio says. "They know I'm writing my will."

"They think they'll end up in your will?" says Ryan, from the hallway. He knows the managers from the one summer he and Zach waited tables the Al Di Là. Zach quit by the Fourth of July, but Ryan stayed on and made a fortune in tips. "Are they on crack?"

As soon as the will is mentioned, Prima notices, Frankie leaves the room. He knows where the rest of the conversation is headed—that their father is about to go on and on about this being his last Christmas alive, how they need to learn how to live without him, they need to take care of Maddalena and the Al Di Là and each other. Every time he talks like this, Frankie shuts down. Prima's never met someone with such a hard shell, but so soft on the inside. "Dad," she says, her hand on his shoulder, when the conversation turns again and Ryan and his *nonna* disappear into the dining room to fix drinks. "Don't talk like that in front of Frankie."

"What did I say?" says Antonio. "That I have a will? That boy's too sensitive. He has to face facts. How many more years does he think I have . . ."

"Just tone it down," Prima says, and she squeezes his shoulder. "Nobody likes to hear that kind of talk. Not on Christmas. It's not sad enough this year?"

"Every year is sad," says Antonio.

She stands for a few minutes, quietly, beside her father, watching him taste and correct the sauce with one hand and arrange lemon wedges on a tray of flounder with the other. On another burner, a different sauce simmers for Ryan, who doesn't eat anchovies; on another tray, the *baccalà* decorated with finely chopped parsley and garlic. He might be a klutzy eater, but his hands don't shake as he fine-tunes each dish he prepares. Decades of work have kept him slim, and while he's gone gray, he's kept most of his hair. Like Maddalena, he's dressed sharply, in a tie and pleated pants. His apron, a gift from one of the managers a few years back, says, "I Don't Need A Recipe—I'm Italian." Prima thinks, You're too alive, too on your game, ever to leave this world. If she'd made different choices in her life, she might have stood beside him like this at the Al Di Là week after week, perfecting the dishes, his right-hand woman, in a team of generations. But that place was Tony's, and once he threw it away, how could she take it, even if she wanted to?

There's a tray of wineglasses on the counter next to Prima. She picks one up to pour herself some chardonnay, but it's streaked and crusty. All the glasses, she notices, are filthy. "You want me to wash these?" she asks her father.

"Your mother already did," he says without looking up.

Prima nods. She wipes the crud from the glasses with a wet dish towel and pours one tall.

Frankie's reading in the armchair by the tree. She sits across from him, but he doesn't budge from his concentration, not even when he reaches over to sip his whiskey, and she can't think of a single thing to say to him that he might find interesting. She wants to turn on the

TV, find a Christmas special, but they don't make good ones any-more, the way Andy Williams did, and besides, she's sure Frankie will hate it.

Having nothing to do makes Prima panicky. Her mother's in the basement and will send her away, demand she relax and enjoy the break, if she goes to visit. She opens the cupboard of the credenza, looking for a magazine or something to help pass the next half hour until dinner's ready, and is struck by a foul smell. At the top of a stack of *Town and Country* magazines, she finds an open pint of heavy cream, spoiled.

She stares at it a moment. Not everything has to be a sign, and yet her heart is pounding. She grabs a cocktail napkin from the coffee table, picks up the carton, takes it outside, dumps the chunky mess onto the grass, the carton into the trash can.

Back in the kitchen, her father is still correcting his anchovy sauce.

"Dad," she says, "did Mom *say* she washed these wineglasses?"

"What? I told you, yes. Why?"

"They're filthy."

"Ask Frankie to wash them. He's not doing anything. You need to relax—"

"I took care of it already."

"Then what's the problem?"

"Nothing," she says. He looks at her funny, and she walks away.

Prima goes downstairs and finds Maddalena at her worktable, wrapping a present. The basement smells of apples and vinegar and grease. "I thought of something else for your father last minute," she says. "It's a joke. Don't ask me what it is because I won't tell you."

Like the dorm room she never had, Maddalena's basement lair is decorated with what defines her: yardsticks and pincushions, bolts of fabric stacked in neat rows, dozens of wire hangers hanging from a clothesline, and gift boxes and ribbons and wrapping paper saved from decades of Christmases. There's a second oven, an older one, so they can keep the kitchen oven gleaming clean. For company she has a television with a senior-size remote, and a radio–CD player set to a dance music station. Prima's ancient dorm fridge hums emptily in the corner by the washer and dryer and the tub in which a pair of Antonio's sauce-splattered pants seem always to be soaking. Framed photos line the shelf above the worktable, where Prima, perpetually thin and twenty-two, kisses Tom at the altar of St. Anthony's; where Frankie stands in his white tux at his high school graduation; where Tony goofily smiles through the huge gap in his two front teeth. Under the padded worktable are school notebooks and report cards, uniforms, and art projects that Maddalena can pull out at any time, show Prima, and say, "You made this for me, you see? I keep everything."

Prima rarely ventures down here. It's filled with too many memories of Tony, of the two of them playing 45s while their mother sewed or making up plays in their own secret hideout behind the old mattresses. But tonight she's on the lookout for signs, and they would be here if they were anywhere. Yet nothing seems to be out of place. "These are ready?" she asks, lifting the tinfoil from the various covered dishes on the stove top (burners off, good) and finding peas and onions, roasted peppers, apple and cauliflower *frittelli,* and potatoes in oil, vinegar, and parsley. She tastes each one, and each is perfect, prepared the same way it's been prepared for as long as she can remember. "You've still got it," she says.

"I'm not a cook," says Maddalena. "I was lucky your father didn't need one. But I can make a few things."

For the rest of the night, Prima studies her. Serving the food, washing the dishes between courses, playing *tombola,* as each gift is unwrapped. Maddalena remembers each gift she's given, and why. She keeps track of her numbers on her little *tombola* card, wins two rounds. The dishes she washes sparkle in the light.

At Midnight Mass, Maddalena recites every word of the Our Father. Still, all throughout the service, Prima can't stop thinking about the spoiled cream, sitting there where it shouldn't belong, its heaviness and stench. She's read the articles, knows the signs to watch out for. She's been watching for a while now, noting each of her mother's "spells," each time she forgets a name, bracing herself for the day she forgets her own. Her father has assured her that her doctors know about it, that they've done scans and blood tests and are not worried, it's just part of getting old, but Prima doesn't believe him. It's Grasso tradition to keep bad news secret, to hide your trouble until you have no choice but to admit it, and Prima is as much a Grasso as anyone.

Eventually she'll have to talk to Frankie. It's the reason for Italy that she's been holding back, but she may not be able to hold it back much longer. Forget what she told Frankie and Maddalena in the car in the mall parking lot. Forget what Nadine said about pleasing others. The kids know nothing about any plans to switch tickets, to substitute Paris for their homeland. As far as the Buckley boys are concerned, they will join the Grassos on the flight to Italy in August. It's a blessing that they're smart enough not to talk about any of this in front of Maddalena.

Yes, Prima wants her boys to see their ancestral village with their grandparents; yes, she and Tom could use a real vacation, a second honeymoon, with good food and wine and fresh mountain air and a midlife kick-start; yes, she wants to give her father the gift he's been dreaming of since the day his brother died; but what she wants most of all is for her mother to complete the circle of her life while she's still able. To have no regrets. To go back to the place in the world where she was happiest. And the realest reason of all? Prima believes that the return to such a place of pure happiness has the power—a magic kind of power—to heal her.

Frankie may talk to his mother every night, but he's not around enough to see all that Prima sees. He doesn't look in credenzas or notice dirty wineglasses; if he did, he'd never leave this little house. But Prima fears she won't be able to protect Frankie much longer. She needs his help. After she finds the courage to tell him what she thinks she knows, he will take her side for sure.

"You really believe this hocus-pocus?" she hears Frankie whisper to Ryan after they've both received Communion.

Quickly, discreetly, Prima covers her ears. She doesn't want to know what her son does and doesn't believe. That's a different fight. She is a person of faith, all sorts of faith, and if she has to have enough for the entire Buckley-Grasso clan, so be it.

THE HOUSE IS finally quiet. Antonio, in his chair, in this room of unwrapped presents and empty, tossed-aside envelopes, watches Midnight Mass at the Vatican on TV. The sound's on Mute because the picture is all that matters. Get the camera off the pope, he thinks. Show the people, show the piazza, and, if you can, swing the lens over the mountains forty miles to Santa Cecilia buried in snow. Show me my old house, the chestnut trees, the frozen spring.

But the picture doesn't change. The pope mumbles on.

From the window he can see St. Mary's, the church that holds his family. Most of his family. Not Tony. Not Mario. Someone is always missing. The parking lot is packed with the cars of hypocrites. He's not one of them. When he needs God, he turns over in his bed and puts his arm around his wife and says, "*Tesoro, tesoro.*"

He doesn't need a new red sweater or a Polo wallet or a gift certificate for a haircut at some overpriced salon. He hates to see his kids and his wife spend money on *stupidaggini*. He feels every dollar they waste on him, on anything, as an insult. You want to show me you love me? Then save your money. Show me respect. Finish your school. Take me to Santa Cecilia, where I belong. I can count on one hand the years we have left together.

He is there now in his village, a boy again, in his heavy coat, the grown-ups around him with candles in their cupped hands, the church cold as a crypt. There is the ceramic baby Jesus at the altar to kiss and adore—or maybe it's plastic? Did they have plastic back then? When did plastic start? The years are a jumble. Antonio was a boy of seven and Maddalena a baby. He remembers the day her parents announced her. They sat her on the counter of the grocery, and customers came to welcome her to the world. Antonio looked up at her wiggling toes, at her *chiacchierone* sisters pinching her cheeks. The Piccinellis lived down the street from his family. They owned that big store, and the Grassos owned a *pezzetto* of land, a three-room house, and a few chickens. The baby Maddalena Piccinelli was pure white, no dirt under her fingernails, no marks on her skin. She glowed in the sunlight of the grocery window. Antonio may have invented all this—the light, the baby on the counter—but it's as real as the fire crackling beside him on this Christmas Eve seventy-two years later. He reaches up to tickle Maddalena's toes. His father is not there to slap his hand away. His father has been gone forty years.

How strange to be at the end of life so soon. Seventy-two years from one midnight to another. The boy at the counter looking up is now the old man in the chair looking back. So what if he feels sorry for himself. He's not allowed? He's never been a brave person. He's not one of those immigrants to write a book about, the ones who came to America with empty pockets. He had a mother and father to lead him by the hand on and off the ship, find him his first job, give him a house with a finished basement and a yard with a grape arbor; he had friends, cars, girls, a brother to put up half the money for a restaurant, a faithful wife. An ordinary life split between two worlds. Soon, when he's gone, a few of those people over at St. Mary's will cry, but only for a little while. Their lives are full enough without him. The customers will still come to the Al Di Là for their calamari and stuffed shells. They'll sit waiting for their tables under the framed black-and-white photo of Antonio and Mario with their arms around each other, and if they notice the photo at all, they'll say, maybe, Aww.

Strange to be a sad old man in an easy chair, the years settling on him like dust, and yet not strange at all. He and his bocce friends at the Vespucci Club talk of nothing but the years. Moments ago, they say, I was a man of twenty-five leaning over the railing of a ship, watching Italy sink into the ocean. Their kids, like Antonio's, like all kids, appeared one day like magic, then disappeared. Why did nobody warn them of the grief of fatherhood: not that your kids grow up and leave you, in every possible way, but that they're strangers from the start. They don't stand still long enough, they let you get only so close, and you work too many hours, and they tell their friends their secrets, and they love you, but with their souls only, the way they love their country or God. Their hearts belong to other people.

He is the only person alive who knew the secret of Tony's heart. He keeps it closer than any he's ever known. It's like a heavy stone in his pocket, one he takes out day after day, turns over, rubs with his thumb, as if it's beautiful and precious, when—he almost has to remind himself—it was the one bit of ugliness in Tony, and it proved powerful enough to kill him. It might have killed him the other way if he'd lived. And yet lately, Antonio wonders if he might one day have made peace with the truth about his son, as his own flesh and blood, the way other fathers have done. (He watches the news; he's paid attention. It's not impossible to imagine.) But Tony didn't give him that chance.

He can't forgive him for that.

His family safely at church, Antonio climbs the stairs to Tony's room. The door sticks. Inside, the air is warm, with the heating vents kept open and the drapes always closed. Antonio can't bear to switch on the lamp. The hallway light is enough. Stepping into this room is like falling back asleep into the same dream you woke from. He runs his hand along the sailboat wallpaper they were just about to replace with a solid, young-man blue; over the stack of records on the bureau;

over the desk with his pens and pencils in their ceramic cup. He falls to his knees, his elbows on the edge of the bed. Antonio Grasso has no faith in God, of course, or he'd be standing now with his family at St. Mary's, but there's no one else for him to turn to, afraid as he is to confess to anyone real—DiSilvio, a priest at another parish, a stranger on Union—and so every Christmas Eve at midnight, this is where he can be found.

They are alone together here, the way believers must feel they are alone with God in their churches. He hears Tony's voice calling, "Babbo!" as he pushed open the door of the Al Di Là after a day at school. He'd throw his schoolbag in a booth, run to his father, and wrap his arms around his waist. It doesn't matter that, by fifteen, Tony had found things about the restaurant to complain about and that he pouted in the corner with his guest checks—the boy calling, "Babbo!" and racing toward him was always there.

If Antonio were a believer, he'd pray for Tony's young soul in the afterlife. But no one's soul, not even an innocent's, can be saved. Instead he comes every year to ask for forgiveness. Because it was his own hand on his son's back that night, pushing him off the bridge. He might as well confess this crime to God, who will never hear him and never forgive him. He doesn't want forgiveness. He deserves to suffer for the crime of failing his precious child, of not reading the signs right, keeping closer watch, stepping in. No good father would have let the boy disappear and then pay no attention to the words he'd written: *Go to the bridge before it's too late.* Did Antonio ignore these words on purpose? Did he not believe them? But then again, how can you believe such a thing can come from your son when he's so full of life, when you think, every time you look at him, You are too alive ever to leave this world?

When Tony got back to the restaurant from his *zia* Ida's that day, the guest checks were gone from his apron pocket and Dante had been fired. The boy was no dummy. He knew why Antonio sent Dante away. Tony wrote more poems, both on the guest checks and in a brown notebook he hid behind his dresser, one of the few places Maddalena wouldn't look in her weekly cleaning. Antonio read every word. And after Tony died, he burned most of the pages, but not all.

Antonio reaches behind the dresser and, in the dust, finds the twelve torn-out pages he stapled into a book with a guest check on top. Even in the half light, he can make out every letter because he has read them over and over for the past twenty-eight years. *I hate him I hate him I hate him* covers every line. This is the kind of poem Tony wrote for his father at the end of his life.

The next page is from the brown notebook. *There is no way out. He'll never understand. I'm a bird in a cage. He'll never give me the key. I see the way he looks at me. He hates me and I hate him and I love him but does he love me? HE WILL NEVER LOOK AT ME THE SAME WAY.*

The next: *It's not fair It's not fair what did I do to deserve this my God it's never going to end, is it? Daddy, it's never going to end. You're never going to let it end and Dante is never coming back and there is no one in the cage but me so why not just let me die It's not fair You're never and Dante and God and coming back and Daddy*

The next: *Where are you, Tony Grasso? Who are you, Tony Grasso? You are a boy with a father who hates you and a mother who doesn't see you and no friends who know you in a world that will destroy you Get out before it's too late before he tells and sends you away before he kills you with his own hands*

The next and the next and the next. There were more pages, but over the years of Antonio's holding them and pressing them to his chest, the thin paper tore and disintegrated. Each time he reads the words is like the first. The same knife to his heart. The blood it draws is a kind of relief. He wants the blood, the questions, the tears, the rage, the thing beyond sadness that there is no word for in Italian or English because it belongs only to him.

If Antonio Grasso were ever to write his son a poem, it would be this: *I want you back. Give me another chance.* But he's not a writer. He says it out loud. Once, then again. Then again. Again.

He rests his head on the side of the bed, the pages in his lap. Behind the closet door, Tony's school uniform hangs with his belts and jackets and clip-on ties. Maddalena still changes the sheets once in a while, vacuums the carpet, dusts the shelves. Everything is as it was. He wants to stay here. He won't tell Prima or Frankie about Maddalena's conversation with Carolina. He won't tell Maddalena what he read in the paper about heredity. He won't tell anyone about his meetings with DiSilvio. But in this room, with Tony, there are no secrets.

A sharp pain shoots from his lower back down to his leg, as if to remind him he can't stay here long. He slides the pages back behind the dresser, far enough so Maddalena won't notice them, and tries to stand, using the dresser for balance. But his old joints and bones fail him, and he falls onto the bed. For a few moments he lies there on his back, catching his breath. The bed is already wrinkled, so there is no reason not to cover his face with Tony's pillow. Except that the boy's smell is long gone.

It's one o'clock in the morning. From the hallway window he sees cars leaving the church parking lot. He goes downstairs, turns on the spotlight, and walks to the end of the driveway without his coat. Before long, his family rounds the corner. Then they say their good-byes and "see you tomorrows" and Prima and Tom and the boys get into their cars—too many cars for one family, a waste of gas and mileage, an extravagance. He takes Prima aside and thanks her for not mentioning the Italy trip the entire night, for helping to give her mother a peaceful Christmas Eve without a single argument.

"I'm on my best behavior," she tells him.

"Tomorrow, too?"

"Tomorrow maybe." Then she sees his face. "Yes, Daddy. Tomorrow, too."

Before Frankie can disappear into his room, Antonio asks him, "So, how was church?"

"How do you think?" Frankie says, smiling. "Smoke, mirrors, and hypocrites."

They share this, at least. Neither of them trusts the Catholic Church to do anything for you except take your money.

"Thank you for going," Antonio says. "It means a lot to your mother."

Frankie shrugs. "It's good people-watching."

They can talk like this only when Maddalena is not in the room. Just as Antonio is about to ask Frankie more questions (isn't he glad he got it out of the way tonight instead of having to get up early tomorrow morning? Are any of his friends in Boston religious? What does he think keeps people coming back year after year for the same nonsense?), Maddalena comes toward them, Frankie winks, and they kiss each other good night.

"I love you, Son," says Antonio.

"Love you, too, Dad. Merry Christmas."

"*Buon Natale.*"

The dining room table is cleared, the dishes are clean, and the hallway swept. Only the den remains a mess: the presents, the wrapping paper crumpled into balls, the pine needles. Antonio and Maddalena will take care of this tomorrow, together, before they drive with Frankie out to Prima's. Now it's time to rest.

Maddalena closes all the lights. She lies on the couch in front of the tree, using her old flowered housedress for a blanket. Antonio goes back to his chair, then changes his mind and sits beside her, her feet and ankles in his lap. They don't talk. They're both so tired.

"Another year," she says.

The TV stays on Mute. The tree glows. They fall asleep this way, eventually, and when they wake it's morning and the tree lights are still on, and Tony's still gone, and they're still older than they've ever been, and it's like any other day, except when Antonio says, "I'll make the coffee," Maddalena asks, "But who are you?"

6   *Beautiful Everything*

FRANKIE HAS BEEN hoping for the phone call. Instead, a week after the January 20 notification date, he gets a letter. There sits the envelope, thin and cold and bone-white, his name scrawled long-hand across the middle like a seppuku scar.

Quickly he snatches it and stuffs it into the front pocket of his backpack. The rest of his mailbox consists of predictable flyers announcing study groups forming for the spring term, a beer night in Davis Square to welcome grad students joining the program midyear, and a long-delayed postcard from a jock in his eight thirty composition class thanking him for an "awesome fall" in which he "learned a ton." The postcard was sent from Bali, as if that's a reasonable place for an eighteen-year-old to spend Christmas vacation. There are no postcards or Post-its or postscripts from Birch. In fact, he's heard nothing from her since January 20 came and went. Before that, she and her husband were on their own exotic trip: a Christmas cruise to Alaska.

For the rest of the day, through his nine thirty History of Ideas class, through a lunch meeting with the Graduate Student Union, through an afternoon lecture called "Derrida's Parenthesis"—at which Annalise Theroux sits in the front row nodding and furiously scribbling notes—he keeps the letter unopened in his bag. As long as it stays there, he still has a chance. He avoids eye contact with Annalise and Dr. Lexus and Professor Yarrow. He skips the post-lecture wine and cheese.

The campus is covered in snow. He walks across it, bundled against the blustery wind, and just as he's about to enter the library, where he plans to spend the next three to five hours grading the semester's first set of essays, he changes his mind and heads home. He wants to be alone. And according to the chatter he overheard at the lecture, a foot of snow is expected by midnight.

He's in the hallway unbuttoning his coat when he hears Anita's voice through her closed bedroom door. He walks to the door and shouts into it. "Anita, are you talking to me?"

It sounds like she says, "A mister called."

"Mr. *who* called?" he shouts back. His heart is pounding. Mr. Yarrow? Mr. Arbuckle?

"YOUR SISTER CALLED," she says, still not opening the door.

"Oh," he says. "Great." He breathes. "When?"

"Like, two minutes ago."

"How'd she sound?"

"It's not an emergency," shouts Anita. "She said, 'Make sure you tell Frankie it's not an emergency.'"

"OK." He can barely hear her and doesn't understand why she doesn't just open the door.

"She said she had a 'work-related question' and that you can call her back whenever."

"She doesn't work," Frankie says.

"I'm just the messenger," she says, or maybe it's, "Well, just ask her." Either way, Frankie has a stack of persuasive essays to grade and no time to go over the same muddy territory with Prima. The next four hours must be spent making marginal notes that complicate his students' generalities about abortion, cloning, and the death penalty. Their syntax must be wrestled with and ultimately tamed by annotating every instance of awkward phrasing and mangled grammar. The end result will be a treasure map that leads to a perfect revision, handed to them by their graduate student lecturer like a gift and with the faith that, by the time the class ends in four short months, they will be able to draw their own treasure maps from essays he will never have to read. He is one of the few GRSLs ("Gristles," they call themselves) who works this hard, who doesn't resent wholesale the hours required to complete his responsibilities as a teacher.

Frankie believes in paying his dues, in serving the process, in hard work as the most potent antidote to bitterness. Simultaneously he indulges in the fantasy that Annalise Theroux—surely $15,000 richer as of January 20, about to complete her thesis in a warm bath of confidence, if the letter in his backpack says what he thinks it says—will be caught plagiarizing and forced to return her fortune to its rightful owner.

He boils some water for tea, puts a Stone Roses CD in the changer, closes the dresser drawers left open all day, and kicks off his duck boots. His socks are wet and cold. He adds them to the pile of soggy socks, scarves, and hats from the day before. He is digging through the hall closet for an extra blanket when he hears a voice other than Anita's through her bedroom door. It's not a man's voice.

He leans against her door, but the floorboards creak, and he steps away. He shouldn't spy. It's none of his business. He's happy for Anita. But what he wouldn't do for a good look at the girl who's finally yanked her over to the wild side! Anita herself has never held any attraction for Frankie, but the idea of her tumbling around with another girl on the other side of the wall provides exactly the sort of distraction he's been hungry for all day. He's read the theories on this. The titillation is derived from the power dynamic, and it's all about the male gaze, and blah blah blah, and because of this he's supposed to fight the desire, but desire—and who doesn't know this?— is invincible.

It's dinnertime, so he boils pastina in milk and tops it with Parmesan cheese and lots of black pepper, a dish his mother used to make when he got home from playing in the snow. The little stars soak up the milk and congeal into a cheesy mush. He eats at the dining room table, with its panoptic view of every door in the apartment, so Anita's lover can't escape undetected. He has to clear the table of old newspapers, catalogs, and cardboard boxes, but it's worth it—or at least it will be worth it when the sapphic beauty emerges.

So he waits. Instead of calling Prima, instead of diving into the persuasive essays or unearthing the letter, he reads a *Globe* article from three weeks ago profiling each member of the harem of women who've claimed affairs with President Clinton. It seems there is no escape from men in power, gazing. He tries the op-ed section. Boston's Big Dig, the most ambitious construction project in American history, is many gazillions of dollars overbudget, and according to Ralph Lind of Quincy, Massachusetts, the greed and corruption is yet another index of the imminent collapse of the Great Satan called Taxachusetts, and therefore Mr. Lind will be moving to Arizona. Frankie knows zilch about local politics, and cares even less. His passions reach beyond long-gone America to countries still forming, still salvageable. If someone paid him to write an op-ed piece for the *Globe,* he would use soaring rents and the citywide ban on happy hour as examples of how blithely citizens collude in their own exploitation.

Eventually he faces the first of the essays: "To Clone or Not To Clone: Thaaaat Is The Question," or so Jim Delaney claims.

Since the dawn of Time, man has longed to reproduce himself. But what happens when there are no fertile women around to satisfy his natural need? Like a Science Fiction movie gone horribly wrong, scientists now have the capacity to create copies of ourselves, and as we speak they are going down a path toward making progenitors not just out of innocent animals like Dolly the Sheep, but out of human beings like you and me.

In pencil, Frankie circles "Thaaaat." He puts a wavy line under "as we speak" and "innocent animals." A question mark over "progenitors." Between this intro and the final sentence is a journey of only three double-spaced pages, but it might as well be a sea of quicksand. Jim Delaney seems like a nice kid, not unlike Ray Savage, the jock from Bali, and not stupid. He deserves Frankie's hard labor. Frankie can rescue him from the wrath of a future professor—Dr. Birch, for one—who would take an essay as clunky and unsophisticated as this, cross out entire sentences, write, "NO!" beside them with a red Sharpie, and crush any budding romance with words Jim might be exploring.

"I can't waste my time on the fixer-uppers," Birch has said to Frankie. "A kid's got to at least have good bones. A solid foundation. A window of insight here and there. That's all I ask. Leave the rest to physics and engineering. It's a mercy killing, really."

Is he crazy for missing her?

She used to arrange her naked body on top of his, rest her chin on his shoulder, and recite Hopkins. "Brute beauty and valour and act, oh, air, pride, plume, here / Buckle! AND the fire that breaks from thee then, a billion / Times told lovelier, more dangerous, O my chevalier!"

In contrast: the last time he saw Kelly Anne McDonald, she read him letters her sixth graders had written to Anne Frank.

He's losing focus. He nukes his tea and adds honey. From Anita's room a Joni Mitchell CD starts up. *Court and Spark.* The volume is raised. Still no one has emerged from the room. Frankie holds Jim Delaney's essay at arm's length, reads to the end of the first paragraph, rubs his forehead in agitation, puts it down. Looks at his backpack, looks away.

He dials Prima's number from the kitchen extension, stretches the cord into the hall so he can sit on the floor and lean against the wall. From this angle, he can see enough of the apartment to detect any disturbance. He hasn't spoken to his sister for over a month, since the uneventful Christmas Day dinner she hosted at her house.

Her phone rings and rings; then the machine picks up. Perfect.

"Hey, Sis," says Frankie. "It's me, returning your call. No need to call back unless—"

"Frankie!" Prima says.

"Oh, you're screening."

"Of course I'm screening. Every other call's somebody selling something. That doesn't bother you?"

"Those people don't call hovels."

"I must be on a list. Do yourself a favor: don't rack up huge mortgage and credit card bills."

"So far, so good," says Frankie. He glances down the still-empty hallway. "So what's up? My housemate said you have a work-related question. I'm superbusy tonight, but . . . are you, like, looking for a job or something?"

"I have a job," says Prima, with a defensive laugh. "It's called raising four sons, cooking six nights a week for my husband, and babysitting two senior citizens." She's on a cordless and, from the jumpy fuzziness of the reception, seems to be running laps around the house. "And you know what? There's no better job in the world."

"Gotcha," says Frankie. God, Birch would despise his sister. Kelly Anne would not. He's been thinking in these comparative terms lately, even though he envisions no scenario in which either woman will meet his family. Frankie has never brought a girl home to his parents, let alone to Prima. He doesn't see the point until—unless—he meets a girl he might consider staying with for a few decades, and even then he wouldn't introduce her to anyone until they'd lived together awhile. No use everybody falling for her, or cutting her down for not being good enough, before he's had a chance to do so himself.

He doesn't understand people who parade their entanglements before their families like it's a beauty pageant, seeking their ratings and
recommendations. Love, like art, has no use for committees. If your
instinct's not an accurate enough guide, you've got some growing up
to do.

"It's *your* work I wanted to ask about," Prima says. "I'm wondering
what your schedule's like in April. You have off Easter week, right?"

"We get a week break around then, yeah. It doesn't always line up
exactly. Why?"

"You know the exact dates?"

"I can look them up. *Why?*"

She sighs heavily, then gets all fake jaunty. "Because I was doing
some research, and you know what? I was totally wrong about going
to Italy in August! Everyone I talk to tells me it's just too darn hot.
So I thought, why not Easter? Better weather, all the churches decked
out with flowers, less crowded with tourists."

"This Easter, as in three months from now?"

"Yeah. The boys are off school. Well, Syracuse's schedule doesn't
quite match up, but whatever. Ryan can miss a few days."

"I thought the tickets were nonrefundable, nonchangeable, engraved
by God on indestructible stone tablets. And, um, isn't the whole thing
off, anyway? Has something happened in the past few weeks to change
that? Because if so, Mom hasn't mentioned a word to me—"

"Let me worry about Mom."

"It's not a minor detail that she'd rather die than go."

"Honestly, Frankie, you take her drama too seriously. I'll worry
about her. Just trust me."

"I need Easter week to work on my dissertation," he says. "I have plans to go down to Providence and New Haven to use their libraries." This is a lie, one he's worried he's used before on Prima to get out of some other family event.

"You can't go to the library some other time?"

"You have no respect for what I do," Frankie says.

"Come on, Frankie, that's not fair. And not true at all. Honestly? I don't really understand what you do. But I figured, you work at a university, and universities get spring break off." There's commotion in the background of her house, dishes being washed or trash taken out. "Listen. I don't tell you this enough, but you're the smartest guy I know."

"You must run with a pretty dim crowd."

"I'm serious."

"OK."

"I want us to be closer."

"OK."

"I don't want us to always be fighting. It makes me sad. We should be on the same side."

"OK."

"Even though you're away. We need to talk more. I want to come up at some point. Me and Patrick. Or me and Tom. Or just me. I've never been to Boston."

"Yeah, I noticed," Frankie says. Then he regrets it. There's a defeated wistfulness in Prima's voice that he can't quite read. Nostalgia? Most of their lives they've been polite strangers, like coworkers who clash on every issue but seek each other out to sit with at the office picnic. Lately, though, their clashing has felt sharper, more charged. Birch would argue this has to do with Tony, but Frankie blames it more on millennial anxiety. Everyone's on edge as they stumble into this jumpy new century. "That could be all right," he says. "There's a lot to see here. Hey! Why don't we just make Boston the big family trip? It'd be cheaper and easier all around."

"Boston?"

He finds himself sincerely excited by this possibility. He's never had the opportunity to show anyone around his city, walk them down the Freedom Trail, explore the historic sites like a tourist. He's never been to the Cape, but the beach cottages there have to be less expensive than their Italian equivalents, even in August. "Mom would love that, don't you think? She'd have no argument."

Again that heavy sigh, and the attempt to power through it with levity. "It's sweet of you," Prima says. "But you don't really want us invading your turf. We'd drive you crazy."

"I wouldn't call this my turf. And I'm asking you to invade it," he says. "I'd . . . like you to. Really and sincerely."

"It not the same."

"Because it's not your idea. Because you won't be in charge of every detail."

"Jesus," she says. "I don't know why you're so hard on me."

Because you have lots of plans, Frankie thinks, but no ambition. No big ideas. Look at the Al Di Là, almost fifty years strong, built from nothing; look at his own quest to ensure that his scholarship not only outlasts him but influences future generations. There's honor there. He's proud of his father, and of himself. The Grasso women, though, sadly, have not transcended. Test their blood: it's half tra-dition, half fear. Maddalena and Prima were taught to maintain, to carry on, to beautify—not to create or renovate. (Look at their living rooms: sterile as museums, plastic on the sofas, Capodimonte figu-rines dusted daily.) No one encouraged them to build or look beyond or even look around. He respects his mother for making the best of her life in a new country, a new language, with a stranger for a hus-band, but he does not respect Prima for the choices she's made. How does she know she's got the best job in the world if it's the only one she's ever tried? "I'm sorry, Prima," he says, because he can't tell her any of this.

"Decide about Easter," she says. "I have to know now. I need you to be aware that we're all going at Easter—Mom, Dad, Tom, the boys—with or without you. There's a reason."

"So much for making sure it fit my schedule. I swear, Prima—"

Then she tells him her reason. But it's a lie.

Afterward, Frankie sits on the kitchen floor. It's not quite eleven o'clock, but he calls his mother, anyway, right away, and she's no dif-ferent, she's fine. Better than fine. She's just back from a lesson at the studio, and Arlene is over for a glass of wine. She ignores Arlene and talks with Frankie for twenty minutes. They've talked for at least twenty minutes every night since he left Wilmington the day before New Year's Eve, and not once has she given him a single reason to believe the lie that Prima told him. She has no evidence from a doc-tor. She hasn't discussed the issue with their father. All she has is her own paranoid assumptions and some bullshit she read in *Redbook*. So what if she put a carton of milk in the wrong cabinet? So what if she can't find the right word every once in a while? He's furious with Prima, with her cruel attempt to exert control over their family. Maybe if she had something of her own in her life and didn't live vicariously through her kids and her husband, she wouldn't create problems where problems didn't exist. Frankie wonders whether it's Prima's mind, not their mother's, that's starting to crack.

The front door slamming shut breaks him from the riot of fears and speculation in his head. He scrambles to his feet, slides down the hall in his tube socks, and makes it to the porch in time to see a bundled-up person of unidentifiable gender trudging toward campus through the blizzard. The gait of Anita's lover is neither manly nor womanly; it is the gait of a cold person, arms folded across the chest, head bowed to the horizontally falling snow. Curse these neighbors and their darkened porch lights! Better yet: curse Prima for distracting him, for putting the wrong ideas in his head. Now they'll fester there, he knows, for the rest of his life. He'll never sleep.

He needs to escape his head. He calls Kelly Anne, but she doesn't pick up. He wanders the apartment, which gets smaller and smaller the longer he circles it. He shuts himself in his room and turns the TV on loud. He takes the letter from the front pocket of the backpack and holds it in his left hand. His pants are around his ankles. He's seen enough of Anita's lover to imagine an athlete—a soccer player, maybe—showing her new girlfriend the ropes. The TV's on loud enough to muffle the sound of his mattress creaking. The coach of the soccer team, a solid but still-feminine woman in her early forties, somehow discovers the girls in the bedroom and teaches them both a lesson they'll never forget. He sustains the fantasy for five minutes, ten, but it's useless. He can't get it up.

He rips open the letter. It's three sentences long.

"Though Dr. Carr admired your—"

"We regret to inform you that, after much—"

"Christopher Curran—"

He pads his way out to the dining room table in his wet socks. Jim Delaney's disaster of an essay stares up at him from the top of a stack of disasters. The words scramble and blur on the page. Chris Curran? Frankie didn't waste a single second of worry on him. It doesn't matter. His mind is on fire. There's only one thing that matters. He calls his mother again, and his own voice on the machine asks him to leave a message, but he can't speak through his tears. She picks up. "Hello? Hello, Frankie? Is that you?" The last thing he wants is for her to worry about him any more than she already does. If there's really something wrong with her, it could make her worse. It's enough to hear her saying, over and over, "Hello? Hello? Frankie? Is that you? I can't hear you." He listens as long as she stays on the line. She sounds like his mother of always. Then she hangs up. And though he has nowhere to go, he puts on his boots, runs out into the snow, and keeps running.

LAST YEAR WAS a good one for the Al Di Là, and look: the first two months of 2000 bring double the profits of the same time in 1999, profits so big the managers ambush Antonio all three together to ask for raises. He's sitting at the front window, linguine carbonara going cold on his plate, when the managers surround him, old

Gilberto, Maurizio, and Olindo, each with his reason. They work too many late hours; they are married men with cars to shine and lawns to keep green; they never see their wives and kids and grandkids and girlfriends; they've been loyal to Antonio through the tough times; the chain restaurants on 202 pay double for less work.

Antonio listens, empty fork in hand. A gentleman doesn't eat in front of his employees.

"I don't see how a raise will solve your problems," he says. "You'll still work the same hours. Sounds like you want me to hire somebody new. I can do that for less than a raise for each of you."

"It's about respect," says Maurizio.

"Let's put the cards on the table," says Gilberto, who's been at the Al Di Là since the day it opened. He almost left in '86 to open his own place in Baltimore, then changed his mind. He's the top manager and, along with DiSilvio, the closest thing Antonio has to a brother. "We don't care so much about the hours. We want the raise."

Antonio unfolds his napkin and lays it across the plate of cold pasta, the bacon losing its shine, the egg in clumps. "You ruined my lunch," he says, "but I'll think about it."

Days later he's in the same spot with the same dish, except Prima and Ryan, who's home for the weekend, sit on either side of him. They're halfway through the meal before Prima finally asks, "So what's the occasion, Dad? Why didn't you want us to bring Tom or Patrick or Mom?"

He calls over the managers, who are here for a wine tasting, and asks them to sit. "How's this?" he asks them. "How about I give all three of you a raise *and* you work less hours?"

"We like that," says Olindo, the newest guy.

"What's the catch?" Gilberto says.

"No catch," says Antonio. He turns to Ryan. "My grandson here, he'll be home from college in June. He's my oldest, very intelligent, very handsome, as you can see. He's got nothing to do this summer. He needs to work—not for the money, for the experience. He's been a waiter here before—Gilberto remembers him—but not a manager. So you three can give him some training. And if you train him good, he takes over some of your shifts, you get the time off, and a small raise at the end of the summer."

"How much is 'small'?" asks Maurizio.

"Um, Nonno?" Ryan says. "Did we talk about this when I was drunk or something? I don't remember ever—"

"*Zitto,*" says Antonio. He puts his hand on the boy's leg.

"So the better job the boy does, the bigger raise we get?" asks Olindo.

Maurizio looks suspicious. "To train somebody is not easy, without a guarantee of funds—"

"Antonio will take care of us," Gilberto says. "You should know that by now."

"You start in June," Antonio says to Ryan. "Your school will be over by then."

"Aren't you full of surprises," says Prima to her father. "It's a great idea, I think. Don't you, Ryan?" She sits up straight. "You want to spend the summer in Wilmington, anyway, right? There's nothing in Syracuse. You've got free room and board at Casa Buckley."

"I gotta think about it," Ryan says. "There's this job at a pro shop my buddy was telling me about . . ."

The wine guy, Enzo, shows up with his crate of bottles, and for the next hour the six of them taste Chiantis and Montepulcianos and some dry whites from the north. The Al Di Là tradition is to serve only Italian imports, but today, as he does every visit, Enzo tries to persuade Antonio to open up his mind to California and France and—*stunod* that he is—Australia. "What's your opinion, Ryan?" Antonio asks.

He thinks a second. "Nobody comes to Little Italy looking for wine from Kangaroo Land," he says.

"You hear that?" Antonio says to Enzo, handing him back the Syrah without a sip. "The new manager has spoken."

Prima is happy—Antonio can tell—but Ryan isn't quite convinced. From what Antonio has seen of his grandson, though, he fell in love with the place from the beginning, not as much as Tony, but close, and he'll learn the manager job quick. Eventually, if the love affair is real, he can take over the place. Two summers ago, when Ryan waited tables, it didn't take long for the customers to ask for him by name. A natural salesman, he was always warm and friendly, but professional, clean shaven, his hair perfect and shiny with that sticky stuff guys put in it now. He flirted with the ladies—young or old, it didn't matter—and made the men feel like big shots when they ordered veal or the expensive wines. He never got tired, not even after working lunch and dinner on the same Saturday. When one of the other waiters asked Antonio if he was sure his grandson didn't take speed, he told him he didn't have to: speed was in the Grasso blood. Hard work at a high speed had built the Al Di Là and kept it running. It didn't matter much that Ryan showed up late once in a while, that he sometimes had beer on his breath, and that once he dropped a bowl of mussels on a customer's arm; the other waiters liked him enough to cover for him, he could just pop a breath mint in his mouth when he needed to, and the customer he burned was a cheap bastard Antonio had never liked to begin with.

Maddalena approves of Antonio's plan for Ryan. He hasn't told Frankie yet, but he knows he will be relieved. The pressure will be off him to carry on the Al Di Là tradition. Frankie might not realize this yet, but he will want and need young family like Ryan and his other nephews in his life down the line. After Antonio and Maddalena go, Prima won't be too far behind, and the youngest will be left alone. Antonio doesn't expect to be alive by the time Frankie gets married and has kids of his own, but Maddalena still believes it will happen soon. She thinks that she sees everything, that she can translate what the kids really mean when they talk and can explain why they make the choices they make in life. In her mind she is inside them every second, like a saint or a witch, feeling what they feel, the pain and the pleasure both. But she's not.

She doesn't see that Frankie's too selfish, that he's one of those types who'll wake up at forty-five a grown man and have to do all at once the grown-man things he should have been doing all along: job, wife, house, kids. Antonio knows lots of men like this, men no more unhappy than anybody else. Frankie's not as complicated as Maddalena makes him out to be.

Does nobody else plan or think ahead the way Antonio does? It used to be considered healthy, but it's not what people on TV tell you to do anymore. On CNN the doctors keep saying that the secret to life is to live "in the moment," but Antonio does not like this expression. The moment is always already past. As soon as you recognize it—as soon as you say, This is right, my heart is full, oh, how beautiful everything is!—the moment is outside you, and you're looking in and can't get it back. The best you can do is stay three steps ahead of tragedy. It's like driving on the freeway. If you keep your eyes on the cars far in front of you, you'll never get into a wreck. Sixty years he's been driving in this country, and not a single scratch. It's not luck. There are no accidents, just people who don't care enough to keep safe, who are too lazy to pay attention.

"We worry about you, you know," Antonio says to Ryan. "Up at that school all by yourself." He's skinnier than he was just two months ago at Christmas. His skin pale. This is what happens when you're away from family too long. "You get enough to eat there? You take care of yourself?"

"You kidding?" Ryan says. "College is the balls!"

"*Language,*" says Prima.

"That means it's good?" Antonio asks.

"That means it's really good."

"Well, I'm glad," Antonio says. They go over some of what the manager job will require—the hours, the uniform, dealing with the kitchen—and Ryan says that he doesn't mind hard work, that the Al Di Là's the coolest thing about his family. His high school friends still bring their dates here. "It's a part of Wilmington history," he says. "Like the du Ponts or the Charcoal Pit. That summer I waited tables? I got more chicks than I could count. Remember, Ma?"

"You spared very few details," says Prima.

"That means you're excited to be my new summer manager?" Antonio asks. "You think it's 'the balls,' too?"

"That means I'll definitely think about it," he says. "Here's the thing, though. If I'm gonna be here all summer, you gotta hang out. This place is more fun with you around."

Antonio draws a long breath, lets it out slow. "You're a good boy," he says. "Don't worry. If you come work for me, it will be like you say, the balls."

"And I'll teach you some new expressions," Ryan says.

Before they leave, Prima takes Antonio aside. "Thank you," she says with tears in her eyes. Antonio watches them get into their car and waves as they drive away.

It's the middle of the afternoon, that time of peace in the restaurant day that Antonio loves most (unless he counts the weekend dinner rush, when the line of customers crowds the entrance and spills out onto the sidewalk—for that he feels a different kind of love). The dining room is quiet and clean, the lights dim; he can hear the dishwashers singing the old songs, and the hum of the freezers, and the bar glasses clinking as they're put away. The TV's on without sound. The front doors are locked, the shades pulled over the glass even though there's no sun. It's a gray winter's day and will be for a long time. Gilberto, who'll stay through the dinner shift, reads the *Corriere della Sera* in the corner booth, no shoes, his feet up on the seat. The paper takes two weeks to show up in the mail, but since nothing ever happens fast in Italy, news two weeks late is right on time.

When the customers arrive, Antonio gives up his table by the window. The early-bird dinner special, Gilberto's idea, ends at seven. So far it's a big hit: they offer a smaller menu that they can xerox in the back office, a few simple pasta dishes and hot sandwiches with a side salad and a glass of wine, and the people can't get enough. Gilberto is proud. Maurizio's new idea, on the other hand—a late-night bar menu on the weekends—Antonio doesn't like as much; it will bring in the wrong kind of crowd. Maurizio keeps telling him that's where the real money is: drunk people after midnight, hungry and alone, and by his calculations, later hours on Friday and Saturday nights mean they can close completely on Mondays, the slowest days. But Antonio doesn't like this part of the idea, either. The slow-day customers may be few, but they're the most loyal. All of this is important. He will teach it to Ryan, and Ryan will carry it through the next forty years.

On his way out, he shakes the hands of the people in line—a young couple new to the neighborhood, the old Irish lady from Forty Acres who reminds him of Giulio's Helen, a priest from St. Anthony's with a colored teenage boy he's trying to save—and they say they're happy to see him, he's not around so much anymore. Antonio promises to change that this summer. Did they hear? he asks them. His grandson (they remember him? the handsome one? the smart college boy?) he's coming back as manager, June 1. And before that, for Easter, the Grassos are all going back together to the Old Country, to the original Al Di Là.

"Won't that be magical!" says the Irish lady.

"Magical, yes," Antonio says. " 'Magical' is a good word."

"*Buon viaggio,*" says the priest.

The colored boy nods.

It will be a good trip, Antonio thinks. If Maddalena could hear him, she'd say, Touch wood, so as he makes his way down Union, he knocks on a shingle of what was once Lamberti's Bakery. It's a rainy rush hour, loud with a whistling wind and cars and buses barreling through the slush. He forgot to pick up dinner from the restaurant, but Maddalena won't mind a simple frittata with onions and some fresh bread. She has no appetite lately, anyway, because of the new pills she's taking, pills Dr. Ferretti hopes will slow down what's going on in her brain.

They sat together in the room with Ferretti, told him about her sisters and what's like a curse in the family. Then, when she went to the lab to get her blood drawn, Antonio asked him how bad it really was, and all he could say was, "The pills could help a little, but it will get worse. We just don't know how long it will take."

It was Antonio's idea, not Prima's, to move up the trip to Easter. He told Prima why, and she said she'd had the same idea all along but couldn't say the words. She won't tell her boys about the meeting with Dr. Ferretti, not even about the pills their grandmother will be taking. But neither Prima nor Maddalena knows the half of it, how bad it could get, and how soon. It's better they don't know, Antonio thinks, that he and Dr. Ferretti keep it between them, the old-fashioned way.

Maddalena will be happy to hear about Ryan. It will bring her joy to have him here, finishing what they cannot. Antonio will start driving her to the restaurant once or twice a week after Ryan starts and will make her eat a full meal, and their grandson will sit at their table even though he's working, and they'll pick out pretty girls for him from the crowd. She'll like that.

A good year for the Al Di Là, yes—good people, good business, and now Ryan on the way in. For all that, he is proud. But he'd burn the place to the ground for Maddalena—burn the money, too, and all of Union Street if that's what it took—to give her a moment more.

AT 11:01 THE rates go down and the news comes on and Antonio walks in from the club and goes straight to the kitchen to fix himself an ice cream cone. Maddalena lies on the sofa in the den with the cordless in the pocket of her nightgown. She hits the buttons on the remote control for channel 4, then Video/TV, then the two little backward arrows, like Frankie taught her, and the phone rings as the tape starts to rewind to the beginning of the story.

"What a stupid show," she says to Frankie. He's always a day ahead because he watches it on his lunch break. Maddalena, who's too busy cleaning or at the dance studio during the day, has to tape the show and watch it late at night, which is good because the story settles her mind. The nonsense of the actors and actresses, with their crazy love lives and mysteries—their familiar faces, the soft music behind them—helps her sleep. As Frankie talks, the tape starts up, and she hits the Pause button, freezing the face of the pregnancy faker on the screen. Antonio stands in the doorway, licking the three scoops of butter pecan so loud she can hear it all the way across the room. Lately he has been watching the story with her in his leather chair. He can't keep the names straight and has no idea who's married and who's evil and who's backstabbing who, and she thinks he just likes to look at the pretty, half-naked girls, but that's all fine with her because at least it's time they spend together.

"Stupid is right," Frankie says. "I can't wait till tomorrow. Friday episodes are the best." He's in a good mood. Maddalena can tell. There's a smile in his voice, no clink of ice from the whiskey glass. "You sound good," he tells her, and she wants to ask, How do I usually sound?

"Things actually happen on Fridays," she says, waving at Antonio to get his attention. "Your father just walked in. He says hello. His mouth is full of butter pecan."

Antonio picks up the kitchen extension. "Hello, Son," he says, swallowing.

"Another late-night bocce game?"

He licks and slurps. "What else? It's Thursday."

"How many games did you win?"

"Three for three. Me and Tomasso twice as a team. Then eleven to five I beat him one-on-one."

"I don't like you driving after three drinks," Frankie says.

Maddalena breaks in. "He can't see good during the day, you can imagine at night half-drunk." She can say this only with Frankie around. Otherwise it becomes a fight. "I tell him, but you think he listens?"

"So I hit a tree," says Antonio. "Big deal. I've lived long enough."

"What if you hit a little kid? How would you feel then?"

"No little kid's out at eleven o'clock," Antonio says. "Use your common sense."

"You know what I mean."

"I gave the drinks away, Frankie. I always do. You don't know me yet? Let's change the subject. Did you eat?"

"No," Frankie says, like he's angry about it. "I sat at my table starving to death, waiting for food that never appeared. Of course I ate."

Now, so fast, he's in a bad mood, all because he worries about his father. "It's just a question," Maddalena says. "What else are we supposed to ask you about?"

"Nothing," says Frankie. "I'm sorry. I had macaroni and cheese, some salad, and an orange. Very balanced. For dessert: about twenty chocolate chip cookies dunked in milk." Again there's a smile in his voice. "Once I start, I can't stop."

"Don't get fat," says Maddalena. "It sneaks up on you. You're not so young anymore."

"Thanks."

"Macaroni and cheese," Antonio repeats. "From a box, I bet. Only an American could eat that slop."

"Like I have time to cook a gourmet Italian meal—"

"What gourmet? It's so simple, Francesco! A can of tomatoes, some garlic, olive oil, a cut of meat flipped over once in a pan. You learned nothing from me."

When her husband's on the phone, everything's an argument. Maddalena enjoys it more when it's just her and Frankie. They can gossip about Prima and she can hear about his students and the weather in Boston. Then they can agree and agree some more about the Italy trip and how neither of them will go, her most of all, Easter or August or ten years from now, and someone should tell the Buckleys to stop making plans and pretending it's going to happen. How long can it go on, all this pretending? Sooner or later, someone has to say the truth, and she's so tired. "Hang up," she says to her husband. "Go put your pajamas on. I've got the story rewinded already."

"Good night, Son," Antonio says. "Be careful."

"Good night, Dad. *You* be careful."

"I love you. Good-bye."

"Love you, too, Dad. Bye."

"Bye, love you, bye. Bye."

"Love you, bye. Bye."

This jumble of "I love yous" and good-byes is how they end every one of their calls, every time, all of them—her children, her husband, always the same, whether they're fighting or not. You can't say it— "Good-bye, I love you"—enough times. The jumble would sound funny to someone listening, some American, but there's only family in the room tonight, no strangers, none of her friends from the dance studio, no neighbors stopping by, so why be embarrassed? You never know if you'll get the chance to say it—"Good-bye, I love you, good-bye, I love you"—again. You never know when everything will disappear.

Frankie tells a story about one of his students, but Maddalena can't quite follow it. In the meantime, Antonio appears in the doorway in a mismatched set of pajamas. The bottom is green plaid, the top red silk and missing a button. His hair sticks up in the back; one of his socks has a hole in the toe.

"You're not so old, you know," Maddalena says to him. "You can do better than that."

"You want me to wear a tuxedo?" he says.

"What's going on?" Frankie asks.

"Your father's looking like a homeless," she says. "I tell him every day: it matters what you wear, all the time, even when you sleep. You never know who's going to see you."

Antonio picks up the extension. "Do you hear this nonsense?" he says. "Can you tell me why it matters what I wear in my own bed?"

This gets Frankie laughing again. Is there any better sound in the world than your son laughing? Especially when he's 355 miles away, to hear it, to hear anything that brings him joy, is like food to the starving.

"I'm gonna let you go," Frankie says to them both. "As much as I'd like to referee this important debate, I have three more hours of reading to do."

"That's fine," says Maddalena. "We had a nice talk."

"We did."

"All our talks are nice."

"They are," he says. "Even when they're not." Then he says it again. "You sound really good, Ma."

"Good night, Son!" says his father. He hangs up.

"Take care of yourself, Frankie," Maddalena continues. "Don't go walking too far."

"I won't. I mean I will. You, too. Good-bye. I love you."

"I love you, too. Bye. Bye."

"Bye, love you, bye. Bye."

"Bye, bye, I love you. Bye."

Maddalena waits until the last possible second, when she's sure he's gone, to push the Talk/End button, then brings the cordless back to her bedroom. She picks up Antonio's pants and shirt and dress socks from the floor, looks at them in the light, turns them twice around, smells them, puts the shirt and socks in the hamper, and hangs the pants back in the closet. She pulls his jeans and a white button-down off their hangers, takes a thin black sweater from the drawer, and sets them on his end of the dresser for tomorrow.

She closes the hall lights and switches on the lamp in the foyer. She straightens the silk flower arrangement on the lowboy and checks the locks on the front door. In the den, Antonio waits for her in his chair, feet up, arms crossed, half-asleep already. She takes an afghan from the credenza and lays it over his legs. She kisses him on the lips, rests her palm a moment on his warm, stubbly cheek—no wrinkles, for a man almost eighty, amazing—and returns to the sofa. The TV is still frozen on the face of the conniving woman, her blond curls and thick lips and eyes blue as her slinky silk dress. She'll get away with everything. That's how the world works now. Women have too much power and no shame. She presses Play and brings her back to life.

"Who's this one again?" Antonio asks.

"*Gesù mio,*" says Maddalena. "She's the star!"

"She's a good-looking woman."

"She's very bad. You don't remember what she's trying to pull? With her baby?"

"She looks like you," says Antonio.

"You're going senile."

"Don't say that."

She takes a deep breath, like Dr. Ferretti tells her to do. But most of the time a deep breath just makes her dizzy, like this afternoon, like yesterday morning. Her head gets heavy as stone.

After a while, in the middle of the show, she says, "It keeps happening." Her eyes are fixed on the TV. "Yesterday I was standing at the sink with the water running and a dirty dish in my hand, and I didn't know what I was supposed to do with it."

"That's nothing," he says. "That's called getting old."

She can't see him. His easy chair is behind her, and they are both facing the same direction.

"You're fine," he says. "We're both fine. The pills will help. Just listen to the doctor."

"But it keeps happening."

"The pills haven't kicked in yet. It takes a few months."

"Is that what Ferretti said?"

"I forget people's names all the time," Antonio interrupts.

He's lying, but how can she argue? "When I was sixty, I thought I was so old. I was a teenager."

"The only place you were a teenager," he says, "was Santa Cecilia." He sits up in his chair. She can feel him leaning toward her. If she turns around, she will see his elbows on his knees, his face begging. She doesn't turn around. "Come back with me there. Stop all this nonsense arguing. Make your daughter happy and me happy."

"Antonio."

"You know what? Forget about me. Forget about Prima. I have a good feeling," he says. "This trip—it will help you. To remember things better. To see your brother and sister, it will spark something. It can't hurt."

Can he see her shaking? She covers herself with her nightgown. He must hear the fear in her voice. Her kids say she can't hide anything. Frankie tells her that she'd have made a terrible actress, that she should have tried to be a dancer instead. Frankie! How will he live without her? What will he become? One night soon he will call and she won't know who he is, and he'll have no one to talk to, no one to settle his mind. He'll never sleep. How can she abandon him?

"Please," Antonio is saying. "Listen to me, for once." He is out of his seat now, makes his way over to the coffee table, where he sits on the edge, faces her, his back to the soap opera that keeps playing, on and on, without them. "From the first day you came to this country, you wanted to go home. That's all I heard for ten years: 'Take me home, take me home.' Now I'm telling you: Don't waste this chance."

Last week, Maddalena was sitting at the desk in her workroom when a man walked by. In her hands was fabric. The fabric had a pattern of daisies. She didn't know who it was for, or how it had come to her, or what to do with it. The man, the flash in the doorway, looked like a man she'd met a long time ago, when she was a girl—the postman, maybe, or an uncle who came to visit from Rome. She wasn't sure. Daisies grew wild in the yard behind her family's store. She used to pick a handful and arrange them in a vase for her mother to find, as a surprise. She sat at her worktable for a while, twisting the fabric in her hands, and the next time the man passed she recognized him (her husband, Antonio Grasso) and the reason for the fabric (Arlene's bedroom windows, Arlene her friend from the dance studio) and where she got it (Jo-Ann Fabrics, in the University Plaza Shopping Center) and what to do with it (sew, sew, always sew). Then she climbed the stairs, walked outside, took deep breaths, and lifted her palms to God, and the houses and sky and trees slid away from her, and the ground out from under her legs, and if she hadn't grabbed onto the iron railing of her porch, she'd have fallen flat.

"I don't want to fight anymore," she says.

"Good," says Antonio.

"Tell Prima whatever you want."

"I'll tell her you're going. We're going. We're all going. Easter is beautiful. Remember the hats?"

"Fine."

"You're sure? You'll see it my way, for once?"

"It will make Prima happy."

"And me."

"And you."

"Yes. And that's a good thing. To make your daughter happy and your husband happy and your brother Claudio and your sister—" He kisses her forehead. His hand is warm on her wrinkled cheek. "And you, too. You'll be happy, too, *tesoro*. This is for you. I promise. I'll make sure."

Part 2 ～ *Spring 2000*

7 *All of Us Are Leaving*

IT'S NOT STALKING if you do it for your kids. This is what Prima tells herself as she idles in the parking lot of Padua Academy, sunglasses on, hair pulled back, waiting for Allison Grey. She's Zach's official girlfriend now, the one who's luring him down from Penn State for her high school prom next month. He deserves to know what she's up to while they're apart.

It's a warm March afternoon, the first of the season. The streets and cars are spit-shiny after the morning rain. Prima arranges herself in the driver's seat in such a way to give her the best view while she soaks up the precious sunlight. Recently in *McCall's* she read about a new disease called SAD, a mood disorder that can develop if you don't spend enough time in the light. More women than men suffer from it, some so bad that doctors prescribe lying under lamps for hours at a time. It got Prima worrying that Syracuse was the wrong choice of college for Ryan. Frankie, too, up in snowy Boston. She can't read anything nowadays without connecting it in some upsetting way to someone she loves.

It's muggy in the car under the direct sun, but the windows are tinted and she can't put them down. She struggles to remove the fur jacket Tom bought her six years ago—can it really be six?—for her fortieth birthday.

At Christmas, Frankie told her, "You can't wear that thing in Boston, you know, if you ever visit me."

"And why's that?"

"They'll scream at you. 'Killer! KILLER!'"

"She didn't club those little chinchillas to death," Tom said. "If I didn't buy it, some other lady'd have it on."

"By wearing it, though, Prima implicitly endorses the process."

"I guess I won't see Boston in the winter, then," she said. "Imagine owning a coat like this and not wearing it."

It broke Prima's heart when Frankie got so excited about a family trip to Boston. Only her parents have visited him there, and just the once, to move him in. Frankie drove them up in the old Toyota he bought from Tom, and they flew back the next day. He's not a parent. He doesn't know there are some things a mother can't bear to see: the run-down apartment where her son will have to clean his own toilet, the city he chooses over you, his life spinning away from yours. Prima has visited Ryan at Syracuse and the twins at Penn State once only, to get them settled. She stayed three hours. It took a lot of effort not to look closely at anything. She didn't want to remember the details—the cinder-block walls, the stinky ginkgo tree outside the dorm room window, the pretty girls in pink jackets bouncing along the paths. She bought no souvenirs from the campus bookstores. She prefers the blue-and-gold high school sweatshirts and pom-pommed hats, which remind her of fuller days.

At two thirty the double doors open and the Padua girls spill into the parking lot. Most are Italians from the surrounding neighborhood, dark-haired teens in matching plaid skirts, white button-down blouses, and chunky black shoes. The blonds and redheads stand out. The first few times Prima checked up on Allison, back in December, the weather was frigid and the girls wore hats and scarves that covered their faces, so she couldn't find her. Then Prima got smart, staked out the Grey house in the early morning, saw the camel peacoat and Burberry-patterned scarf and hat she left for school in, and later that afternoon spotted her right away.

Today, Allison's hair is in a ponytail. As she struts out, she gabs nonstop with a girl on her right, waves to one of the teachers, then giggles into the girl's ear. Last week, she walked out with a different girl, got into her car, sped off to a house in Fairfax, and didn't emerge before Prima had to get home and fix dinner for Tom. Today, Allison leans against this other girl's Jeep while she fishes for something in the trunk, chattering the whole time even though the girl's not paying any attention. Prima wishes she could hear what she's going on and on about and report back to Zach that Allison's got her eyes on a different boy. It's obvious to Prima that she can't be trusted, but what's not so obvious is how Prima will prove it.

The girl closes the trunk and hands Allison a tin of something. Allison opens up the tin, looks around, picks out a small tablet, and pops it in her mouth. She laughs. The other girl laughs. She hands back the tin, and the girl stuffs it guiltily in her sweater pocket. They stand there, waiting, Prima guesses, for another girl to meet them and join them for whatever trouble they'll get into. So far, Prima's followed Allison and her various friends to the mall, to Bert's Music, to Fairfax, and to Brandywine Creek State Park, and while she hasn't caught them red-handed in anything major yet, she's certainly never caught them volunteering at a senior center or planting trees. She's noted that each of them drives over the speed limit, the Fairfax girl smokes cigarettes, and now today there's this suspicious little tablet Miss Allison Grey won't put in her mouth unless she looks around first.

Between her car and Allison is a large maple tree that, when the wind comes, obstructs her view. The branches were bare in January, but now they're sprouting leaves and making surveillance more of a challenge. Leaning over on the passenger's side doesn't help. What is she hoping to discover? She doesn't know. She knows only that the girl is bad news. A corrupter. She can't say this to Zach without him asking how she could possibly think that. She needs evidence. For three months she's been looking. *I happened to be at the mall, and what did I see but Allison Grey stoned out of her mind . . . what did I see but Allison Grey stealing a pair of earrings . . . what did I see but Allison Grey kissing a Puerto Rican boy . . .*

Someone pounds on the window. Prima jumps out of her seat, hits her head on the sunroof. When she looks over, she finds Patrick. Patrick! He's pulling on the handle, but the door's locked.

"*Mom?*" He peers into the car, his hand shading his eyes.

"Fuck!" Prima says. She tosses her glasses on the passenger seat and opens the door for her son. "You scared me!" she says. "What are you doing here?"

"What are *you* doing here? I noticed the Beamer and I was like, That looks like Mom's car. Then I checked the license plate."

He's all smiles and happy to run into her, but she's so flustered she can't find a way to turn the keys in the ignition. "Shouldn't you be at practice?" she says.

"I am at practice. We jog over here sometimes, then jog back." He's wearing his baseball jersey, but with shorts instead of the uniform pants, and now she does see a group of boys running sprints on the grass next to the main building. Prima's always worried that Allison Grey might catch her here; she's never once thought of Patrick, even though his school's five minutes down the road.

She starts the car. "I was just about to leave," she says. "You scared the heck out of me!"

He looks over at his team, then back at her. "I still don't get why you're sitting in the parking lot."

"Oh," she says. She musters a big, goofy smile. "I'm not 'sitting in the parking lot.' Barbara asked if I could pick up some tax form from the school office and drop it by for one of your father's clients." Barbara is Tom's secretary, and every once in a while, when things get busy at the firm, Prima will spend a few hours in the office and run this sort of errand. The excuse doesn't sound too far fetched, especially because Tom's working double-time to get his clients' taxes done before the trip. She picks up a manila folder from the passenger seat and shows him. Inside the folder is all the documentation for the

Italy trip, but it could very well include a tax form for Barbara, as far as Patrick needs to know.

"Oh, OK," Patrick says.

Prima looks over at where Allison Grey was standing, but she and the girl and the car and the tin of little tablets are gone. Fuck, she thinks, and Patrick must see the word on her face.

"You sure you're OK, Mom?" he asks.

"Of course, sweetheart. Why wouldn't I be?" She leans over and kisses him on the cheek, but when she pulls away, his eyes, those starry blue eyes that keep her awake at night, are narrowed at her. "What is it?"

"Dad told me not to say anything," Patrick says. "But to be honest, I'm kind of worried about you. You seem really stressed out. More than usual."

"Oh, Patrick," she says. "The last thing in the world I need is to worry about you worrying about me."

"That's what I mean. You say stuff like that." He looks down. "And you forget things you never used to forget. Like, last week. You were supposed to come get me after practice, but you never showed up. The Gooch had to drive me home."

"What?" Prima says. "When? What day?"

"Last Tuesday," Patrick says.

Last Tuesday, her father had called in the middle of the day to say, "Come to the house soon as you can."

Some guy from the team yells out, "Buckley!"

"Oh God," Prima says. "I'm sorry. Your *nonna* wasn't feeling well last Tuesday, and Nonno was busy at the restaurant, so I had to run out and get her something. Why didn't you say anything that night?"

Patrick shrugs. "Because you were all stressed out then, too." He looks out toward the street, away from his teammates. "And then I think, when I leave for school, after we get back from Italy and you don't have enough stuff to do, are you going to be OK all alone, just you and Dad?"

"BUCKLEY!" the guy calls again. "Let's *go!*"

Again Patrick ignores him. "I can catch up," he says to his mother.

This, too, is Prima's fault. She's joked too many times how badly she wishes Patrick were graduating from kindergarten instead of high school. It breaks the rule she set for herself as a mother long ago, then forgot: Never give your kids a guilt trip for something they can't control. Like growing up. Like becoming men. "You should be with your team," she says. "Don't worry for one second about me, do you hear? I'm going to be just fine. The Italy trip's a big deal, and your *nonna*'s been having a hard time with it. And yes, I'll be very sad when you leave for school, but I've been through this before, right? With your brothers? I can do it again. And you're coming back every break, so I won't even have time to miss you."

He's listening. Then he says, "I don't want you to be lonely."

Prima looks over his shoulder to make sure the team's gone, then pulls him close. She holds him there for as long as he lets her, which is a long time, longer than he's allowed her in years. She wants to ease his mind, to protect him from every sadness and worry and mistake. "You're too much of a Grasso," she says, and he half smiles, rubs his forehead, embarrassed that he's caused this scene, that he's opened his heart, that his mother's sitting in a car alone in the middle of the day with her hair up. And then, as suddenly as he appeared, he breaks free of her, without so much as good-bye, runs across the parking lot, turns the corner, and is gone.

Prima has to get out of here, too. She's one of the few cars left in the parking lot, and if she stays any longer the conversation with Patrick will stick to her. She drives down Delaware Avenue, scanning her mind for something to focus on. Only then does it occur to her how close she came to being discovered. She's lucky she's quick on her feet with a reasonable lie, but what will happen the next time? Twice she stops herself from pulling in to the Columbus Inn for a glass of wine to calm her nerves. Instead, at a pay phone in the 7-Eleven parking lot, she digs out a quarter from her purse and calls Tom.

But no surprise, he's too busy to meet her for a sandwich or a cup of tea.

"You OK?" he asks. She's never invited him out like this, in the middle of the week, with no occasion to celebrate.

"Of course," she says. The phone feels dirty on her chin. "Don't worry, I'll entertain myself."

"Is it your mother again?"

If she says any more, her voice will break, and he'll ask what's wrong, and she won't have a lie at the ready. She'll have to say: It's everything. And I'm afraid. So she gets back in the car and drives, with no destination in mind, into the glare, on the shiny roads, for an hour at least, through neighborhoods and in and out of strip mall parking lots, until she finds herself on Main Street in Newark, in the heart of the University of Delaware campus.

She has to stop every few blocks for the crossing college kids, boys as handsome as hers and girls as bouncy and baffled as she and her girlfriends were when they were students here. As she watches them and imagines herself as one of them, she realizes she hasn't come here by accident. It's a place where her only memories are happy ones.

She pulls up in front of the old row house on Academy Street, where her girlfriends lived when they were twenty-two and fresh out of U of D. Linda, Jill, Colleen, Audrey. The place looks no different than it did in the seventies: the sagging porch, the prickly holly bush, the rusted chain-link fence. This was the party house, and Prima has always been—it's true, why not admit it?—a party girl. She wasn't the prettiest in that circle, but guys flocked to her. She wasn't as prissy as Colleen, or as timid as Jill; she wasn't afraid of beer (like Linda) or dancing (like Audrey) or letting a guy take her for a ride on his motorcycle (like all of them). She had been, as the expression goes, around the block. In the years after Tony died, when she'd run wild with Dante Marconi and his friends, a high school crowd much different from this one, she got comfortable talking to boys, teasing them, flirting. She shocked herself, the things she said and did in parking lots and the back seats of cars and across state lines. Dante encouraged her. Then they went too far. But that's not the memory she's here for. She needs a happy memory today.

One night, Prima was standing next to the holly bush when a new guy showed up. She was always standing in front of that holly bush, snapping off one leaf at a time, tearing it at the seam, snipping each thorn with her nail, a circle of friends around her. She got so she could do that with her left hand while holding a beer in her right and making small talk with a boy.

She wasn't into baseball at twenty-two, but from her time with

Dante's crowd she'd learned enough key phrases to impress a boy. "They have no defense," she'd say, a fact that seemed to be true enough for every team in history.

"You think?" some U of D frat guy would say.

This new one's eyes were a glassy blue. He parted his hair in the middle. On his feet were boat shoes; tied around his neck was a pastel polo. These preppy qualities were pluses, light-years from the boys on motorcycles and souped-up Camaros she usually took to. His friends were friends of Linda's brother, whom no one had ever met. The house parties on Academy Street were like that then—a revolving door of tangentially connected strangers bearing six-packs and joints and armfuls of record albums. There was a lot of sitting around, asking each other who they wanted to be. No one planned to spend her life as a Wilmington housewife or a teacher at the local elementary school or a graveyard-shift nurse, though that's how each of the girls turned out. Prima used to say she dreamed of parlaying her high school theater career into a recurring role on *Days of Our Lives;* and in the meantime, like all the girls (except Colleen), she made out with various guys on the couch and on the curb and on roof decks and anywhere else they could be alone.

Thomas Patrick Buckley, this new guy, was the first to request a kiss; the others just dove in. They'd been standing on the porch, Prima asking him about his twin sister, when he'd interrupted her question with the question.

"I'm sorry," he'd said afterward. "I couldn't concentrate on anything except how much I wanted to kiss you."

Now a blond girl in pink sweatpants opens the torn screen door halfway and squints at the middle-aged woman in the silver BMW. When she doesn't recognize her, she slams the door. The entire porch rattles. Prima doesn't drive off. She has as much right to sit here as the girl does to be young and suspicious. She could tell the girl a thing or two about men and marriage, how quickly they come, how you have to prepare for them like you would an exam.

Tom's first kiss was enough to hook Prima. His Grand Prix, his cleft chin, his steadiness—those kept her on the line. She and Amy hit it off, too, though the girl was stoned most of the time and would have hit it off just as well with a palm tree. Tom liked numbers, Prima liked people; this seemed complementary. So after three months, she informed her father that she was bringing somebody around. She had to pretend she'd just met him, because even though she was in college, if her father knew she'd already let this young man drive her to the beach and buy her dinner and meet his own parents, he'd have called her a *disgraziata,* and maybe even closed the bank account he'd opened for her the day she graduated. Dazed as her father was at the time, he knew nothing of the running around Prima did after Tony died; by the time he came out of his daze, Prima was going to church with Linda on Sundays and had enrolled at the U of D after putting it off a semester, and father and daughter silently agreed to pretend those years never happened.

That first night at her parents', they sat in the den, Antonio in his recliner with his arms stiff on the rests, Tom and Prima on the couch opposite him, hands folded in their laps. Maddalena clattered around the kitchen, making coffee and assembling a tray of cookies and chocolates. Tom wore a blue button-down shirt and pressed dress pants. His face was pink and clean shaven. He called Antonio "sir." They discussed his goal of starting his own accounting firm with two friends from college. He'd liked UPenn, he said, but wasn't a fan of the city, which was too loud. As soon as he could afford one, he'd buy a house on a golf course. No, he didn't want to become a dentist like his father. No, he had no plans to settle down in another state. He liked Delaware; his family had settled here in 1802.

"Your mother, she's still living?" Antonio asked.

"Yes," said Tom. "Of course."

"You don't mention her once. Why? You say 'my father,' 'my sister,' even 'my uncle with the boat business.'"

Tom looked at Prima, then back at him. "She's at home, Mr. Grasso. We play golf together sometimes; she's better than me." He laughed and put his head down. "Besides that, she's just, you know, my mom. Not the best cook, but otherwise like any other mom."

"Hm," said Antonio. "The mother is everything."

They stared at each other.

"Her name is Diane. Maiden name Blanchard."

Antonio looked at his watch. "Maddalé!" he called. "You're coming to meet this Tom Buckley or not?" Then finally he smiled at him. "We raised our daughter right. She's a good girl. The best. She belongs to us first, always, no matter what. Husbands come and go. You'll do all right in life. You have a good head on your shoulders. But don't forget what I'm telling you: She's not yours. She's ours."

"We just met, Dad."

"What are you saying to him?" said Maddalena, appearing in the doorway. She loved to make an entrance. She had her hair up and wore blue eye shadow, red lipstick, and a party dress. Frankie was a toddler then, and she'd quickly lost the pregnancy weight. Right away she went to Tom and took him by the hands and kissed him on both cheeks. She was playing a part—the flirty housewife, Sophia Loren in *A Special Day*—and so was Antonio, the vaguely threatening mafioso. "Don't pay any attention to him, sweetheart. You two have fun together. Don't get married too soon. You end up like us."

Soon Maddalena brought in the tray of amaretti, and they ate them with spiked espresso, though in real life Tom never touched caffeine or liquor. His leg kept shaking. After a while, they turned on the TV and sat in stress-free silence, like two middle-aged couples after a bridge game.

"Handsome," said Maddalena later, pinching Prima's side. The Grand Prix pulled away, and Tom honked twice and waved. "And nice. Rich. You really did it, Prima. I was so afraid for you, but now—"

"Don't jump ahead," Prima said. "We barely know each other yet."

Maddalena leaned in. "You don't have to lie," she whispered. "Not to me, OK?"

Though Antonio said nothing, Prima knew he was as pleased as he could be with a *'merican*. British, Irish, German—they were all the same to him. They didn't love their families the way Italians did; they had no sense of humor and lacked warmth; they ate mayonnaise and sour cream and watched too much football; but this one, this Tom Buckley, seemed as good as those people got. Prima didn't disagree with any of these assessments. At the very least, he'd be an excellent provider, and she could relax into a long marriage. At best, he'd be strong and decisive and romantic—a rock with flowers growing underneath.

As Prima lay in bed that night, beneath the canopy her mother had sewn for her, a Carpenters album on the turntable in the corner, her father lingered outside her bedroom door. Just stood there, listening. She could hear him shift his weight, breathe. He paced for a little while. Then she fell asleep.

On New Year's Eve came Tom's proposal. Ten months after the wedding, Ryan was born. Prima never made it to nursing school. Tom and one of his buddies opened the firm right on schedule, and since then the money's flowed like a fountain. January to April—tax season—her husband's a ghost, but the summers are their rewards. When summer comes, they take walks around the development in the evenings and eat ice cream cones and chat with the neighbors. They listen to baseball on the radio even though they have a big TV. They've road-tripped with the boys through thirty-six states. Together the Buckleys have seen everything.

The pretty girl appears again in the doorway. This time she's dressed for class: jeans, pink fleece jacket, backpack hanging off one shoulder. Another girl's right behind her. Then another, each in fleece with a ponytail and backpack. It's a clown car still, the old Academy Street party house, and might be forever. There will never be a shortage of girls. They narrow their eyes at Prima when they walk by her car, but she's not moving.

She could visit her mother, but even she is too busy. She has a dance lesson today, or so they discussed last night on the phone. The tango.

Her friend Arlene is driving her, and afterward Arlene is taking her to a flower show at Winterthur. Her seventy-two-year-old mother is doing the tango, fighting for every step, as full of life as she can be, strolling among flowers. And Prima is alone in her car, scanning her mind for happy memories.

She gets out of the car, pulls off a branch from the holly bush, gets back in, and drives off.

IN BED WITH Kelly Anne McDonald, the fog in a chilly hover outside her dorm window, their bodies entwined under her pink down comforter, George Winston on her stereo, Frankie is stalling. He should be showered by now, at least, and on his way to the passport office downtown. Instead he nuzzles his head deeper into the glorious warmth of Kelly Anne's breasts and shoulders, holds her tighter against the morning. For Frankie, she has set aside the first few hours of her Fridays, her days of relative rest, free of classes and appointments with her mentor in the Education Department. Leave it to the paternalistic US government, which requires Frankie to show up with his birth certificate in order to obtain a document that allows him to escape it, to disturb this one brief stretch of peace.

"So, what you really mean is, your family hates the Irish," says Kelly Anne playfully. "That's why I can't go to Italy with the Grassos."

"They *do* hate the Irish," Frankie says. "And you *can* go with us. I'm just saying you'll regret it. You've heard of the Warren Commission? That was nothing compared to the grilling you'll get."

"I'm a big hit with families."

Frankie can't tell how serious she is. They've been dating only three months. She has zero funds for a plane ticket. She'd never miss Easter with her beloved clan of McDonalds. And yet she's been passive-aggressively inviting herself on his family trip since Prima rejiggered the schedule and sent him his ticket certified mail.

"Here's a plan," she says. "I come home with you on the twenty-fifth. I meet your family, turn on the charm, flirt a little with your brother-in-law, talk recipes and gardening with your sister, they get inspired, and before you know it they're paying my way."

"I don't think so," says Frankie. "This trip's all about family. And you're not." He's aiming for matter-of-fact, but it comes off harsh. Does she really think three months gets you a seat at the table?

"Not *yet*," she says.

Sometimes he forgets she's a Catholic girl of twenty-two who's seen too many romantic comedies.

"I'll meet them anytime, anywhere," she continues, "but no pressure." She tugs on his earlobe. "Well, OK, *some* pressure."

Frankie's instinct tells him that this thing with Kelly Anne McDonald, whatever it is, won't survive the semester, let alone her summer internship at a bombed-out youth shelter in Jersey. Here's how he sees it going: over the next few months, before and after they part ways at the end of the school year, she'll write him letters and call every other night, and maybe even persuade him to rendezvous with her in Philly or New York some June weekend, but by the end of July the interest on both sides will have moldered. They are similar creatures of habit, he and Kelly Anne, unsuited to the randomness and unpredictability of summer. He can see all this as clearly as the sad face of James Dean, which stares back at him from the life-size poster on her dorm room wall. Before long, Frankie's cynicism and persistent flirtation with bleakness will have exhausted Kelly Anne; likewise, her sunny enthusiasms and dogged faith in the essential beauty of humankind will have bred contempt in him. Which is why he should enjoy her body and her sunshine and her adorable dabble with him now, while it still pleases them both. Which is why there is no need for her to meet his family on March 25 or anytime after.

"Call me," she says after he has showered and dressed and slung his satchel over his shoulder. "Let me know how it goes." On his way out, she hands him a fistful of quarters from the top of her dresser. "There are lots of pay phones downtown."

"You're going to make a great teacher," he says.

"And for the record, I already have my passport."

It had taken two months of movie dates and Socratic questioning and hand-in-hand walks through Harvard Square for Kelly Anne to agree to sleep with him, and since that night (February 1, a date to which she refers with gravity), she has shown alarming flashes of wifeliness. More than once, she's braved the dorm kitchen to cook him real dinners—Irish stew, broiled salmon, turkey tetrazzini—and served it to him on real plates, with stainless steel silverware and linen napkins, in the lounge. She's called him from the Rite Aid pay phone to ask which toothpaste and soap he preferred, since she was restocking and might as well get something they both liked.

The window for telling her about Birch has closed. Before February 1, she might have found the information intriguing and sexily dangerous; after February 1, it would count as a betrayal, a symptom of his rotting soul. She has given herself to him, and in return she expects his loyalty, if not his consistent emotional availability. As a lover, Kelly Anne is, surprisingly, as wild and generous and attentive and thorough as Birch is impatient and demanding. Sparing no part of him, she approaches each act with the assured serenity of a sculptor or a surgeon. One day she will find a better man, her own age, to spoil.

As he walks across the BC campus, past the towering cathedral, through the dissipating fog, a poem comes to him. The first lines: "Well, I have lost you; and I lost you fairly; / In my own way, and with my full consent." Edna St. Vincent Millay, Frankie remembers, minor but notable. The poem had spoken to him, though he'd yet to lose anyone he'd loved in a romantic way. The next lines: "Say what you will, kings in a tumbrel rarely / Went to their deaths more proud than this one went." Even then, he'd found that metaphor fitting: relationship as sovereign in an execution cart. He has forgotten the middle, but the last lines go something like, "Should I outlive this anguish—and men do—/ I shall have only good to say of you." Sentimental, yes, Millay, but a fine craftswoman, like a weaver of intricate but tacky baskets. Frankie turns, walks backward, as if he can see Kelly Anne from here—sitting up in her bed, textbook on her lap even though it's her day off, a pack of multicolored highlighters on the pillow where Frankie's head just lay, a mug of English breakfast tea steaming on the windowsill—and repeats the last nine words of Millay's poem. *I will have only good to say of you.* There is no sadness to outlive, of course—not yet, not yet—but Frankie's philosophy has always been to expect the worst, to steel himself, to inoculate.

To that end, he reaches into his satchel, finds the smallest interior pouch, unsnaps it, and fingers the bag of pot that Chris Curran, the

stoner medievalist, the Big Winner, unloaded on him after the dissertation fellowship convinced him he should quit once and for all. The
bag had been full when Curran handed it to him in the West Hall
men's room two months ago, but since then Chris has dropped by the
apartment more than a few times to "say hey," his code for a raid of his
old stash. Rarely has Frankie joined in. He's had no urge. The drug
makes him giddy and slow witted and excitable—in other words, useless if he's to sleep or get work done or satisfy two demanding women.
To brave the passport office, on the other hand, to wait in line with
the masses of the American traveling public, Frankie couldn't ask for
a more useful tool.

He walks several blocks through the hilly neighborhoods of Tu-
dor mansions and wide, sloping lawns that surround BC, looking for
a gardener's shack or a patch of densely packed trees, but can find
neither. There are stone pillars and gates at the feet of the driveways.
Daffodil beds surround the mailboxes. He thinks of Birch, who likely
lives in a house like this, Dr. Z. having made a fortune in the private
sector before sliding down the ladder to academia. She calls Frankie's
Stowe Street apartment "Iron Gates" after its pitiful attempt at a
grand second-floor terrace. In the beginning of their entanglement,
back when the stakes were low, Frankie and Birch had role-played
caretaker and lady at Iron Gates and used to joke that they'd have
been better off as a couple in nineteenth-century Britain, where people knew their place.

The last time he saw Lady Chatterley, there was no conversation,
not a single word, to record in his journal. He found the note in his
mailbox, hoofed it home, left the front door open, stripped down to

his boxers, and beckoned her into his room; less than a half hour later she was fully dressed and grunting good-bye. No more repeat performances, no more pillow talk. D. H. Lawrence might have approved of this exchange, and Frankie can't say it doesn't scratch a certain itch that even Kelly Anne's sweetly ferocious stamina can't reach, but he misses the *words*. They'd had the words back in the early days, when they would spend equal time in the sack and at the kitchen table, gossiping, revisiting arguments from her African lit seminar. Obscure lines from Soyinka and Spivak and Salih spilled forth from Birch's lips as naturally as her name and address. The Professor's mind had thrilled Frankie before he'd even registered the litheness of her body, and at first he'd felt he'd won both on a game show, the grand prize! Now her body is a consolation that fails to console.

He turns the corner and ends up on Commonwealth Avenue. There's a gas station–minimart that backs up to some woods. He buys a tin of breath mints and a lighter and trudges down a faint path through the trees, a shortcut no one seems to have taken in a while. The ground is hard, the leaves stiff and cold. March in Boston. Under the branches of a dried-up pine, he fishes Curran's bowl from his satchel, packs and sparks it, and fills his lungs with smoke. He holds in the smoke as long as he can, then coughs it out. When Curran does this, the entire process is as smooth and natural as peeling a banana, and afterward Frankie notices no change at all in the guy's demeanor. That's what makes Curran an addict, he supposes. Frankie's own inability to stop coughing at this moment confirms his amateur status, as does the cloudiness that immediately fills his head. Still, the woods, as he finds the trail again, go as pleasantly flat and distant as the set of a school play, and he is the lone actor stepping across the stage.

He arrives at the passport office on Causeway Street in time for the lunch rush, takes a number, and waits on a bench among a crowd of surprisingly normal-looking people. He expected the blighted supplicants of the DMV, but of course anyone in line at the passport office seeks to abandon the United States for another culture, for a while at least, and that alone lends them virtue.

He sits, red pen in hand, rereading the chapter on *Midnight's Children*, which he's finally finished, twice revised, and had peer-reviewed by two of his cohorts. Try as he might, he can't find a single example to cut. No matter what his cohorts say, if the example wasn't essential to his argument, he wouldn't have included it in the first place. The chapter is ready. The other chapters—some Birch-approved, some Birch-ignored, each skimmed in recent days with the help of his red pen—are also ready. He's approaching the next phase of his work, which will require him to choose the right chapters to put in the diss, then make resonant links among them. He will start this next phase the day he returns from Italy. In the meantime, he'll attempt to take what's known to the wider world as a "vacation," even though he's ill equipped for such a thing. If he didn't have the Rushdie chapter with him today and was forced to sit alone on this bench with his undirected thoughts, he'd have succumbed to panic.

When his number is called, the agent, a possum-faced guy with cheeks so dry they look burnt, greets him with the charm and enthusiasm of a cigarette machine. Still, he takes Frankie's money and DS-11 form and birth certificate and IDs and eyebrow-ring-less photo and does a bunch of joyless stamping and typing. He hands back the IDs with a receipt and says to expect the passport to arrive in the mail in four to six weeks.

"Four to six *weeks*?"

He points to the part of the form that clearly states, PASSPORTS ISSUED 4–6 WEEKS FROM DATE OF SIGNATURE. "Is that a problem?"

His heart skips a beat. "I'm supposed to leave for a family trip on March twenty-fifth!"

The man looks at the calendar, looks back at him, wrinkles his nose.

Frankie's eyes well up. For a moment it's just the two of them in a duel of stares. Except Possum-Face has all the power, and Frankie can only beg, though he's filled with rage. This smug man will keep him from his family, from walking his mother through the olive grove. Without this man's help, Frankie will not be there when she walks up the hill and, for the first time in fifty years, finds her brother and sister and first love waiting for her at the top of it. They are hoping for a miracle in Santa Cecilia, for time to go in reverse, for her to find her memories, but Frankie won't see it, won't make the trip he's come not only to want but to need. He hasn't quite known this until now, when it's about to be taken away. "Oh God," he says, rubbing his eyes. "You don't understand. My mom—she's sick. This might be the last time she can come with us. Isn't there anything you can do—"

"Sir," says Possum-Face, "this is a regional office. You can have your passport *today* if you need it. Most people don't. It takes just a few minutes."

"Today?" Frankie says. He rubs his eyes. "Jesus. Why didn't you say so?"

"I was about to," he says kindly. "You didn't give me a chance." And then Possum-Face smiles in that earnest way, with his lips turned in—a smile that says, I'm my mother's son, too—and when he does, he's not so ugly, not so burnt.

"Thank you," Frankie says. If there were a tip jar, he'd empty his pockets.

When Frankie does reach into his pocket, on the way out of the passport building onto blustery Causeway Street, he finds one of Kelly Anne's quarters. She expects an update. But he knows what she'll say if he gives her one: that he should have sent in his application weeks ago when she reminded him, that he should see this as further evidence that he needs her in Italy to manage his affairs. He checks his watch: twelve thirty. Birch is in office hours. She holds them on Friday afternoons because they are the least popular with students. He finds a pay phone, dials her West Hall number. When it rings, he hangs up. The phone eats the quarter.

There must be a Bruins game at the Boston Garden tonight because, all around him, packs of grown men malinger in gold jerseys, shouting at each other. Frankie doesn't come to this part of the city, with its dingy sports bars and screeching elevated trolleys, unless he's on his way to an Italian restaurant in the North End, but even those visits are rare. He avoids the Italian section. All those restaurants, one after the other up and down the narrow streets, remind him of the Al Di Là, except in none of them would he find his father sweet-talking the customers or his mother adjusting the drapes or Zio Giulio with his accordion or his ten-year-old self hiding under a booth. He certainly won't find his father's homemade pasta and veal cutlets and garlicky sautéed spinach, or his mother's *frittelli* and deep-fried smelts, all prepared with hundred-year-old recipes and fresh ingredients and love. When he's home, Frankie devours every dish his parents set before him, thinking, with each bite of the endangered and unrepeatable flavors, that they will soon disappear, irretrievably, and the rest of his life will be spent in longing. Does Ryan, who will eat at the

Al Di Là every day this summer, and possibly for the rest of his life, understand how lucky he is?

He hits a 7-Eleven, buys a large bag of salt-and-vinegar chips, and stands at the window overlooking the street, stuffing the chips in his mouth like a junkie. Then he buys a chili dog with extra chili.

He calls her again. This time, he lets it ring, and his fear comes true: she answers.

"This is Professor Birch."

"Hey" or "hello"? He chooses, "Hey there, it's Frankie. Are you with a student?"

"No," she says. "Students don't like me."

"I can't imagine why."

He hears the sound of her office door closing. "Are you calling for a reason? It's Friday, isn't it?"

"Yeah, it's Friday," he says. "I just—this is a business call, actually. I'd like to discuss my diss soon. Just the diss, that's it. We haven't really, you know, *talked* lately. About that."

"Well, these are my office hours. I'm on the clock, so let's talk." She must sense that this stings him, because right after she says it, her voice changes. "Or did you want to come by? No reason why you shouldn't come by."

"I'm not on campus," he says. "I'm downtown. Are you free in, like, two hours? I know that's off the clock . . ."

"I'm driving Amos to the airport," she says. "He's going to some conference in Perugia. That's fair, right? We go to Pittsburgh and Saint Louis, and the engineers go to Tuscany."

"Umbria," says Frankie.

"What?"

"Perugia's in Umbria."

He hasn't told her about his own trip to Italy. He doesn't want to hear her reaction to it. He wants her take on his work, not on his parents and siblings. On the rare occasions he mentions them, he can almost see her mind spark, eager to pounce with her expert analysis of his family dynamics. What he's pieced together of Birch's family—a distant and long-dead father, a nervous mother remarried to an insurance salesman in Cincinnati, a sister in Lansing—calls to mind one of those bleak Rust Belt upbringings people of substance spend the rest of their lives renouncing and American novelists try, lamely, again and again, to illuminate. No wonder she is attracted to the tragedy-marked immigrant saga of the Grassos.

"Next Friday, then," Frankie says, though he doubts he can wait that long to share with her his newest idea, the one he began to form at the grimy 7-Eleven window between the bag of chips and the chili dog. The idea will require one or two new chapters, but he thinks that he can mine two of his existing ones for material and that, moreover, the idea will help create links among the other chapters, if he can nail the introduction. He wants to get to work on this idea *right now.*

She must have heard the wistfulness in his voice, because after he says, "Next Friday, then," she goes soft again. "How about this, Frankie. Have you ever been to the Oak Room?"

"I don't think I know what that is."

"It's a restaurant. In the Fairmont Copley hotel. The prices are obscene. We can meet there, you and me, tonight, for dinner. It's a good place for talking."

"Isn't that . . . very public?"

"Nobody in the English Department can afford to eat there, trust me. Someone got Amos a gift card a hundred years ago and he's never used it. I'm sure he won't notice if I take it."

"Do his friends go there? What if they see us?"

"I'm your adviser. You've just gotten your PhD. Congratulations! We're celebrating! Et cetera."

It's the least Birchy idea she's ever had. He can't resist. "If you're OK with it—"

"It's my suggestion, so obviously I'm OK with it."

They agree to meet at seven. He has five and a half hours to kill, so he heads to the BPL, conveniently located next door to the Fairmont Copley, to check out a few titles the university library wouldn't have. His plan is to take a break and call Kelly Anne to update her on the passport, but then he loses himself in the stacks and, while examining the bottom row of the lit-crit section, dozes off on the floor. When he wakes, it's 6:40, he's got slobber on his lips and carpet burn on his right cheek, and an enormous homeless man is hovering over him with his arms contemptuously crossed. By the time he makes it through the circulation-desk line and rearranges his satchel to stuff five new books in, it's too late to call Kelly Anne, and besides, what would he tell her he was up to?

He arrives on time, if a bit woozy and disheveled, at the Fairmont Copley Plaza. It takes him a few minutes of wandering the glittery, gilt hallways to find the Oak Room, but otherwise Frankie is well within the margin of error punctualitywise. Birch runs her life like Mussolini ran the Italian train system, and grows exponentially more peevish with every minute someone keeps her waiting.

This time, though, he's the peevish one. Seven fifteen comes. Seven thirty. Twice he asks the maître d' to confirm the reservation, and both times, yes, it's for a party of two at 7 p.m. Name: Césaire. Birch's favorite theorist. Seven forty-five. Eight. Dozens of other reservations arrive and cast down their disapproving eyes on Frankie, waiting on the leather banquette in a faded blue oxford unbuttoned to reveal his Nine Inch Nails T-shirt, obsessively checking his watch. Eight fifteen. He could read the books in his satchel, but he's too angry to focus. "Can I use your phone?" he asks.

Frankie's fear—that Kelly Anne has been waiting for him—comes true: she picks up on the first ring. "Where've you been?" she asks. "I was getting worried."

"I'm taking you out to dinner," he says. "Have you ever been to the Oak Room?"

She hasn't, she says, but she's heard of it. He rebooks a table for Grasso for eight thirty, tells the maître d' he'll be right back, and walks across the square to Boylston Street. At Marshalls he purchases a white button-down shirt, a striped tie, and khakis. He tries on the cheapest pair of dress shoes, but even these are too expensive, and besides, he's already compromised too much for the sake of the maître d' and his snooty assemblage of diners. His Converses will do just fine. He changes in the fitting room and stuffs his jeans and T-shirt into his satchel.

He returns to the Oak Room to find Kelly Anne already waiting for him at the bar. Walking toward her, he is struck again by his gut-level attraction to her all-American looks; this surprises him now, as it did that first night on Amtrak, because he's spent much of his adult life chasing the exotic. Tonight she's pulled her hair back and wears a simple blue-and-white polka-dot dress, her gold cross front and center at her throat. She's half on, half off the barstool, legs delicately crossed, drinking through a straw from a pint glass of ice water. When she sees the scrubbed-up version of Frankie walk through the door, she covers her mouth. Then she stands, adjusts her dress over her thighs, and holds out her arms.

"Look at you!" she says as Frankie steps into her embrace. "What's going *on*?"

He shrugs. "I'm not sure. I just thought, For one night, let's be adults. See what it's like."

"Well," she says, extending her hand. "We'll pretend this *isn't* my prom dress, then. Let's say we bought it at Saks. It cost three thousand dollars."

"And I'm the chair of the Department of Engineering," Frankie says. "I saw you across the crowded campus center."

"That's creepy."

"Is it? You're not a student, though, remember? You're in the Ed Department. You're a professor, too. Not the chair, though. Not yet." He smiles.

"An ed professor in a three-thousand-dollar dress?" says Kelly Anne.

The maître d', surely eavesdropping, waits impatiently with their menus. They follow him to a table in the back corner, likely on account of the sneakers. Frankie doesn't care. The chair backs are padded with thick, satiny material that reminds him of his mother's drapes. They're surrounded by oak walls on all sides and those little brass light fixtures that stick out—he can't remember what they're called—and then Kelly Anne says, "Sconces. We're eating in a room with sconces."

He folds his napkin over his lap. A fern tickles the back of his head. He's starving. While he was waiting for Birch on the banquette, he read from a thick coffee-table book of clipped magazine and newspaper articles, all of which argued that the experience of dinner at the Oak Room is singular and unmatched. One writer devoted three paragraphs to the Dover sole alone, and so, when Frankie sees it on the menu, he orders two. And Waldorf salads. And a manhattan. Kelly Anne, not a drinker and only recently twenty-one, orders a Coke.

They discuss her day (busy), the passport office (no sweat), and the prices on the menu (one decimal point off, surely? Should they bring this to the waiter's attention?). But Frankie has a sky-high limit on his credit card, and at this point, who cares? They're on the cusp of spring. His diss is in its final stages, thanks to the New Idea. He'll ditch Birch, as an adviser and a lover, once and for all, now that she's made her blatant disregard for him abundantly clear. Until now, he hasn't minded being a kept man, but being stood up at the Oak Room changes a person. He'd imagined he and Birch would discuss the New Idea over wine the way they used to discuss it over cereal, like adults, then have sex in the oversize lockable bathroom, among the fresh flowers and Elizabeth Grady scents, like rock stars. But she didn't give them that chance. She could still show up, of course, catch him canoodling with Kelly Anne, about whom she knows nothing, and make some sort of scene, but Frankie's aware of the more likely scenario: she wussed out and didn't have the balls to tell him.

Kelly Anne is watching him think. "Did you take me here because you don't want me to go with you to Italy?" she asks.

"That wasn't my thought process," Frankie says. He takes a sip of his manhattan. "But now that you mention it . . . Can we agree not to talk about that? Can we just enjoy this place and make fun of it?"

"I want us to be closer," she says. "A real couple."

"We can't get any closer than this," Frankie jokes. For such a fancy restaurant, the table is so small that their salad plates touch. "Besides, we are a real couple. We don't have to take some extravagant trip to prove anything. This isn't *Pretty Woman*."

She laughs. "Did Frankie Grasso just reference a Julia Roberts movie? You really did have a brain transplant today. *That's* why you couldn't call me."

A busboy appears and whisks away their salad plates. Behind him, the waiter wheels over two big, scaly fish, heads and all, on a cart draped in tablecloths. As Frankie and Kelly Anne watch, he scoops off the heads with a spoon, deposits them out of sight on the second tier of the cart, and goes to town on the rest of the bodies. He splits and unfolds them like they're antique books, teases out with precision the delicate white bones, and leaves only the juiciest, lemoniest flesh, which he places before them with the confident flourish of a magician.

"Dinner theater," Frankie says.

There's peril in eating here, he thinks, as he brings a forkful of fish to his lips. It's dangerous to know what you're missing, what's available to the man willing and able to pay for it. He eats most days like there's a depression: lunch on bread from the Pepperidge Farm outlet and market-brand ham and cheese, washed down with tap water. For the rest of the day he snacks on energy bars and peanut butter. His fridge is filled with cubes of cheese left over from department parties. If he didn't have a freezer full of his father's lasagnas, he'd be swimming in his new size 28 khakis.

"It's really good," he says, of the sole.

"It's amazing," Kelly Anne says. "I want to learn how to cut a fish like that."

"I've seen my dad do it. He teaches the waiters at the Al Di Là, too."

"I want to eat there one day."

Maybe it's the second manhattan, or the perfection of the fish, or the sense that nothing matters that comes after you spend lots of money you don't have, but whatever it is, Frankie hears himself say to Kelly Anne McDonald, "You will," and after he does, it's as if he's just plugged her into an electrical socket. Her eyes widen. She sits up two inches taller. It's possible that her teeth get whiter. She calls the waiter over and orders a manhattan for herself. In her mind, the occasion calls for a libation. Plus, she says, she likes the heavy tumbler, the red glow of the cherry on the glass.

Dessert is Irish coffees and crème brûlées. The waiter is their new best friend. With tip, the bill comes to $150, more than Frankie spends on groceries in two months. He doesn't blink. They consider staying another hour, maybe grabbing a final drink at the bar, but then Frankie decides against it; the splurge feels good, and when something feels good it should be held and admired, not stretched thin.

They push through the revolving door of the hotel into a busy and rainy Copley Square. They take the T back to BC, to the warmth of her bedroom, where they immediately undress and dive under the covers. Though they're jazzed and tipsy, the gluttony has made them more sleepy than horny. They pass out in each other's arms at eleven thirty. At 2 a.m. he bolts up in bed: he's forgotten to call his mother.

He pads out to the pay phone in the hallway, dials her number, assures her quivering voice that he's fine, he's great, he was just out walking after a double feature at that movie theater in Harvard Square he's always telling her about. No, he wasn't alone. Yes, he was with nice people. Smart people. Yes, he's excited to see her in a couple weeks, and yes, he's already bought his train ticket to Wilmington using his father's credit card. No, the Italy trip's not going to be as bad as she thinks, but now's not the time to talk about it. It's late. It's too late. Now's the time they should both get some sleep.

"You sound good," he says at the end, because she does. It's one of her good nights. And she says, "So do you."

8   *The Grasso Brain*

IT NEVER FAILS: just as Prima settles in to relax, the telephone rings.

She's alone in the house, a six-hundred-calorie dinner of boiled chicken, mesclun greens, and one baked sweet potato in front of her. Patrick's next door and Tom's at the office late again to bank as much time as he can before Italy. Her parents are on their way to the dance studio for the weekend social. All Prima wanted from this lazy Friday evening, the last Friday before the big trip, was to take a break from the plans and the double checks and sit in front of the TV with her sensible dinner (because she, too, is banking) and her March Madness brackets. It scratches her gambling itch, and she must admit, watching the fresh-faced college men spin around in their shorts and tank tops is a perfectly fine way to pass the time.

A ringing phone never fails to worry Prima. She wasn't always like this. But then one day she was called out of US History and told that Tony was missing and asked, over and over, if she had any idea where her brother might be hiding. A day later, the police called to say he'd been found, and she can still see her mother on the floor of the kitchen, weeping, wrapped in the long green cord. The ringing phone is a constant threat to the years of peace Prima has had since high school, this blessed span of sidestepped tragedies, this golden era she knows won't last.

The girl on the phone is crying.

"Who is this?" Prima asks. "Who's *call*ing?"

Prima's been preparing for this call, the one that changes her life with unbearable news: Patrick's flipped his car, Ryan's gotten drunk and fallen off a roof deck, her father's had a stroke, Tom a heart attack, her mother's left the oven on and burned the house down. Frankie has been home with Maddalena the past few days, though, and this has eased Prima's worry. He arrived earlier in the week to help get them ready for the trip. So who will it be tonight, then? How has Prima lived this long with these wolves outside the door?

"It's Allison," says the crying girl. The connection is scratchy, and there's a sound like thunder in the background. "I need your help, Mrs. Grasso."

She's pregnant, thinks Prima immediately. Then: Zach's beaten her up. Both options are all too possible. Her son, like all men, is a lover and a fighter, capable of anything. Whichever it is, Allison drove him to it, and now it will be up to Prima to fix the situation.

"Tell me," Prima says.

All in a rush it comes: "I ran out of gas and I'm on the road to Penn State and I can't call my parents because I'm not supposed to visit Zach without them knowing and I didn't ask their permission to take the car all the way out to State College and they don't even know we're dating, Mrs. Grasso, they think I'm spending the night at my friend Katie's house and I don't know what to do, so I was calling you because you're a cool mom and you'd tell me what I need to do or maybe Patrick—"

"Allison, slow down," Prima says, catching her own breath. "This is a relief. You made it sound much worse. I thought something happened to Zach. Did you even think of what might be going through my mind?"

"My parents are going to KILL me!" she wails.

"It'll be fine," says Prima. "Eventually, though, you have to pay the piper."

"What?"

Prima switches the phone to her other ear. Relief washes over her. In three minutes she'll leave Allison to solve her own problem, and she'll get back to her brackets. "What are you expecting me to do for you, Allison? I won't call your parents and lie for you, if that's what you think."

"No," she says. "That's not—is Patrick there? Because I thought, maybe Patrick could drive out to meet me? Like, with a gas can, the kind you have for a lawn mower?" She babbles on: Her father had to do that once for her mother. He drove out in the middle of nowhere, which is where she is—somewhere on 41, near Harrisburg—even though her dad was so mad at her mom and didn't say a word to her when he got there. Her dad just filled the tank and left, and that's all Allison Grey says she needs from Patrick Buckley: to waste his Friday night to drive forty miles looking for her blue Honda Civic on the side of the road, then turn around and come home so she can make the rest of her journey without her parents finding out.

"No. Way," Prima says.

"What? Really?"

"Really. No way. I may be a 'cool mom,' but I'm not letting my son go all the way out there by himself."

"Can I talk to Patrick?"

"Even if he was here, Allison, I wouldn't let you. No seventeen-year-old should be making that trip alone, not you and not Patrick. It's not safe. You need to call your mother, or I'll do it for you. Why don't you just call Zach? His friends have cars. You're halfway there."

"I still want it to be a surprise," she says, her voice shaking, from cold or nerves or both. There's more of that thunder in the background and car horns and wind. She's quiet for a minute, then starts to cry again, louder than before, a kind of whimpering wail, but Prima is unmoved. The sooner Allison learns that actions have consequences, that you have to prepare for any and all calamities, the better.

"You need to figure this out on your own, Allison. I'm sorry."

"But Mrs. Grasso, I'm scared. There's, like, nothing around here."

"If there's a phone, there has to be something near it, right? You're not at a restaurant or rest area?"

"I'm near a gas station. But it's closed. It's right off the exit. I had to walk on the highway to get here. My car's on the side of Forty-One. I could see the gas station from the road. I thought for sure I'd make it. I didn't even notice I had no gas at first. I was so excited to see Zach.

It's our six-month anniversary. Six months. Isn't that crazy? But it's all farms around here. And really, really dark. Some crazy guy's gonna come out of the woods with an ax, Mrs. Grasso. I swear that's what'll happen if I'm stuck here."

"You need to call your mother," Prima says again firmly. "Or give up the surprise and call Zach or one of your other friends. Doesn't Katie have a car?" Surely this is not Prima's problem to solve. Meanwhile, Allison continues to cry and asks if she can stay on the phone while she figures out what to do.

"Fine," says Prima. Then she offers, "Nine one one, maybe?" But Allison is a minor, and the police would have to notify her parents, anyway. She looks out her window at the neighbor's house, where Patrick is having dinner and watching a movie with one of his classmates he doesn't particularly like. Prima could easily run next door and get him—she'd be rescuing him, too, in a way—and ask him to come with her out to Harrisburg to rescue Allison Grey. They could stop for ice cream on the way home. Soon enough, she won't have Patrick around for such a thing.

The operator comes on and demands that Allison put in more coins. This causes her to sob even louder. "Go back to your car and lock the doors," Prima says to her, firmly. "Patrick and I will be there in an hour."

"Oh my God, really?"

"Yes."

"Thank you so much, Mrs. Grasso."

"You're welcome."

"It's, like, an hour and a half, though, from you, I think. Just so you know."

Prima is silent.

"I'll make it up to you, I promise," says Allison Grey.

Prima switches off the TV, walks over to the neighbor's, and explains the situation to Patrick and his classmates and the parents, and soon they're on 41 speeding toward Harrisburg.

"This is why I sent you to Boy Scouts," Prima lectures. "So you can *be prepared*. You have to think ahead for every step you take. You have to imagine all the worst-case scenarios. You don't just expect that the easy route's going to open up in front of you. That's easy to imagine when you're a teenager, I know, but sooner or later you find out life doesn't work that way."

Patrick yawns. It's tired advice. Prima's father used to ramble on to her like this, in that blur of years after Tony. The words had the opposite effect on her then. They made her push him and her mother further away, give up on anything safe and reasonable, throw herself harder and harder at Dante Marconi—but she prefers to think that they weren't wasted, that they meant something later, after she'd settled down with Tom and started a family.

They're almost to Lancaster. Prima keeps her eyes out for horses and buggies, though she's not sure if the Amish travel at night. Patrick's in his track pants, sweatshirt, and tube socks, his feet up on the dashboard, and she almost tells him it's not safe, but she's done enough lecturing for one night. To change the subject, she tries, "What do you think of Allison, anyway?"

"She's hot," he says.

"Not her looks. How she *is*. *Who* she is. You think she's a good person?"

He shrugs. "She's not mean or anything. Her best friend's Katie Campo, this big-time bitch, but Allison's cool to everybody. I don't know anyone who doesn't like her."

Prima's already aware of all this. She's made some inquiries about Katie Campo and has since indicted Allison with bitchiness by association.

"Zach still likes Allison as much as before?"

Patrick doesn't answer, but a certain smile comes to his face. Prima can see it even in the darkness of the car. It's that particular smile that guards his world from her intrusions. She'll never break through it, though she's come as close as any mother could. She'll never stop trying to discover the lives her children lead out of her sight, to piece those lives together from the glimpses they give her.

"I think he's in love," Patrick finally says, and when, in disbelief, she looks over, he's pulling something from the pocket of his sweatpants. It's one of those tins. He opens it, takes out a white tablet, and pops it in his mouth. He hands the tin to her. "Want an Altoid?" he asks. "I'm, like, addicted."

"A what?"

It's not the last thing she remembers. The last thing is the wooden fence flying at her, taking up the entire windshield, like sunlight does when you turn into it.

THE MAN ON the phone is crying. It takes Frankie a long few seconds to realize that it's Tom and that Tom is telling him that

Prima and Patrick are at Lancaster General Hospital, they've been in a car accident, and Frankie needs to get there right away and bring his parents.

"They're in bad shape," Tom says, and after he does he breaks down and another man takes the phone from him, a man who turns out to be Tom's brother, Steve.

When Frankie heard Tom crying, he'd thought instantly of his mother. As if on cue, his mind spun out the worst-case scenarios: she'd collapsed on the dance floor, she was missing, she was disoriented, she was, in some way or another, gone. Now his head and his heart are too crowded to consider the implications of the relief—there's no other word, he's sorry—that he'd felt upon hearing the names Prima, Patrick. "They're going to be OK, right?" Frankie asks.

"The doctor says there's a very good chance for both. But he won't let us see them. Tom's losing his mind. He won't believe anything the doctor says until he can see them. The twins just got here, but Ryan can't get a flight until tomorrow morning. I told him not to drive down from Syracuse, but I think he's going to, anyway."

Frankie isn't sure he remembers the way to the Crystal Ballroom in Claymont, where his parents dance on the weekends, and it's late—they might be on their way home already—but still he puts on shoes, throws on a jacket, and takes off to find them. He can't just stay home and wait by the front door.

He drives fifteen miles over the speed limit, makes two wrong turns, and nearly slides into another car as he tries to read the map unfolded on his lap. When he arrives and makes his way down the wide pink staircase into the main room, which is still very much partying, it doesn't take him long to find his mother. She's in the middle of the dance floor, her arms around a tall man half her age, her back arched and head turned dramatically to the side, tangoing or waltzing or something. Her face is serious, full of attitude, focused on nothing but the tall man and the music. From behind a column in the foyer, Frankie watches her, letting her finish out the song, bracing himself for the scene that's about to erupt, not wanting to wrench her from this moment of joy, and amazed that, from this distance at least, she appears no older than Prima, without a care in the world. And there's his father, sitting at a table in the corner with a group of men. His eyes, full of pride, are fixed on Maddalena. His foot taps along to the music.

They have been married more than fifty years. They lost a son and might now lose a daughter and their youngest grandson. One of them will soon be lost to the other. It is more than anyone should have to bear.

At the end of the song, he weaves his way through the crowd to his father's table. The old man's face lights up when he sees him, pure joy at his son's surprise visit, at the interest he's spontaneously taken in his parents' dancing life. Then the Grasso brain kicks in. "What's wrong?" he asks. Quickly he pulls him out of his mother's line of sight. "What are you doing here? Is everything OK?"

"No, Dad," Frankie says, even as he's annoyed that his father assumes the worst. Then suddenly his mother's there, too, between them, her hand on his back, her panicked face searching theirs for an answer. "You here, Frankie? O *Dio*!" Her eyes well up. "What happened? Something bad, I can feel it. Tell me!"

A group of their friends—fifteen of them at least, a crowd of scared faces—walks with them up the pink stairs and out into the parking lot. Arlene helps his mother into the backseat of the car and gives Frankie a kiss on the cheek when she's settled in. "You kids should come more often," she says inanely as Frankie takes the wheel.

Maddalena lies in the backseat, praying in short mumbling bursts and screaming Prima's and Patrick's names. His father is beside Frankie in the passenger seat, his face turned toward the window.

"I want to leave this world," his mother screams.

"No, you don't," says Frankie, though he should just let her say what she has to say. "They're both going to be fine. I know it. I promise."

"I WANT TO LEAVE THIS WORLD," his mother screams again.

Frankie starts to cry. The headlights coming at him from the other side of the highway go blurry. "Don't say that, Mom," he says. He grips the wheel. "Please. For me."

"Don't pay attention," says his father, his face still turned away. His hand on his lap is clenching and unclenching a fist.

They've lived through a war. The Germans came through their village in tanks. They spent the best years of their lives in kitchens and factories. Dancing or no dancing, their bones are old, their joints stiff, their minds going soft. They don't deserve another tragedy. All Frankie's life, they said, "Let us do the worrying, let us suffer, so you don't have to."

They find Tom and Steve and Steve's wife and Tom's parents in the waiting area of the emergency room. The twins, looking crazed and angry, rush in soon after, with some girl who's attached herself to Zach and doesn't stop rubbing his shoulders for one second.

Maddalena goes right for Tom, and the two of them stand there holding each other, her head against his chest. After a few minutes, a nurse comes in and offers to take the entire family to a room where they can wait in private.

Maddalena rushes the nurse. "They're going to be OK?" she wails. "Tell us!"

"I'm sorry, ma'am," she says. "Dr. Morrison will be out real soon, I promise."

"*Disgraziata!*" she says. "They never tell you anything! I'm her mother!"

"It's not her job, Mom," Frankie says. "We have to wait for the doctor."

"*Disgraziata!*" she yells again as the nurse leads them through the swinging doors. Antonio walks beside her but doesn't try to settle her.

"Did you see her badge?" Steve says to Frankie. "Her last name is Patrick. That's a good sign. I believe in signs."

"We all do," Frankie says.

9 *Close the Light*

MADDALENA WALKS AROUND the outside of her house, pulling weeds, inspecting the windows that need washing now that June is here. In June she washes all the windows, inside and out; in July she launders all the drapes; at the end of August she goes through the summer clothes they didn't wear and donates them to the church. When they were young girls, Carolina used to tell Maddalena that she was special, meant for a big life. Is this what she meant? Is this a big life? Now that she's near the end of it, can she finally say, No, Carolina, you were wrong?

If Maddalena had stayed in the village, chosen Vito Leone over Antonio Grasso, she'd have had all she has here: a house and children, a car to drive to a dance studio, a family business of some kind, and flower beds to keep up. Vito would have failed at his businesses just as Antonio failed at his in the early years. What would have been the difference between that life and this one? She's been a seamstress, a wife, a mother, and an old woman terrified of the years ahead—no more special than any of her sisters, after all, just thousands of miles away and six hours behind.

The mongoloid next door, a boy born the same year as Tony, is now a middle-aged man. He sits on his back porch with a dog in his lap and talks to his mother through the open kitchen window. Maddalena waves hello to him as she walks along the fence that separates their houses. She used to feel sorry for him, before Tony, but then over the years she came to think him better off never having had brothers or sisters or a wife or children to die on him, no romantic regrets, no rides down the hill on a bicycle in the arms of the girl who loved and left him. The Italian way is to think that the more people you love, the more insurance you have, but Maddalena doesn't believe in the Italian way anymore.

Inside the house, the floors are waxed and shiny, the drapes washed, and the sheers resteamed. There's no dust in the air or on the furniture. The sink is empty of dishes. She's already trimmed the dead leaves from the plants, made the beds, and checked the hamper. It's too late in the day to start on the windows, and with the gnocchi and pork chops and roasted apples left over from two nights ago, there's no reason to make dinner. Antonio won't be back until five o'clock at least. Maddalena opens the refrigerator—not a crumb or a smear on the bright white plastic. She is too good at her job. Lately she's been working faster and hurrying home from church instead of staying to talk to Father Larson, just in case she gets one of her spells. When the spells come, she'll take to her bed for an hour or two, waiting for her head to clear. If they don't come, she can finish her day's work, and there is no better feeling.

Today, all week really, she's been lucky. She knows who and where she is. She's strong. Yesterday afternoon, she pushed Prima's wheelchair for five minutes in the Brandywine Creek Park, until they got to the big hill, and then Tom took over. The weather was perfect, and instead of talking about that, about how good it was to be alive on a sunny day in June, they were talking about the end of the world that was supposed to come last New Year's Eve when something happened to the computers. Maddalena stopped paying attention because they talked too fast and used words she didn't recognize, but also because they were wrong. The world will never end. The world will keep going with or without them.

"Stop with this nonsense," Maddalena interrupted. "Talk about Patrick. Tell me how good he's doing."

"He's back to normal, Ma," Prima said. "You saw him at the house, remember? You remember being at the house this morning, and having breakfast, and Tom driving us here?"

"Of course I remember," Maddalena said. "He showed me how to swing a golf club."

"OK, good."

At the park, Maddalena looked out over the green hills, down to the lake, where ducks were moving slow over the water, then up to the big stone mansion, where the road split. There were two horses in the yard of the mansion. She pointed them out to Prima, but then Prima snapped at her, saying that she'd pointed them out to

Maddalena just five minutes ago. She snaps at Maddalena a lot these days, ever since the accident. She'll have trouble with her legs for the rest of her life, the doctors told her. It's Maddalena's job to keep her from giving up. It was her idea to come to the park in the first place. She saw the weather and said to Prima, "You have to get out."

A mother is never at peace. It's the price she pays, and it's worth it, but sometimes Maddalena wishes she could get a break. The worrying makes her so tired. In the days before Prima was born, she used to take five minutes of every day to sit on Mamma Nunzia's porch swing. Five minutes of peace, music on the radio, neighbors stopping to say hello. She hasn't done anything like that since becoming a mother, and then a grandmother. Her spells are no break. When Maddalena comes back from them and doesn't remember where she was or for how long, it's not peace she feels but fire spreading over her skin. How much longer will it be, she wonders (no one will tell her—no one tells her anything—and she can't read enough words to find out for herself), until the spells take over, until she's lost completely to her children and to Antonio, unable to protect and pray for them, unable even to say, "I love you," or "I miss you," or "I have a story for you."

"Take her to a nice dinner tonight," Maddalena said to Tom. "Hotel du Pont. I'll pay the check."

"Like we really need you to buy us dinner," snapped Prima.

The path took them into the woods. Birds flew up all around them, escaping into the blue sky. It was dark and cool, a good place to talk honest, like church, like the living room of Mamma Nunzia's house in the middle of the afternoon, when the men were away. She had things to say to Prima. She wanted to tell her that what happened to her and Patrick wasn't a tragedy, that she'd gotten off easy. Then Prima decided they should turn around, something about the woods being dangerous, kids taking drugs and punks waiting to steal your purse and some other dirty nonsense she read about in the paper. So they walked back toward the parking lot.

"This is good practice for us," Maddalena said.

"Practice for what?"

"For when we go to Italy. There are a lot of hills in the village."

Prima sighed. "We're not going, Ma. Remember? That's all over now. We were supposed to go, but then I had an accident—"

"I know all that," Maddalena said, and this time she was the one doing the snapping. "I'm talking about next summer. When we try again."

"You're sure singing a different tune," Tom said.

"People change," Maddalena said.

Except she hasn't. She was trying to help Prima, to give her something to look forward to, to let her think she'd been right about the trip all along.

"I'm through pleasing everybody," said Prima. "I'll tell you that much."

Maddalena wasn't sure what she meant or how it connected to what they'd been talking about, so she let it go. The parking lot was filling up—people with dogs on leashes, a van with Catholic-school students. Tom had one hand on Prima's shoulder as he pushed the wheelchair with the other. "We'll go somewhere just the two of us," he said to her, as if Maddalena couldn't hear them. "Yes, we should. We will," Prima responded. Maddalena wanted to tell them, That's what you should have done from the start.

The perfect weather continues today, and so Maddalena sits for a while on the back porch, hands folded in her lap, admiring the violets and the wrought iron patio set she's had for thirty years. She takes deep breaths and says a short prayer for Prima and Patrick, and then Arlene, and then she feels guilty and ends up saying prayers for everyone she knows, one by one, the same way she did last night and will do again tonight.

They will go to Italy after all, Prima and Tom, on a second honeymoon. Just the two of them. A romance. She imagines Prima stepping out of her wheelchair and walking hand in hand with her husband through Piazza Navona, stopping for coffee and pastries, kissing in the spray of the fountains. They should skip Venice, with its dark alleys and tourists and dirty pigeons, and spend the extra days in Lake Como or Portofino. They'll never make it to Santa Cecilia. They'll quit halfway up the mountain, on those little roads with no fence between the car and the cliffs; they'll get dizzy and lose their nerve. They won't believe people live so high up, in the middle of the clouds.

Funny how Prima's told everyone Santa Cecilia will be a resort, like the Poconos. She's shown Maddalena the brochures: stone buildings with terraces on the roofs, boutiques with gold clocks in the windows, air-conditioned bedrooms. Good luck! Prima should know that Italy is a country of exaggerators, the villagers worst of all. Maddalena would like to see her face when she drives into Santa Cecilia and finds only one run-down fabric shop, one café, one man playing his accordion in the street, one angry old woman renting out rooms with cracks in the walls; when the villagers tell her, You like, yes? Is charming, no? and she has to agree or hurt their feelings; when she brings Tom and the boys and Frankie into the Piccinelli store and tells the old man sweeping the floor, Zio Claudio! We are your family . . .

Here, alone on the porch, is where it finally hits her, what fate's decided. She will not go back after all. She will never go back. Never again will she see Claudio, the store, the olive grove, the gorge, Carolina. She will take them all to her grave. She always expected she would, but now that it's certain, more certain than ever, she feels no relief or contentment or satisfaction in having won, after all, this battle with her family. After her first and only victory, she feels, suddenly, shaken.

This is why it's dangerous having nothing to do. Your mind takes over, plays tricks.

She goes inside and locks the door behind her. Turns down the air conditioner. The grandfather clock chimes four times. It's ten o'clock in Santa Cecilia, still early enough. In the top drawer of the lowboy she finds the wrinkled slips of paper with Claudio's and Carolina's phone numbers. She sits in Antonio's chair at the kitchen table, picks up the phone, starts to dial the numbers, then hangs up. Then again. Again. If she reaches them, what will she say? How will she make up for the years in between? Should she try? People don't understand. They say she's been cold and cruel. Words that don't sound like her at all.

"Heartless," Frankie had the nerve to call her once, back in the fall when they were fighting all the time about the trip. Imagine! They'd been talking about homeless people. He was feeling sorry for the little kids, growing up on the streets hungry, no fathers, stuck in schools with no books or paper or pencils. Maddalena had said she thought those children are better off, like the mongoloid. They have little to lose; their lives can only go up.

"Better off?" Frankie said. "You're kidding me."

She told him it is much worse to have everything—a family who loves you, plenty of money, food on the table—and then lose it. You never recover. You try to get back to a place that's not there anymore, and nothing, no matter how beautiful, can compare.

"Most of those kids don't live long enough for comparisons," said Frankie.

That is a shame, Maddalena agreed, but there has to be a reason for it. God doesn't do anything by accident.

"There's an expression," he said. " 'Better to have loved and lost, than never to have loved at all.' I'm guessing you don't believe in that. What it means is—"

She knew that expression, she said. Every time she hears it, she wants to scream. Americans are too much in love with love. Look at the soap operas. The women and men both, they want a love affair like they want new clothes, and then as soon as they wear the clothes, they're tired of them. Italians are different. More balanced. When we romance, we do it with our hearts, but we love our husbands and wives with our brains; our children and our parents we love with our souls. You have to keep them all separate, she told Frankie, or you get in trouble, mixing one kind of love up with another. Americans are in this kind of trouble all the time. Look at the talk shows: that man who shot his family so he could run off with the stewardess, that mother who stole her daughter's teenage boyfriend—it was all the same problem with an easy solution.

"That's compartmentalization," Frankie said. He was always using that word. She still doesn't know what it means.

Maybe she's doing it now, as the phone rings in the room on the other side of the ocean, and Claudio's confused voice calls out, "*Pronto? Chi è? Pronto! Pronto!*" Maddalena listens, drinks in her brother's voice, then places the phone back on the receiver with a gentle click. Good-bye, good-bye.

Moments later, before the regret takes her nerve away, she dials the other number and hears, after many rings, the voice of Vito Leone. It's been fifty years, but there's no mistaking it. It is as clear and near-sounding as Frankie's from Boston. She closes her eyes and feels Vito's breath on her cheek. His hand on her hip guides her to the back room of her father's store.

He calls out the same words Claudio used — "Hello? Hello!" — and the same question — "Who are you?" — but she can't answer.

She listens for more voices in the background. Is Carolina there? Does she remember her? In a few seconds, Vito will hang up and be lost to her again. What a hypocrite I am, Maddalena thinks. What an American. I should have loved him with my heart only, from the beginning, but somehow along the way I let him slip into my soul.

"Vito," she says.

"*Sì.* Vito Leone. *Chi parla?*"

"*Mi dispiace,*" she says. I'm sorry.

"*Ma chi parla?*" he repeats. But who's speaking? His voice is quiet, just above a whisper. She imagines him on the edge of his bed, in his slippers and shirtsleeves. Is Carolina asleep beside him? She has no right to disturb them, she should leave them in peace, but still she holds the phone against her ear.

"*Mi dispiace,*" she repeats. It's not a lie. She is sorry for never writing to them, for leaving them in the first place, for never knowing the people they went on to be. What she would have given, all these years without her beautiful Tony, to find a number in a drawer and use it to call him, just once, to hear the voice of the man he'd have become, to tell him, I miss you, to ask him, Why did you give up on us? What could we have done to save you? Everything is the answer. She'd have done everything. And to think that she'd had Vito and Carolina and Mamma and all the others at the other end of the line most of her life and never reached out for them—she recognizes this now as her deepest sin. Antonio, Frankie, Prima—they recognized it all along. They kept trying to tell her, but she'd convinced herself otherwise. Heartlessly. Cruelly. Those words that suddenly sound like her.

She stays quiet as long as she can. Doesn't Vito recognize her voice? Has it changed so much? She listens to him ask his questions—Who are you? Who are you?—until he gives up, and the line goes dead.

ONE MORNING, ANTONIO is dressing for the Al Di Là when Maddalena comes home early from church. She sits on the edge of their bed, her hands in her lap, watching him put on the polo shirt and pants she laid out for him the night before. She's got a dark look on her face, and Antonio thinks maybe the priest scared her again with his talk of hell. Her face is dark a lot lately, like she's pulled a veil over it, but then, sometimes in the same minute, she'll lift up the veil and her face will fill with light again.

"*A cosa pensi, tesoro?*" he asks her. What's on your mind, my treasure? They speak mostly in Italian these days. The old words, he's noticed, come easier.

"I'm sorry we're not going to Santa Cecilia," she says. "You wanted to go, and now we're not going, and it's my fault."

He kneels beside her, his belt half looped around his waist, in just his socks. "It's not your fault," he says. "You don't remember this, but Prima, she had an accident—"

"I know about the accident!" Maddalena says. "It's my fault, too. She had too much on her mind. She was worried about me. She wasn't paying attention."

"Maddalena, no."

She shakes her head. "I need to tell you: we won't go next summer, either. I heard them talking. They're going by themselves, as soon as Prima can walk. A second honeymoon. I ruined our chance, and I'm sorry."

"Please don't worry," says Antonio. "You get yourself worked up for nothing. You think I can't change Prima and Tom's mind about some second honeymoon? Listen: I talked to Claudio yesterday. He sounds so happy. Like a teenager. He says Carolina's doing much better. She's keeping up her garden. When she heard you were coming, she started making you a *crostata* with figs. Her daughter's been asking her every day, 'How long before we meet our famous American *zia* Maddalena?'"

"Prima and Tom are going alone," Maddalena repeats. "That's the only trip anybody's taking. As soon as she's out of the wheelchair. They won't want anyone else around, not even the boys, and especially not me, not anymore. I'm not strong enough. And they should have their romance."

Antonio doesn't tell her what Claudio really said: that he'll never forgive Maddalena if she doesn't come to see him one last time in Santa Cecilia, if she doesn't make peace with her sister before she dies. It's a matter of months for Carolina, not years, according to Claudio. There's no garden. No *crostata* with figs. Claudio, too, eighty-eight this spring, weakened by emphysema, wonders if he will see Christmas.

Antonio's lies, which he will keep telling as long as he can, are for Maddalena's own good. So no matter what Prima and Tom want from a second honeymoon, no matter what new excuse Maddalena will come up with not to go, he will find a way to get her on a plane with him before long. This summer. Next week, if it comes to that. He doesn't know how this will happen, but he has to imagine it's possible.

"You can go with them, just you," Maddalena says, and her face lightens. "Prima won't mind. She loves to have you around. They can drop you off in the village so they can have a few days in Portofino for the romance. I'll be OK here. Frankie will stay with me. I think you should go, Antonio. It would make me happy to see you go back."

"Maybe I will," he says, bluffing, thinking, I'll never leave you alone, thinking, Before you know it, you and I will be walking together up the steps of the church of Santa Cecilia. We'll drink a toast on your father's terrace, where I asked your father for your hand. We'll lean over the railing and wave to the customers at the Al Di Là across the street. I'll play cards with Claudio late into the night, and you'll sit next to me with your hand on my knee. You won't deny me that, will you?

"Good," she says. "It's about time somebody had some common sense."

Later, as he leaves for the restaurant, she reminds him: "Talk to Prima. Tell her we have a new plan." She's in the living room, spraying Pledge on tables that are already shiny.

"If you promise to rest," he says, "I promise I'll talk to Prima."

DiSilvio comes to the Al Di Là for lunch. Ryan is there, serving them and managing the rush. Antonio's been watching Ryan since he started two weeks ago, and he was right: the boy is a natural. The customers love him. The kitchen guys listen to him. He earned their respect right away. Just yesterday, when some rude big-shot business-guy customer with gold rings complained that his meatball sand-wich was cold and that his floozy of a girlfriend's salad had too much dressing, and called the restaurant an "overpriced dump," Ryan re-placed both dishes right away with a smile and threw in two glasses of (bottom-shelf) wine, and nobody got agitated. Gilberto would have told the big-shot guy to warm up the meatballs between his floozy's legs; Maurizio would have given him a free dinner and a hand job. But Ryan has a way of calming people down without too many freebies; he makes them feel right, even when they're wrong. He speaks to the dishwashers in the Spanish he learned in college, and *un miracolo,* the dishes come out cleaner. He stays past midnight to get the books right and still has time for fun with the girl waiting for him at the bar. Al-ready he knows the loyal customers by name and walks them to the sidewalk at the end of their meals.

For two weeks, Antonio has watched his grandson like a girl

watches a boy serenading her. It brings him back to the early years
with Mario, and more than that, it gives him hope, for the first time
since his brother passed, that the Al Di Là will end up in good hands.
It's not too soon to tell, no matter what his lawyer might say. The
signs are always there.

Antonio says as much to DiSilvio, who for thirty years has helped
keep him and his books legal. Now on a Monday afternoon in the
middle of June, Antonio is finally redoing his papers. The meeting is
eight months overdue.

It takes Ryan to show Antonio what he should have seen all along:
that Frankie will never give up on his degrees and fall in love with the
Al Di Là the way Tony did. Only now that Ryan is a possibility can
Antonio fully remember how Frankie suffered through his summers
as a waiter, how nervous and impatient and clumsy and resentful he
was.

DiSilvio asks, "You don't worry this is just a passing phase for your
grandson? Two weeks is nothing to judge, especially at his age."

Antonio shakes his head. He knows people. He listens. It's maybe
the only joy of being old: you're allowed to sit on the couch and
rest your eyes during the family parties, the quiet hours of the Al
Di Là afternoon, take in all the gossip, the complaints, the secrets.
He's learned a lot this way, eyes closed, arms folded, mouth hanging open so people think he's asleep. But he doesn't sleep; he studies.
Antonio's been studying each of his grandsons since they stopped being kids, but it wasn't until the twins' birthday party in October that
they came clear to him. The twins and Patrick have too strong a wild

streak, but Ryan, who showed up to surprise them, who had tears in his eyes when he hugged his brothers even though he'd seen them just a few weeks before, is a man of the family.

DiSilvio is skeptical. But Maddalena, if Antonio discussed such things with her, would agree that Ryan is the Al Di Là's best chance. Lying beside her in bed at night, after the soap opera is over and she's hung up with Frankie, he tells her a lot more than he used to, but he still won't discuss what will come after them. His talking helps to settle her mind, she says, it's what she's wanted for many years, to hear what he's learned from his day. So he tells her that Ryan is the strongest of the four, that Patrick drinks too much, that Matt's not as smart as Zach, but Zach's not as good at sports. He tells her that one of the line cooks is cheating on his wife with a girl who works at the Rite Aid next door. He tells her that Frankie won't stay in Boston forever, that, like Ryan, he won't last long so far away from them; that Tom's got a temper Prima tries to hide from them; that Prima is lonely. Most of these, Maddalena claims to know already. Only when he tries to tell her things about herself—that she's a better dancer now than when they first met, that Arlene is jealous whenever the teacher picks her to demonstrate, that she wants nothing more than to make peace with Carolina and Vito—will she say, "Close the light," and turn her face away.

There are some things Antonio won't say. They wake him long after Maddalena's finally fallen asleep, and won't let him rest, and take him downstairs and outside to the yard, where he walks under the neighbors' dark windows. But he's not safe here, or anywhere. What follows him is the certainty that he will outlive her, the beautiful baby girl he first saw asleep on the countertop of her father's store, the young woman he met again years later, his love of fifty-four years. That her end will come soon, and hard. That he'll not last long without her, alone in their house of dreams. That there's more. That Tony, the son they loved more than anything in the world, much more than they loved each other, was cursed, and fought a war of his own, and lost. To know all this is a heartbreak Antonio can't bear. It comes to mind in the night and when DiSilvio forces him to open his eyes to the future.

"The way you have it now," DiSilvio reminds him, wiping the crumbs from his second dessert off the documents between them, "your wife inherits one hundred percent of your assets, should you precede her in death. After she passes, all assets, including the house, are to be divided equally among your two children, minus the sum you've set aside to be distributed among your grandsons, *and* minus the sum you have put in trust for Ryan Buckley should he fulfill your wish to inherit the Al Di Là and all its assets and liabilities outright."

"Yes," says Antonio. "And if he doesn't want it, you sell it to the highest bidder and give the profits to the kids, fifty-fifty."

"You don't want to include an option for another grandchild—or Prima or Francesco—to take it on?"

Again Antonio shakes his head. "It took me twenty-five years to buy that land and make that business what it is. If they don't want it now, they'll never want it. After I'm gone, they might think they should hold on to it, for—"

"For sentimental reasons," interrupts DiSilvio.

"That's right, sentimental, because maybe they miss me, but then soon enough they stop missing me, and they're left with this business they don't want and don't understand, and they start to hate it, and they fight with each other, and the whole thing's a mess. I'd rather a stranger buy it and tear it down, and the kids and grandkids get the money, than for any Grasso to hate it. Mario and I built this place from love."

Heavy wood pedestal tables line the dining room, upside-down glasses twinkle above the marble bar, photos of mayors and senators line the front hallway. The dessert fridge hums, filled with home-made zuppe inglese and tonight's special, *palle di neve.* "Ciao, Ciao Bambina" plays on the stereo. Antonio could run up and down kissing the walls and the floor and every woman and man who steps through the door. If only he could hold this room as it is today, keep it from passing into the next stage, whatever that stage would be—but that's more sentimental feeling.

"In a few days, then," says DiSilvio, "I'll come back with the papers ready to sign."

Mario stands on a chair in the corner, opening night 1955, tapping his wineglass to get the room's attention. Maddalena's at the front door, at the five-year anniversary party, to welcome the customers, take their coats, show them to the bar. Tony's at her feet, his arms around her knees, and then, as she turns to kiss one of the guests, he's grown, he's carrying a tray of dishes to the kitchen. Prima's at the far booth taking an order, her hair long to her shoulders—when did she cut it? These rooms have held them all—even Frankie, over at the chalkboard, writing down the specials when he should be memoriz-ing them. They're all still here.

"You'll talk this over with your family in the meantime?" DiSilvio asks. "Antonio?"

"Of course," Antonio says. He shakes his old friend's hand. He has no intention of discussing this conversation with anyone, and DiSilvio must know this, too. It's not what their fathers would have done.

FORSAKEN, WANDERING. SUCH is Frankie's life, the life of the scholar, in summer in a college town. The libraries close at dusk and open at noon, equipped with a skeleton crew of international students who can't help Frankie locate the men's room, let alone the obscure journal that just might include the missing piece of his jigsaw-puzzle dissertation, the piece that will convince his new adviser of the brilliance that is the Big Idea. For weeks, Frankie's traversed alone the stark, sunbaked terrain of Boston's many educational institutions, his knapsack of provisions (Fanon, Freud, Foucault) strapped to his back, searching for that missing piece among the various archives and special collections with which Boston is famously lousy. He avoids BC, lonesome at any season, unbearable with Kelly Anne in Jersey. Most days he ends up back on his home turf, beleaguered, grouchy, squeezing what blood he can from the familiar stones.

The view from Frankie's West Hall office is of inner-city kids on the quad, shrieking in their cornrows and tennis camp T-shirts, gobbling up boxed lunches. Last week he watched a garden club tour the flower beds and peel bark from the ancient elm behind the admissions building. It's distressing how the college whores itself out to such groups. He knows of at least one professor forced to hold his seminar in his apartment because the university rented all leftover classrooms to a national conference of phlebotomists. If the trustees treat the place like a low-rent convention center, should it be a wonder the students and faculty don't aspire to excellence? There is a direct correlation, in Frankie's unsolicited opinion. He doubts Harvard would allow thousands of needle-packing phlebotomists to trample its sacred ground.

Today, restless, Frankie wanders up and down the corridors of West Hall reading outdated flyers, inanely checking his mailbox every half hour, chitchatting with one of the work-study kids about the creatures thriving in the communal fridge, and generally wasting time. In an hour he'll head home for lunch and his soap. There's that, at least, to look forward to.

The mailboxes have been newly updated for the incoming fall master's candidates. Gone are the slots for the two (two!) students who managed to finish and defend this academic year: old Maud Benson and, of course, Annalise Theroux. Frankie harbors no ill will toward Maud, who began her dissertation in the late sixties, survived two forms of cancer in the seventies, climbed Mt. Kilimanjaro in the eighties, and spent the nineties revising. Maud's ideas are long irrelevant, and she'll never find a job in the current market, but good for her for closing the loop. Not so Annalise. Much ill will remains harbored, fellow loser or not. Her work is unfailingly au courant, and rumor has it she'll soon jump full steam onto the tenure track at Amherst.

As for Chris Curran, he's used his windfall to spend six weeks in England, where, he assured Frankie the last time he raided his stash, the landscape will serve as his muse.

Frankie's day will come. It's just a matter of time. Patience is required, along with thoughtful synthesis of his ever-multiplying dissertation chapters, ruthless cutting, and the connection of seem-ingly randomized dots. His new thesis adviser, Professor Avery Gadkari, himself a biracial product of postcolonial India (a human emblem of the document's most salient arguments! Why did he not choose him from the start?) has been clear about the above require-ments, much clearer than Professor Rhonda Birch, herself a tangent, a digression, a symptom of the dissertation's fatal flaw: its ambitious, at times radiant, but ultimately incoherent *sprawl.*

When Frankie told Gadkari he just needed one more text to bring the New Idea together before he could start pruning, Gadkari eyed him skeptically. It was the end of the term, and no doubt he'd hoped to wash his hands of Frankie before summer, given how far along the boy was and how "enthusiastically" Dr. Birch had recommended him. "Addition by subtraction," Gadkari told him. "Trust me. The last thing this thesis needs is another text."

Gadkari, like most of the professors, rarely appears in West Hall in the summer. Mostly it's Frankie and work-study college kids and the department secretary, barricaded in her air-conditioned room at the top of the stairwell. Still, when he passes the professor's office, he stops for a few moments to listen for shuffling or the tapping of keys.

Frankie's mailbox, when he checks it for the last time before lunch, contains, to his astonishment, a single sheet of department letterhead. He looks quickly around. Birch's door has been shut all morning, he's sure of it. What would she be doing here, anyway? Last he'd heard, she'd planned to spend the summer on Martha's Vineyard, where Amos had built her a house; but that was back in April, when they'd run into each other in the hallway and were forced to speak. The note is unmistakably Birch's: a smiley face and, beside it, a question mark. Frankie stares at it and then, because he is a weak man and has little, if not nothing, not even his pride, to lose, now that she's initiated the backslide, crosses out the question mark, writes "why not" in lowercase letters (uppercase would be too conciliatory), slips it under her door, and waits a few moments for her shadow to pass across the slit. It does.

Halfway down College Ave, just before Vinny's Pizza, he senses her. When he turns, she is there, a block and a half behind, keeping discreet pace. After the Oak Room snub, she'd sent him a maddening e-mail apology at 1 a.m., one that, if he read it correctly, blamed Frankie—yes, Frankie—for getting himself stood up, for not recognizing her idea as terribly unwise, un-Birch-like, and unlikely to transpire. If he truly understood her, the e-mail had implied, he wouldn't have shown up, either. He didn't write back.

Rather than acknowledge him now on the street, Birch checks her watch. He speeds up. As he turns the corner, his hand's in his right pocket to adjust his boxers, to maintain discretion.

His room's a wreck. Two weeks ago, he'd printed out all 478 pages of his dissertation—200 or so too many—and arranged them in piles on the dresser, desk, bed, and floor. Among the stacks of paper: dirty and half-dirty clothes, coffee mugs, plates crusted with peanut butter, shoes, books, mix tapes. Earlier this summer, at one of their rare house meetings, Anita had asked him to be "more mindful" of the common areas now that her "friend" Whitney was visiting 25 Stowe on a regular basis. Now all his stuff has moved into his bedroom.

The front door slams, and he stands, arms crossed, at the top of the stairs to greet her. "So, look who actually showed up."

"Let's not talk," she says. "Not yet, OK? We'll ruin it."

"Fine," he says, because what other response can a man have—even a man of letters, even a man scorned—to her too-tight "Rosie the Riveter" T-shirt, jean shorts rolled up at the thigh, tanned legs, and red toenails, her body moving closer, removing her sunglasses, crooking her arm around his shoulder? They kiss right there in the dining room in full view of the neighbors, a first, until he pulls her into his room and guides her around the trash to his futon. Her eyes are closed. She could be kissing anyone, he thinks, but he doesn't mind, not in this moment, at least. He's missed their electricity. They fall onto the mattress, half on, half off the Ngugi chapter he'd needed her opinion on nine months ago. Below her navel is a new tattoo, a goddess—Athena?—whose face he kisses. He unsnaps the top button of her shorts, scoots her toward the window. Her ass smashes the pages. He goes for the second button, but she stops his hand.

"I shouldn't be here," she says, her eyes finally open.

"No shit," he says. "That just occurred to you? If you leave now, I swear—"

She scoots away from him, lowers her head. "I'm a mess, Frankie. The human equivalent of this filthy room."

"Embrace the filth." He tries again for the button.

"I want you to tell me something," she says.

"Oh God," he says. "I thought we weren't ruining it."

She straightens her back, rolls her eyes.

"Look," Frankie says. "I'm still pissed off. You've got all this guilt. I've got all this rage. Let's channel it." He smiles. "Then I'll tell you what you want me to tell you."

"I'm serious."

He sits back on his ankles, still straddling her. They're barefoot but otherwise fully clothed. "Fine, Rhonda. What do you want?"

"I want to know how I'm seen."

"How you're *seen*? Which means . . . ?"

She turns her head toward the TV. "This morning, when I was putting my T-shirt on and fixing my hair and deciding if I could get away with these girly sandals, I thought, for the millionth time, It's a costume, I'm playing a part. That's no big shocker, of course; we both know everyone performs their genders, blah blah blah. Then it occurred to me—again, not the first time—how transparent the part is, how obvious I am, and that people see me as this—" She stops, holds out her hands. "But I couldn't fill in the blank. I thought, Rebel? No. Agitator? Maybe. Each word felt so hollow. Because the part I see myself playing, Frankie, is truly subversive and uncompromising and stubborn and exacting, not just with my students, with everybody. But what if people really see me as a sappy old throwback, like Maud Benson, or a small-minded narcissist, like Lexus? What if this role I try so hard to cultivate, and reinforce in my work and my classes and my home life, such as it is—what if nobody's buying it? Because we never get called on our bullshit, not in a serious way at least, not without the person apologizing afterward and saying, You know I didn't mean that, and then we forget or dismiss it, even though it was real."

"Well—" Frankie says, but she keeps talking.

"So I thought, Shouldn't I know for sure how people see me, so I can change or adjust or something? And I realized—this was the traumatic part—I had no one I could trust to tell me the truth. Nobody without a stake in impressing me or telling me what I wanted to hear. Then today I saw you in the department—you were in the doorway of the lounge with one of those yappy work-study kids—and I thought, I can trust Frankie, I always trusted Frankie. Frankie will tell me the truth so I can stop making a fool of myself."

She's not backsliding, he thinks; it's punishment she's after. He's not quite ready to give her what she wants. Plus, he's never been able to lie to her.

"You want honesty?"

"Yes."

"The problem is," he says, "I see you exactly the way you say you want to be seen. Subversive, exacting, brilliant, all that. That's how I describe you to—well, I can't talk about you with anyone, but that's how I *would* describe you if I could."

"That's just you. What about everybody else? Your classmates, and Lexus, and Gadkari?" Out of nowhere she's almost crying.

"I'd add one word to your self-description," he says. "Selfish. Un-generous. OK, two words. They shouldn't surprise you. But those aren't exactly negatives, or inconsistent, in our field."

"What about everybody else, Frankie?"

"Jesus, why do you care so much all of a sudden?"

"Just tell me."

He thinks for a moment. He has her on the hook. This can go one way or the other. "Everybody else, too, then, as far as I know," he says, which is true enough. "You're not a fraud, Rhonda. I mean, everyone's a fraud, but you're less of a fraud than most." She turns to look at him. "You did screw me over, though. Twice. You even broke my heart a

little. Not just when you stood me up. Before then, a bunch of times."
He leans back, props himself up on his palms. "But hey, you could say
that's my own fault. Since I know how selfish and ungenerous you are,
I should have seen it coming."

"Now you're being a prick."

"Isn't that what you wanted? You said so yourself."

"Not for you to act like a child."

"I am a child."

"You're making fun of me. But you're better than that. It's not
like you." She tries to slide out from under him, but his legs have
her pinned.

"Tell me what *I'm* like, then," he says.

"This isn't about you."

"Come on," he says. "I can take it. Besides, we'll never see each
other again. Today is the last day you'll be in my bed."

"You sound like your soap opera."

"*This* is the soap opera."

"Fine," she says. "Fifty words or less? Frankie Grasso is a funda-
mentally decent, deceptively sentimental, overly deferential scared
little Catholic boy who misses his mommy."

"No argument there."

"So this is the last time?" she asks.

"Sure," he says. "So say what you're gonna say."

His prediction: In a few minutes, after they're done punishing
each other, and she stops crying, and his legs release their grip, she'll
go for his fly, and their clothes will come off, and they'll fuck two or

three times for old time's sake, until all the poison's out. By the end of it, their unprecedented candor will have made them indifferent to each other and snuffed whatever electricity remained. Already her need for validation, her lack of self-awareness, has diminished her in his eyes. He longs for the swaggering Birch, the one who, not long before, behind her dark sunglasses, said, No talking, don't ruin it.

"OK," she says. "Let me add this, then. You see yourself as a serious scholar, that's the part you're playing, that's how you think people see you, but really—and Gadkari would tell you this, too, if he had any balls—you're a dilettante. That missing piece you keep looking for in your dissertation doesn't exist. There's not a text or a lens in the world that can make these pages cohere." She picks up one of the Ngugi pages that has fallen onto the floor. "The more parentheses you jam into your words, Frankie, the less meaning they have, not more. You have to decide on the meaning *you* want."

There is no exhausted relief. No indifference. There's only him telling her that she has misread his work, she's always misread it, that even when she used to praise it she was misreading it, that she's got blind spots and a lack of vision and, worse, a mean, ungenerous little heart. There's her trying to make light of it all, to say that this, too—the riling up—is part of the act, is why she came, is what she's missed.

"I feel better now," she says, "now that it's all out in the open."

She goes for his fly—he was right about that—but he pushes her hand away. His body won't cooperate anyhow. He stumbles out of bed and kicks his way to the front porch. He leans over the railing, the sun on his face, waiting for her to come up behind him, lean her body alongside his, say, I didn't really mean it, Frankie. He expects and deserves that, at the very least, even if it's a lie.

Instead he hears footsteps on the stairs. Moments later, he watches her walk down Stowe toward the college. It's like she's walking in slow motion. At any moment, he expects her to turn around, take it all back. What a fool. She stops at the intersection, turns, and gives a little noncommittal wave, like a princess in a motorcade. Then she walks on. Good-bye, I don't love you, good-bye.

That night, at 11:01, he gives his mother some news. He's coming home for a little while, a month, maybe until Labor Day, who knows? He'd mentally blocked out August for the Italy trip, anyway, a long time ago, and now that the trip's not going to happen, he might as well spend the time with her. Prima could use his help driving her places and dealing with her house; he could spend some time with Ryan at the Al Di Là. (What he doesn't tell her: that Wilmington's two hours from Newark, New Jersey, where a girl he likes is spending the summer.) Not that he'll be socializing, he says. He'll be sequestered in his old bedroom, where he'll put the "finishing touches" on his dissertation — "I'm so close, Ma. I can feel it. Wait till you see how many pages" — and if she doesn't mind, if she's feeling up to it, could she do his laundry and keep up his room a little?

"Are you kidding?" she says. "You, home? For the whole summer? Did you hear that, Antonio?"

His father picks up the extension. "Hear what?"

"Francesco's coming home."

"I said the summer *at most*," Frankie says. "I don't want you to get your hopes up."

"You don't know what you do for me right now," she says to Frankie. "You answer my prayers."

"He wants a job," says his father. To Frankie: "I told you, one day you'll get tired of living on prestige."

"I'm so happy," says his mother.

It doesn't take him long to pack his dirty and half-dirty clothes into his suitcase, stuff his knapsack with books and a toothbrush, and write a brief note to Anita. First thing in the morning, he buys a round-trip ticket on Amtrak, using his own credit card. This decision belongs to him, not his parents. He keeps the return date open. By the end of July, he'll be back in Boston; if not, then Labor Day at the very latest, in time for the fall term and his yawning English 101 kids with their two-dollar pens. Until then, it will be him and his pages and his old room with air conditioning and the sailboat wallpaper and a box of Dixon Ticonderoga pencils and his mother and father's daily bene-dictions. More than enough to live on.

At the campus computer center, he prints out two clean copies of his dissertation chapters. "Wow," says the sari-clad girl at the help window when she hands them to him. "You wrote all these?"

"Yup."

"Is it, like, your final?"

"Most of it."

"There's more?"

"Maybe."

"How long's it have to be?"

"About two hundred."

She looks at him.

"Most people have the opposite problem I do."

Maybe that's it, he thinks, walking back across campus, checking his (empty) West Hall mailbox for the last time, taking the long way around the admissions building. Maybe Frankie Grasso will always have the opposite problem. His fellow scholars are blocked, but he can't shut the floodgates. His friends resent their parents; Frankie courts them like lovers. His lovers want to be courted; Frankie resents them for not pinning him down with brute force. It's all so postcolonial, really, he thinks, walking down the engraved stone steps toward College, this buried desire for (benign?) domination by your oppressor, this ambivalence toward home rule, this exceptionalism. Or not. The connections are half-baked, the metaphors tortured. They've always been, according to Birch, according, apparently, to Gadkari. He has a long way to go to make sense of himself, of what he's creating, of the firings and misfirings in his brain. And now, to figure it all out, he's going to his parents' house, the place he fled in order to gain clarity.

10 *Volare*

FRANKIE SITS ON his mother's worktable, legs dangling, while she irons his shirt. She and his father are throwing him a party tonight, and he is glad. Officially, the party is for both Frankie and Ryan, to welcome back the son and wish the grandson a happy twenty-second birthday, and for the first time this year, all the Grassos will be together for a happy reason.

They're expected at the Al Di Là in a half hour, but Maddalena doesn't rush. She takes each crease with passion and precision, bent like a pianist over the crumpled button-down he extricated from his suitcase. Say what you want, Birch, Frankie thinks, I'm taken care of here at Casa Grasso. Call it patronage. Call him a mama's boy, or developmentally arrested, or sentimental. Say he can't be serious. He'll embrace every epithet. He has his mother and father close, and work to do, and Kelly Anne driving down from Newark, and that is all good and right.

Frankie has always loved his mother's workroom. In college he'd drive his laundry the half hour home to her once a month, and she'd spend most of her day washing and ironing while he wrote his papers upstairs at the kitchen table. He'd come down every couple of hours to keep her company, sit for a while on her long padded table, and listen to her stories of the village and Vito Leone's bike and the olive grove, and of working in various sweatshops in the fifties alongside Greeks and divorced ladies and "colored people," and of his father's tight fist and stubbornness, his frustrating tics and tricks. The years were a jumble to her, even then, while Frankie lived in the narrow and buzzing present of a college kid. Week after week he tried to explain what he was learning in his classes, but the fancifulness of the subjects, their disconnect from anything she found familiar or applicable in the world she'd just brought to life in her stories, embarrassed him; so he stuck to character sketches of his floor mates and profs, whom she imagined as more spoiled and distinguished, respectively, than they were. She'd show him the drapes she was sewing for a lady she met at church; he'd show her the photos in the campus directory and his byline in the monthly newspaper. She'd show him the missing ruby in the ring her mother gave her when she left for America; he'd show her the broken zipper on his jacket.

"What rich material!" she says now, spreading the collar of his shirt flat. Frankie found it at a vintage store on Newbury Street, convinced by the owner that Allen Ginsberg once wore it in an author photo. "I'm scared to ruin it."

"How much you pay for that?" asks his father. He's appeared in the doorway, at a distance, arms crossed.

"He got a good deal, I bet," says his mother. She looks him up and down. He's wearing a T-shirt with yellow stains in the armpits and green army pants three sizes too big, with frays at the cuffs. No shoes. His socks have a hole in the big toe. "You know clothes don't mean too much to Frankie. He cares about his inside." She taps her forehead.

"That's true enough, I guess," Frankie says.

His father is staring at him. "You're OK up there, though?" he asks. "In Boston, I mean. You're happy?"

"It's not my job to be happy, Dad," he says.

"Why you bring up Boston now?" says his mother. "He's home. Forget Boston."

Antonio ignores this. "What I'm asking you is, was it the right thing to do, all that graduate school? You'll get a good job soon, at least?"

"Is this really the best time to discuss my career path?" Frankie says. "How many times have I explained it to you? I'll get a job, but it'll be a shitty one for a few years, and I'll make no money, and the college'll work me to death, and then eventually I'll get what's called tenure, and then I'll be all set."

No college would hire a man in those pants, Maddalena thinks. He looks like a Vietnam vet. Antonio goes on. "And you'll make what, a hundred thousand a year, with the summers off? That's what some professor customer told me he makes, and you know what he teaches about? Flowers!"

"Not quite. More like fifty, if I'm lucky. That's guy's probably a botanist, Dad. And he's old, right? The longer you teach, the more you make."

"Fifty thousand? With all those degrees? You could make more as a bricklayer."

"But then I'd be a bricklayer," he says.

Frankie and me, we're snobs, thinks Maddalena, but in different ways. It was her doing, and she doesn't regret it. It makes him want a better life than she had, slaving over sewing machines and irons, the tips of her fingers bleeding from the needles. Still, though, there's honor in laying bricks. The blocks fit together. At the end of the day, you have a house, a wall at least, that will stand up after you're dead. What will Frankie have?

"I won't get any job at all if I don't finish my dissertation this summer," he says, putting on the Ginsberg shirt. "That's where you come in." He walks to the other end of the room, checks himself in the mirror. He looks older than twenty-seven. Neither Birch nor Kelly Anne has ever seemed to mind that he doesn't care much about his outsides. His hair is not as thick on top as it is in the photos on the basement shelf. His skin is pale. Is this dullness professorial? Is he *wizened*? Should he take afternoon breaks and walk around the park? Prima told him something recently about vitamin D stimulating the mind.

"Hurry up," his father says on the way up the stairs. "I don't want to be late. We have a big party coming in after we leave."

Maddalena makes the sign of the cross, as she's been doing lately, every time someone she loves leaves the room. She can protect them while they're in her sight, but once they're not she calls on God. It's a lot of work, all this calling and watching, and it's making her very tired.

She's onto ironing Frankie's dress pants now, the ones he wore to the Oak Room. As he waits, he notices two books on a shelf behind her sewing machine. They're shoved into a cracked plastic desk organizer along with a motley assortment of pens, pencils, crayons, and markers. He pages through one of the books, word games for kids ages three and up. Next to a drawing of a cat is the letter C, followed by two blank lines; next to a dog is a blank line, followed by an O, followed by another blank line. The handwriting belongs to his mother. She must be practicing letters, learning to spell basic words: COW, MOUSE, PONY. Many of the answers are wrong. The ink she's using keeps running out. He looks over at her, but she's so focused on his pants that she doesn't see what he's reading.

He picks up the other book, which isn't a book at all but two pads of guest checks from the Al Di Là held together with a rubber band. In it are random disconnected phrases, the letters in all caps, blocky, with little Old World loops at the tips. HAPPY BIRTHDAY TO A SPECIAL DAUGHTER. FREE OFFER FOR SUBSCRIBERS. HAPPY HOUR SPECIAL. Some of the s's are backward. There are periods where commas should be. NEW SUMMER PASS SCHEDULE. REMEMBER TO VOTE THIS TUESDAY. He keeps flipping through. The front section of pages are filled, one after the other, with these odd phrases, some in pink marker, some in pencil, some in ink, whatever she had lying around probably. FIFTY PERCENT OFF SALE. PHILADELPHIA PRIDE.

The other pad of guest checks is different. Starting from the last page and going backward, she's copied out the same sentence—*I love you*—over and over. The words are scrunched onto the lines in tiny lowercase letters. She's separated the sentences with commas and dated the dozens of sections going back two years. The ink is smeared in places, the paper torn loose at the edges from the spiral hooks.

Thousands of times, over dozens of pages: *I love you, I love you, I love you.*

"What are these?" Frankie asks. He's got the word games in one hand and the rubber-banded guest checks in the other.

She looks up, smiling. Then her face falls. Fear comes to her eyes. "*O Gesù mio,*" she says. She knocks over the iron as she rushes to him and wrenches the books from his hands. "Those aren't for you to see."

"But what are they?"

She shakes her head and stuffs the books in her pocket, where they don't quite fit. "I'm just—I'm silly."

"What are you trying to do?"

She shrugs, her head down. "It's just to pass the time."

"But what does it mean?" Frankie asks. "You know, if you want to learn English, there are plenty of night-school classes you can take. I think they're even free."

"I know English," she says. "I went to night school five years when I first came over. I know English. I just can't write, I don't know the spelling, so I practice on what I see in the mail or the newspaper or cards people send me. To keep my mind sharp." She goes back to the pants, determined. She turns them inside out. "I saw it on the Lifetime channel," she continues, not meeting his eyes. "They say the senior citizens, they should try to learn something new every day to help the brain. So that's what I do. It's like a muscle, the brain. I get a little confused sometimes, Frankie, I forget what I'm doing, my head goes cloudy. You know some of that already, yes? You've noticed? It's nothing to worry about. But then I think, why not try to help myself? Maybe I can make my mind stronger on my own. I don't want to go to night school again, with all those strangers. I'm too old, anyway, so I try to learn myself."

"You're never too old," says Frankie.

She waves him away. "Only the young person believes that."

"But what's with all the 'I love yous'? What are you teaching yourself there? And why are they on guest checks?"

She's still looking down at the pants. For a few seconds she says nothing. "You saw that, too, then." She turns the pants over. "It's another silly thing. Don't pay attention."

"But what is it?"

"Oh, Frankie. It's nothing! Every time I say my prayers, I write down, 'I love you,' so I don't forget to say them as many times as I should. I keep count. It takes a long time—I pray for you and Prima and all the kids, and Tony, and my brothers and sisters and my father and Mamma, and my friends, I have a lot of people—and if I don't get them all done, I don't sleep, I feel scared, like I didn't do enough for them, for you. I've been praying now, the whole time you've been here, in my head. One prayer after another. And when you go upstairs, I'll write again 'I love you' in the book. And at the end of the day I count to make sure I've said the prayers enough times in case I forgot."

"I can get you a real notebook," he says. "So you don't have to scribble on guest checks. Dad's too cheap to get one for you?"

"The checks—they were your brother's. From when he used to be a waiter. He still had empty ones in his room." She shakes her head, looks down at her ironing.

He goes to her, and without asking, without resistance, he takes one of the pads from where it sticks out of her pocket. He turns to the back, counts. Beside each date are at least ten "I love yous" crowded onto the lines, covering the back to the middle over fifty pages at least, like she's afraid to waste the paper. Her hands move over the pants as he reads. He slips the pad back in her pocket.

"How do your clothes always look and smell so good?" Frankie's girlfriends, in college, used to ask him.

"My mother," he'd say, and, exaggerating her accent, *"I clean you clothes with love."* Then the girl would unbutton them and pull them down and throw them in a heap on the bed.

"Try to look good tonight," his mother says now. "For me. For this girl you bring. To be dressed up is not so bad once in a while. It's a special occasion: you back, the birthday of Ryan . . ." She looks him in the eyes. Hers are welling with tears. "I still can't believe it, you here. When you're in the house, I don't worry as much. I feel safe."

Has Frankie not known how hard she's been trying to keep her mind strong? To protect him, to protect all of them? How much she prays and begs God? Of course he's known; she's told him on the phone every night for years. But to see it, the sum of her life, scratched into the little pads, Tony's pads, dazzles him. He goes to her, puts his arm around her shoulders, looks down at the bargain khakis she's treated like silk—they look brand-new. He casts his eyes around the room, the swags and cornices and pillows all sewn and arranged by hand. "I'm amazed by what you do," he says. "It takes real talent. Rare talent. I hope you know that."

"This?" she says. "This is nothing."

"It's not nothing," he says. It's almost a scold. She needs to understand him, to hear him loud and clear on this. He holds her by the shoulders. "It's beautiful," he says. "It's your work. It's everything."

THE WAITERS HAVEN'T brought the antipasto, and already Prima's a little drunk. She's not the only one. Frankie, too, keeps refilling his glass, and the twins aren't shy, either. There will be no surprises tonight. No speeches or tricks. No arguments.

On the table are candles and the good white linens and fresh flowers. "All Ryan's idea," Prima's father told her, when the sight of it, and her son standing in front of it in his black graduation suit, took her breath away. Ryan's at the head of the table now, explaining the dinner, as if the Grassos haven't eaten here a hundred times, as if the carpets and the ovens and the very air aren't in their blood. But it's charming. Her son will charm the diners here for years to come.

When Prima can train her focus on Ryan, on not only his summer at home but the other Al Di Là restaurants that he and his charm and his business degree will open and scatter over the tristate area, she is happy. Otherwise it's a great deal of work for Prima to convince herself that the battle she's fighting is worth it. She talks to herself like this now, like a soldier, and she hates it. The talk has led her here, to the rocky border between one kind of life and another. Rage comes in waves, and though Tom won't tolerate self-pity, she has to lash out every once in a while, at him or at one of the boys, or at her mother. It's unfair, but she has no control over it. Prima waited all her adult life for another terrible thing to happen to someone she loved, but instead it happened to her, and she wasn't prepared.

Tomorrow morning, Tom will pack her into the car and take her to a rehab facility in Princeton. She'll be an outpatient for a month, three weeks if they're lucky. Her doctor is optimistic that his new idea, which he explained to her and two other doctors in incomprehensible detail, will work. She and Tom will stay in a hotel nearby, one of those efficiencies with a kitchenette, where Tom will work from the room. So much for a second honeymoon.

He sits on one side of her, Patrick on the other. Her mother across. Frankie and his shockingly normal-looking girlfriend and the twins are with her father at the other end. Prima forbade Allison Grey's presence, and Zach didn't fight her. The girl has sent Prima at least a dozen cards since the accident, but Prima hasn't opened a single one. Did she not know from the start that somewhere, somehow, the girl would ruin her? Zach's lucky that Prima still lets him talk to her, let alone call her his girlfriend.

Ryan's explaining about the complexity of the wine. Then he brings the pasta—"Penne *ah-ma-tree-cha-na*," he says, in forced but technically correct Italian—and then veal Milanese, and then bowl after bowl of sides: roasted peppers, sautéed onions topped with bread crumbs, peas, broccoli rabe, all of which they scoop up with thick cuts of warm bread. The restaurant fills around them. Music piped through the corner speakers—crooners from the fifties—gets louder, and Tom, of all people, sings along. He must be drunk. Prima looks at him with a bemused pride, nudging Patrick in the ribs. Frankie tells a Clinton joke that nobody quite gets and that may be too dirty for a family dinner.

"I have a joke, too," Maddalena says. She raises her hand like she's in school. "How does a cat eat spaghetti?"

They all look at her.

"He puts it in his mouth," she says. She throws her head back in full-throated laughter. No one else laughs. "You don't get it?" she says. "The cat eats spaghetti like everybody else!"

"Stick to making drapes, Ma," Frankie says playfully, and he flicks a bit of crust at her.

"I'll get you!" she says, still laughing at her joke, and she flicks one back.

"It's a little corny," says Patrick.

"The priest told it," she says. "I was going to save it for Thanksgiving. I'm glad I didn't!"

"Yeah, stick to dancing, Nonna," says Ryan, now seated at the table beside his father.

"I'll get you, too," Maddalena says, tearing out a big chunk of the bread. "You watch out!"

"Have another drink," Antonio says with a smile. When Maddalena tries to protest, she knocks her glass of wine into the bowl of onions. Kelly Anne starts laughing, too, and soon so does everyone.

"She's invented a new recipe," says Zach.

"Who says I don't cook?" says Maddalena.

Prima thinks she should be enjoying this laughter, and this celebration, and this teasing of her mother, who has her very good days and her very bad days, and the food fight with her sons and the buzz that's warming her in her chair, but she's so tired, and this celebration's not planned the way she would have planned it. If Prima had had her way, they'd have taken Ryan to a nightclub, to make up for not doing anything for his twenty-first, and invited some of his friends down from Syracuse. If she'd had her way, they'd be here retelling stories from the trip to Italy, passing around photos of the Grassos in front of various monuments, of her mother with her arms around her brother and sister. They'd have memories of arriving in Rome, driving first to Terni for a day, then Rieti, then Santa Cecilia in time for the feast on the fifteenth, then Florence, then down to Assisi, and finally back to Rome for three days of guided tours. Prima had it all organized. Ten magical days it would have been.

Instead, the guidebooks and brochures, once arranged in personalized gift bags in the backseat of her car, have become the trash run over daily by tractor trailers and motorcycles on Route 41. The tickets and reservations are partially refunded, the Buckleys are out thousands of dollars, and doors are shutting and dead-bolting around her. In the thin air of the restaurant, all the laughter and love that surround her—it's the happiest she's seen her family in a year—is a cruel kick in the gut. She's doing an adequate enough job passing for happy for the sake of her sons and husband.

From her seat she can see cars pass on Union. The occasional driver looks over, catches her eye for a moment, then moves along. The headlights make shadows on the windows, which are open on this warm June night. The honking horns rattle her. Coffee appears, and plates of tiramisu, and a bowl of sliced fruit passed around family-style. When the plates are cleared and someone mentions grappa, Frankie stands.

"I know this day is half in my honor," he says, "and it's probably bad form to make a speech, but since Ryan's working on his birthday, I guess we're not following any rules."

Oh my, Prima thinks, is he going to propose to this girl? Right here in front of everyone? She watches Kelly Anne, who looks as confused as the rest of them. Frankie is not the speech-making type, and Prima can think of nothing else important enough for him to say. Kelly Anne seems nice enough, and not wild in any way, rather like Tom; when Prima realizes this and sees her mother and father light up at the sight of their son, her love of surprises kicks in. No one can resist a man getting down on one knee in a restaurant. But how could he afford a decent ring?

"I just want to say happy birthday to Ryan and a big thank-you to Dad and Mom for the delicious dinner, and for, well, the free rent the next couple months."

"*Free?*" jokes Antonio. "Who said it was free?"

"*Stai zitto,*" says Maddalena. "Let him talk!" She's thinking, With that shirt on, and your hair not a mess, and standing tall with your hands in the pockets of your dress pants, you look like a professor, Frankie, like someone who knows things. "You can stay a hundred years for free!" she calls out.

"I also want to say"—here Frankie turns to Prima and Patrick—"how lucky we are that you guys are all right." He picks up his glass. "To the Grassos!"

They all fumble for whatever's on the table in front of them: coffee mugs, water glasses, half-empty glasses of wine. They reach toward the middle and hold there, until everyone's touching.

"To Ryan and Zio Frankie!" Zach says.

"Welcome home and *buon compleanno!*" says Antonio.

"To my beautiful wife," says Tom.

"Yes, beautiful!" says Maddalena.

Prima wants to say something, the right thing, to convince them, and herself, that she's grateful, too, but she can't, not yet, and so she's left with only a feeble "thank you" fading on her lips.

"She's speechless," says Tom. "That's a rare sight."

Maddalena looks at each of them, all of them together, here in this circle, half-drunk and silly. She wants to hold them here as long as she can. But the moment doesn't last. Just a few minutes later, the waiters take the last of the plates and glasses away, and Antonio and Frankie are yawning.

"Already?" she says to no one in particular.

"It's late," someone says.

"It's only ten o'clock!" Maddalena says. In the early years, Saturday nights like this, they used to push the tables against the wall and make room for a few couples to dance. All the men liked dancing with her. She knew how to follow in a way that made them feel like Fred Astaire. She'd try to sit down and they'd come after her, sometimes two at a time, with their hands out. She won't suggest dancing now, not with Prima how she is, but she wishes she could. "When'd you all get so old?"

"I'll stay," Matt says. "Nonno?"

"Whatever she wants," Antonio says.

"I'll put music on," says Ryan, and he disappears into the kitchen.

Tom takes his wife's hand, squeezes it, checking in, the way couples do. One squeeze asks, Is it OK if we stay another half hour? Are you tired? Will we be OK? She squeezes it back, saying, Yes, yes, and yes, I guess we will.

Music comes on, and Ryan returns from the kitchen to take a bow. Taking charge suits the kid. It's as if he's always been here, calling the shots. Maddalena gets up and stands beside him. She sings the words. Eventually he joins in. The others stand around them, and then Antonio joins in, too, and the customers turn to watch, whispering. Crazy Italians, they must be thinking. But isn't this why they come to a place like the Al Di Là? Why they'll keep coming to the Al Di Làs that her son will build for them? To sit among people so full of life. To soak up the color and the drama and the love.

The song is "Volare." Frankie puts his arm around his girlfriend's shoulder. Neither of them sings along. They must not know the words. Prima does, but she's too embarrassed. She hasn't sung in public since high school.

Let's fly way up to the clouds . . .

Antonio walks over to Maddalena, takes her hand in an invitation to dance. She says, "No, no, I can't." She looks over at Prima. She's asking for permission.

"You should dance, Ma," Prima says, and, no argument, that's all it takes. The bus boys move the chairs on the other side of the table and push it against the wall to make more room. Maddalena and Antonio dance a fox-trot or a cha-cha, Prima doesn't know the difference. The entire restaurant watches them. Tom keeps holding on to Prima, squeezing her hand with more questions, but it's OK, she can handle it. She's aware that other people will keep dancing whether she can or not. She keeps her eyes on Zach and Matt and Patrick, who stand beside each other, clapping along to the beat. They sing a little bit of the chorus, the only part they know—all those *oh oh oh oh*s—then Matt grabs Zach by the belt, and they're dancing, too, with the customers laughing and pointing.

Patrick flicks the chandeliers on and off, rapidly, to make a strobe. Service comes to a halt. The kitchen guys come out and wave their spatulas at Antonio and Maddalena, the owner and his wife, the reason they are all there in the first place. The flames from the grill leap up behind them. The honking of the horns from the cars on Union is in beat with the music. The headlights are fireworks on the windows.

Penso che un sogno cosi non ritorni mai piu . . .

The song speaks the truth, Prima thinks. *It will never happen again, such a dream.*

She is right.

It is the last time she will see her family together like this, fully alive, happy enough. When she gets back, in five weeks, from New Hope, she will be walking, as back to normal as will be possible, but everything else will have changed.

The music stops, and after the clapping the place returns to its dull roar. Ryan hasn't cued another song. He's occupied, cheek to cheek with some girl who showed up at the front door asking for him, whispering into her ear. "More!" Maddalena calls out. The customers go back to their pastas and desserts. Antonio sits down. Frankie and Kelly Anne are chatting with one of the chefs.

"More!" Maddalena calls again. She shakes her head. She looks over at Prima from across what used to be the dance floor. "That's all we get?" she asks. "One little song?"

LABOR DAY, AND Frankie's still home. Maddalena tries to ask how, and why, but he snaps at her. He tells her he's stressed out and that "things just aren't coming together" with his paper, but it's not the mother's business to ask for more details than that? The snapping is like Prima, but it's also like the Frankie of three years old and the Frankie of fifteen years old, so much the same Frankie, it's true, as the Frankie of almost thirty years old, locked in his room with his books. Now that he's been home more than two months, it's funny, they don't talk as much as they did when he was in Boston. Eleven o'clock comes and the phone doesn't ring and there's no "good night," no "I love you," only the light under his door that doesn't go off until three in the morning, when Antonio's been snoring already four hours but Maddalena's awake, walking in and out of the rooms because she can't sleep praying for Tony, who's upside down in a way no one will explain.

If Maddalena could drive, she'd go out and look for Tony. He goes walking after school sometimes, to clear his mind. She'd like to see where he walks, but she doesn't know the streets and won't be able to find her way back, and Antonio is no help, he lies to her, him and Prima and Frankie, they all tell her lies about Tony that don't make sense, they just don't understand him the way she does. The only one who's not a liar is Frankie's *fidanzata,* the Irish, who calls five times a day and will talk to Maddalena when Frankie's too busy to stay long on the phone, which is always. When Prima comes over, she brings yogurt and blueberries and vitamin B tablets and starts to wash the dish Maddalena's just eaten her lunch from, but Maddalena takes the dish from her and washes it herself and asks her what happened to her leg, and isn't she embarrassed to have to use a cane like an old woman? She has no reason to be embarrassed, Prima tells her, and she's fine, she can wash a dish, she's not a cripple, and then she shakes her head and promises to come over again tomorrow to bring more blueberries and yogurt, but how much blueberries and yogurt can a person eat?

In the meantime, Maddalena has Frankie to watch over. Every day when he gets up, never before noon, he bangs his door open, half-asleep, on his way to the bathroom. Soon as Maddalena hears the bang, she runs to the kitchen to microwave the coffee Antonio made before he left. The coffee and one biscotto are waiting for Frankie on his desk when he's done on the toilet. His room is a disaster. Piles of papers everywhere, bedsheets all twisted and full of crumbs, drawers open with clothes hanging out. The only chance she has to straighten up is when he's in the shower, usually around four o'clock after he watches *General Hospital,* but if she's not out of the room before he comes out, he snaps. She tries to read his papers, but they make no sense. She's never seen such words. She copies out as many letters as she has time for. HETEROGLOSSIA. INEXTRICABLE. BOOMERANG EFFECT. She'll never understand what he's doing with these words, why they matter so much to him, make him angry with himself and with her and with the world. Frankie tries to explain his degree to her, but she gets lost the first minute. No one's a tailor or a doctor or a priest anymore. The jobs are so complicated nowadays, and people go from one to the other like rides at a carnival.

Around two o'clock every day she brings Frankie a frittata with extra onions or leftovers from dinner the night before. For dessert, a peach and two hard chocolate chip cookies (his favorite kind, in the blue wrapper). If she has time, she cuts up a watermelon and picks out the seeds and brings him the chunks. If he's in a good mood, he'll say, "Hey, hang on," and she'll sit on the edge of his bed feeling like she's won a prize, and they'll talk about *Days of Our Lives* or the nice cool air conditioning or the dances she'd like to learn at the studio, but never about Tony or anything serious, like how he's really making out with his big paper, and doesn't he have students to teach up in Boston? Will he get fired if he doesn't show up? She's afraid to upset him with her questions. If she upsets him too much, he will leave for real, like Tony did. If Maddalena has her way, he will stay forever and ever in his room like the Frankie of three years old and the Frankie of fifteen and twenty-two years old, and she will keep bringing him whatever she can, plates of food and cups of coffee and armfuls of clean underwear, to make his life easy.

Between him and Prima coming by and the girl calling and Arlene and Father Larson visiting all the time, it seems like Maddalena is never alone. If it's late enough in the afternoon, she drinks a glass of red wine with whoever's there with her, or if it's not too cold or dark now that the time's changed, she goes for a walk. Prima tells her to eat more bananas and take her fish oil pills (so many pills!) and do what the doctor tells her, and to stop worrying about Tony or Frankie or anyone, and to let go, let go, let go, because, according to Prima (who never takes her own advice), to worry is not healthy, and it must be the worry that's making her spells worse. What Prima and Tony and Frankie don't know is that there's no hope, that fish pills and bananas and yogurt and blueberries and vitamin B and doctors can't change the plan God put in her brain and her blood, the same brain and blood that killed her sisters at her age.

One day it's freezing and the wind is blowing the dead leaves around outside, and someone lets himself in the front door and

Maddalena gets scared when she sees him in the hallway. But then she sees it's not a man but a woman and she looks just like Mamma in the light, and right away Maddalena thinks it's a trick, that what Tony's been doing all this time away at a special school—that's what Antonio said, a special school for smart people, a place far away where he can concentrate and learn—is finding Mamma in Italy and bringing her over as a gift. Then the worry melts away and Maddalena is so happy, because there is Mamma, after fifty years without her and a thousand letters and pictures, there she is, with that bump in her nose and her shoulders Roman-straight, there for Maddalena to run to and fall to her knees and grab around the waist. And then, when Mamma bends down to lift her off the floor, kiss every inch of her face, the face switches, and it isn't Mamma's face anymore; it's Prima's full of tears, yelling at her like she's a stupid child, pulling her out of the dream, then taking her onto the porch for air. It stays with Maddalena, though, the dream that was real, the surprise gift, her arms around Mamma again, touching her lips to her smooth skin, her clothes smelling of Santa Cecilia ashes. She didn't want her to turn into Prima. She wanted her to stay Mamma so she could show her the little house she had in America, all the rooms she'd decorated herself, the pots of violets, and Frankie working hard at his desk like a professor, and sit her down on the sofa to ask what to do about Tony, and never let her leave.

If Teresa and Celestina and Carolina had to go like this, it's only fair that Maddalena should, too, and if it means she can see her sisters again, alive, here on earth instead of in heaven, when there's still time to introduce them to their nieces and nephews and grandnieces and

ALL THIS TALK OF LOVE ∽ 297

grandnephews, it's not the most terrible thing, it's like falling asleep into a dream in the middle of the afternoon on a chair in the sun. It's what old people do. But Frankie will be leaving before she can prepare herself to say good-bye.

As it is, he's around less and less lately, her Frankie. He's disappearing like Tony did, except not all at once. All night he's gone sometimes and for a few hours in the afternoon. At first it was lonely, but then Celestina and Teresa and Carolina came to keep her company. They're here off and on all day, gossiping about the boys back from the war in their uniforms, how handsome they are, and the movie that's showing in the piazza on a big screen brought over from Avezzano. For years they've been waiting for a movie to come to Santa Cecilia. If Babbo lets them, they'll bring blankets and sleep in the square to save a spot in the front, does Maddalena want to come?

Yes, she does. She wants very much to come. She wants to lie beside them on the soft grass, with the stars so close she can reach up and scoop them into her hand and dab them on her face like glitter. There's a man coming from America, she's been told, a man with money and a ticket on the boat across the ocean, and she has to look as pretty as she can if she wants to be his wife.

No one has told Maddalena the trouble Tony's in, but she knows it's big, it's not a camp for smart boys because it's not summer and no camp goes on so long except prison. She knows this like she knows the hole in Frankie's eyebrow he thinks he's hiding, like she knows Prima's lonely heart she won't admit to. Mamma agrees. She's around most of the time now. She doesn't like that Maddalena's hair is getting so long and gray, so she has to ask Prima to color and brush it, like Maddalena used to do for Mamma Nunzia, the nights Antonio stayed out all night with his derelict friends. Prima stands behind Maddalena on the cushioned chair in the vanity in front of the mirror, brushing one hundred strokes on one side of her head, one hundred strokes on the other. They count together.

Frankie goes out more and more. The coffee she brings him gets cold on his desk. A girl in a blue truck picks him up, and when he gets into the passenger side he kisses her. If she's the Irish girl from the phone, why doesn't she stop in to say hi? Maddalena watches from the powder room window, and after they're gone she goes into Tony's room and covers herself with his sweet-smelling sheets and sleeps in his bed for hours and hours, and only a few times does someone catch her and lead her by the arm to her own room down the hall, where Antonio's put in a new TV-VCR on a stand so she can watch her stories with her feet up on a pillow and the phone next to her on the table with framed pictures. So many more framed pictures than there used to be! There are as many pictures as pills. Too many. Frankie's much better now about the mess in his room, there aren't as many papers in piles as there used to be, and he's bought new clothes—ties and dress shirts that show up in his hamper, clothes she's happy to wash and iron when she can, when she can hold the iron without losing the strength in her arms. When that happens, she has to stop or she'll fall down, even with Antonio or the nurse lady there next to her propping her up so she can do what gives her so much happiness: iron the shirt of her handsome son so he can wear it with one of his professor ties and look so good, so grown up, walking to the car with his briefcase to go teach his class at the university.

The nurse lady is strong for a girl so skinny, and she smiles and speaks in a soft voice, but Maddalena hates the little moles across her nose that look like cockroach shit, and every time she comes, Maddalena hides, but the rascal girl always finds her, calls out her name, and says it the wrong way, with some Spanish accent, and it's a disgrace to have that girl in the bathroom with her doing what she has to do to keep her clean. Maddalena hates her for that most of all. And in the meantime Antonio and Frankie and Prima (not Tony, Tony is gone) are in the kitchen making their plans and not inviting Maddalena to anything anymore, not letting her even walk outside by herself, not even with her coat and scarf. They talk loud, not caring if she hears, but who needs them? Sometimes she hates them more than she hates the Spanish girl.

She has Mamma to help her put the garland on the chandelier and crack open the chestnuts and wrap the gifts Prima bought and left on the workroom table next to the yards of fabric she can't make into drapes anymore. She tries. She tries so hard. The measurements keep coming out wrong. One time she tries and rips up the fabric afterward and throws it into the oven and turns the knob to Broil to destroy it so she'll never have to see the mistake again, and after that the fabric disappears from the table, along with the gifts, and it's not Christmas anymore all of a sudden, the tree in the backyard is raining down its pink petals on the lawn, but Prima and Antonio and Frankie (not Tony, Tony is gone) are still in the kitchen making their plans. It's where they always are anymore, and Maddalena loves them so much, she misses them so much, all she wants is for one of them, any one of them (and Tony? What did she do to Tony to make him hate her?) to visit her for longer than a minute and put their hands on her cheek and kiss her hair, and she wants to tell them, Don't forget me, I can still see you, Prima, you are so pretty, Antonio you have a hole in your sweater, Frankie, you're getting fat in the middle, and you know what, it looks good on you somehow. But the words don't come, and she tries to call them to her but their names don't come, either. It's just her in the room where not even Antonio sleeps anymore, with the blond actress on the TV screen jumping up and down because finally the man she's been chasing all her life is on his knees in front of her with the ring, and Maddalena thinks, Good luck, both of you, it's a long sad life you're in for, and when she calls out this time, it works, she makes noise from her mouth, loud, like a siren, but nobody comes.

Part 3 ❧ *Summer 2003*

11 *Miracles*

THE NEW DOCTOR at Christiana is not the first to make the suggestion. He's the first Italian specialist they've seen, though, and his last name, amazingly, is Grasso, and if a sign like that worked for Prima and Patrick, it can work for Maddalena.

"Take her home," Dr. Grasso tells Antonio.

He's young and tan and has a degree from Harvard. He doesn't say, Take her to Santa Cecilia. But that's what he means. He says, too: Forget her resistance to the trip two years ago. She might as well have been a different woman. Her body is healthy enough for the plane ride, her heart and bones are strong. Flood her mind with the happy memories of youth. The stage she's in, she's regressed to her childhood and can only be made more peaceful if what she sees with her eyes matches what's going on in her head.

These last words Antonio hears most clearly. *She can only be made more peaceful. Your wife, Signor Grasso, can only be made more peaceful.* They leave the office and drive straight to another Italian, Ombretta, the travel agent Antonio's never had the chance to use until now. She gets Frankie on the phone, then they call Prima, and then she's buying them four tickets for Saturday's Alitalia flight from Philadelphia to Rome. It's crazy. It's not like Antonio to act this fast. But nothing is as it used to be. His life has changed more in the past two years than in the fifty before.

The fourth ticket is for Kelly Anne, not Prima. She doesn't agree with Dr. Grasso's prescription. She calls other doctors and begs Antonio and Frankie to listen to their concerns, to consider the dangers of taking a woman so frail on such a long trip. But she's wrong. *She can only be made more peaceful.* If she were Prima's child, she'd do whatever it took to help her.

When Saturday comes, Prima shows up early in the day to say good-bye. Maddalena sits in the living room in the flowered dress Prima bought her last Christmas, a dress Kelly Anne helped her put on for the plane ride, and right there on the spot, seeing Maddalena in that dress, Prima changes her mind. She calls Alitalia and buys a last-minute ticket for the flight. Two thousand dollars. But nobody blinks.

Antonio and Maddalena have flown only twice in their lives: once to Las Vegas, once to Miami. Both times on senior citizen vacations organized by the dance studio. Both times, Antonio had to take tranquilizers for his nerves. Tonight he wants nothing deadened. He presses his face to the window through the long night hours, while everyone around him sleeps. Then, shade by shade, the sky lightens, and when Italy finally appears below him, it's like a woman stretched out on a bed in the morning. He can climb on top of her and wake her with his kisses, or he can watch her sleep a little longer, taking in her beauty. Either way, she is his.

At the Rome airport, they rent a car, and before long they're on the *superstrada,* which cuts through the mountains like a thing from the future. Frankie, from behind the wheel, tells Antonio it's called science fiction, the kind of movie Antonio feels like he's in, where everything's real and familiar and at the same time impossible and strange. Maddalena sits beside him in the backseat, humming, her hand gripping his. Prima's on the other side of her. Kelly Anne's in the front reading the map. All of them, even Maddalena, are talking, pointing at the views of Valle del Salto, Antonio talking most of all. He can't shut up. The stories come one on top of the other, so many stories as they climb up and up and around the mountains, where memories hang from the trees and are soaked into the heavy stone. And then the sign for Santa Cecilia appears (a tall green metal sign, the same as you'd see in Rome or on the Jersey Turnpike, impossible!), and they exit the *superstrada.* The road up the hill through the olive grove used to be dirt. Now it's paved. The olive trees, though, are in the same place, like they've been waiting for Antonio all these years. At the first row of houses the car goes quiet, or at least Antonio can't hear a word they say. He's crushing the tiny bones in Maddalena's hand, his heart is exploding, it's been fifty-seven years, and he is home.

They pass his father's house with the crack above the door. "Slow down, Frankie!" he says. He points out the Grasso farm that never grew enough, and now, look, it's bursting green. There's the stoop where the old witch Guglielma Lunga used to sit, and there's the window where Gabriella Puzo used to stand and change her blouse. He says these names aloud, watching Maddalena's eyes for a spark, but the spark doesn't come. Still he keeps talking.

After the bend in the road, they come upon the grocery store that once belonged to the Piccinelli family. They park in front. Antonio can't bring himself to step out. Not yet. He leans across Maddalena, points through the back window, and reads her the sign in the window: DROGHERIA PICCINELLI. "Can you believe that?" he says to her. "That's your old name—you remember it? Before you were a Grasso, you were a Piccinelli." She smiles, but maybe only to match the wide smile he gives her, like a baby does for her father before she's old enough to know it means she's happy.

"What do you think, *tesoro*?" he asks again.

It's two o'clock in the afternoon, and the village is quiet. Frankie and Kelly Anne stretch their legs in the sun. Prima rings the buzzer of the house above the store. Taped to the glass of the *drogheria* are posters for discounted meats, for bands appearing in the piazza later in June, and for parties at Pensione Granara and Pensione Lupo. Antonio reminds his wife that, back in their day, these hotels were his friends' houses. Bands came through twice a year if they were lucky. The meat was always on sale, or you could barter or beg for it if you told a sad enough story. "You remember?" he asks again.

Frankie opens the door on Maddalena's side and helps her to her feet. A young tourist couple walks out of the store carrying flowers and a jug of wine and bread in a long paper bag. They stare at them, smile, and move on.

From the house comes an old man with Maddalena's same wrinkled face. He goes to her and pulls her close without a word.

"You know him," Antonio says. "This is your brother Claudio."

She doesn't know him.

Claudio wipes his eyes with a handkerchief he pulls from his shirtsleeve. He puts his arm around his sister's waist and leads her into the store. The aisles stand where they've always stood. The barrels of nuts are the barrels from 1946. The radio is where it used to be, except it's half the size and has flashing lights and stacks of tapes and CDs next to it. A teenage boy works the counter.

"You want her to look around the store?" Claudio asks. "Or is she ready for upstairs?"

"Are they there?"

"Yes."

"Let's go up, then."

They climb the back stairs to the rooms where Maddalena lived until she was nineteen.

Everyone is watching her, looking for a spark, for anything, but her eyes stay blank. On the walls are framed color photos of nephews and nieces and cousins they've never met.

In the hallway of the kitchen, Vito Leone waits for them. He's skinny as ever, wearing a wrinkled off-white suit. His tie is crooked, his belt tied too tight. The strap of the belt hangs halfway down the front of his pants. Here is the great romantic, an old man now. He's the mayor of the village and the three little towns around it, and has been, off and on, for two decades. He holds out his hand to Antonio, American-style, but Antonio kisses him on both cheeks. He is his brother-in-law, after all. Whatever war they fought over Maddalena fifty-seven years ago is long over. And if it's Vito Leone, not Claudio or Carolina, not the sight of her old house or the church or the olive grove, that brings Maddalena back, just for one second, then Antonio will be grateful to the man for the rest of his life.

But Maddalena Piccinelli Grasso looks at Vito Leone like she'd look at an empty wall. He takes her hands in his and says, "You look beautiful, signora. To see you is a miracle."

"*Grazie*," she says.

"He's the one who made that bike you always told me about," Frankie says. "With the big silver tires and the rock for a seat."

"It goes too fast," she says.

"No *freni*," says Vito. "No *brakes*." He learned a little English from his daughter, Donatella, he explains. He asks Antonio, in Italian, "They don't speak the language?"

"No," says Antonio. "We didn't teach any of our kids."

"*Che peccato*," Vito says.

"What's going on?" Prima asks.

"Fiorella makes such a fuss," Maddalena says. "She wants a boy-friend too bad. Who's going to put up with her?"

"Fiorella was her friend," says Claudio. "She died of cancer five years ago."

"Is there any happy news in this place?" Frankie asks after Antonio translates.

"Not anymore," says Vito. He puts his hand on Frankie's shoulder. "You two to be married?" he asks.

"Us?" Frankie says. He looks at Kelly Anne. She looks at him. "Too soon," they both say at the same time. Vito laughs.

"Don't wait," Vito says. "You have a coin in your hand, close your fist."

They're crowded in the dark, narrow hallway that separates the kitchen from the rest of the house. Claudio shuffles his feet, checks his watch, asks if they're hungry, if they want some wine. No, says Antonio, they're not, and not yet. Then they have no more small talk to make.

"Your wife," Antonio says to Vito. "Where is she?"

"In the living room," Vito says, "watching TV. It keeps her calm."

They walk through the dining room, past the table and chairs where Antonio ate his first dinner with the Piccinelli family. The same wooden table, the same shiny chairs, arranged in front of the window under the silver crucifix. Antonio could have chosen any of Aristide and Chiara's daughters. He was a rich American with paid passage to New York and a way with words and a trunk full of promises. But he chose Maddalena, even though she didn't love him, even though she'd promised herself to the man now leading him down the hall.

It was always Maddalena. The night after that first dinner, he invited himself back, and then again the night after that. For two weeks he tried to impress her. In the meantime, he and Aristide talked and made plans, and the night all the details were settled, the two men met on the terrace and drank a toast to Maddalena's future as an American wife. That's how Antonio remembers it, at least. He promised Aristide many things: to keep his daughter safe and never let her worry for money and give her whatever she asked for no matter how crazy it sounded. He's kept every promise the best he could.

The old woman who sits in the corner of the couch has a blanket over her knees. Her hands are crossed in her lap. Her hair's long and gray with streaks of white; it flows over her shoulders down to her elbows. Her face resembles Maddalena's—the wrinkles in the corners of her eyes and above her lip, the high forehead, the eyes blank as a field of snow. She's watching a game show where girls onstage dance around in bikinis and throw pies at a fat middle-aged man. She looks up from this nonsense to see, after almost sixty years, her sister, her best friend, on the arm of the man who took her away. She squints, leans forward, and the tears come. She holds out both arms. She runs to her.

Who is this old lady? Maddalena wonders. Why's she so happy to see me? First there was the man in the white suit, now this *strega*-looking woman with dry skin and a chicken neck and veins all over her legs. The weather's too nice to be cooped up in here. And it smells funny. Baby powder and bleach. The handsome young man and his girlfriend look so sad. The lady with the limp, too, in her sundress too small in the waist. They want to get out of here as bad as she does. If they can escape the old fogies, she'll take them to the café. She can hear the music. "Turn the TV down, will you?" she says, angry, to the man who brought her, squeezing his arm. "You hear? Shh. They're doing a waltz."

"Who?"

"Across the street."

He's not paying attention. He makes Maddalena sit down next to the old lady on the lumpy couch. They tell her she's Carolina, but that's a joke. Carolina's in Rieti with Teresa and Celestina buying fabric. Maddalena wanted to go, but Papà made her stay and work in the store, and now all of a sudden there's a new boy behind the counter and she's in the room with these strange people. Somebody died, maybe, because the old lady is crying. "What's the matter, signora?" Maddalena asks her.

She lays both her hands on Maddalena's face and looks deep into her eyes. "*Sorella mia,*" she says, over and over. "*Sorella mia.*" My sister, my sister.

"Your sister died?" Maddalena guesses. It happens to old people. It's what they do. "I'm so sorry. What was her name? I'm sure she was very nice." She looks up, shrugs her shoulders. What else can she say to this woman she met two minutes ago? She decides on, "Can I get you a drink? Or do you want us to leave you alone so you can watch your TV show?"

But instead of eating or drinking or walking to the café, they sit and watch the silly TV show. A half-naked *putana* type is writing in lipstick on the head of a bald guy with a crazy mustache. The audience laughs and laughs. Maddalena can't sit still. The handsome boy sits on the arm of the couch next to her. She rests her head on his shoulder. Francesco, his name is. She likes the name. She feels comfortable with Francesco. The girl he's with has a friendly face; there's something foreign about her, American or German. They sit around for such a long time, and Carolina keeps crying and hugging her and kissing her all over her face, talking about her sister, how much she misses her. It's so depressing. Maddalena feels her own tears coming, even though she didn't know the sister.

"It'll be all right," Maddalena tells her. She dries her tears with her sleeve. "You'll see your sister again in heaven, you know. Think of it that way. There's no reason to be sad if you remember she's up there waiting."

Good for you, Vito Leone, Antonio thinks bitterly. Your wife's not so bad off as Claudio made it sound. He can't stay in this room another second. He hands Maddalena his handkerchief and walks out to the terrace. Claudio follows. Big clay pots overflow with flowers. Claudio offers Antonio a cigarette. Antonio hasn't smoked in years. The sun and the flowers are bright on their faces.

"She's like a stranger," Antonio says.

"So is Carolina, most of the time. What you saw back there, that's a miracle."

Antonio wants to take each of the flowerpots, lift them over his head, and smash them onto the street. Shatter the windshields of the cars parked below. There shouldn't be cars in Santa Cecilia, anyway. There should be carriages and donkeys and dirt.

Claudio disappears, and now Prima comes out with Kelly Anne.

"Anything?" Antonio asks.

Prima shakes her head. "We knew not to get our hopes up, Dad. It was a long shot at best."

"If it doesn't happen now," Antonio says, "it's never going to happen."

"You don't know that, Mr. Grasso," says Kelly Anne. "Not even the doctors said that, right?"

"You should enjoy being back here, Dad," says Prima. "You've been wanting this for a long time. You deserve it."

"I need to check on her," he says. "The three of you, go walk around. Before it gets dark. It's easy to get lost here."

"Seriously?" says Kelly Anne.

"He's joking," says Prima.

Antonio walks back into the room where his wife is sitting, whispers in her ear, takes her hand, and leads her away from Carolina, without a word to Vito or Claudio.

"Thank you," she says in the hallway. "What do we do now?"

"I think it's time for a nap," Antonio says. "It's been a long day."

"No!" she says. "I'm not even tired!" But by the time they reach the end of the hall, she's yawning and shuffling her feet. "I could rest my eyes a little," she says.

Her old bedroom is now the guest room where they will be staying the next three nights. Antonio shuts the heavy wooden door, newly fitted with shiny brass hinges. In the window is an air conditioner on high. There's a cordless telephone attached to a fax machine and, in the corner, another TV. Antonio eases Maddalena onto the bed and unstraps her sandals and rubs her feet to help with her circulation. Her toenails are pink, painted by Kelly Anne the day before they left.

He helps her take off her dress and hangs it in the closet. She bats her eyes at him as he buttons the front of her nightgown, one of those flannel old-lady kinds with lace around the neck, nothing stylish. Her hair, which he paid the Michael Christopher Salon eighty-five dollars to make pretty earlier in the week, is going flat. He'll ask Prima to fix it later before they see more people, the distant cousins in the village who will come calling before long. Maddalena would want to look her best—no witch hair falling all over the place, no bare legs, no ears without earrings or fingers without rings. For now, though, he wants only for her to be comfortable and rested, not to worry how she looks. He tucks her in. He closes the blinds and finds music on the clock radio to help her sleep. He's about to say good night and step out of the room when he notices the way she's looking at him.

Something in her face is different than it was just minutes ago, in the room with Carolina, and in the hallway, and on the bed when he was removing her clothes.

"You know me, don't you?" Antonio says.

"Of course I do," she says. She smiles. "Antonio."

It's the first time she's said his name in months, since one night in the spring, when she woke up in the middle of the night calling to him. He sits beside her. His heart is racing. "How do you feel, *tesoro*? Do you understand where you are? Are you happy? Can I get you anything?"

"Did you eat?" she asks.

"We all ate," he says. "You and Frankie and Prima and Claudio and Carolina. All together. And now you're in your old bed. You know that? You used to sleep right here with your sisters. All four of you on this little mattress." The words can't come out fast enough. He wants to tell her everything.

She closes her eyes. "You work too hard," she says.

"I'm not working tonight," he tells her. "We're going dancing at the Al Di Là." And there it is, that smile in the corners of her mouth. He hasn't seen it in so long.

"My shoes," she says, her eyes still closed. He wishes she'd open them. He wants to see them see clear. "The gold ones, the heels," she goes on. "I can't find them."

"I have them. Don't worry."

"Tomorrow," she says. "Tomorrow night we'll go dancing. It's late now. Isn't it late?"

"Yes," he says. "It is pretty late." So he takes off his clothes and, in his underwear and shirtsleeves, lies beside her under the covers. The sheets are cold. The room is dark. The air conditioner blows across their bodies. The drapes ripple like a child is playing a game behind them. Maddalena turns on her side, she lays her arm across his chest, her head on his shoulder, and her right leg alongside his left, and before long they're both warm.

They've come all this way, and he is the one she remembers. Not her sister. Not Vito. Not even her own children. That has to mean something. It has to mean—it's possible, at the very least—that she loves him best, and has for some time. It could mean he wasn't wrong to take her away from here after the war. It could mean their story was a romance after all.

They can stay in this room, in this bed, for the next three days if she wants, pretending it's always night, that they are always about to fall asleep together. Whatever brings her peace. So what if they've flown across the ocean? Let Frankie and Prima and Kelly Anne enjoy the scenery, soak up the air, make their own memories. Leave Antonio and Maddalena alone here in their bed for a while. At this moment, there's nothing and no one else worth seeing.

SANTA CECILIA REMINDS Frankie of a place you'd take your eighth-grade social studies class: Quebec City or Williamsburg, authentically ancient in pedigree but preserved in a flimsy, manufactured way. The church charges a fee. Alongside the Italian options, the Al Di Là Café menu lists a hot dog and fries. No old men sit in folding chairs in the piazza, and no old ladies hang laundry, as

Frankie saw in the other villages he drove through to get here. Most people, even Vito Leone, speak some English. On the side of the bus that roars by, an ad for *The Lord of the Rings*. In the window of the Pensione Fiorentina, a poster of Michael Bolton.

The sun is strong and close. Frankie takes off his long-sleeved shirt and wanders the streets and the crumbling cobblestone paths in shorts and his white T with Kelly Anne and Prima. Kelly Anne wants him to talk more, to say what he's feeling, to "share," but most of what he's feeling is rage. If he could talk, what would he say? That he hates himself for getting his hopes up. That it's just like him. That miracles are for people of faith. That nine times out of ten, what's most likely to happen, happens. People get old and lose everything and die. They leave you bereft and clamoring. Villages and cities and entire countries relinquish what came before them, fall victim to progress and oppression, wipe themselves off maps.

To walk down this road in his ancestral village is a luxury. To reach up and pull a grape from a vine that's been growing for generations is an extravagance. None of it belongs to Francesco Grasso. He's a descendant of Santa Cecilia, and of this convoluted country, but not a player, not an actor. He knows little of Italy's history, of the history of his own family, beyond the romances his mother filled his head with, and his father's fermented nostalgia. His gut tells him that they shouldn't be here, he and his girlfriend and his sister, that they are mere tourists in the lives of others. They shouldn't have brought their mother back and experimented on her like nineteenth-century quacks. They should have honored her wishes when she was present enough to express them.

They walk up and down the road for what might be hours. They wait in a long line in the piazza to drink from the "authentic natural water" at the spring and drop a few coins in the donation box beside it and take pictures of two Canadian newlyweds on the steps of the church. With a crowd of couples, Germans and Belgians, they watch a young, muscular butcher carve up a pig through the large picture window of a *macelleria,* but even this seems for show. There's too much flourish in his handling of the cleaver. A cigarette dangles Brandoishly from the corner of his mouth. When he's done, the crowd applauds. Frankie shakes his head.

Where is my village? his father must be asking. You can't go home again, Frankie should have reminded him when he called from the travel agent's, but how can you deny your father when he's begging you, through tears, to bring peace to his wife, your mother, the woman you miss more than you can bear? Bring the Irish girl, he said to Frankie. Make it a vacation. You have the summer off, don't you? You work too hard as it is—and don't worry, I'll pay for the tickets, the hotels, everything.

Frankie defended the idea to Prima. The trip seemed like the right thing to do. They had no other choice; it had the potential to bring joy, transformation, the poetry and crescendo of reunion. The same rationale Prima had once applied to her own cursed family adventure.

When they reach the olive grove, they take off their shoes and walk through the knotty grass. Frankie takes a photo of Kelly Anne under the canopy of one of the trees, her elbow resting on a branch, her lovely, smooth, tanned bare legs crossed at the ankles. Prima gets a picture of them both in the same spot, then sitting on the grass, then holding hands. She's Kelly Anne's number one fan and has pretty much insisted Frankie propose to her before she comes to her senses and dumps him.

Vito Leone hobbles toward them with his cane. He's changed into a pair of sagging jeans, a thin V-neck sweater that shows a thick mound of white chest hair, and a wide-brimmed panama hat. Not what Frankie expected from the great love of his mother's life, but a kind man nonetheless.

He takes the camera from Prima and snaps a photo of the three of them. Prima's arm is tight around Kelly Anne. "*La famiglia Grasso,*" he says.

It doesn't feel strange to have Vito lead them around, talking in his broken English. His mind zigs and zags all over the place, switching from one memory of Maddalena to another without transition, and they have a hard time keeping up, connecting the dots, but his English gets better the longer he goes on. Something about him reminds Frankie of Zio Giulio. He puts his arm around the old man's shoulders as they walk.

"Follow me," Vito says. "Something special to see."

He leads them down a path toward a darker part of the grove, into the woods. The trees grow taller and closer together and block the sun, which has fallen a bit now that's it's almost five o'clock. "*Qui,*" he says when they reach a clearing. "Here. This was Maddalena's favorite place." The girls used to gather in this clearing, he explains, and tell secrets and put on plays. They wrote the plays in their head and somehow kept them straight without writing them down. If she'd had the chance, Maddalena would have made a very good actress. She used to do impressions for her friends. Carolina was the bully and ran the shows, dictating who performed what and when. The girls didn't know it, but Vito and his friend Buccio used to hide behind the trees over there and spy on them. "Every time Maddalena took the stage," Vito says, "I cannot breathe."

"That's how you feel about me, right, Frankie?" says Kelly Anne.

"*Ganzo,* eh?" Vito asks.

"*Ganzo?*"

"*Ganzo* means, how you say, cool?"

"*Ganzo,* yes, I like that," says Frankie.

"Something special else I have for you," Vito says. "Follow me."

ANTONIO WAKES TO a dark room and the smell of anchovies and roasted peppers. It's five thirty in the afternoon, and someone in the Piccinelli kitchen is cooking the *merenda*. For the first time in their lives, he and Maddalena have slept through lunch.

He dresses her and puts back on the clothes he was wearing when he arrived, and together they walk through the empty house. There's laughter coming from the terrace, and when they walk out into the cool June evening, they find a crowd waiting for them. Carolina is lying on a lounge chair with a wide, blank smile and a glass of wine in her right hand. The woman standing behind her braiding her hair introduces herself as her daughter, their niece, Donatella. Donatella's brother, Sergio, in his own lounge chair, stands to greet them and introduces his wife, Anna. The teenage boy from the store is there, Ignazio, son of Celestina, and a group of his buddies. An entire family of strangers has gathered in honor of their American visitors. Sergio promises that more will come, and keep coming, for dinner and cards, long into the night.

On the table is a platter of *supplì* and peppers and figs and cheese—too much food, in Antonio's opinion, for the traditional *merenda*—but it's been so long since he's eaten like this at this time of day that he doesn't question them when they fix his and Maddalena's plates. Instead they sit on a bench by the railing and eat greedily with both hands and say little, the juice of the figs running down their chins. They refill their wineglasses. He asks where his children and Vito are, but no one knows or seems to be concerned that they haven't returned from their walk. Donatella turns on the stereo, and Maddalena taps her foot to the beat of an Italian song from the eighties. The next song is a rumba from the fifties. The one after that used to be played by the traveling bands during the war. Antonio can't help smiling.

"What is it, Zio?" asks Donatella.

"One thing I forgot about Italy," he says. "The years are all mixed together."

"Every day is yesterday here," says Sergio.

After a while, Carolina comes to sit beside her sister on the bench. They grip each other's hands and look into each other's eyes but say nothing. "La Piccinina" comes on. Carolina knows the words, and Maddalena seems to follow the tune, and in this way they sing along. The sun is quickly going down over the mountains. There's almost a chill in the air. This mountain chill, too, Antonio has somehow forgotten; this and the music of the slamming shutters and the women snapping their sheets out their windows and the ringing of the church bell. He stands at the railing and looks down at the cars and buses and the tourist couples left on the street, thinking, morbidly, how the last Grassos and Piccinellis of his generation are here on this porch, and that soon, very soon, they will be the stories hanging from the trees, stories no one will be interested enough in to tell. Any old person worth his bones knows this, it's nothing new or profound, but when you see it up close, it's a shock, it stops you.

There's some commotion in the street, and when Antonio looks up, he sees, in the near distance, Prima and Kelly Anne and Vito Leone walking toward them. In the middle of the street, weaving slowly among them and the passing cars, is Frankie, riding a bicycle.

Antonio nudges Maddalena. "Do you see?" He helps her to her feet, steadies her at the railing. "Look who's coming."

They lean side by side against the railing, his hand on the small of her back, and watch as Frankie pedals toward them on a rickety heap of silver metal with one oversize front wheel and the chain hanging down and two half-deflated tires lumpy on the asphalt. Leave it to Vito Leone to hold on to that jalopy for half a century. Antonio wouldn't be surprised if he still rode it himself—in the middle of the night, maybe, while Carolina slept, under the moonlight, day-dreaming. It's a wonder the bike moves at all, but here it comes, carrying Frankie up the hill in a tipsy wobble, about to collapse under his weight.

"Ma!" Frankie calls out. "Hey, Ma! Check me out!"

Maddalena leans forward to get a better look. As she waves to the handsome young man on the bike, what she's thinking is, How will I choose? Even from here, she can see the love in the boy's eyes. He's offering her his best life. An adventure. She's tempted to run down the stairs, jump on the handlebars, and say, Take me to Broccostella! and together they'd glide down the hill into the woods, like they did last week. But not only is Maddalena too tired to run, there's the old man beside her, his strong hand on her back, holding her in place. She feels safe with him. In his eyes, too, there is love. She turns, and everywhere—even in these strangers on their lounge chairs—love stares back at her. The white-haired man lifting his cane at her from the street. The fat lady with the limp. Even the young German girl. They look at her with their big, shiny eyes waiting for her to choose which man she'll spend her life with. But what if she wants them both? Can't she have both?

The boy on the bike comes closer. She's worried he'll fall. She blows him a kiss to stall while she tries to decide what to do next. Then the old man whispers something in her ear. It makes no sense, but she considers it. She nods. I don't know this play, she thinks. But she's an actress; she can do it. It will be good practice. So she calls out, as loud as she can, to the young man on the bike: "Frankie!" she says. "There's my Frankie!"

He calls back, "Ma!" and starts waving like a crazy person, almost crashing into a car. "Ma! Ma!"

The man beside Maddalena whispers to her again, and she calls out to the woman with the bad leg, "Prima!" and then she, too, starts waving back and jumping up and down. You've never seen two grown people so excited for something so simple. It's fun, like being onstage in the olive grove. The old man notices what a hit it is and keeps giving her words to call out and telling her what gestures to make with her arms, so Maddalena goes along, keeps saying the lines—"Frankie!

Prima! Come here! I've missed you!"—until the young man jumps off the bike and, the woman not far behind, runs up the stairs and onto the terrace and into her outstretched arms.

THAT NIGHT, THEY walk to the gorge to look at the stars. It's the highest point in the village, Donatella explains, up a dirt road beyond the church and the graveyard, at the end of a path too narrow for cars. Vito carries a flashlight but doesn't switch it on. The stars are enough.

Prima walks with him, her arm looped around his, in the middle of the pack, her father beside her, her cousins in front smoking and talking a mile a minute, Frankie and Kelly Anne behind. Prima can't stop looking at the sky. She's never seen it so close and bright and inescapable. It should be scary how it presses down on them, the stars sharp as spears, and yet she feels powerfully enormous, a wandering giant. The top of her head brushes the heavens. She could blame the four glasses of wine she had at dinner, or the thin air, but in fact, neither has had any effect. She blames the sky. Her mother's sky. Now that she's under it, she understands how impossible it would be to leave it, how you spend the rest of your life feeling small and strange and far away.

For a minute today, just one minute, Prima had her back. Her mother called her by her name, and it was a miracle. If the miracle happens again, somehow, before they leave in a few days, and lasts long enough, Prima would love nothing more than to tell her she's sorry, that she understands now, finally, why she didn't want to be reminded of this place she lost, where she walked gigantic beside the boy she loved up the path to where the sky began.

Prima has other apologies to make, starting with Allison Grey. The girl has no sense, but neither did Prima at her age, neither does any woman who loves with her soul. Prima doesn't pretend to understand how men love, but she suspects it's from the body and the heart and can't compare. It's a kind of poverty, being a man. Arm in arm with Vito Leone, stepping slowly over rocks and wildflowers, it occurs to her that her mother must have loved him with her heart only, the lesser way; otherwise she could never have left him, and their home, for Antonio Grasso. And if that was true for Maddalena, it was also true for Prima and Dante Marconi.

Now that she knows this, she can apologize to him, too. When she gets home, if she still has the nerve, she'll look him up.

At the end of the path stands a stone wall, chest high, that connects two lines of trees. Beyond the wall and the trees is a steep drop to a river thousands of feet down. The river is so far away that they can't hear or see it, even in the daytime, and yet, her father explains, this is the river where the women used to wash clothes back when he and Maddalena and Vito were young.

They climb onto the wall and sit, in a long row, legs dangling, facing the drop and the dark valley below. They can see the lights of other villages at the tops of their own mountains, miles in the distance. In English, with his daughter's help, Vito explains that the wall they're sitting on is the only part left over from the original church of Santa Cecilia. The church stood in this very spot for hundreds of years before it collapsed in an earthquake. If you notice, he says, switching on the flashlight and running his hands along the side, this is the same stone you see in the new church down the hill.

"How new is the new church?" Kelly Anne asks.

"Very new," says Donatella. "A hundred and fifty years."

Frankie laughs.

"It's OK," says Antonio to Vito. "You can tell the real story." But Vito says nothing.

There was never a church up here, Antonio begins. There was only the cliff and this one big patch where nothing grew, where people came to look out at the valleys without the trees blocking. For hundreds of years nothing grew in that patch, probably from all the people stomping around and the boyfriends who brought their girlfriends up here to hide from their parents. Then, about the same time Vito said they built the new church, a woman came up here carrying her baby. For no reason at all, she threw herself with the baby into the gorge. Weeks later, after some villagers found them, the woman's husband, the father of the baby, built the wall with his own hands, stone by stone, so no one else would think to do such a thing. "But of course the wall made it easier to jump," says Antonio, shaking his head. "And that woman wasn't the last one to do it."

"There are ten stories for every rock in Santa Cecilia," Vito says. "I don't like that one. I like better the one my mother told me."

"I want to hear a happy story," Prima says, a chill running through her.

"We had one today," says Frankie, from the other end of the wall.

Because they're all sitting in a row facing out, it's as if they're speaking not to each other but to the gorge.

"I can tell you one," says Donatella. "Papà knows it, too."

She's even farther away than Frankie, so far Prima can't distinguish her dangling legs from Kelly Anne's, her voice like an echo from the trees.

"My friend in Avezzano had a friend, an old man who's dead now, who used to be a pilot. The pilot told him once that if you fly a plane over the valley—the Valle Del Salto here, where we are—and you look down at Santa Cecilia from the air, the shape of the roads and where the trees grow makes the village into the body of a woman."

"I don't understand," says Frankie.

"The *shape*," Donatella says. "Like the—how do you say—the *contour*?"

"I understand what you mean," says Frankie. "The *outline*. But how is it a woman? Isn't it just a person?"

"That's the romance talking," says Sergio.

"No," says Donatella. "It's the trees at the top, where the head is. And down at the bottom, too, if you can excuse me, between the legs, they look like hair. Long hair at the top. This is what my friend in Avezzano told me the pilot told him. The piazza is the head, down by the olive grove the legs. If you think hard enough about it, and you know the village back and forth, it makes sense."

"Leave it to the Italians," says Frankie. "How come you never told us this, Dad?"

"I'm hearing it for the first time," Antonio says.

"*Ganzo,*" says Kelly Anne, and Vito laughs.

"Maddalena would think so, too," says Antonio.

"She already knows," says Donatella. "Zia Celestina told her in one of her letters. Zia loved that story, for some reason. She wanted to tell everyone. She believed it was the image of Saint Cecilia herself, painted onto the earth by God."

Maddalena never read any of those letters, Prima could say, but she stops herself. Her father and Frankie, too, say nothing. They found all the letters in the basement, tied with a ribbon, unopened. Behind those, letters to her mother written years after she was already dead.

Prima's lower back aches, and her leg, her crushed but functional leg, starts to throb. The long day is catching up with her. Her family must be tired, too, especially her father. It seems impossible that just yesterday she was in Wilmington madly packing her suitcase, and this morning she landed in Rome. It was as easy as she always thought it would be to get here, but she takes no comfort in that. She wishes Tom were with her. She wants to talk to him, tell him everything that's in her heart. It's surprising—she's been thinking of him more than of her boys. She's been wondering what he'll do for Saturday dinner, which of his T-shirts he's put on to mow the lawn. She wants to tell him about the miracle of the bicycle, the shape of the village, the sky. She wants him to know she picked him for a reason, whether she knew it at the time or not, and has no regrets.

"Listen," says Vito. "Keep very quiet. Don't even breathe. You can hear it."

"Hear what?" asks Frankie.

"The river."

THE SAME GROUP gathers two nights later on the Piccinelli terrace. Prima's glad that Maddalena is with them this time, eating the *merenda,* drinking the white wine chilled by the creek, wearing sunglasses though the evening light is fading. She's in a lounge chair beside Carolina, who has become a new friend.

There are four languages on this terrace, Frankie thinks: Italian, English, the hybrid that Vito stammers through, and the mystery tongue spoken by the sisters. The words are real Italian, of course, but the sentences don't follow a track. Still, Maddalena and Carolina laugh and answer each other's disconnected questions, and when one of them mentions a name, the other places it and offers news of the person they're discussing, something no one else on the terrace can do.

In the morning, Maddalena will leave and Carolina will stay and they will never see each other again. To Prima, it seems cruel not to tell them this so they can say good-bye, but then again, it's all been cruel. The years of silence between them. The ocean that kept them apart. Their minds rotting before their bodies.

It doesn't take long for Vito Leone—a chatterbox if there ever was one—to again steer the conversation to his favorite topic: when will Francesco propose to this pretty Kelly Anne?

Prima's embarrassed for the poor girl, sitting beside Vito in a strapless yellow dress that shows her sunburnt shoulders. She's a good sport, all smiles through the teasing and his hand on her knee and his asking, over and over, how she can be so *simpatica* and not Italian. Is she sure her grandfather, maybe, or great-grandmother, didn't have some Italian blood? To Frankie he says, up close in his face like an accuser, You don't realize how lucky you are?

"Leave them alone, Papà," says Donatella.

"I won't," he says.

Prima sits beside her father, her hand on top of his. How strange it must be for him, she thinks, hearing Vito's advice on love when he knows that he means every word for the Maddalena of sixty years ago, for the life Vito would have had with her if it weren't for him. Even so, she can see in her father's eyes that he's sad to be leaving. She's already suggested they stay a few more days, change their tickets, who cares about the money, Ryan and the restaurant and Tom will be fine, but he said no, it was time.

"All this talk of love," Prima says to him while Vito rambles on to Frankie and Kelly Anne on the other side of the terrace, "—it reminds me: Do you know whatever happened to Dante Marconi? Is he still in Wilmington?"

He looks at her. "Dante Marconi? Why?"

"It's OK, Dad," Prima says with a laugh. "I know why you fired him. You don't have to pretend."

He blinks at her, seeming confused.

"You don't remember. That's a good thing. Or maybe you really didn't know? When I was sixteen and working at the Al Di Là? We used to sneak around, me and Dante Marconi. Before Tony died. And . . . and after, too. For just a little while. It was nothing big. But there was no way I could tell you back then. It was obvious you didn't like him. That ponytail—"

"You and Dante?"

"Yes. Why do you think I was such a terrible waitress? All I could concentrate on was him. I thought I was in love. Can you imagine." She laughs. It's a relief to get that part of it, at least, out in the open, even though she could have done so a long time ago, after she'd settled down with Tom, when it wouldn't have mattered anymore to her father. "I thought for sure Gilberto told you. He caught us in the alley once. We both assumed that's why you fired him all of a sudden."

"Who are you talking about?" Frankie calls out from the other side of the terrace.

"Nothing," Prima says. "Just a crush I had once. This guy Dante Marconi. A waiter at the Al Di Là."

"*Dante,*" Frankie says. "How literary of you, Prima."

"*Dante e Beatrice,*" says Vito, who's half following them and half gazing at Kelly Anne's shoulders. "An Italian love story."

"It wasn't a love story," says Prima.

"What was it?" asks Kelly Anne.

"You OK, Dad?" Prima asks him. "You're not mad at me, are you? It was such a long time ago. I was stupid. You can't be mad at me for something like that—"

"Did Tony know?" he asks.

Everyone's looking at him because now he's shaking. "Dad, what is it? Why does it matter?"

"Just tell me if Tony knew about you and Dante Marconi."

Prima casts her mind back. "At first, no," she says. "Then—yes, I think I did tell him. Because I was worried he'd find out from Gilberto and tell you. I made him swear not to. I remember for sure now. We were sitting on his bed one night after a shift. He didn't rat on me, though, did he?"

"No," Antonio says.

"We kept each other's secrets," she says. "I would have done anything for him."

"He hated you, too, then. Not just me."

"What did you say?" Prima asks. "He didn't hate me, Dad. He didn't hate any of us. You shouldn't talk like that. Do you need a glass of water?"

He shuts his eyes and squeezes them tight like he's trying to stop tears. "I'm sorry," he says. Then he stands up. He's still shaking. "I'm going for a walk."

"I'll go with you," Frankie says, shooting Prima a look that means, Don't worry, I'll figure this out.

"No," says Antonio. "Stay here."

He goes to Maddalena, kneels beside her, and whispers something in her ear. She nods. He takes her hand and helps her to her feet and together they go into the house without a word to anyone.

Minutes later they appear on the street, walking toward the piazza. Prima and Frankie watch them. From above, they look like any white-haired village couple: the lady in a housedress, the man with a sweater tied around his shoulders. Except she can only be Prima's mother and he can only be her father, and Maddalena was always going to pick Antonio over Vito Leone, and their first son was always going to jump from the bridge, and they were never not going to grow old together or take one last walk hand in hand through the village, up to the church. In their long lives, Prima thinks, she and Frankie have played only small parts.

When they turn toward the gorge, Frankie asks, "Do you know what that was about?"

"No idea," Prima says.

Kelly Anne comes over to stand with them. "So you lost track of Dante?" she asks. "How sad!"

"It's not so sad," says Prima. "He hates me."

"For what?"

It's been torn down now, Prima's checked, but back in her day, there was an abandoned house in the woods behind Brandywine Creek State Park. Kids called it the devil house, but it was really just a small cabin people had stopped living in. The land was owned by two old women, cousins, or so they said, who lived in a big house up the hill from the shed. There were lots of rumors about the shed. You never heard the same one the same way twice. The most famous rumor went that devil worshippers gathered there to sacrifice animals and there was a hole in the floor that led straight to hell. Kids used to go driving around drunk at night looking for the devil house but never finding it. It was just a little workman's cabin hidden from the road by trees. What some of them must have known, though, and kept mostly to themselves, was that it was a place where a girl could get a doctor to come if she needed one. The two women in the main house were connected to the doctor. You had to go through them first, and pay the money, which is what Prima did, with her friend Linda, and then a night or two later, when she told her parents she was going to Linda's house, instead she went to the cabin.

"He caught me with his best friend," Prima says to Kelly Anne. "We were just making out, but—it was enough."

"Classy," says Frankie.

"I know, I know," Prima says, with an "I surrender" wave and a smile she forces through, though her heart is breaking in the same raw place it broke that night in Linda's car on the way home from the cabin, and has broken, again and again, with the same ache immediately following, each time she's with her sons.

"I never saw him again after that night," Prima says, and this part is true. "It really hurt him, what I did. He had so much pride. I didn't know then about an Italian man's pride. I was just figuring it out."

Prima can still see him, Dante, beside her on the hood of his blue Camaro, in his jeans and white T-shirt, arms out, making her promise that she wouldn't do it, that she'd think as hard as she could about marrying him and living in his grandmother's house at the Jersey Shore with their son, their daughter, whatever God gave them. He was too young and stupid to be angry or scared. He felt nothing but joy at their twist of fate.

I promise, Prima had said.

"He's forgiven you by now," says Kelly Anne.

"Seriously," Frankie says. "No offense, but he probably doesn't even remember it. We Italian men go through lots of women in a lifetime."

"Is that right?" asks Kelly Anne.

The next morning, when they're gathered outside the store with their luggage, and the entire village, it seems, comes to wish them off, Vito Leone's face is full of tears. Carolina can't understand why. Maddalena, too, is confused. But he makes sense to Prima. He's a romantic. And because Prima is not—not anymore, at least—she envies him.

Maddalena sits in the backseat of the rental car next to her husband. Up until the last possible second, even after Frankie's turned on the ignition, she holds Carolina's hand through the open window.

Then they pull away, and Prima's last glimpse of Santa Cecilia is her army of a family, who'd been strangers just days before, walking fast toward them in a pack down the middle of the street, waving their handkerchiefs, shouting their names, calling, *ciao, ciao, buon viaggio, arrivederci,* see you soon, see you again!

12 *More*

LATER THAT SUMMER, Frankie and Kelly Anne take a proper vacation. A week in Rehoboth, just the two of them, with nothing to do but read and swim and play games on the boardwalk. They spend a couple of mornings on the stretch of beach where Matt and Zach work as lifeguards. Kelly Anne looks delicious in a swimsuit, the freckles across her chest, her hair a strawberry blond for just a few precious weeks. The beach trip is a gift from her parents, offered and accepted without fuss. They don't want the week to end but aren't sad when they leave. Their little life together in Newark is a satisfying one. So in the car headed north on Route 1 they turn up the radio and sing.

Once a month, every month now for the past year or so, they meet Prima and Tom for dinner at the Al Di Là. When they do, Antonio cooks the meal himself to show the cooks who's boss and to keep up the old recipes. Frankie's in constant disagreement with Prima—over politics, whether Patrick should join a frat, why he and Kelly Anne don't need to get married, all the conversations they had in Santa Cecilia rehashed and added to—but at the end of the night they put their arms around each other and say how fast the months go and promise to see each other more. Ryan's always there buzzing around the tables in a tie and blazer. A newly minted graduate of Syracuse, he spent a small fortune of his parents' money to secure the job at the family restaurant he could have had out of high school, but nobody complains.

This fall, Assistant Professor Frank Grasso is on the U of D campus five days a week. A Monday three-hour lecture, a Tuesday-Thursday intro course, and a Monday-Wednesday-Friday postcolonial survey. Not to mention office hours (Tuesdays and Fridays, 10 a.m. to noon, the time most popular with the students, and by appointment). Not to mention the endless thesis-committee meetings, and the reams of essays he grades in the cafeteria between commitments. Throw in research time on new papers for MLA and the Pitt and BU conferences, and the revision of his dissertation-about-to-become-a-published-book, and his volunteer role with the Graduate Student Union, and his schedule becomes unmanageable. Yet he takes more when more is offered to him. Because every minute on campus, hard at work, at the podium in front of scribbling coeds, is one of distraction.

It's not until he gets in his car—a 2001 Toyota, the first car he's bought with his own money—and tosses his satchel and empty thermos on the passenger seat, that he's reminded what a fool's paradise *more* has turned out to be. *More* is never enough. The undistracted minute always arrives, and there beside him is his sadness, that hulking giant that follows him wherever he goes.

The one magic afternoon in Santa Cecilia was the last time Frankie's mother recognized him. He conjures it up more often than he should: Maddalena calling his name, taking him in her arms. A miracle. Conjuring up the day gives him hope when hope is necessary. Once something beautiful unfolds before you, isn't it human nature to replay the moment over and over, take it like a drug when you need it?

He calls Kelly Anne on his cell phone to plan dinner. She's a decent cook, but neither of them is much of a housekeeper. Against her religion and her parents' wishes, they rent an apartment off Academy Street. She teaches in the Delaware public school system. He helps her with her bulletin boards, making sure she doesn't pass along the naive understanding of America's reprehensible colonial history her professors at BC taught her. She drags him to church once a month. In these ways, they corrupt each other. Though she's patient with Frankie's skittishness, he knows she'd like a ring, to feel legitimate in the eyes of the priests at St. Ann's, and one day he'll break down and get her one, but for now he prefers not to mess with a good thing.

At night, if he doesn't have too many papers to grade, they watch documentaries. Or they grab a beer at Klondike Kate's and hope they don't run into any of Frankie's students. Whatever they do, most nights they're home by ten, an old unmarried married couple. And at 11:01, in bed beside her, he calls his parents' house from the extension on his nightstand.

His father plays bocce on Tuesdays, Thursdays, and Saturdays, the nights Prima and Frankie take turns sitting with their mother. There's a new nurse in the daytime, an expensive one Tom and Prima pay for.

Tonight's a Wednesday. His father answers on the second ring, groggy, startled, half-awake. They make sure they've each had dinner, that their cars are running OK, the same conversation they had yesterday, and have been having for two, five, fifteen years, and will have as long as they can. In the middle of it, his mother picks up. She's in a different room, the cordless always beside her.

She tells him about people he's never heard of, who may not even exist. She mixes Italian and English in the same sentence. He recognizes some of the names from previous conversations, on the Piccinelli terrace and elsewhere, but most of the names are inaccessible, unattached to any of the multiple story lines that have been building over the years. But how happy she sounds tonight to know these strangers, to report on their progress.

Their soap is on in the background; it plays over and over most of the day in her room; he can hear it, it's on so loud; and though she may or may not understand him, he fills her in on what's going on, who's in love, who's missing, who was thought dead but has come back to life. All the silliness and drama and sex and heartbreak that is the stuff of life. It's too late to go on for long, they are all three so tired, but the time is tradition.

His clock radio says 11:13. "Good night to you both," he says. "I love you."

"Good night, Son," his father says. "Be careful."

"Good night, Dad. I'll see you tomorrow night at the restaurant. *You* be careful driving."

"I'll be there," he says. "Love you, Son. Good-bye."

His father is always the first to hang up.

"Good night, Ma."

"Bye, bye!" she says brightly.

"I love you."

"Love you, too. Bye, bye!"

"Good-bye," Frankie says. "I love you, good-bye."

Acknowledgments

FOR THEIR GENEROUS and expert feedback on early drafts, I am forever grateful to Heidi Pitlor, Antonia Fusco, Bret Anthony Johnston, Kristin Duisberg, Ladette Randoph, Mary Evans, and Margot Livesey.

Thank you to my editor, Kathy Pories, for giving this manuscript a chance and then making it better with her invaluable time, attention, and insight. I feel lucky to be part of the dynamic Algonquin family.

My agent, Janet Silver, is supremely wise, dedicated, savvy, and more patient with me than I could ever have hoped for.

The following people have helped me in crucial ways by offering their encouragement, space, advice, and/or companionship: Eve Bridburg, dear friend and mentor; Sonya Larson, Whitney Scharer, Michelle Toth, and everyone at Grub Street, my happy and inspiring home for over a decade; Jennifer Grotz, Michael Collier, and the pure joy that is Bread Loaf; C. Dale Young, Ellen Bryant Voigt, and the faculty and students of Warren Wilson; Steve Almond, Maud Casey, Stacey D'Erasmo, Scott Heim, Michael Lowenthal, Steve McCauley, Tom Mallon, Anita Shreve, and Sebastian Stuart; Steve Buckley, Adam Lavielle, and the Diesel Café; Jenna Blum for three months at Sweet 5; Wolfgang Wesener; Rachel Careau; Elisa Piccinelli (no relation?), who corrected my very bad Italian; Jonathan Jensen and the Latchis Hotel; and my brother, Emidio Castellani, who has shown extraordinary acceptance and love.

Speaking of love: Michael Borum has it all.

All This Talk of Love

A Note from the Author

Questions for Discussion

A Note from the Author

In December 1995, my parents took me back to Italy for the last time. They had grown up in Sant'Elpidio, a small village at the top of one of the highest mountains in the Valle Del Salto, and it was the return to this village that I most eagerly anticipated. I'd visited Sant'Elpidio and the major Italian cities as a child, but my memories were distant and dreamlike. I recalled kicking a soccer ball between two olive trees to score an imaginary goal; sticking my hand between the stone lips of the *bocca della verita,* the mouth of the truth; and sitting at my mother's feet over long, rambunctious feasts, begging her to translate what my relatives were saying.

In fact, my most enduring memories of Italy consisted of my mother's face smiling down at me as she smoothed my hair and retold the stories, jokes, and legends that formed the centerpiece of every family gathering. A few of the stories, she said, would have to wait until I was older; some of the jokes wouldn't make much sense in English;

but most of what my relatives discussed she faithfully and patiently recounted to me there at the table or later in the night, as I fell asleep. In that strange and beautiful world, my mother was always my guide, my voice.

We didn't go to Italy to sightsee. We went so that my mother could visit the family she'd given up to marry my father, who'd emigrated to America after World War II. We went so that my parents could introduce me to the "real" world — vivid, honest, and unspoiled — and so they could escape the harsh and colorless "new" world. We went because my mother missed her best friends, her six brothers and sisters, who were still relatively young and very much alive.

In 1995, I was a shy young man of twenty-three. I was a student of literature with the dream of becoming a writer, and I was also anxiously closeted. Compared to my parents' lives and the ones led in their ancestral village, my future seemed unchartable, unprecedented. The apparent simplicity of Sant'Elpidio, little more than a cluster of stone houses linked to other clusters by one narrow and bumpy road, bewitched me. Wandering through the village with my parents at my side, I thought, All the answers are here! If only I observed it and my mother's family closely enough, I thought, I'd understand more fully her nagging sadness, and my father's pride, and, somehow, my own inexpressible longings. By seeing where we came from, I'd find out who we were.

Night after night, we feasted. On Christmas Eve, we ate the traditional seven fishes at Zio Ernesto's and played cards and *tombola* late into the night; for Christmas Day we headed down the street to visit Zio Totò, the greatest of the joke-tellers; we stopped into Zia

Clara's for her famous *pizza sfogliata,* rivaled only by Zia Carolina's *crespelle;* in the middle of the day we found ourselves dancing across Zia Maddalena's concrete basement floor; and on Saint Stephen's Day we gathered at the home of Zio Nello, the oldest and the keeper of the family history. We were never alone. At meals, on car rides, on walks up and down the village street, my aunts and uncles surrounded us. They seemed to have one hand on my mother at all times, on her shoulder or her lap or the small of her back, as if to keep her from leaving them again.

This month of feasts did show me who we were, both as a family and as a people: we loved each other with abandon. Of all the ways of expressing love that Italians have in their repertoire, the feast, with food and stories at its center, is among the most powerful. Knowing this, seeing it up close, made me less afraid of the future. No matter what, I thought, I was rich in love and would never be poor.

Within a year of that trip to Sant'Elpidio, Zia Maddalena and Zia Clara both passed away, and my mother vowed never to go back to Italy. She couldn't bear the country without them, she told me, and so she turned her back on it completely. *All This Talk of Love* is about a woman much like her, someone who was born into the riches of family and then renounces it. I named her Maddalena and gave her two lives: the one she left behind in the village and the one she built with her husband and children in the United States. What would happen, I wondered, if the two lives collided?

Questions for Discussion

1. In what ways does Tony's absence continue to affect each character's perspective and the way the characters see their role and future?

2. One reviewer called the Grasso family codependent. We generally think that codependency occurs when one person is addicted, physically or psychologically, while the other person is psychologically dependent on the first. Does this sound like any of the Grassos to you? If so, how?

3. Maddalena, Antonio, and Prima each give their own definitions of love as it relates to their hearts, minds, and souls (see pages 156, 167, 255, 256, 324). How do these definitions reflect on them? Maddalena tells Frankie (page 255), "When we romance, we do it with our hearts, but we love our husbands and wives with our brains; our children and our parents we love with our souls. You have to keep them all separate . . .

or you get in trouble, mixing one kind of love up with another." What does she mean?

4. Why do you think Prima is so obsessed with Allison Grey? What in Prima's past might affect her reaction to Allison?

5. What keeps Frankie with Rhonda for most of the novel? Do you think he's better off with Kelly Anne? Why do you think Frankie ultimately chooses to settle down with her?

6. How does Prima's accident change her?

7. At the end of Frankie and Ryan's party, Maddalena says, "That's all we get? One little song?" (page 292). How might this be a theme for the entire novel?

8. What do you think the epigraph refers to? Do you think it applies more to one character or to all the characters equally?

9. What does Italy represent to each of the characters, and how does that change by the end of the novel?

10. What about this particular immigrant family is similar to other immigrant families you've read about? What is different?

WOWE

Christopher Castellani is the author of two previous novels: *A Kiss from Maddalena,* which won the Massachusetts Book Award for Fiction, and *The Saint of Lost Things.* He lives in Boston, where he is the artistic director of Grub Street.

Other Algonquin Readers Round Table Novels

A Reliable Wife, a novel by Robert Goolrick

Rural Wisconsin, 1907. In the bitter cold, Ralph Truitt stands alone on a train platform anxiously awaiting the arrival of the woman who answered his newspaper ad for "a reliable wife." The woman who arrives is not the one he expects in this *New York Times* #1 bestseller about love and madness, longing and murder.

"[A] chillingly engrossing plot . . . Good to the riveting end." —*USA Today*

"Deliciously wicked and tense . . . Intoxicating." —*The Washington Post*

"A rousing historical potboiler." —*The Boston Globe*

AN ALGONQUIN READERS ROUND TABLE EDITION WITH READING GROUP GUIDE AND OTHER SPECIAL FEATURES • FICTION • ISBN 978-1-56512-977-1

West of Here, a novel by Jonathan Evison

Spanning more than hundred years—from the ragged mudflats of a belching and bawdy Western frontier in the 1890s to the rusting remains of a strip-mall cornucopia in 2006—*West of Here* chronicles the life of one small town. It's a saga of destiny and greed, adventure and passion, hope and hilarity, that turns America's history into myth and myth into a nation's shared experience.

"[A] booming, bighearted epic." —*Vanity Fair*

"[A] voracious story . . . Brisk, often comic, always deeply sympathetic."
—*The Washington Post*

AN ALGONQUIN READERS ROUND TABLE EDITION WITH READING GROUP GUIDE AND OTHER SPECIAL FEATURES • FICTION • ISBN 978-1-61620-082-4

The Puzzle King, a novel by Betsy Carter

This is the story of unlikely heroes, the lively, beautiful Flora and her husband, the brooding, studious Simon, two immigrants who were each sent to America by their families to find better lives. They found each other and built a life—and a fortune—together. Now they are the last chance for their loved ones' escape from Hitler's Germany.

"The kernel of Betsy Carter's third novel is a powerful bit of family lore . . . A work of genealogical fiction from the late 19th century to the eve of World War II . . . It balances the Jewish immigrant experience in New York—both the achievement of the American dream and the curdling of it—against the insidious anti-Semitism of Germany and Eastern Europe." —*Los Angeles Times*

"A fine novel with twists and turns and pieces that interlock tightly . . . Carter at her best." —*The Miami Herald*

AN ALGONQUIN READERS ROUND TABLE EDITION WITH READING GROUP GUIDE AND OTHER SPECIAL FEATURES • FICTION • ISBN 978-1-61620-016-9

Until the Next Time, a novel by Kevin Fox

For Sean Corrigan the past is simply what happened yesterday, until his twenty-first birthday, when he's given a journal left him by his father's brother, Michael—a man he had not known existed. The journal, kept after his uncle fled from New York City to Ireland to escape prosecution for a murder he did not commit, draws Sean into a hunt for the truth about Michael's fate. *Until the Next Time* is a remarkable story about time and memory and the way ancient myths affect everything—from what we believe to whom we love.

"A mysterious, sweeping family saga reminiscent of the work of Meira Chand and Julie Drew, Fox's novel is a suspenseful tale of lost love, rediscovered family, and the importance of history." —*Booklist*

"A taut suspense novel, a history lesson on a people's enduring struggle, and a chronicle of a star-crossed pair's everlasting love."
—Sandra Brown, *New York Times* bestselling author of *Lethal*

AN ALGONQUIN READERS ROUND TABLE EDITION WITH READING GROUP GUIDE AND OTHER SPECIAL FEATURES • FICTION • ISBN 978-1-56512-993-1

A Friend of the Family, a novel by Lauren Grodstein

Pete Dizinoff has a thriving medical practice in suburban New Jersey, a devoted wife, a network of close friends, an impressive house, and a son, Alec, now nineteen, on whom he's pinned all his hopes. But Pete never counted on Laura, his best friend's daughter, setting her sights on his only son. Lauren Grodstein's riveting novel charts a father's fall from grace as he struggles to save his family, his reputation, and himself.

"Suspense worthy of Hitchcock . . . [Grodstein] is a terrific storyteller."
—*The New York Times Book Review*

"A gripping portrayal of a suburban family in free-fall."
—*Minneapolis Star Tribune*

AN ALGONQUIN READERS ROUND TABLE EDITION WITH READING GROUP GUIDE AND OTHER SPECIAL FEATURES • FICTION • ISBN 978-1-61620-017-6

Pictures of You, a novel by Caroline Leavitt

Two women running away from their marriages collide on a foggy highway. The survivor of the fatal accident is left to pick up the pieces not only of her own life but of the lives of the devastated husband and fragile son that the other woman left behind. As these three lives intersect, the book asks, How well do we really know those we love and how do we open our hearts to forgive the unforgivable?

"An expert storyteller . . . Leavitt teases suspense out of the greatest mystery of all—the workings of the human heart." —*Booklist*

"Magically written, heartbreakingly honest . . . Caroline Leavitt is one of those fabulous, incisive writers you read and then ask yourself, Where has she been all my life?" —Jodi Picoult

AN ALGONQUIN READERS ROUND TABLE EDITION WITH READING GROUP GUIDE AND OTHER SPECIAL FEATURES • FICTION • ISBN 978-1-56512-631-2

In the Time of the Butterflies, a novel by Julia Alvarez

In this extraordinary novel, the voices of Las Mariposas (The Butterflies), Minerva, Patria, María Teresa, and Dedé, speak across the decades to tell their stories about life in the Dominican Republic under General Rafael Leonidas Trujillo's dictatorship. Through the art and magic of Julia Alvarez's imagination, the martyred butterflies live again in this novel of valor, love, and the human cost of political oppression.

A National Endowment for the Arts Big Read selection

"A gorgeous and sensitive novel ... A compelling story of courage, patriotism, and familial devotion." —*People*

"A magnificent treasure for all cultures and all time."
—*St. Petersburg Times*

AN ALGONQUIN READERS ROUND TABLE EDITION WITH READING GROUP GUIDE AND OTHER SPECIAL FEATURES • FICTION • ISBN 978-1-56512-976-4

Water for Elephants, a novel by Sara Gruen

As a young man, Jacob Jankowski is tossed by fate onto a rickety train, home to the Benzini Brothers Most Spectacular Show on Earth. Amid a world of freaks, grifters, and misfits, Jacob becomes involved with Marlena, the beautiful young equestrian star; her husband, a charismatic but twisted animal trainer; and Rosie, an untrainable elephant who is the great gray hope for this third-rate show. Now in his nineties, Jacob at long last reveals the story of their unlikely yet powerful bonds, ones that nearly shatter them all.

"[An] arresting new novel ... With a showman's expert timing, [Gruen] saves a terrific revelation for the final pages, transforming a glimpse of Americana into an enchanting escapist fairy tale."
—*The New York Times Book Review*

AN ALGONQUIN READERS ROUND TABLE EDITION WITH READING GROUP GUIDE AND OTHER SPECIAL FEATURES • FICTION • ISBN 978-1-56512-560-5

Mudbound, a novel by Hillary Jordan

Mudbound is the saga of the McAllan family, who struggle to survive on a remote ramshackle farm, and the Jacksons, their black sharecroppers. When two men return from World War II to work the land, the unlikely friendship between these brothers-in-arms—one white, one black—arouses the passions of their neighbors. In this award-winning portrait of two families caught up in the blind hatred of a small Southern town, prejudice takes many forms, both subtle and ruthless.

Winner of the Bellwether Prize for Fiction

"This is storytelling at the height of its powers . . . Hillary Jordan writes with the force of a Delta storm." —Barbara Kingsolver

---

AN ALGONQUIN READERS ROUND TABLE EDITION WITH READING GROUP GUIDE AND OTHER SPECIAL FEATURES • FICTION • ISBN 978-1-56512-677-0

Coal Black Horse, a novel by Robert Olmstead

When Robey Childs's mother has a premonition about her husband fighting in the Civil War, she sends her only son to find him and bring him home. At fourteen, Robey thinks he's off on a great adventure. But it takes the gift of a powerful and noble coal black horse to show him how to undertake the most important journey in his life.

"A remarkable creation." —*Chicago Tribune*

"Exciting . . . A grueling adventure." —*The New York Times Book Review*

AN ALGONQUIN READERS ROUND TABLE EDITION WITH READING GROUP GUIDE AND OTHER SPECIAL FEATURES • FICTION • ISBN 978-1-56512-601-5

Join us at **AlgonquinBooksBlog.com** for the latest news on all of our stellar titles, including weekly giveaways, behind-the-scenes snapshots, book and author updates, original videos, media praise, detailed tour information, and other exclusive material.

You'll also find information about the **Algonquin Book Club**, a selection of the perfect books—from award winners to international bestsellers—to stimulate engaging and lively discussion. Helpful book group materials are available, including

Book excerpts
Downloadable discussion guides
Author interviews
Original author essays
Live author chats and live-streaming interviews
Book club tips and ideas
Wine and recipe pairings

twitter Follow us on twitter.com/AlgonquinBooks
facebook Become a fan on facebook.com/AlgonquinBooks